PR
QUEEN OF NONE

"A captivating look at the intriguing figures in
King Arthur's golden realm."

*Kirkus*

"A layered, engaging retelling, sure to please
fans of the Arthurian tales."

*Publishers Weekly*

"Readers feel as though they could slip from the
mundane to the fantastical at any moment..."

*Library Journal*

"Barron's take will leave readers with entirely new
insights into Arthurian legend."

*Booklist*

"A brilliant reimagining of the Arthurian canon,
*Queen of None* balances pulse-pounding action
with Byzantine intrigue."

**S. A. Cosby**

"A tale of love, magic, triumph,
and heartbreak, all set against a rich and
beautifully-described background."

**A. C. Wise**

"A unique and amazingly vivid
perspective on Arthuriana."

*Nerds of a Feather, Flock Together*

# QUEEN OF NONE

# QUEEN
# N(OF)ONE

## NATANIA BARRON

SOLARIS

This edition published 2024 by Solaris
an imprint of Rebellion Publishing Ltd,
Riverside House, Osney Mead,
Oxford, OX2 0ES, UK

*www.solarisbooks.com*

First published 2020 by Vernacular Books

ISBN: 978-1-83786-061-6

10 9 8 7 6 5 4 3 2 1

A CIP catalogue record for this book is available from the
British Library.

Designed & typeset by Rebellion Publishing

Printed in Denmark

MIX
Paper | Supporting
responsible forestry
FSC® C104608

*For Dorothy*
*who first followed Anna into the shadows.*

# FOREWORD

WHEN I BEGAN *Queen of None* over a decade ago, it was with the intent to tell Anna Pendragon's story. Anna, the full sister of King Arthur, was first mentioned in Geoffrey of Monmouth's *De gestis Britonum*, or *Historia Regum Britanniae* (*The History of the Kings of Britain*), written in the twelfth century. Subsequently, she merged into the myths of her more well-known sisters Morgan and Morgause, and vanished from the narrative altogether.

That I began writing Arthuriana is not surprising. I had spent the better part of my twenties entrenched in Arthurian literature during my graduate studies. I read widely and with joy. But to my knowledge, no one had ever tackled Anna's tale. Almost 900 years of legends and adventures, yet Anna—such a simple, unpretentious name—remained a mystery. Even among the myriad other female characters, she never had a chance to share her perspective.

So, I decided I would write the story myself.

This new edition from Solaris will bring Anna's story to a larger audience, but also expand upon the family saga of

Pendragons, Orkneys, and du Lacs that has since become the *Queens of Fate* series. Anna begins as our guide, but subsequent narrators pick up the tale as it moves through over twenty years of time throughout the series. Each build upon the legends of Braetan and Carelon until, by the time of *Queen of Mercy*, it is truly an ensemble across a sweeping realm, encompassing dozens of elements drawn from the long and winding road of the Matter of Britain.

That said, there are a few things you may want to know about the books before you go off on this adventure.

First, this is not intended to exist historically. Although I do try to maintain a sense of consistency within the realm of Braetan, I consider the *Queens of Fate* world a secondary world, and therefore there are no date equivalents. If you are here for medieval historical accuracy and attention to detail, you will be disappointed. I have molded time and indeed, continents and islands, to my will.

Braetan and Avillion were inspired predominately by the Pre-Raphaelites and their visual depictions of Arthuriana. Like my hidden Anna, there are dozens of Pre-Raphaelite women—painters, models, writers—who have fallen to the margins of art history. If you look at paintings of Elizabeth Siddal, Evelyn de Morgan, Emma Sandys, and Marie Spartali Stillman, you will see many of my muses for the women of this series.

Linguistically I have chosen to further blur the line between fantasy and history by presenting alternative spellings for character and placenames. These are all rooted in older spellings or simply regional spellings of familiar names, as English had little standardization for centuries. The name Guinevere has more iterations than you can imagine, to say nothing of even minor characters like Sagramore. It is an endless source of amusement for me. Not everything sounds as good in French as it might in Welsh, after all. Especially names like Myrddin. Likewise, I cannot be blamed for some naming conventions, including the trio of Orkney brothers Gawain, Gaheris, and Gareth, who often must occupy scenes together.

Fantasy is generally rather unkind to mothers, relegating them to passive roles, or killing them before they can develop into characters at all. They are valued as the progenitors of heroes, but rarely as heroes themselves. My most treasured reader responses are from mothers who thank me because they see their own reflection in Anna's experience. Yet being motherly does not mean sainthood. Anna is not always a good mother, nor does she always see the whole picture. As the series continues, readers will not just experience the world growing, but reshape their understanding of Anna's own story.

Ultimately, these books are my love letter to Arthurian Legend. Rather than tales of bloodshed and glory upon the field of battle, the *Queens of Fate* series focuses on the conflicts that occur between fate and choice, family and love, and duty and loyalty.

I often say there are no happy endings in Arthuriana. But that isn't quite true. There are no real *endings*. The legend is a circle, a great tapestry of fate, and it has been made and remade century after century: the once and future queens here within are but one more reverberation across the loom.

*Natania Barron*

Then [Uther] returned to the town of Tintagel, which he took, and in it, what he impatiently wished for, Igerna herself. After this they continued to live together with much affection for each other, and had a son and daughter, whose names were Arthur and Anne.

**Geoffrey of Monmouth,**
*History of the Kings of Britain*

The gods only go with you if you put yourself in their path. And that takes courage.

**Mary Stewart,**
*The Crystal Cave*

And so there grew great tracts of wilderness, Wherein the beast was ever more and more, But man was less and less, till Arthur came.

**Sir Alfred, Lord Tennyson,**
*The Idylls of the King*

# CHAPTER ONE

## THE BEGINNING OF THE GREAT END

I OFTEN PICTURE the scene of my birth: the dark room, the pulled drapes, the stench of incense and blood. I see my father, Uther, scarred and haggard, limping across the floor, then gazing at me for a fraction of a heartbeat. He nods his acknowledgement then leaves, letting the midwives whisper in his wake.

I see my mother, Igraine, well past the flower of her youth, pale and weary. She turns her face away from me, closing her eyes with relief, knowing I could have no claim to this bloody throne. Just another daughter like all the rest. Another girl to add to the litany: Elaine, Morgen, Margawse, and now Anna.

In my mind I watch as my brother, golden Arthur, is ushered in to examine the wrinkly squalling child, his wide eyes transfixed and perhaps a little frightened, unsure what to make of the new presence making so much noise in his mother's room. He leans forward, trying to get a better look at the strange, shrieking creature. "This is your sister, Arthur," my mother says. And then he buries his head in his hands and cries. I am so ugly and small and useless, and he was hoping for a playmate. Forever his disappointment.

And lastly, and perhaps most clearly of all, I see Merlin taking me into his arms. He wasn't there before, but then, there he is, as if emerging from the walls themselves like a ghast. He leans over me, brushing his thumb over my forehead—still sticky with blood and caul—and speaks in a voice like the roaring of the sea: "Anna Briallen Carys Pendragon. Through all the ages, and in the hearts of men, you will be forgotten."

My prophecy. My burden. My curse.

THIS TALE, NOT of slaying beasts and saving helpless maidens but of shaping Fate, begins shortly after the death of my first husband, Lot of Orkney. I had been away from Carelon for twenty years, having been married off at twelve, and bore my first son, Gawain, shortly after. Lot, though decidedly dead when this particular chapter of my life began, undoubtedly drained me of my worth. He leveraged Arthur's gift of our marriage and used his political power to strengthen his lands, make strategic alliances with local lords, and emerged with a house richer for it in value and in reputation. While Lot's influence grew, he kept me in the north wing of his old fortress with none but my servants, my books, and the ghasts. And once the boys were born, Lot only paraded me bout for occasions, to display Arthur's only full-blooded sister, tamed and fettered to Orkney. When he was angry, he would beat me and let me linger on the bruises. He did not love me, and he did not expect me to love him.

"There are no princesses in Orkney," he would tell me as I lay, voiceless and motionless, to his violence. "Your blood is this land's blood now."

When I returned to Carelon as a woman grown—a widow and a mother of three boys, I was weary from the month-long journey, but not broken. As we traveled the rolling hills and wheat-rich fields and away from Orkney, I thought only of seeing my son Gawain again, whom I had not seen in five years. Not even at his father's funeral. They were steely, my boys, in ways many of the other knights at court were not. Perhaps I can thank Lot for that. My children grew hard in hard places, and it did them well in the years to come. For of course this is not a happy tale. It does not end with triumph and glory, the right of things champion over the darkness: but it is memorable. It is Arthur's story, and even if you do not know my place in it, the tale remains.

I had seen the twins off at the barge in Striveling weeks before, as I rode toward Carelon: Gaheris trying to hide the tears that were both over departing from me and knowing his father was truly gone, and Gareth staunch and staid as any twelve-year-old boy can be. They were now in the care of Luwddoc, Lot's younger brother, and I hoped his similarity to Lot was comforting for the boys. I only hoped that Luw's habit of bedding any woman within ten miles would not rub off on the boys. Luw was kinder than his brother, Lot, and I trusted him to bring up his nephews in ways I could not.

Yet I had another son. My eldest. There is so little in Lot of Orkney I ever found to be of worth. From his gluttonous vices and deadly temper to his insufferable singing voice, from the bunions on his feet to the reek of his breath, everything about the man repulsed me. And yet, though conceived in grief, Lot granted me an unexpected boon: Gwalchmai, my little Gawain.

Not so little, I reminded myself. Not anymore. But he was a babe, once, and I cradled him to my breast, watched his perfect pink lips suckle greedily, and felt a joy which has since eluded me altogether. I hated Lot as I have hated anyone, but had it not been for him, I would never have borne Gawain, would never have loved as I loved him.

We crossed over the magnificent stone bridge to the north of the castle I recalled dangling my legs off of when I was a child, the rough stones ringing against our horse's hooves. I half-expected to see young Elaine, my eldest and once dearest sister, in her cloak carrying a basket of a variant of flower that only bloomed in the rain, hair plastered to her face, and smiling serenely.

I had not heard from Elaine in quite some time. Like me, she was married young in a marriage of state, given as a spoil of war, not valued for cunning mind and nurturing soul. Our last parting, bitter and brief, still lingered in my thoughts. I did wish her health and joy in my heart, even if it was hard for me to accept those things for myself. We did not often write one another, content in our separate spheres: I in the frigid North, and she in the South of Gaul.

The trees along the road to Carelon arced over us, but thinned, trimmed, and twisted into shapes more befitting of a royal garden than a natural forest. Such was the way of the world and man's unending desire to bend nature to his will. Gone was the wildness I remembered with such fondness; the thickets and brambles I had gamboled through as a child were no longer. I always pictured Carelon as a jewel in the center of a great, rugged wilderness, but now it was tamed to reflect Arthur's unending quest for rule and order. It did not surprise me. I knew the little boy arranging his soldiers in neat lines by the roaring hearth, though he stood taller now and wore a heavy crown.

It was late spring, the leaves clustered on the edges of the branches, ready to unfurl, but still cold enough to chill me down to my underpinnings. I needed some hot liquor and a fire. I felt a rattling in my chest, and a growing cough I suspected came from the long miles and terrible weather during our journey.

It was perhaps that moment, entering the outer gates of Carelon, coughing into my scarves, I at last accepted the truth: I was no longer a queen. Once, I entertained dreams of courtly love, elegance, and ruling wisely. Ten years as Lot's captive burned away those visions, naught left but ashes. Queenship, I decided, would never be my fate.

Though my relationship with Arthur was fraught on a thousand counts, I agreed, as our father before us, in the vision of a unified Braetan. A Braetan of peace. Fewer crowns means fewer conflicts, and in that a hope that Braetan could be whole—just as Avillion had been for the last three thousand years. One King, one Rule.

As Queen of Orkney, upon my husband's death, I was granted the most significant choice of my life: I could pass Lot's crown to my sons, or to my brother. Lot desired no part in unification. The few times I attempted discussion on the matter he silenced me swiftly with his fists. Instead of immediate retribution, I waited patiently. As the years went on—as lichen crept up my walls and ice filled my veins— Lot finally breathed his last. And when he gasped that final, desperate plea, naked and alone before the gods, I vowed my defiance.

So, I carried the dead King of Orkney's crown, tied around my waist in a silk and ermine lined satchel, like a weight dragging me to the bottom of a lake. Drowning in the rain, in memories, and in regret.

Certainly, I was melancholy, but who could blame me? Perhaps I expected Carelon to remain unchanged, for my familiar friends and family—Arthur, Cai, Bedevere, Elaine, Margawse, and even Morgen—to be waiting for me, preserved as if in amberglass in my absence. It was a childish, naïve wish. But it was the wish of a child who was forced to grow up far too fast, of a girl who lived in shadows so long that even a ray of sunshine through thick colored glass felt like the sun.

I had just begun to nod off again, when I heard Culver, my chief servant, at the head of my entourage, barking an order to stop. I squinted ahead and saw the red and gold banners of Arthur, and under them, two riders approaching at an impressive pace. I shivered, noticing for the first time the spires of Carelon in the distance, though misty and gray in the rain.

The riders drew closer, and after exchanged welcome and laughter—laughs I recognized but could not place immediately—the shorter rider removed her hood, and I saw it was Morgen, my half-sister. Her red lips stood out brilliantly, like a gash across her pale face, and her soot black hair fell in straight braids on either side. Morgen's face bore the same ethereal beauty, untouched since our last meeting, save the lines at the corner of her mouth and subtle hollow of her cheeks.

Morgen was ever Merlin's protected child, and it was no surprise to me the old conjuror was the other rider. I should have seen it in his gait. He turned to look at me, new streaks of white in his brown beard. His eyes were the same intense black I recalled, the lines in his face deepened and hardened but not changing the breathtaking strangeness of his face: his forehead was a twisting gyre serpentine of tattoos, his black brows bushy and unkempt, his small nose flanked by high cheekbones deeply scored with skeletal precision.

"Why, Anna, you have returned," said Morgen, upon seeing me. Her berry-green eyes bright in contrast against the drab that cloaked the world. "It is so good to see you, sister."

She was as sincere as she could be, yet I knew the words were out of courtesy rather than true compassion or feeling. My half-sister's cold affections for me were no secret. Still, I would have settled for a quiet neutrality, but the daughters of Gorlois never had seen me as an equal.

"The Queen of Orkney returns at long last," said Merlin, his voice carrying over the rain, and I shivered. I heard the words of my prophecy when he met my eyes, as fresh in my mind as new ink on parchment: *Through all the ages, and in the hearts of men, you will be forgotten.* "I trust the journey was not too difficult, though it was undoubtedly trying. You wear the distance on your face."

I gave the best imitation of a smile I could but felt a twinge in my lung and coughed rather unseemly into the crook of my arm.

"You're soaked through," said Morgen, bringing her horse up beside me, reaching up to touch my face. Her fingertips were like fire on my skin. "And you're burning up. How long have you been out in the open? You should be in the caravan, sister. You're not a servant."

"It is stifling in the caravan," I said, but it was not the only reason I opted for the saddle rather than cover. Anette, one of my woman servants, was recently with child, and I did not want her in such inclement conditions. So, the previous day I gave up my seat for her, and insisted the medic, Jain, stay with her; it was a small covered caravan, and certainly too cramped for three.

Instead of elaborating, however, I continued, "I am surprised to see such a greeting. I did not know if my herald arrived in time to—"

Even before I finished speaking, out of the corner of my eye I saw Culver wink at me, grimacing. I fell silent, knowing I had made an error.

Culver cleared his throat and turned the attention from Morgen's embarrassed face as he said, "Merlin and her Ladyship are on their way to greet King Pellas and his entourage—they are arriving for Lugh's Tournament. It is a happy accident we've come upon one another for such a fortuitous reunion."

"Of course," I managed, glad for the fever to cover the blush creeping into my cheeks. "You will forgive me, I have been away from court so long, and we have been preoccupied with the arrangements since Lot's passing."

Merlin narrowed his eyes, piercing, sifting through my words. Calculating. I could have done without seeing him for weeks. And here I was, not yet within sight of the castle, and the old bard was already trying to break me apart. "Yes, may his soul pass through the final door in peace," said the sorcerer.

"Yes, we wish him a swift arrival to the far shore," Morgen said, a little hurriedly. "You know, sister, Arthur will be so pleased to see you. Though you've arrived a bit earlier than we were expecting. I'm not sure Gweyn has brought everything up to her standards at the moment, what with the tournament just around the corner."

Lot had barely cooled in the crypt, it was true. But I could not wait another day in that moldering prison of a fortress.

"The winds were in our favor, it seems," I replied. Then to Culver: "We shall make do, shan't we, Culver? We can always help the Queen. It isn't as if we are unfamiliar with keeping a castle."

"Of course, Your Highness," replied the coachman.

"Her *Ladyship* will suffice, you recall," I said to him, and he nodded a little reluctantly. He was intentionally asserting my former title in order to remind Morgen and Merlin of whom they were dealing with, and I admired him for the pluck. They would never assume such a man as Culver, a man more at home among dung-strewn stables than at court, would ever be as capable as them. It is one of the reasons I brought him with me to Carelon.

"If you will excuse us, then," I said, letting Merlin and Morgen pass on their way. "We are tired and, as you can see, a bit worse for wear. The promise of a warm fire and a hot meal will get us these last few miles."

"Of course," Morgen said, her smile fading. "But promise me you will have your woman look after you as soon as possible. You do not look well, sister."

Merlin shook his head. "Morgen, Morgen. Your sister has plenty of attendants, and we are behind schedule. She does not need a midwife to hassle her."

I bid farewell to my sister, and watched her leave, her black braids like perfect lines down the back of her cloak. As was always the case with wise Morgen, I knew I would see her again soon. And I was curious what our next conversation, without the presence of the looming bard, would bring. There were messages in her expressions I could not put together.

The road grew busier as we approached the spires of Carelon, the towers coming into view in gilded red and yellow, and it was so much more expansive than I remembered. What had once been an impressive central fort in my childhood, the life's project of Uther Pendragon, was now a rambling collection of towers and bridges, all comprised of the same pink granite and shiny ivory limestone. A veritable city rose from its feet, inns and markets and temples and homes crouched together like penitent pilgrims.

Housed within Carelon's walls lived approximately one thousand souls at its height, only about one-tenth of whom were nobles. But that number did not take into account the city surrounding it, supported it, and supplied it. Carelon itself hosted its own brewery, winery, bakery, armory, smithy, an aviary, and extensive stables, both for the King's personal uses and the needs of the castle itself. There were forty bedrooms, and five separate apartments with two-to-three chambers in each which accommodated the King and various members of the royal family. One tower was Merlin and Morgen's, which housed the vast library below, and their elaborate quarters above. There were all kinds of wonders within, including a cloister that was, in fact, a copse of trees, a natural spring, a variety of fruit trees, and a glass-paned orchid garden. All about the castle, the stonework was a marvel of craftsmanship, depicting intertwining dragons, oak trees, and a variety of assuredly beautiful designs all in deep red and blush stone.

Yes, *beautiful*. Beautiful as anything made by man's hands. Perhaps Carelon was one of the greatest wonders on the face of the earth; I do not know; I have seen so little of it. But know this: such beauty came at a price, for every arc and line, every flapping banner told the story of the people who lived and died under them; the common people, the workers, the servants, unseen mothers and daughters and courtiers who do not find their way into the songs. Arthur always enjoyed decadence, as did our father Uther before him, and every inch of Carelon was steeped in grandeur. But it was a cold, drafty place in the winter, and unbearably hot in the summer months. There were more mice in the walls than people between them. The West wing was prone to flooding and then to mold and mildew by turns. One of the sewing rooms always smelled of cow manure. And not to mention, moving from one place to another in Carelon was an endless succession of stairs and hallways, no small task even for someone as accustomed to walking as I.

I am sorry there is less romance in the description. But Carelon, even glorious Carelon, was like a polished quartz embedded in the ground: if you could turn it over with your heel, all sorts of creatures would scuttle out from beneath, dark and deprived of the sun.

Culver led us down the slope and across the many bridges, through the busy streets, and into the common stables to board our horses, then arranged to send word of our arrival. I checked on Jain and Anette, and they were both well enough. Jain had come with me from Carelon to Orkney and was eager to be with her family and friends again, but Anette was born to the desolate isles to the North and was clearly nervous living among such strange folks. I tried to reassure her as well as I could, but I knew it did little good. Anette was the sort of woman who would always fret, regardless of reason.

My cough was getting worse, and at the insistence of Culver, rather than wait for an escort, I was taken through to the main entrance with Jain, Anette, and Haen—another of the groomsmen I brought with me from Orkney—for a formal announcement followed by, what I hoped, would be a swift retreat to a warm bath. It was one luxury I looked forward to at Carelon: the ease of hot water. Lot's drafty old pile of stone in Orkney contained no pipe-works to speak of, and to get enough hot water for a bath required at least an hour's notice.

We entered through the great doors, forged mostly of iron and inlaid with scrollwork, an ancient remnant of my childhood. Those doors still felt imposing, even though I had grown a bit taller. The air from inside moved my hair, bringing with it the scent of sawdust, baked bread, and musky perfume. It did not smell like the Carelon I remembered, the fortress of flux, of sweat, of hay. As a child, it was not uncommon for animals to still graze the halls. No more. It was transformed.

I was informed at the door by a knight I did not recognize that the King was not seeing anyone, let alone penitents. The knight may have said his title, but I was so incensed by his arrogant manner, and assuming I was some wandering serf, I blurted out:

26

"You will tell Arthur at your nearest convenience that his one *true* sister, Anna of Orkney, is languishing, awaiting his word," I said.

The knight looked confused and blinked at me. "You mean *you're* Anna?" he said.

"I realize I am slightly bedraggled, but I assure you I know my own worth," I said, removing my hand from my sleeve to reveal the twin crests of Orkney and Pendragon on my rings. They glittered rather impressively in the light. "He knows of my arrival—"

"Anna?" said a voice, as another knight approached. It was Cai, limping over to me on his bad foot, his limp so much more pronounced than I observed just five years ago when I delivered Gawain to Arthur as his squire. Now, Cai's once striking crimson hair turned to white at the temples, and one of his shoulders was significantly lower than the other. Had Arthur brought him to war again? He was immense and homely as ever, though, waxy complexion pockmarked and sallow, his squinty eyes widening as he took me in. Still, seeing him filled my heart with affection.

To the young knight, Cai said: "Gods, boy, this is the King's *sister*."

"But I thought His Majesty said—" attempted the knight.

"You thought *what*?" bellowed Cai, turning on the younger knight and squaring his shoulders. Cai may no longer have been able to compete in the tournaments or knock heads off of his enemies, but there was no doubt to his capabilities in close combat. He was strength embodied, and of such a stature I wondered, when I was younger, if he was been born of giants rather than men.

When the knight did not answer, and only blinked his

dusky brown eyes, Cai asked, again, "You thought *what*, Sir Lamorak?"

Lamorak gulped and said, staring over my head and at the door, "I thought her Queenship—her Ladyship—was part of her retinue, and not herself. Sir."

Cai frowned, clearly disgusted by Lamorak's explanation, and rolled his eyes. "You, Lamorak, are an embarrassment. Can you not see the resemblance? Gods, man, she is as like as he is as would be a twin."

"Y-yes," stammered knight. He was shaking, beads of sweat springing out at his temple, darkening his ash blond hair. Handsome he was not, but he had a certain uniqueness to his features, a memorable face. It was the sharpness of his nose, and the distance between his eyes— not a combination I often noted.

The seneschal took a deep breath and took my arm in his, protectively. "See to it you do not forget your place, Lamorak. She has come home to us. I do not suppose you have offered her condolences for the recent loss of her husband, have you? Or informed her that her son will be brought to her as soon as possible?"

"No—no, Sir Cai, I have not," rasped Lamorak.

"Well?" He flapped his large hand in the air, his fingers as long as sausages.

Lamorak licked his lips and said, "My condolences, your Ladyship, on the loss of your husband, King Lot of Orkney. I will send word to your son—"

"*Sir* Gawain," interjected Cai.

"Sir Gawain," repeated Lamorak, "Ah… immediately."

"Many thanks," I said, suppressing a shiver, and squeezing Cai's arm slightly. I would have laughed save for my weary soul; Cai was always Cai, the over-protective brother I never had.

As Lamorak walked away, I said to Cai, "Must you be so hard on the poor boy?" I said it with a smile, though.

"Ah, it will help him toughen up. He needs a good scolding every now and again, truth be told. Spends much too much time impressing the lasses with his fancy title rather than earning it, I will tell you that much. A little work, and he would be a match even for your Gawain."

My heart leapt again at the mention of my son. "He is so good? Gawain, I mean."

"The best," said Cai, his face all seriousness. He was not a man to give a compliment, that was for certain.

With as much pomp and circumstance as a limping seneschal could manage, Cai walked with me through the entrance hall, asking a number of questions I could scarcely answer quick enough. He wanted to know about Gareth and Gaheris, of course, and was loath to learn they were now with Luwddoc. Cai disliked the Orkneys in general, my sons withstanding of course, and Luw even less than Lot. I believe he called him "worse than the nether bits between arse and cock" but I could be wrong.

"We are headed toward Mother's chambers..." I said, finally getting my bearings. There was so much in the way of redecoration since Gweyn arrived, from tapestries to mirrors and unfamiliar statues, I almost lost my bearings entirely. When I realized where we were at last, I came to an abrupt halt. "I—does Arthur really mean to—?"

Cai paused, a little relieved to take a breath, and looked sidelong at me. Jain and Anette waited patiently behind us, talking to each other in low voices. Anette had never seen

Carelon, of course. The simple girl was out of her mind with wonder as we rushed by the dizzying delights of the castle compound.

"It is a compliment," said Cai, almost asking rather than saying. His crooked shoulders slunk. "You see—it has been entirely renovated, and awaiting, well, *you*. She has so put her heart into it, she would be devastated if you refused."

"She?"

"The Queen," said Cai, softly. "Gweyn. She took it upon herself to redesign the room when she knew you were coming, though it isn't quite finished in the way she'd hoped. Fresh flowers, and all."

"Fresh flowers?"

Cai nodded solemnly. "She takes the study and meaning of plants very seriously. The rest, she wanted to be a celebration of... well, you'll see. Half of the furniture is from Avillion, specially brought in, and though it is certainly not the sort of decoration I would consider a necessity to the day-in and day-out activities of one's life, I am certain you will find it—"

"Hideous," I said, barely whispering it.

Cai grimaced.

I sighed, searching, as I always did, for something comely in Cai's features. But I found none. I put my hand on his chest and spied a small golden cross pinned to his cloak, crudely made but lovely. So, the Christ men had come to Carelon. Ever-suffering Cai would be an ideal convert, but I never considered him the religious sort. Still, time changes us all. Even a man born with bloodlust and rage in his veins could be swayed toward peace and self-flagellation in the right situation.

"Ah, well, it is little matter," I finally said. "I hardly need an entire apartment. I requested something simple, but if this is what Her Majesty desires, then it will be so. So long as there is hot water, I shall be delighted."

"There is that," said Cai. "Aplenty."

"And it comes from pipes, not hauled up stairs by knock-kneed servants?"

"Every drop from the bowels of the castle," said Cai.

"And it is clear, not the muddy, murky sludge Uther used to favor?"

"On my honor, pristine as the Lake itself."

"Thank the gods," I said. "Every last one of them."

# CHAPTER TWO

## UNDIGNIFIED ENDS

STANDING AT THE threshold of my new apartment, I recalled something Mother said to me one day after she found me sitting in the fountain in the central gardens at Carelon, reading a book and covered in mud to the knees as I was so often.

"You must act as if your father could see everything you do"—for of course, in those days, Uther was still alive—"and when Arthur is king, act as if he can see everything you do, and consider your actions in light of that. Anna, dear, you have none of the gifts of my other daughters but do try at least to be modest and practice discipline now and again."

I understood, cruel as her words sounded. I was neither dainty nor pretty in the way her first daughters were. Instead, I was hardy, lanky, and rather plain. Try as she might to encourage me, I had no proclivity for needlework, no propensity for spellcasting, and, certainly, significant difficulty keeping my mouth shut when offended.

And now, Arthur had given me Mother's old quarters.

How strange it was I would be the daughter to inherit them and not one of her three jewels. I recalled only dim details about the rooms: she favored marigold yellow and spruce green, and collected small statues from Avillion the common folk made to represent their household gods.

However, I need not have worried about the room retaining any of my mother's design, for now it was awash in brilliant crimson, sky blue, and dazzling swaths of silver—the colors of Avillion. I was almost blinded by it. Every wooded surface was gilded, scrolled, and embossed, every tuffet and cushion a swirl of silks and metallic threads, every table and chair swathed in embroidery. The walls were hung with tapestries of maidens frolicking naked in streams, dryads dancing by the banks. Charming, in a way, but entirely unlike anything I would have chosen. Had I been asked, likely I would have selected natural wood, woven carpets, and simple, but elegant, coverlets. Perhaps living in the staid ruggedness of Orkney muted my own taste, but what I beheld made me dizzy.

Jain and Haen helped Anette to a seat, into which she crumpled with a sigh of relief.

"This will be home," I said, softly. "For a while, at least. Thank you, all of you, for making this journey with me. But now, before I fall to pieces, I must wash and rest."

Jain helped draw the bath—the apartment even boasted a separate chamber for bathing and dressing, which was a welcome luxury—and I soaked for a good hour before the water went cold. Gweyn supplied a wide array of soaps and soaks, but due to my congested state I could not enjoy the herbal aromatics. The warmth was enough, though, and when I emerged and wrapped myself in a fur-lined robe which under any other circumstance I would never have considered wearing, I felt refreshed.

The feeling did not last long. I received notice Arthur wanted an audience with me immediately, which meant I would be unable to lounge in comfort and would have to put on more suitable raiment, the trappings of silk and brocade befitting the widowed Queen of Orkney. It was little matter. I was used to being summoned, and I knew how to play the game with words as much as with fabric and presentation.

Of course, Gweyn thought ahead, and provided me with an extensive new wardrobe, most of which was too small. Gweyn, who was not a mother, had no idea how much one's body could shift and change with the years. Jain and Anette helped me find a suitable gown. The color was dark plum, which did naught for my complexion, but it would have to do until my things were brought back to my quarters. Arthur was not interested in the play of my golden hair against the dress: he wanted the crown of Orkney. I would arrive, we would exchange pleasantries, the court scribes would record, and then…

Well, I did not know what came next, what steps Fate would reveal to me. As Anette fixed the beaded cuffs about my wrists, set the pearl-studded pins in my hair, and tied the laces tight about my kirtle, I tried to shape my future life in my mind, and it was like wandering a dark corridor with the torches guttered out.

When my maids finished their work, I studied the result. It would do. My youth still lingered, albeit reluctantly, about my brow and breast. I did not look quite so haggard as I felt. This would suffice.

"You're trembling, Ladyship," Jain said as she finished tying my sash.

"Am I?" I asked, looking down at my hands. Apparently so.

"Perhaps you should rest first. You are unwell," the medic said softly.

"Nonsense," I said, knowing the trembling had more to do with nerves than the cough, but saying naught to Jain. She would not understand. She was a practical woman, without room for frivolous emotion. It was one of the reasons I kept her near.

I was thinking about seeing Gawain again, who did not return to Orkney for his father's funeral. I'd not seen my firstborn in five years. Was he still so brilliantly red-haired, or did the color fade like Lot's, to a dark auburn? Had he grown taller? Already mighty for his age at fifteen, he could have outgrown even Cai by now. Surely, he would attend Arthur, as he ought, as first knight—but would he want to spend time with me? Would I embarrass him? Certainly, the last thing such a celebrated knight as Gawain would want was the presence of a meddling mother.

There were times I felt I could never let go of the little boy he once was to accept the man he had become.

"The King awaits," I said to Jain, brushing her off as she tried to set one of the pearl pins toward the center of my hair. "I have a crown to deliver, after all, and it cannot wait for vanity. At least, not mine."

Arthur did not receive me in the main hall, but rather the smaller, more intimate Argent Foyer, as it was called. The room once served as our father's military planning center, and I would often sneak there as a child to look at the grand maps. Now, it was Arthur's secondary receiving hall, meant for more personal, intimate matters. He often sat with Merlin discussing matters of state in the Blue Foyer, enough to garner the nickname "the Owlery" by those at court with a less than favorable view of the old conjuror.

I looked for Gawain as soon as the doors opened, but I knew immediately he was not in attendance.

Instead, I was surprised to see another knight attending Arthur, one whose face I had spent the last ten years trying to forget: Sir Bedevere. He stood next to Arthur, hands linked behind his back, and looked to me immediately. Bedevere's still, brown eyes widened, and he smiled—a bit perfunctorily—and I saw the new lines of wear, the erosion of his once charmingly round face. Taller and, I always thought, more handsome than Arthur, betimes he was mistaken for the King with his lithe build and easy manner. But bedecked in brown and maroon as he was, Bedevere nonetheless cut a rather somber figure next to Arthur.

Golden and fit as always and draped in his more casual king's garb with a scarlet sash and yellow brocade, Arthur stood immediately upon the announcement of my arrival. He had grown a beard since last I saw him, and his hair was long, tied back. As ever, I marveled at the similarity in our features but thought the age did him well; he looked less pinched with the years, his nose drooping to near hawkishness and his eyes deepening, hinting at his occasional intensity.

I did not think long on Arthur, for Bedevere commanded my thoughts, as ever.

Bedevere, my first love.

Ours always was a complicated relationship. We scarcely were allowed to see each other in our youth, as I was as yet unmarried in those days. Arthur once said he hoped to make a good match of us, and he suspected we would be a suitable political alliance—his sister and his most loyal friend. Providing Merlin agreed.

Instead, Arthur married me off to Lot. At the time, I did not understand. But years of life in Orkney taught me the power of politics, and Merlin's constant guiding hand. Far beyond that, Arthur depended on Bedevere to be his conscience; Arthur was not a shrewd man, not a man of logic, but Bedevere always was. I do not think Arthur could have endured any doubt to Bedevere's loyalty, marriage or no.

Though it is not to say that Bedevere and I remained blameless. We enjoyed many stolen moments of indiscretion in the ensuing years; oftentimes under my husband's own roof. That my heart leapt to my throat upon seeing Bedevere could not be helped. The man's very presence illuminated my soul.

"Sister—great gods, it does me good to see you," said Arthur, placing a hand to his chest, as if I was a ghast arisen from the grave.

I bowed lowly, the sleeves of my dress touching the floor, beadwork tinkling against the gold-streaked marble. "Hail Arthur, King of Braetan."

When I stood straight, he was before me, and took me in his arms, holding me close before kissing my cheeks, my mouth, and then clasping my hand. He would not let it go, but continued to look down at me, smiling serenely, staring through me with my own pale grey eyes. A strange reflection.

"Anna—dearest sister," he said, helping me to one of the high-backed chairs in the room. As he pulled it away, it scraped against the marble floor, reverberating through the room like a wailing mother. When I sat the scent of beeswax and old straw rose around me. "My heart breaks to hear of Lot's passing. He was a king among kings. We all regret we could not make the trip for his pyre-lighting, but as you know the winter was particularly cruel this year."

"My gratitude, Your Majesty," I said, smoothing the front of my skirt. A butler immediately came to my side and offered me cordial out of a jeweled goblet, which of course I took. Knowing Arthur, it would be bereft of alcohol, and I was the last person to deny his hospitality, especially considering he was taking me in as his own. Granted, I was laying a kingdom at his feet... but I was still at the mercy of his kindness.

"Gweyn is in her chambers, unfortunately, and ill," Arthur said, at last letting go of my hand. He startled, then laughed. "Not to worry you! I suppose you have not heard: she is with child. Four months, now."

"Congratulations are in order," I said, trying to hide my surprise. I was not sure Arthur was up to the task; five years married to Gweyn and not even a whisper of a child. Some husbands would have called for an annulment in such time, but I knew with Arthur the difficulties in the bedchamber lie much deeper than Gweyn's womb, and our father had broken him in ways I could not fathom regarding Arthur's proclivities. "I would very much like to call on her soon. To thank her for all the truly dazzling work on my chambers."

"She would be most pleased," said Arthur. He glanced over at Bedevere and chuckled. "Oh! And of course,

Bedevere is here! Oh, ignore me. I admit, I am more than dizzy with all the preparations for the Tournament. But you're old friends. You hardly need introductions."

I could have smiled at Bedevere, done a thousand little things to let him know I noticed him, I was happy to see him, and that I desired him; but I was weary down to my bones from my travels, and perhaps feeling a bit petty. He had not written in a long time. Instead, I simply nodded, and said: "We have a matter to attend to, Your Highness, before there is time for any reunions."

I pulled at the pouch at my waist and stood.

The crown of Lot of Orkney, the storied heirloom passed down generations spanning at least two hundred years, slipped easily out of the bag, and in the light of the Blue Room the dark iron and silver filigree looked unearthly and cold, the red garnets set around it like fresh blood. Lot meant that crown for Gawain. So he'd said a thousand times. However, the decision fell to me upon his death. I may have lied to him, promised to honor his wishes to allay his fears. I knew what obstinance and defiance got me, so I played his game until he could breathe no more.

As I stared at that golden wonder of my husband's ancient house, the crown in my hands, I almost smiled knowing Lot of Orkney was naught but ash and memory. The decision was mine now, mine alone. Wherever his soul lingered, he could not hurt me.

"Truly—this was his?" asked Arthur, taking it gently in his hands, his eyes wide with childlike wonder. For all of Orkney's roughness, the crown was impressive even by Arthur's standards. "You brought it all the way with you?"

"Symbolic, perhaps," I admitted. "But yes, my lord, it is

the true crown of Orkney. The very same Lot wore upon his coronation, and all the kings of Orkney before him."

"Surely, a treasure of this sort is beyond measure…" Arthur began, trailing off to admire the ermine lining. He may have spoken to the contrary, but I noted the way his fingers intertwined with the fittings on the crown, smoothed over the stones, fawned over the whorls and indentations. He was smitten by beauty, as always.

"The Orkney Isles are yours, King Arthur," I said. Then: "Hail King Arthur, King of All Braetan." Bedevere echoed me a moment later. There were other knights in the room, around the perimeter, and they replied in kind. Arthur did so enjoy a show of loyalty. As I said, I knew the game well enough.

Arthur sat back down, placing the crown on his lap, drawing circles around the garnets, which were as thick as his thumbs. He looked like a cat with a new plaything.

"I am humbled, sister," he said, not looking up at me. "This is a gift of such generosity and sacrifice." His shoulders dropped slightly, and he was silent, then looked over at Bedevere. "Do not you think we should celebrate? Have a feast? Something—I know this is a busy time of year, but it is fitting that we should make up for our inability to attend the funeral; I feel terrible about it." He turned back to me, his brows down and eyes near the point of tears. "Truly, Anna, I feel terrible. The timing…"

"Perhaps after Lugh's Tournament," said Bedevere, as helpfully as he could. "With so many guests arriving in the next few days, we are hard-pressed as it is for time—and the kitchens are fit to bursting with orders. They will be backed up for days. But a show of solidarity would be wise, afterwards."

"I see," I said, meeting Bedevere's eyes and holding them for a moment before he looked away. I covered my smile with a cough. "It is of little concern, of course, Your Majesty," I said, turning to Arthur, watching him as he continued to run his hands over Lot's crown.

"Her Ladyship is likely tired from her long journey from the Isles, my lord, having just returned today," said Bedevere, breaking what was a strange silence. "Shall I escort the Lady Anna back to her apartment, Your Majesty?"

Arthur looked up at Bedevere and nodded. Poor Arthur. Bedevere and I could have coupled on the floor and he likely would never notice. Our king was a man of passion and learning, but not of cunning. He even married Gweyn on a whim of passion, and not with good logic—without the support of Merlin, to the wizard's fury. Certainly, an alliance with Avillion was a sound decision, but he had fallen for Gweyn for her storied beauty, which was impressive, and not on her character. Even worse, he was previously engaged to her sister Hwyfar, and the entire situation had been a near fiasco. That he and Gweyn were so mismatched was a secret source of pleasure for me. Arthur's wants forever overshadowed their consequences.

"Of course, of course," Arthur said. "Sister, do rest yourself. The tournament is in two days' time, so we will ask very little of you until then. I expect you will want to be in attendance to see Gawain in the events, of course—and, why, have you even had the chance to see the lad yet?"

"I have not," I replied. "I was hoping he might be here upon my arrival."

"Oh, he's a busy fellow," Arthur said with a wave of his hand, as if it explained everything. "Indispensable, really. I rely on him for so much. He's got an impressively tactical mind once the temper is mitigated. As of yet there are no rumors of war, but when there are—for it is inevitable—he will prove himself on the battlefield. For now, we leave him to the tourney. He's a favorite among the knights, and a wonder with the lance."

"It makes my heart glad to hear such praise," I said, even if it was not entirely true. The idea of war made my skin prickle with fear and the idea of sending my eldest boy into the fray was difficult to comprehend. I was not the first queen to see her child taken to battle, but I had lived in the times of plenty and peace between Uther's death and Lanceloch's treachery. Those years were reserved for my own personal violence of a kind I learned to endure and, when needed, control.

"We have arranged Gawain to meet Lady Anna this evening for dinner," Bedevere said, to my honest surprise. I had not been informed. "He should be able to make the time between trainings."

"Excellent good," said Arthur. "As usual, Bedevere, you have the whole business tied up rather handily. Please, see Anna back to her chambers and when you return, we can attend to the lists again together in preparation for the Tournament."

"Yes, Your Majesty," said Bedevere, and he held out his arm to me, which I took without question. Were I considerably more refreshed, I might have scrutinized such an intimate gesture. Even touching him through the fabric of his tunic was enough to send a flush to my cheeks and my thoughts down scandalous pathways.

Carelon was a bustling place in those days, so Bedevere's

escort was by no means reason for tongues to wag. He was a knight; I was a lady. Such things were expected. We walked through the halls, unspeaking, passing hundreds of servants and knights, lords, and nobles. It was overwhelming for me, as I was by then accustomed to the quiet of Orkney Castle, as decrepit and empty and ominous as it was. I had become rather used to moving around undetected. But in Carelon we drew many eyes as we wound our way to my new apartment, tall Bedevere with his dark eyes and sharp features, and I, pale and fair and so like Arthur.

Still, I was not aware the presence of so many people, coupled with the exhaustion from the trip and the emotion of giving Arthur Lot's crown, had put such a toll on me. I was taken just as unawares as Bedevere when I lost my footing quite completely and half-swooned as we mounted the stairs.

"Anna—" Bedevere said, quickly steadying me with his strong, fair hands. Thankfully I did not fall completely, and my dignity was still intact.

My eyes fluttered shut, but when I opened them again, I noticed how despairingly close Bedevere was to me, his lips just a breath from mine.

"Anna, you aren't well," he said. "You never should have come to Arthur so soon—the matter of Orkney could have waited. You need sleep… after all you have been through—"

"I am hardy and hale," I insisted, taking some liquor from his proffered hip flask. It was lukewarm and spicy, some sort of foreign drink no doubt, as he so often preferred. But it did help me revive somewhat. "I needed to settle my mind before I truly rested; I cannot tell you what a burden carrying that relic around has been…"

Bedevere realized then how close he was to me, his arm still around my waist, and gently let go—but not before squeezing my side with familiarity and affection. "Would I could help you with your burdens, lady."

Ah, it had been an age since I heard such words. The effects of compliments never cease to move me, considering I have been given so few in my life. To look at Bedevere watching me, I could have mistaken myself for one as lovely as Gweyn. I commanded power over him; I knew I need only say a word and he would be mine.

Such knowledge always made me a little drunk.

No, I am not proud of the way I conducted myself with Bedevere, nor in the way I had toyed with his heart, ever letting him on, year after year. I told myself it was my right, as a woman whose prime of life was sold to an old lecherous dotard, to hoard my power somewhere, to assure myself of my own womanliness. I believed it was the key to my sanity and a well of strength beneath my ever-mounting weaknesses.

"How... how are you, truly?" he asked. When I did not reply, his voice grew tender. "I hear you left the boys— Gareth and Gaheris, that is—with Luwddoc?"

Yes. There was the matter of the twins, as well, and Bedevere knew all too well, though we certainly never spoke of it to one another. One of our indiscretions had been nine months before their birth and though I arranged it in such a way Lot would not suspect, Bedevere was shrewd. They did not take after Lot in the least. They were dark-haired, tall and lean where Gawain was soaring and broad. Lot either did not care or did not have the strength to deny them, such a gleaming pair they were.

"For a few years, yes," I said, gently as I could, still feeling as if my breath had been taken from me, but gaining composure. "But when they're of age, Luw will bring them to court. It seems it is the fashion these days, after all, to see our boys in the tournament."

"Better than at war," said Bedevere.

"For now," I said. "But… you'll excuse me, Sir Bedevere, for cutting our conversation short. You see, I have only just arrived and one of my maids is with child—I would like very much to see to her before catching a short nap. I've a dinner to attend, later, for which I must prepare."

Bedevere frowned slightly, the edges of his lips turning down. He had no idea how much I wanted him, then. Always. Living in the same castle would afford us some luxuries we never considered before, but it would also bring other complications. There were so many eyes on us, so many gossips just waiting for Arthur's chief advisor to make a mistake, to do something unseemly. It was a thrilling kind of pressure, but a true threat, too.

He stared at me, waiting for me to say more, and then took my arm, bringing me all the way to the door of my apartment. A pair of guards posted there uncrossed their lances to let me through.

"Good eve'n," I said to Bedevere. "Will you be joining us for dinner tonight?"

"Afraid not," he said. His nostrils flared, and I could tell I had angered him. "I am required elsewhere."

"Perhaps we can have breakfast together in the coming days, or tea?" I asked, giving him what smile I could manage.

"Perhaps," he replied. His back stiffened and he looked at me, almost with a challenge in his dark eyes. I wanted to touch his lips, to take him with me, to lay with him and release myself of the darkness I could not dismiss, even after the submission of Lot's crown.

But I was not so easily conquered.

"You can send word to my grooms, Haen and Culver, if you like," I said, softly. "If you decide you'd like to."

"Yes, Ladyship."

"Goodnight, Bedevere."

"Goodnight, Lady Anna."

BEDEVERE ARRANGED FOR dinner between Gawain and myself in one of the balconied breakfast rooms on the third floor of Carelon, a rather uncomfortable distance from my apartment. As I made the long trek, I recalled Bedevere and I had once snuck into the very room and smiled. It seemed he was growing bolder in his age. He wanted to remind me.

However, the third floor was quite different from what I recalled. Someone, presumably Gweyn, judging by the similarity the decoration held in comparison to my new apartment, had draped everything in saffron silk and blue linen, replaced the old wood furniture with plush pillowed versions. The room itself, once I was ushered in and given a seat, was now home to a series of gaming tables as well as breakfast trays and featured a newly refaced central hearth in the rounded Avillion fashion. The smell of quince and cinnamon wafted through the room, but I avoided the food and looked around anxiously for Gawain.

He had not yet arrived.

One of the side-doors opened, and a voice announced the arrival of my sister Margawse.

Gods damn Bedevere for inviting her! Perhaps he was playing a more dangerous game than I originally thought.

I will say this: many of the things you have heard about the women of Carelon are false. I have heard the rumors, the suppositions, the mythologies built around them. And nearly every woman I would defend to the last, unless the rumor happened to be regarding my youngest half-sister, Margawse. There is naught I would put past that woman.

As she entered the breakfast room, she drew my attention magnetically. Margawse arrived out on a chaise lounge, eating ruby red grapes from a bowl, her eyes half-lidded, her lips turned in a smile.

My mother was once remarkably beautiful, but by the time I was old enough to remember her clearly, she had faded with age and sorrow. I have been told Margawse favored Mother more than any of us. Her face was heart-shaped and dimpled at the chin; eyes dark as oak bark, her hair a riot of black curls fell far past her waist. Those lips, so full and sensual, teased every word she spoke. Her form was more flawless past her middle age than I managed in my prime: Full breasts, round hips, and a waist so narrow most men could encircle their hands about it.

And many had.

When Margawse rose languidly from her chair, her long skirts slid after her like crimson waterfalls. She was smiling so serenely I wondered if she remembered just how much I disliked her; I had never made a habit of hiding it, and even then, I struggled to look anything but furious.

I found myself standing and took a few steps toward her, feeling dowdy and diminished in borrowed attire. Gods, but Margawse was a walking vision of womanhood.

"Sister. Anna, dearest," she said, her voice low and seductive. It was not a ploy merely with men, it was how she spoke to all. Musical, captivating, and entirely superficial. "How good it is to see you—oh, you look ghastly. What a trip you must have had! In the rain I hear! How shocking. Please, have a seat so I can congratulate you properly."

I did not sit. Instead I felt my knees lock. "Congratulate?" I asked, just as I saw Gawain enter.

I could not miss my own son, not with the shock of red curls and broad shoulders, even if he was a head taller since I had last seen him. I saw Gawain both as my sunny, freckled child, and as the striking warrior he was now, a vision in yellow and blue, his vivid eyes wide and still with a hint of mischief.

And just as I felt a swell of pride in my breast, it was quelled. Someone followed behind him—a wisp of a girl with a mane of gold tresses falling to her shoulders, wearing a stunning green gown. She was beautiful, I suppose, but in a pinched, rather washed-out way.

I had no time to wonder further, for Margawse said: "On Gawain's engagement, of course. It's not every day a woman is set on a path to become a grandmother."

# CHAPTER THREE

## DEAD ENDS

"It is Gawain again," said Jain, handing me one of his notes. He had been trying to gain entrance to my apartment since I abruptly stormed out of our dinner the hour before in cold-faced horror. "He is outside the door, and threatening to knock it down if you do not let him in."

"Let him bellow," I said, turning away from Jain. "He always did tantrum when he didn't get his way."

"Yes, your Ladyship," Jain said, and I did not miss the note of exasperation in her voice.

Gawain's voice bellowed all the way across the apartment, the door rattling on its hinges. I had aroused his ire. I knew him well enough that once his temper was ignited there was little to quell it. He would find a way to destroy the beautiful front door if I let him to it long enough, regardless of the scene. That child of mine was impervious to the opinions of others, a considerable frustration when rearing him, though it would serve him later on in life.

"Fine, then. Gods above and below, just let him in," I said, sitting up in bed, and smoothing the furs atop my legs. My hair was combed out and fell down my shoulders, curling and gold. I twirled a lock around my thumb and watched the individual shafts catch the dim light of the oil lamp. Not entirely diminished, I hoped. After Margawse's antics, I would have to make a stern impression, and beauty was power.

Jain showed Gawain in a few moments later, and he was positively seething, half sputtering words and curses and oaths before I held up a hand to silence him.

"Calm down before you speak," I said, looking over at him. "I have not seen you in five years. I demand a moment to gather myself."

He towered over the bed. Gods, but he was immense. Taller than Arthur, taller than Uther, his grandfather. There was so little of Lot in Gawain, but it was enough to enhance the diluted colors the Pendragon side granted him. His hair was dark red, red as dried blood, and his eyes gooseberry green rimmed in blue. The high cheekbones reminded me of my own, but the round shape of the face was all Lot. It was an improvement, I think, over Arthur's own looks. Ever expressive, his brows were darker even than his hair, and thick, making it difficult for him to hide his emotions. He was still as freckled as a robin's egg, but gone were the last vestiges of youth, lost to experience and battle in the intervening years. This was a man grown.

He clenched his teeth and I saw he was missing one of his incisors. Likely from a brawl. And he sported a thick scar through one eyebrow, barely missing his bright green eye. A pity. It gave him an almost brutish air. "Mother. How can you refuse me entrance? I am your *son*. Now you refuse me to my face in front of my beloved!"

As if I needed the reminder.

"I am tired," I replied, and I sounded as weary as I felt. "I have traveled a great distance, and I have had numerous unsettling encounters in the half day I have been here. You'll forgive me for not wanting to be dragged into childish notions of marriage and love when I have just seen my husband at the pyre." I coughed, a little dramatically of course, but it did the trick. His face softened, the stern line between his brows diminished. For a moment I saw him again as the child I once adored.

"I am sorry, Mother," he said, kneeling by my bed. He looked pale. Worried, perhaps. "I have just been under a torrent of pressure. With your return, and the tournament and… Elaine…"

"Elaine?" I asked.

"That is her name—not Aunt Elaine of course, but my betrothed."

Would she could have had any other name. Would my life be ever plagued with Elaines?

"Gawain, I do not wish to speak of this now. You will not like what I am going to say," I said, warning with my tone. How did he think I would approve of such a thing? He was far too young for marrying, too impetuous. Young men made bad husbands, even worse than old dotards.

"She is wonderful, Mother," he insisted, taking my hands in his. My fingers looked like a child's in contrast to his; how strange, I thought, having once cradled his tiny ones in the same way. "With your blessing, we can be married at Midsummer—"

"I do not wish to speak of it."

"Mother—this is *important to me*."

51

"No, it is not," I said, taking my hand from his and sliding it under the covers. Part of me only wanted to take his head in my hands and stroke his red curls as I once had when he was so young, to tell him that to love is to be cherished, and with hard work and determination he and Elaine would have a long, happy life together.

But I was a coddling mother and I did not want to lie. I decided, with Gawain at least, fostering such ideas would lead him away from his true talents, and his ambition. He could not risk such recklessness. Not with his position at court, not with his proximity to Arthur. He could no more afford a pretty young wife of middling nobility than I could afford marrying Bedevere.

"Tell me, how did you meet this Elaine?" I asked, feigning interest. "If you need to tup a girl, you don't have to marry her, you know."

Gawain frowned at me, confused by the question. "Mother. It isn't about that."

"Isn't it?"

"No. I didn't just drag her from an inn. She has been at court."

"Under whose attendance? Women just do not appear at court, Gawain. You know precisely what I am after," I said.

The question left Gawain flustered. He knew I wouldn't like the answer, and so I said it for him. "It is Margawse, is not it? Margawse brought her to court. Of course she did. And do you know why?"

"Mother, it is not like that. Elaine is not Margawse."

"She doesn't *seem* to be, but Gawain—dear Gawain, you must listen to me. Margawse is a calculating woman, of powers and abilities I do not think you comprehend. She delights in trouble, in trickery, and above all, playing with people's hearts. Tell me, have you ever seen Margawse perform acts of good purely for good's sake? No, it always ends in her benefit, somehow. It took me ages to learn, as a young woman, and now I pass that knowledge to you."

He was staring at me, pain in his eyes. He knew the words I spoke were true.

I began more softly, now. "She tried to ruin me once, and I will not see her do it to my son. I will tell you this, and heed my words: if you marry young, Gawain, you give up your freedom. Your father was fifty when he first married, and nearly sixty the second time around. He was able to enjoy his family—" Gawain snorted at this. There was little love between he and Lot; death had not warmed his memories. "Above all, you are a knight—Arthur's knight. And you are beholden to him above all else. What would he say to this match?"

His eyes moved away when I said Arthur's name: he hadn't asked for his permission. I was surprised to find, yet again, a subject which I would have to agree with my brother. So I pressed onward.

"But if the King has given you his blessing then I suppose there's little I can do to dissuade you…"

Gawain flushed. "I did not ask him. Not yet. I was going to—it is only—"

"Oh, well. I am sure he has got a very keen stance on his best knight marrying young, having a brood, and being harangued to stay home and attend to his delicate wife. After all, with you off the market, everyone will be rushing to the stands to see other, more available, fight. Can't think of anyone more interesting than a *married* knight at Tournament."

He bristled, folding his arms across his chest. "People come to see me fight, not to see me prance around like some sort of stallion fit for stud."

I couldn't help but laugh, bitterly and long. "Oh, Gawain. You are so innocent! Of course you're a stallion! You may not like it, but it is all part of the game. And a grand game it is. A game you must play to survive. You're but a part of the show in Arthur's play. As am I. We all must learn our place."

"Mother. Enough." He rose from the bedside. I had taken the fight out of Arthur's best champion with a few words; he looked as tired as if he had battled a dragon, which left a rather unflattering view from my end.

I sighed. "You love her?"

"I think... Hearing you speak of Margawse, and of all her wiles, I feel like an imbecile set up to make you upset," he said. "But you do not know Elaine, Mother. She is so—"

"You can have women," I said, as pointedly as I could. "Don't look so stricken, Gawain. If I had the luxury to engage in dalliances in my youth, I would have. You were given a childhood, time to grow and experience nature and the freedom of your own body. Rejoice and do not seek to grow up too soon. I promise you; it will be worth it. You're practically expected to have an affair, or ten! You need practice. Otherwise you'll be the talk of all the handmaidens at court. And you don't want that."

"Mother—"

"Gawain! Listen to me. Enjoy yourself. Enjoy the young women you want—be careful, mind you, and be certain they're seeing a midwife if needs be, but do not sell yourself short in a marriage to a woman you scarcely know. If it is her buxomness you're after, you can certainly find such features in other women who will not need a ceremony to lay with you."

His skin was swiftly approaching the same hue as his hair.

"I have embarrassed you."

"A little," he admitted.

"You'll come to appreciate my forwardness in the future," I said softly. "I know it cannot be easy to have a meddling mother all of the sudden, but I will do my best."

"No," said Gawain, grinning a little. He looked relieved. "It is good to have you here. I have felt a bit adrift, and Margawse is... persuasive."

"She is that." For a brief moment I wondered to what levels Margawse lowered herself these days and prayed she had not tried to seduce her own nephew. I gave him a tight smile.

"You didn't ask about your father," I said lightly, now the air between us had calmed.

"There is naught to ask. His ashes are cold. You're home now."

"Home? I suppose I am. I cannot help but wonder what he would have thought about today, though. The crown in my hands, his kingdom dissolved in a single gesture."

Gawain looked out the window a moment, the filtered light through the stained glass dotting his skin with even more motley spots. I did not know what went on in his mind, but it broke my heart he had been given such a wretched father.

"I'm glad you gave the crown to Arthur. Carelon is my home; Braetan is my country. As it should be," Gawain said sharply.

"You do not desire your own kingship?"

He looked at me with a pitying kind of expression, but sad, too. "I am many things, Mother. A fool, sometimes, it seems. But I have no kingly heart, no mind for such politics. As you said: I know my part."

"It is not an easy truth to accept, but one that will serve you well," I replied softly, taking his hand again and squeezing it. "There are worse fates than at the right hand of Arthur Pendragon."

He nodded somberly. "I suppose you are right, Mother."

"I know it must be strange to have me at court now, after years of freedom. I do hope we can become closer."

"We will. And I am glad you are here to guide me, now." He leaned over and kissed my head. "Well, dinner awaits. I am sure the King will send word for you again—he tried to send Bedevere with the invitation, but he reported he was not allowed in." He grinned a little, scratching the back of his head. "The way Bedevere goes on about you, I swear he is half in love with you."

The only expression I could manage was a grimace, which he took to be rather amusing. He laughed. "Oh, come Mother! And you're no longer married. You should keep your options open, as well."

"I have no desire to marry again, even if I could pose as a willing prize," I said. "Now, leave me to my ruminations. Promise to visit me before the tournament."

"Of course. Goodnight, Mother."

"Goodnight, Gawain."

THAT NIGHT, I fell asleep thinking about my own childhood, lived within these very rooms. Different as they now were, the lingering smell—rose with a hint of old, burned wood—drew my thoughts time and again to my days of innocence.

While some would recall I was a moody child, a dark child, I do not think this is the case. I was happy in those first bright years, blissfully so, content as the ever-present shadow of my eldest sister Elaine and quite unbothered with my lot in life. My greatest concern was the collection of flowers in the fields, the categorization of insects at Carelon, and sneaking sweets when Cook wasn't looking.

I was always well taken care of. I might have been overlooked on occasion, but I was still a part of the most remarkable family in Braetan. Father, still hale in those days, would occasionally sit us down and tell us stories by the great hearth at Carelon's family chamber. I would get lost in the sound of his voice, the low rumbling baritone, and find myself quite transported to the Braetan of old, back before Avillion was given to the Old People, when there was more connection than simple diplomacy and tolerance between our islands. Before the Christ's men came. Before Bedevere. And Lanceloch. And Nimue.

But I get ahead of myself, as I am wont to do. The longer I live the harder it is to piece the memories together in the right order.

Yes, I had great happiness in those days, in those moments.

My closest friend and companion was always Elaine. My mother was never doting, and already ailing when I was young, so Elaine was my surrogate. We shared a room, and I followed her like a small, pale ghast, learning from her all the arts she had mastered so diligently: embroidery, weaving, herbalism, and music. She tolerated my very middling capabilities and taught me to read, to write, and to dance. Elaine's unending support helped shield me, I believe, in those early years at Carelon, before the Great End began. Before everything fell apart.

But my own Great End began just after I turned ten, on the day Elaine left me. She warned me the day would come, but I was resistant—and still am—to such changes. I believed if I simply kept it from my mind, I could prevent the inevitable.

Late one evening I returned to our room to find her bed stripped of linens and furs, her things packed in a trunk, and beautiful Elaine perched on a chair, trying her best not to cry. She was never good at hiding her emotions, which her other two sisters seemed to excel at, and upon seeing me she burst into a cavalcade of tears so intense I scarcely knew what to do. She had never cried so before me, and she looked so like our mother Igraine at that moment, and I wondered if Mother's face eroded away from sorrow and not from sickness or age.

Yes, the more I think on it now, the more I see it as a viable reason for the sharp lines and marks about Mother's once fair face. Her life was a lesson in grief. But I learned such consequences well after she was dead, and I was capable of understanding the lengths mothers go for their children.

So, I was ten when I learned my beloved Elaine would be sent south to the Gaul, which might as well have been the other end of the earth to me, and marry Ban of Benwick, the recently widowed king of that particular province. He had four sons, it was said, and this marriage was certainly a matter of state and allegiance, not love; Ban promised to send his sons to court in exchange, and this made Father very happy. The youngest, who was just a babe and the cause of his mother's death, would be sent much later. I remembered his name because it sounded so beautiful: Lanceloch.

We sat together in the room we had inhabited for ten years and Elaine looked up at me, her clear blue eyes rimmed red, her slender fingers entwined with her embroidered handkerchief and said, "Do not look so surprised, Anna. I told you I must leave someday. I am nearly twenty now, and I'm lucky to have made such a match."

"But you do not *have* to," I said, stupidly. I said many stupid things at that age, and I am not entirely sure the habit has left me years later. "You can hide away, in the kitchens, pretend to be a scullery maid. You can stay with me always—"

It was perfectly plausible to me, as it was the sort of thing romances were made of. I often dreamed she and I would be part of a great story, two sisters traveling to the edges of the realm and challenging the old gods and the new, and in my innocence, it seemed no less plausible now. I was ten and I did not know the pain of the world, even if I was lingering just on the precipice of my own marriage.

My suggestion did not ameliorate Elaine's frustration. She began to cry again, and I could not understand why.

"I… could come with you?" I tried, again, offering a smile. "I wouldn't be much trouble."

Elaine took a deep breath and closed her eyes. "Anna. I have told you a thousand times. Our childhood is our only gift. Father has been more than generous in allowing me more time at Carelon, but the time has come. Lives are at stake. We must strengthen the realm."

"But who will take care of me?" I blurted the words before I could think what to say. "What will I do here alone?"

She frowned, and an expression of fury cut through her sorrow; I had never seen her angry at me, and I startled. "I am to be married to a man twice my age, doomed to live in a land far-off and alone, and you worry about yourself? Your selfishness knows no bounds."

I had no idea how to react, so I ran away from her and hid myself up in a cupboard in the kitchens until one of the serving women opened it up in search a tureen.

By the time I was hauled in front of my father for a good scolding, Elaine was gone. I had not been able to let her know, to share with her what I meant to say, all the promises and proclamations my befuddled ten-year-old mind confounded with emotion. I would have told her that I loved her, more than I loved anyone on the earth, that when I sat next to her, when she spoke to me, I felt more alive than with any other. That now she was gone, I could not breathe properly. I had made her an embroidered handkerchief, being one of my only talents, but it lay in my hands, crumpled and tear stained.

Four months after Elaine's departure, my father died abruptly when a wound he acquired during a hunting accident festered, and Arthur was crowned Braetan's king at the age of twelve. Elaine did not come, and I do not blame her. Uther was not her father. The only one of my half-sisters present was Morgen, and only then because she was Merlin's acolyte.

She, however, did not have to stand on the dais before half the realm. I stood there, awkward and boyish, scratching at the uncomfortable garb my mother selected for me, my knobby knees aching to run, my hair tickling my neck under my cap.

For all the distractions, however, I could not help but be as enraptured as the rest when Arthur and Merlin took their places up on the dais. No, it was Arthur, especially Arthur, who captivated me, the sibling I remember most from that day. Set like a scene in a triptych, I can see the whole scene before us. It was as though I were standing there with him, looking up into Merlin's face. As if the sun shone on my hair and set it ablaze. As if...

You see, we were so very alike in our youth. I had seen my face in my mother's copper mirror, studied every line, and I recognized the same fullness of the bottom lip, the same heavy-lidded blue eyes, that I saw in my brother. Neither of us favored our mother with her shiny black locks and hazel eyes, like our sisters Morgen and Margawse, but were the very image of our Pendragon father—fair, freckled, and angular. It is a strange thought, but as a child I sometimes forgot where he ended and where I began. Fosterage made no difference. We were cut from the same flesh and bone. But he was not property in the way I was. And I envied him and desired to stand inside his skin, to see the world with his eyes: full of promise, bright destiny, and power. I loved him fiercely.

Arthur approached me fresh after his crowning and embraced me so hard I was left breathless. He was weeping after the coronation, though whether over the grief at the recent loss of our father or the emotion over such an experience I did not know. But he took my cheeks with both of his hands and stared at me.

"Let us become ever closer together, Anna. I pray you will only find happiness in the days to come."

I could not suppress the feeling of dread those words

left behind. Arthur did not understand. He was a man; I was a woman. Elaine warned me. Even though we of the same parentage, he was heir and I was a pawn. I would be sent off and married off like Elaine. And soon. Happiness was just another word for betrothal. I would be miserable, and Arthur would remain king of all Braetan. The whole kingdom bowing at his feet.

As if he had heard my thoughts, he said, "We will make you a happy match, dearest sister. I promise you. You will want for naught."

I hated him for those words, hated him because I could not believe them. And because I loved Carelon and its surrounding fields and forests and I wanted simply to stay. Arthur was always in search of another horizon—another conquest, another battle, another adventure—but I was happy within safe walls, protected and left to wander. I just had no idea how much it meant to me until it was too late.

Just two years after Arthur's coronation I was married to Lot of Orkney, a man three times my age whose previous wife had been a barren disappointment. Lot and his wife's sundering was long and difficult, but at long last it was approved at court with a great deal of help at the hands of Merlin. Within days of the ruling it was decided, in light of Lot's impressive army and imminent allegiance to Arthur, I would be the best reward for him.

Merlin personally delivered the news to me one evening, chiding me for the tears I wept, impatient with my childish behavior. But I was a new creature, still, unschooled in the game. I had only just begun my bleeding and still sometimes played with the dolls Cook made me out of old grain sacks. I stared at the seals draping from the King's decree, dangling before me, the light catching on their shiny red surfaces. So many people had known. Least of all me.

"Do not weep tears of sorrow," he said. "Arthur has made you a queen."

So at thirteen, I became Queen of Orkney, abandoned and forgotten. I arrived on the windswept, desolate chain of islands in the North on my fourteenth birthday, returning only twice to Carelon—once for Mother's funeral, and again for Arthur's wedding to Gweynevere of Avillion—in twenty years.

Thankfully, nothing lasts forever. Especially marriages to dotard men.

THE DAYS LEADING up to Lugh's Tournament passed quickly, with little in the way of concern, at least for me. I have never liked the brutality of such games and always found the Tournament to be a loud and preening distraction for knights, an alternative intended to exercise their burgeoning muscles like prancing stallions, while the women—and other men—are given license to gawk. I had conflicting emotions about it, knowing Gawain was playing into the expectations I abhorred, yet felt intense pride for his accomplishments, most of which were fostered by his father.

The brawn was all Lot ever wanted of Gawain. Lot was not a present, patient, or a supportive father. He informed his sons what he wanted and expected them to act accordingly without question. He was arrogant and cold, and desired naught of me save my womb and my connection to Arthur. I only know Gawain was his because I was with no other at the time of his conception, but the same cannot be said of Lot. Lot spent more time—in his own quarters nonetheless—with his long-time mistress, Maira, than he ever did with me during our marriage.

The adultery might have been difficult if I harbored any gentle feelings toward the man, but after consummating our marriage in terror and in pain, barely a child myself, I needed only Gawain for the next seven years. Orchestrating additional marital conjugation around my second pregnancy required a great amount of whiskey and compromising on my behalf. He never suspected the twins were aught but his own. At least, if he had doubts, they never went expressed.

Then again, Lot never expressed much to me. We did not have a marriage of that sort.

And yet, in spite of all of Lot's many shortcomings, Gawain continually sought his father's approval. I suppose it is the curse of children, for I felt the same way about Uther for the short time I lived in Carelon as a child. We strive for the attentions of our fathers, even if we will never please them. That Gawain was unable to make his father's funeral was a final cruel blow to their complicated relationship, though I do not think Gawain regretted it. I was only privy to some of their arguments; they were bitter and violent enough to curdle milk. When words failed Lot, he used his hands. Sending Gawain to court not only kept him safe, but likely prevented him from strangling his own father.

The morning of the Tournament, I received my first official summons from Arthur since my arrival, requesting I break bread with the knights before the games. Resigned, I accepted; I knew Gweyn would be there and I had been avoiding her on purpose for the last three days, making the best of my illness and trying to keep a low profile. I sent her a few short letters, thanking her for her hospitality, but spent the majority of the time in my new quarters, rearranging furniture and making requests for decoration.

For breakfast I chose a new dress, one made of silks Arthur sent specifically for me in green and light gold, colors befitting my station and complimentary to my complexion. I was not fond of the current styles seen at court, which included moronically long sleeves and darted waists, so I had Anette design something more traditional, based in part on a dress Mother wore at my wedding. Instead of darting the waist, we used a broad green sash, beaded intricately in a pattern I thought, from a distance, looked almost like dragon skin. Fitting for a Pendragon, and elegant.

My hair was a different story; I felt silly having it down, like some flirtatious virgin. So, we pinned it up and studded it with the emerald pins I had been given by Elaine when Gawain was born. A simple veil and tasteful jewelry were all that was required to finish it off.

I was overwhelmed when I arrived at breakfast to find so many familiar faces assembled together—not to mention the unfamiliar ones. I sat to Arthur's left, and Gweyn was placed on his right. The Queen sat only for a few minutes before she excused herself, so I did not have a chance to speak with her. It was just as well. This left Gawain next to Arthur, and then Bedevere beside me. This pattern of knights and ladies continued around the feasting table, which was U-shaped to allow guests to see one another.

I will tell you, in a few words, that most of the knights in attendance that morning were the most famed and celebrated of Arthur's court. Sir Bors: stubborn, loyal, dull. Sir Ector: old, irascible, ornery. Sir Caradoc: quiet, romantic, competitive. Sir Dinadan: raucous, charismatic, clumsy. Sir Lucan—Bedevere's brother: temperamental, boisterous, impetuous. Sir Cullwch: peacemaking, gentle, kind. Oh, there's more, plenty more, many of whom you have heard and others you have not. Of the women there were a few of note, including both of my half-sisters and the Queen herself. The majority of women seated at the table, however, were minor ladies, most of whom were simply married to a handful of those placed. King Pellas of course, was widowed, and instead he brought his daughter.

King Pellas' daughter was Gawain's Elaine. I found it hard to believe she was of such a pedigree, although I should have guessed by her anemic looks.

Elaine had been crying, delicate skin beneath her eyes puffy and red, and did not touch her food throughout the meal; if her father noticed anything unusual, he certainly made no indication. In fact, as I watched them over the three-course breakfast, picking my way through seasoned venison sausages, the grizzled old king all but ignored his daughter. I couldn't help feeling a little guilty knowing I was likely the cause of her pain.

Gawain did not so much as look at her. He failed to mention she was a princess, and as Pellas had yet to pledge his loyalty to Arthur, it made for a slightly more precarious situation than I initially thought. What was Margawse up to?

Bedevere ate slowly, disinterested, as I continued to sit proper and alert. He used the excuse of nearly toppling my wine glass to begin a conversation.

"Well, must be my nerves," he said, brushing drops of wine from his hands on the tablecloth.

"Your nerves?" I asked. "I didn't know you were on the lists."

"I'm not," Bedevere replied evenly. "But I'm the one who has spent the last two years working with Gawain on his form. He had quite the injury to his knee last summer, and we were worried he might not recover in time for Lugh's Tournament."

"You underestimate the strength of the Orkney boys," I said. Some wench was going around bestowing white garlands on all the knights participating

"I never underestimate anyone coming from Orkney," said Bedevere.

I laughed. "Then you enjoy all of this puffed-up pageantry?"

"The food is good. But it is very expensive." He lowered his voice: "I am, along with Cai, tasked with the royal treasury."

"The rose garlands are lovely."

"They were a last-minute addition…"

"Let me guess: Gweyn?"

"You are wise and shrewd, Lady."

"Anna!"

It was Arthur. I started at his comfortable use of my name and turned to give him a placid smile.

"Yes, Your Majesty," I said, giving him my full attention.

"Have you had a chance to place your bets? I would assume you, like me, are putting your coin toward our young Orkney boy here," Arthur said, elbowing Gawain, who was busy eating three times the food of anyone else. My son lifted an eyebrow, grunted, and then tucked in again.

"Ah, well, when I was at court it was not seemly for women to indulge in such things," I said somewhat meekly. I found the idea of gambling on my son's life and prowess beyond foul.

Bedevere added: "It has become a custom of late, the ladies of court are voracious in such matters. It's quite the fashion."

"So are sleeves so long they drag through trenchers," I said, observing Lady Dindrane doing just that.

"I forget your wit, sister," said Arthur, with genuine brightness. "But, be warned, my wife tells me the court of wives has its own delicate dance. It would behoove you to dally along with them now and again."

"Of course she will," said Bedevere. "It will just take time. Once she is finished mourning her husband, Your Majesty, I'm sure Lady Anna will be renewed as these roses."

The uncomfortable argument was cut short when the maiden bestowing wreaths to the knights leaned a little too close to Gawain, and Elaine left in a flurry of skirts, silks, and tears.

As the meal blessedly came to an end, a servant announced that all ladies of court, as well as the kings not participating in the tournament, were to be escorted out to the sparring fields. Gweyn, who had returned from her momentary absence, meandered through the widening crowd straight to me, and embraced me like a sister, tears in her magnificent violet eyes.

It was the eyes, I think, that drove men mad for Gweyn. Because all in all, she was not unusually beautiful. Oh, I could not deny she possessed grace and a certain striking figure: Hair the color of honey wheat tumbling in braids and curls down her back, set with pearls and delicate lace, and a round, smooth figure—yes, Gweyn shone. But there was little else remarkable about her, especially in comparison to her two sisters, Hwyfar and Mawra, whom I met at Arthur's wedding. Until Gweyn appeared at court, along with her father and a few other diplomats from Avillion, I did not think Arthur would find any woman beautiful. I certainly never heard he favored women at court, though opportunities abounded from the youngest of ages to dally in any manner he chose. But when Arthur set eyes on Gweyn, all changed. He wanted her at any cost, and for the first time in his life he ignored Merlin's counsel and made his own choice.

Merlin, you see, was not of Avillion, though he trained there for decades—he was a conjuror calling upon powers unconnected to those of the Old People. Some of the principles were the same, I suppose, but having never been formally trained in such things I couldn't give you the precise details of his magic. Morgen, in one of her moments of warmth toward me, explained that the people of Avillion depended on the power of the gods to do their magic, calling on their patrons and house gods to instill powers through them. This required much in the way of prayer and preparation. But Merlin's magic, and by extension Morgen's, had more to do with the power within oneself.

When I was young, I was half convinced Merlin was a god himself. There was something off about the man on a very basic level I could never put my finger on. He moved about our world in a different time than everyone else, as if we all moved very fast, and he was slow. Whenever Arthur needed him, he appeared; whenever I dreaded he would be somewhere, he was. Both expected and unexpected, a storm of his own, he, and not Arthur, was the true ruler of Carelon.

And so, for my ills and afflictions, it was not on Arthur whom I laid the blame, but on Merlin; for he had interpreted my prophecy, and he moved Arthur's hands in all things.

Of course, as in the case of Gweyn, when it did not. It will forever perplex me that Arthur did not listen to Merlin regarding Gweyn. Merlin was against the idea entirely, asserting with all his power that Arthur should marry a priestess, daughter of King Leodegraunce or no. His first betrothed, Hwyfar, Gweyn's sister, the eldest and certainly no priestess, possessed charm, wit, character, and beauty of which I never saw parallel. But one glance at Gweyn, and Arthur knew he must have her at any cost. He would disobey the wishes of Merlin if it served him, but not if it meant he would have to do without something he wanted.

Arthur always got what he wanted.

I have no idea if Carelon ever made Gweyn happy. She smiled a great deal, but she smiled as one who does so to hide tears. Never a dull moment with her, she moved about like a nesting bird, a constant flutter of silk, lace, and hair, sitting down only when commanded. Perhaps she dealt with her own difficulties at court by continual motion.

"Oh, Anna," Gweyn said, touching her hands to my face. I do not know why so many people felt as if my face were their personal property but having arrived in Carelon it seemed to be the proper way to greet me. Perhaps it was tactile confirmation that yes, I had returned, and indeed I was Arthur's sister. Our bearing to one another could be no more quaint. "It is so good to see you again, sister— my heart warms just knowing you're here, and now you'll know the joy of Amhar's birth firsthand. What a deviously lucky little boy he will be!"

"Amhar?" I asked, distracted. Bedevere caught my eye across the room and gave me a rather sympathetic grin. He knew well my limited tolerance for Gweyn's state of constant joy and movement.

She touched her hand to her belly, which was not yet showing. I was the same way with Gawain; until the sixth month, most scarcely believed I could be with child.

"I had a dream," she said, violet eyes half-lidded and strange. Ah, the priestesses of Avillion, back with her dramatics. "And in the dream, I saw him so clearly. Oh, Anna, he was a beautiful boy, with golden hair like mine, and eyes like you and Arthur's. And the name of course—"

"Our great-grandfather," I said, knowing this. Amhar was the first Pendragon. While some found Gweyn's ways odd to the say the least, I found her charming in limited quantities. For all her curious prophesies and ecstasies, she was far from boring. Unlike most women at court, she was not complacent with embroidery and gossip.

"He is excited about the Tournament," she said, voice hushed and tinged with a little laughter, patting her stomach. "He has been turning about all day—it is so remarkable to feel him move. The first time I straightaway began weeping tears of gladness."

"How joyous," I said, genuinely as I could. I knew she would make a good mother, but my concern remained with Arthur. Kings rarely make good fathers, as I learned with Lot, and Uther before.

"You must be so proud of Gawain," she said, grasping my hand in hers as we made our way down the corridor with the rest of our group toward the sparring fields. We proceeded through the central courtyard, under the boughs of yew and ash trees; beside the gurgling fountains and flowered walkways. Birdsong rose about us, as if welcoming the Queen. "Arthur will not stop boasting about his abilities, so much so King Ban has brought his own champion— the strange knight has refused any kind of hospitality and has been holed up in the stables for the last two days. The stables! It is the queerest thing. In a full suit of armor, no less, praying to Lugh, from what my ladies tell me."

King Ban was my sister Elaine's husband. She had not written, not on this matter or any other, but I wondered if she was aware of this curious knight's appearance.

"And, not to be outdone, there's King Pellas's champion," continued Gweyn. I did not recall the Queen having such a love of the tournament. She sounded as giddy as a kitchen maid gifted with extra livers. "Have you seen him? He was sitting there at dinner—very swarthy and wearing the fashion of the desert, all draped in gold and tan and cinched with leather. From Akkadia, you see, the son of a tsar, or whatever they call kings in the south, we hear. Palomydes, I think is his name. His brother's to be sent to court as well. It is quite a collection of champions."

"Indeed." I recalled the man she spoke of and had wondered myself. His bearing and visage struck me immediately: an angular face with amber eyes set in oak brown skin.

We walked up a flight of stairs, permanently carved into the stones of Carelon, for access to the Tournament field. Before we emerged, I already caught the smell of the crowd rising, the collective aromas of sweat and food and horses, bringing to mind my first tournament, when I was fourteen and a new mother.

As nobles, we arrived above the fray, under crimson and gold awnings, three rows above the crowd, to seats bedecked with pillows and blankets. Before us rested carved wooden tables laden with rich food and drink, and toward the back of the pavilion, our own minstrel group tuned their instruments, should we find the event boring.

The crowd, seeing the King, rose to their feet, and cheered so raucously I shuddered. The entirety of the tournament field was a marvel of construction, with twenty rows built in an oval shape, interrupted by two large gateways made of hewn stone on each narrowed end and set with grotesque gargoyles holding spear. The gargoyles, painted red and green with inlaid scales, presented the day's banners: Pendragon, Pellas, and Ban. Pendragon higher than the others, for Arthur would suffer no insult. The grounds themselves were packed dirt and shorn grass, edged in stone with remarkable trace work depicting shields, devices, and a complicated scene of hounds and harts running the perimeter. The first row was some six feet from the floor, however, to ensure the spectators were not injured by flying detritus during the fight.

Squeezing Gweyn's hand quite involuntarily, I felt a rush of fear course through me. I did not want these people looking at me; I felt laid bare. Time crawled to a stop, and my heart thrummed in my chest, and finally the crowd quieted down. At last, the herald called my name, and I took my seat. I was breathless, exhausted, and quite in need of good wine.

The ceremony began, and the procession of the shield, lance, and sword commenced while I gathered myself. Three priestesses and two priests from Avillion first emerged, their long white robes hemmed in scarlet, processed around the field, holding the implements high in the air. These were symbolic of the gods' three gifts to the warrior Ayr, the ancient hero of Avillion. The versions they paraded out were not the true relics, as those had been lost to time long ago. I admit, as a child, having stumbled upon them in the armory one day, I thought they were the famed weapons of old—they were but regular weapons, simply painted gold and wrapped with scarlet silk ribbon. Still, the crowd was in awe of such beautiful, presumably holy implements, I understood why Arthur kept up the tradition. There was power in them, even if it was a lie.

I was thankful to be seated next to Gweyn, if only because I was so unaccustomed to the tournament, I would have likely missed Gawain's entrance without her guidance. We watched two knights spar, and one win. The winner proceeded to best another knight. It was a matter of endurance and cunning. And loud, incessant clanging. The knight to win the most consecutive fights in a row won the event and his score followed to the next—the three events were shield and mace, hand-a-half sword, and mounted lance. Their positions in the list were determined by previous, smaller tournaments or, in some cases, blessings by the King.

Gawain's strengths were the last two events, but he would first have to master the shield and mace against his opponent.

When Gawain walked into the arena, I felt my heart twist in my chest. Although he was clad in mail from head to toe, I could not mistake the colors of Orkney—green and gold, with a reared unicorn sigil. The shield was a gift from Lot, or more properly, a gift I insisted Lot give Gawain when he was knighted. I had brought it out of the dingy armory in Orkney and reapportioned for him, repainted and repaired by the best artisans I knew. It was a stunning piece now, complementing the green sash he wore about his waist— very much like mine, I realized with a smile of pride.

I do not think I breathed for the next hour. Gawain fought so well, he dazzled. Due to his size, he would never be a fighter of dexterity, but he showed remarkable endurance, and he made feats of strength otherwise considered beyond an average man's capacity look effortless. Time and again his opponents tired in their attacks, and he parried and blocked, dodged and even rolled, never seeming to slacken under the rising heat of the sun.

Finally, after seven worthy opponents, he was bested, knocking his shield in anger and bellowing at the crowd. A good show even in defeat. Still, seven was a hearty number—a solid number. The highest wins to date in the shield and mace event still stood at eight, Bedevere's own record, years before. Gawain was expected to go ten and ten in the next events, at very least, as I knew now from the gambling lists.

"Breathtaking!" said Sir Cai, who limped toward me. I hadn't even noticed he was among us; he must have come in after Gawain started. "Seven? I wagered a win with only five in the shield and mace, and here he is gaining already. Remarkable lad you've got there, Ladyship. Every bone a warrior."

"Thank you," I said, finding breathing a little easier now Gawain was no longer in the fight. I wished I could go to him. At very least, I sent Jain his way to attend as a personal medic. If he suffered any cracked ribs or bruises, she would be the best to handle them between bouts. "He is a born fighter." In Orkney, you had to be.

Gweyn was keeping a tally for herself on a tablet, and glanced up at me and grinned, squinting in the sun. "You must be so glad to have made it back here in time to see this."

"Yes, I have never seen him fight so arrayed and celebrated. I wonder, though—the third knight Gawain bested, what was his name?"

"Sir..." Gweyn said, running her finger down the list to find it. "Sir Lamiel, I believe."

"Lamiel. Not a name I know."

"Nor I," said Cai. "But he got quite a beating from our Gawain."

"It looked like he fell unconscious," I said, having barely managed to watch the fight, which ended abruptly with a decisive blow to Lamiel's head. "Is he quite all right? Do you think he will fight another day?"

Cai looked grim. "I do not know. But that is part of the risk, you know. Why, when I fought, I once took a knock to the back of leg with a mace. Shattered it—and it is my good leg. I was in bed three weeks after, after it festered and—"

"Quite enough, Sir Cai, if you do not mind," said Gweyn. "Lady Anna has gone a bit green."

Ban's knight, Palomydes, then went on to win five matches, losing the last to Sir Caradoc, his sigil a glorious phoenix entwined with snakes. His fighting style was unusual, and the knights of Arthur's court had no real course of action against him. It was an impressive sight, even to me.

And though I wished to be curled up somewhere else, perhaps with some intricate embroidery work, my attention was taken by the entrance of another knight, one I had not seen before. He displayed no device on his shield and wore only gray: gray armor, sash, plume, shield, and mace. A bore, entirely, and yet in his understatement he drew a remarkable amount of attention. Those in the stands gasped for he looked so incongruous.

"Who in Braetan is that?" asked Cai, leaning forward and squinting.

Gweyn grinned, a conspiratorial glint in her eyes. "You hadn't heard, Sir Cai? It is King Pellas' champion himself."

"Why no device?" asked Cai, who clearly disapproved of the lack of sigil and more than unusual presentation. "This is ridiculous. Lugh's Tournament is not some pageant. What's Pellas getting at?"

"According to my Lord Arthur," said Gweyn, "he carries no device because he is as yet untested. He is to win the right to carry arms today."

"And successful means what, besting a knight?" grunted Cai.

"Winning the entire match," corrected Gweyn. "Apparently the King and Pellas placed a bit of a bet, themselves."

Cai snorted. "The whole tournament? He has heard of Gawain of Orkney, has he not? This is idiocy."

It was not idiocy.

To our utter shock, of the ten knights left on the lists including stalwart Caradoc, the Gray Knight bested them all. Worse even, he did it with all the flair and lightness of foot Gawain did not possess. He was mesmerizing to watch, tiring his enemies and dizzying them with a dancer's grace

I never before observed in a fighter. Even Palomydes could not last against the Gray Knight, and tired quickly. At first the audience was in awe of the strange unnamed knight, but they soon began to grow weary with his constant success.

The last knight to come against the Gray Knight was thrown back so hard against the stonework that his helmet came off, making a racket that set my teeth. Apparently, it did not escape the Gray Knight. He approached the fallen knight and checked for possible wounds—unheard of in the Tournament. Even I knew it was no place for compassion.

The crowd exploded into dissonant cries, some cheering the knight on for his sensitivity to the situation—the fallen knight was quite unconscious, and deathly pale—while others booed and jeered for showing weakness.

At last the herald resorted to blowing his horn in order to keep the peace. Arthur was crimson with rage. He stood at the edge of the balcony, glaring down, hair blowing in the wind, like spun gold in the sun, swirling around his ears and temples, curling slightly. A figure of beauty in so many ways, and all eyes turned to him.

"What is the meaning of this, knight?" demanded Arthur.

The Gray Knight did not remove his visor but quirked his head toward Arthur. He said something, but I did not catch much of it. Arthur asked for him to repeat himself.

"I believe he may be dead, Your Majesty," said the knight, his voice clear now, but not without strain. I thought I heard the edge of a sob in his voice.

The priests and priestesses made their way out onto the field, followed by a handful of medics and a stretcher.

"Get on with it, get him off the field," said Arthur, irritated. He did not like when people broke the mood of a day, especially not Lugh's Tournament. I could tell he was livid; like me, when angered, the skin around his mouth went white.

We did not learn until later what the fate of the fallen knight was, but if the incident truly bothered the Gray Knight, it did not show. Gawain fought next, besting ten knights before conceding; Palomydes bested an admirable six—but the Gray Knight bested nine, and was once again the last standing. There were others who won, considering there were over fifty knights still on the lists, but none outshone those three.

At last it was time for the lance, which was Gawain's best event. He could still catch up if he worked harder, if the numbers were with him as they said. Though the numbering of the games was not exactly fair from a mathematical point, Arthur—and Uther before him—believed the lists had a way of exacting the fate of the gods. And I must admit, it usually looked that way. The best knights walked off with the titles, and the lesser ones to the infirmary. It was so much easier before the Christ's men came. We could accept Fate, could accept chaos. I did not know what a strange, lucky thing it was to have such a world view, until it was gone.

This time Palomydes went first, as he was the third lead. He bested another seven, of thirty-nine left well enough to fight, before falling. Gawain was a bit further down the lists. Someone helped bang the dings out of his armor, and he stood very straight on his horse, a great statue of a man with a great red plume rising from his helmet.

When the fight finally concluded, Gawain bested a total of twelve before conceding, and the Gray Knight was again left standing, undefeated in combat, his mount gored and liming.

But the crowd was dissatisfied, in spite of the caliber of the performances. The problem remained that the Gray Knight had, in fact, tied with Gawain—they each stood at twenty-nine wins, and no winner could be determined. There was much discussion and debate among the heralds.

King Pellas muttering under his breath, and Arthur tried to confer with Cai and Bedevere.

"He has bested without a concession once," said Pellas of his knight. "He is the clear winner. Your champion looks in no state for fighting."

"It is not a matter of concession, with all due respect, Your Highness, and judging by the state of your champion's horse, I feel we are on even footing," said Bedevere, ever the peacemaker. I watched, unnoticed, as he did his best to calm King Pellas, who hobbled around the dais, limping on his gouty leg. "It is numbers and numbers only."

"Then have them fight it out," snorted Pellas. His daughter Elaine was nearby, standing ill at ease by her father, tiny white hands twisted around a handkerchief.

"We've never had a tie before," said Cai, scowling. "There's protocol to follow—perhaps it would be better to have them fight tomorrow, when they're rested—"

Pellas let out a rough laugh, like shale scraping. "Tomorrow? What do you take my champion for, a sniveling woman? If your champion is too tired to fight today, then I will claim the victory as mine."

"How about a fight with the sword and shield?" asked a resounding voice. We all turned to see Merlin standing at the edge of the dais, gazing out over the field. The field was transformed, blood staining the ground, dirt clods loosened along every step. All beauty was gone from the landscape, and in a way Merlin's presence was appropriate. He reminded me of carrion fowl, perched over the gore of the field, surveying the wreckage.

When no one spoke in response, the conjuror continued: "The knight left standing will take the title. After a brief reprise, mind you. I think you would agree, King Pellas, that even your young knight could use a cool drink and a bit of attention from his medics before throwing himself headlong into another fight. Both men have fought exceptionally well, but we must not ask them to have the constitution of gods."

Merlin's explanation quelled Pellas's ire, and he agreed to the terms. Cai was furious; he put money on Gawain and was rightfully worried. We were all worried. As impressive as Gawain was, there was no denying the prowess of the Gray Knight. He fought like a man possessed. And his style was so contrary to Gawain's I worried my son would not be able to keep up.

I supposed I must, like the rest, leave it to the numbers.

When they met at last, there was much delay. Neither wanted to strike first. Gawain carried a short sword given to him by Arthur, inlaid with the Pendragon crest. It glittered in the hot sun, setting now just above the stands, shining into the combatant's eyes and shedding an unearthly golden hue on the earth below, deepening every shadow.

I could not breathe. I could not eat, could not drink. I leaned as far forward as I dared, willing all my strength to Gawain.

Still, for all my pleading and petitioning, he failed.

Gawain was a horseman and a wonder with two-handed weapons; but the shield made him clumsy, the sword unfamiliar in his hand. He fell first, missing a very obvious feign from the stranger, and then simply tripped over his own feet. The Gray Knight danced maddeningly around him, always swerving out of the way, able to anticipate Gawain's blows. The clang of ringing swords reverberated around the field, cutting through the grunting and groaning of the two knights. The stands fell silent as we all watched our champion fall. And fall.

*Concede!* I willed in vain.

But Gawain would not. He stood again and again, his legs trembling underneath his own weight as the Gray Knight met him blow for blow, each resounding ring against his armor like a bell tolling his end.

I felt panic rise and feared Gawain would fall as the other knights before him, perhaps to his death. The stranger had already killed one man. This was not worth the spectacle. This was my *son*, not some untested squire—he was the nephew of King Arthur of Braetan. It was a mockery to put him in such danger. And damn him, but he was too stubborn to recognize it! And damn Arthur for allowing it, and Merlin for suggesting it.

"Do something," I said to Merlin, too desperate to talk myself out of approaching him. "You cannot let this happen."

"I am not letting anything happen, Lady Anna," he said, not taking his eyes off of the field. "I merely suggested an alternative."

"Gawain could die."

"Children die, men die, women die... Fate turns the wheel, and who are we to say?"

"Merlin, you old goat," said Gweyn, rushing to my side. "Lady Anna is terrified for the life of her firstborn son. It is unseemly to speak to her in such a manner."

Merlin turned his eyes away from the fight and glared at Gweyn a moment before saying, "My apologies. I was caught up in the moment. Your son will not die today, Lady Anna."

His words gave no comfort. But Gweyn had called Merlin an old goat, and I must admit, it gave me an enduring sense of satisfaction.

A great rending sound drew my attention, and a shout of surprise. Gawain barely stood, blood coursing down the front of his greaves, head lolling side to side as if drunk.

The crowd began cheering the Gray Knight, as fickle and senseless as they were, laughing as Gawain fell again, his knee twisting. He managed to catch himself by driving his sword into the ground, but the Gray Knight kicked him in the chest, and he fell onto his back, the sword shattering at the hilt, the Pendragon crest sundered.

*Concede!*

But Gawain did not. With his shield only, he attempted to protect himself from the continual onslaught, tried desperately to fend off the Gray Knight's advances. The paint on his shield splintered and chipped off, falling like white and green snow to the ground the unicorn slashed through, until at last he held it up above his head as the berserker Gray Knight buffeted it over and over again.

*Concede!* I wanted to scream it. I wanted to run there to him; I wanted to murder the man who caused pain to my son.

"Arthur," I gritted out, putting a trembling hand on his. "Please…"

We stared at each other a moment, and I knew he was afraid. There were tears in his eyes. He squeezed my hand and broke from me, running to the edge of our pavilion.

"He concedes!" yelled King Arthur, in a voice so loud it reverberated throughout the entire field. The Gray Knight stopped as if Merlin had magicked him into a statue. He dropped his sword, and his hands fell to his side, and his head fell forward.

Gawain, though, would not have it. He took the opportunity to muster what fight remained in him and barreled forward, knocking the Gray Knight over and taking him unawares.

That damned temper.

It took a dozen knights to separate them after the final explosion, and Gawain was rushed to the infirmary, for one of his ribs broke straight through the skin and possibly his lung, not to mention the pulpy ruin of his left leg. If he did not receive help soon, he would be of no use to anyone in the future. If he ever recovered from this wound to his pride. No longer Arthur's shining champion. He had been bested not just on the field, but in matters of chivalry as well.

"Who in the kingdom was that?" asked Arthur, turning on Pellas. The elder king must have seen the fire in Arthur's eyes, for he did not answer cryptically this time. He said simply:

"He is King Ban's youngest son. Lanceloch. He has been a guest at my home these few months, and I asked him to enter the lists for me. Look—see him there—" pointed Pellas.

Lanceloch stood close to the dais now and removed his helmet. He was battered, his eyes blackened, but graced with such singular beauty I caught my breath. Amber eyes like a wolf, black hair cropped in curls at his brow, a strong jaw and fine nose, skin the color of fine bronze. He was flushed from exertion, but he held out his sword, unwavering: a pledge of fealty.

"I surrender my sword to Arthur, King of all Braetan," he said, in a voice clear as cold water.

I recognized the look in Arthur's eyes, and it unsettled me. I never did concern myself with my brother's dalliances. He was king, he could do as he pleased. I would not judge his heart's affections, man or woman it did not matter. However, open affection for another knight, burning desire, in the eyes of the court, could be interpreted as weakness. Our father tried, without success, to stop Arthur and his "depraved appetites" as he was so fond of calling them. He could no more stop Arthur from loving other men than he could stop himself from seeking power.

A prickling sensation fizzled across my skin and I looked across the way toward Merlin, where I noticed the conjuror frowning at the travesty on the field. He caught my eye for the briefest of moments. I had to look away. He understood, as well. This was the beginning of a new era, or the end of a golden one. I did not know which.

Arthur always got what he wanted. No matter the cost. Both Merlin and I understood, just in very different ways.

# CHAPTER FOUR

## SPLIT ENDS

Jain granted me access to the infirmary to visit Gawain in the following days, as he slowly recovered from his wounds, and I was often left alone to attend my son. He was often unconscious; when lucid, he railed and raged. But he improved with time. I smelled constantly of comfrey and mint, of poultices and astringents, but I did not mind.

Under the cover of common dress, none dared assume I was anything other than a casual visitor. As so often in my life, I discovered I could move about without drawing attention, especially if I gave off the air of purposeful action.

I was perhaps a little too confident in my disguise as I returned from bringing Gawain some books to read from the library—histories on the Pendragon family and one or two romances on the bloody side that I thought he might enjoy—for I ran headlong into Sir Bedevere. It took a moment to register the surprise on his face.

"Anna," he said, bowing quickly, hand to his chest. "Where is your escort? What are you doing alone down here?"

"Taking a walk back to my apartment after visiting my ailing son," I replied, softly. His eyes shone wide with surprise. He had clearly forgotten my penchant for breaking rules. I almost laughed were it not for the true concern in his expression.

"In—you're dressed—so very—" he tried to avert his eyes but did not do a terribly good job.

"Simple and common," I said, swirling the brown homespun dress and cloak I wore, then shook the long straps of the leather belt. It was one of Jain's ensembles. "Nothing wrong with that."

"You are the King's sister," Bedevere reminded me, taking a step closer. We were very alone in the long corridor between the infirmary and the residences at Carelon, torchlight illuminating the nook we found ourselves in.

I grinned at him. "I am aware."

"And it is not appropriate for you to be unescorted, especially in a place such as this. We take in locals, peasants—someone could recognize you—"

"No one ever does," I said, shrugging. It was true. So long as I was not in the company of other nobles, it was as if I walked about cloaked in mist.

"You give too much credence to such a ridiculous notion."

"I most certainly do not. Merlin said I would be forgotten, and that is my fate. I walk into a room, and the moment I walk out, a mist falls on the mind. Even Arthur forgets me sometimes."

"You still believe the prophecy," Bedevere said, accusing. Clearly, he did not.

I sighed, watching him as he watched me, his eyes hungry. I ever marveled at his desire, etched on every line of his body, muscles drawn across his skeleton taut as bowstrings. Of course, I desired him as well, but I was able to keep it comfortably to myself, a quiet kind of wanting I only released when convenient.

Such is the gift of being a woman, I suppose. Our thoughts linger so deliciously in secret.

"It is not that I believe it," I corrected. "It is that *others* do."

"And being away for twenty years has no impact on the fact people mistake you for common serving women?"

"You think I look like a common serving woman?" I asked with a coy grin.

He blinked at me, then cleared his throat. "I only think you hold too much credence to Merlin's ranting. He is not always right; he often misinterprets prophecies."

"Perhaps. Yet somehow, Merlin always has a hand in where my path leads, and I know he instructed Arthur to send me to Orkney, rather than stay here and marry..." I almost said it, but my words fell short in the air like flightless birds.

"Well, you're here now—and there is no time Arthur has needed you more."

"For what?" I asked.

"Support. He could use your blessing for Lanceloch's presentation at court," he said. "You've been spending all your time here, apparently, when you'd be well served by his side."

"My son almost died," I said.

"I know, of course I know. But he's in the hands of the best healers in the realm. Arthur feels terribly guilty."

"His decisions are his own. If he wants to knight a murderous brute, it is his choice—" I began, but Bedevere interrupted me.

"Lance is a good man," he insisted. "He will do great things if given proper direction—you haven't even met him aside from the tournament. And besides, Arthur will be pressing you soon to marry again. You cannot expect him to let you dangle free for much longer—you're a prize too valuable. Be on his good side, or he might marry you to someone even older than Lot."

*A prize too valuable.*

Dread washed over me. I could not bear another marriage. I would claw my eyes out rather than again endure the pain of marriage. What a fool I was to think Arthur would grant me peace from another tortuous marriage.

Rather than argue, I said only, "I hope His Majesty will be... judicious in his decision."

"But what if you were to speak to him about it—to have more of a say in the marriage?" I hated the look he was giving me, mixed between adoration and frustration.

"Bedevere, I have no choice in my own life. It is something I relinquished the moment I was pronounced a girl. You cannot understand this."

"No, but I can love you all the same," he said, taking a step closer. I had no idea what his business was in the infirmary, likely simply to visit the wounded knights from the Tournament, but he smelled of lilac soap and fresh leather and it clouded my better judgement. His tunic was pristine, his beard combed. My heart squeezed in my chest, then fluttered as he brushed his fingers down my cheek, the calluses rough.

"We have discussed this before," I said, finding it very difficult to think straight. My body was responding to his touch quite automatically; I was never very good at refusing his advances, likely because I did not want to. He was always a most beautiful man and a passionate lover.

"And we can visit this issue again," he said, his fingers finding their way into the long locks of my hair, winding down the curve of my neck. "It would be a good match—a safe match. Then we would not have to hide."

"It is not... my decision," I said, breath catching in my throat as his lips met my cheek, lingering just for a scant moment before retreating. Lust burned in my belly, edging me on, pulling at me as naturally as waves to the shore.

It had been a very long time.

"But it can be mine," Bedevere said, staring at me, eyes wide in the torchlight. He held my face with both of his hands. "I have refused every match Arthur has made for me, hoping against hope that one day you would be free to be mine again. I have written to you, Anna, written letters upon letters, and all go unanswered. Some days you look at me as if I were the lowliest of beings and others you throw yourself into my arms. What am I to do with this? Have I forsaken my chances at having children..." he paused, indicating the unspoken: Gaheris and Gareth? "Have I wasted happiness on a phantom of love?"

I could not answer him. There were words to explain my actions. In some ways I felt I was still a confused fifteen-year-old girl. My indiscretions with Bedevere were an attempt to reclaim part of my power, to pay back Lot for bedding me like a rutting monster. Bedevere would never refuse me.

Instead of words, I answered him with actions. I kissed him, pressing my lips softly to his, teasing him with the tip of my tongue. I ran my hands down his fine, strong arms, finding his fingers with my own. The tension in him melted away like snow in the face of the sun.

I pulled away and said, "There are places we can go. Secret places I know... I will send Jain to you, or Haen. There we can speak more fully, without worry of interruption."

BEDEVERE AND I met the following evening in a side-room once designed as a storage place for the brick and stones used to build Carelon. It was mostly sealed, but there was still a stair access to it, which Elaine had shown me years ago. It brought little in the way of comfort; still, we brought candles and blankets.

I shut the door behind me, checking one last time for passersby. I had sent Haen on an errand, making it clear to him he was not to return until the eleventh bell; in the dim light we spoke of our heart's desires.

To look upon Bedevere... oh, I cannot say it well enough. I searched my sons' faces for his features through the desolation of Orkney days, I dreamed of him in the frigid night; no, dreaming was nothing compared to the face I beheld that evening. In our sparse space, we lay down like newfound lovers and reveled in the beauty of coupling, of pleasure. When he entered me, I was so completely overwrought with joy I began to weep; I bit down on my lip, stifling the cries. He did not notice, so involved was he in the act.

When it was finished, we cradled together; he circled his arms around my back and rested his chin on my shoulder, breathing softly. His fingers twined through my hair, as we had done when we were young and bold and innocent to the snares of court politics and the reality of Merlin's power over Arthur.

"I will see this through," he said in my ear. The bristles of his beard tickled, and I smiled. "I promise, Anna. We will be together."

Gods, I loved how he said my name.

"I am too afraid to even wish it," I admitted, squeezing his cheek with my uplifted hand.

"Arthur listens to me," Bedevere said. "He knows he does not have a mind for marriage matches. If you told him what you endured with Lot—"

"No," I gasped. "Please, do not ask it of me. And do not say his name ever again."

"If Arthur knew, he would consult with you more often."

"He should consent with me because I am a person, not because he has been shamed into it. I do not need his pity. Nor do I need yours."

"Anna…"

"Kiss me again," I said. "Remind me why I have dreamed of you so often."

It was not our last escape. Now that I think upon it, I am embarrassed for succumbing to such childish whims, hiding away with Bedevere, acting as if our secrecy was sacrosanct. In all truth if anyone found out, even Arthur, I doubt he would have been upset. We were adults, neither married at the time, and very careful.

Still, it was good to lose myself in the act of love, to delight in the caress of flesh upon flesh, and to be doted upon. It was a welcome counterpoint to Gawain's growing black temper amidst his healing, and the irritation I felt over Lanceloch's popularity at court.

I called our secret meeting place our Enclave. And for a time, I was happy.

Bedevere believed he was making headway with Arthur, and that in a few days he was likely to announce his ruling on the subject of our marriage. He agreed with Bedevere: I should be kept close at court, and sending me away again would be ill-advised, considering my proximity to the King. A knight, he said, a knight with good pedigree would be an ideal choice.

When Bedevere failed to come to me at the Enclave two evenings in a row, I wrote him a rather scathing letter and sent it to him by Haen, hoping to remind him of his promises to me. He came to me, then, in my own chambers, much to the shock of all.

He was furious.

I ordered Anette to the kitchens and Haen to post at the door, but I felt entirely put out having Bedevere there; there was something strangely inappropriate about the action, in spite of the fact we dallied in secret for months.

He gripped the letter in his hand and held it to my face. "This is unacceptable, Anna. You have no right—no right—to speak so!"

I swallowed. I had drunk the better part of a bottle of wine the evening I penned it and could not recall the majority of it, but was not about to lose face over such trivialities. "You left me no word. You did not come to me—" I stammered before closing my mouth altogether.

His dark eyes glimmered with tears.

"Do you doubt me so much?" he whispered, shaking his head, rubbing the area at the bridge of his nose.

"I know very well of what truly happens in Carelon, Bedevere, you know that…"

"It wouldn't have been hard to find out. Or did you miss the tolling funeral bells?"

I could not recall hearing funeral bells, but I did note a relative quiet about the castle. I had avoided formal dinners for a week, instead enjoying the quietude of my room when I was not meeting Bedevere.

I sat down at the edge of my chair, looking down at my hands. "I am afraid I must have missed it—"

He interrupted me again. "One among our knights died, Anna. A squire I had seen through a thousand drills. A good man. A messenger. Sir Valinar. You wouldn't know him, but he couldn't have been much younger than your Gawain. We've been in mourning, as knights do when one falls."

My letter had been terribly rude, but I was loath to fall to pieces. "I simply thought I was worth more to you, Bedevere—you could have let me know, or let one my servants know."

"There was no time for it," he muttered, wiping his brow with the back of his hand. He had stopped weeping, but sorrow clung about him like a cloak.

"If we are to be married, I hope Arthur learns he cannot have you all the time. I will be your wife; he will have to understand—"

"I am a knight first," Bedevere said, looking me in the eye. He backed up to the door and wrapped his hand about the latch. "I had a life here, without you, for twenty years. You mean so much to me, Anna, but I am just a man. And you cannot be my only world."

"Bedevere—"

"Good night, Anna. I think it best we wait Arthur's announcement. In a week's time, at breakfast, he plans on speaking to the court regarding your marriage options. I will be there. I have done all I can. I hope you know that."

I watched him go, saying nothing.

So, on a buttery bright morning in the fairest part of spring, I was summoned to Arthur's chambers. It was the first time I had been invited to see him since the debacle at Lugh's Tournament, and I was nervous as a new bride considering my fate lay in his hands. Gawain was still convalescing, but I was glad he was not there to observe this part of my life. He did not need to see his mother pawned for power.

If I could marry Bedevere, I could tolerate another marriage.

My heart thrummed in my chest as I followed Sir Cai to the King's personal quarters—not the hall, or even one of his greeting chambers. I did not recall having ever been there before and was rather entranced by the proliferation of crimson and gold decoration, the gigantic carved wooden chairs, and the endless suits of armor stood, uninhabited, about the periphery of the room, ghostly and intimidating. I could not have slept at night with such an intrusion.

Arthur sat on one of his large, straight backed chairs, leaning to one side, wearing a long tunic of deep maroon. He looked both bored and slightly depressed, and when he rose to greet me, I saw the lack of sleep written in the circles under his eyes.

"Sister," he said, forcing a smile.

"Your Highness," I said, bowing low. Cai helped me to a seat, and then excused himself.

It was just Arthur and me in the room, alone. I do not think we had ever spent such intimate time together in all our years, and it struck me as very odd. Whatever news he wanted to give me was to be done in private.

"I have been speaking to Bedevere," he said, cutting to the chase. He resumed his seat, and drummed his fingers on the armrests, carved to look like huge lions with open jaws. Each tooth was set with ivory. "About the subject of your... current state, dear sister."

"My current state?" I asked, trying to sound surprised. I had no idea how frank Bedevere was with Arthur, and I worried looking overconfident would be to my disadvantage. Arthur never liked being out thought, though it was painfully easy to do. Those of us in the habit of doing so learned to hide it well.

"It has been three months since the death of King Lot of Orkney," said Arthur, as if this information was new to me. "Three months is the traditional accepted time for a widow to mourn. Are you—ah, do you feel as if the time of mourning has been sufficient?"

What a strange way to ask the question.

"Indeed, my lord," I said.

"You are yet young enough, and you and your sons are the closest in succession to the throne, as we speak. Yes, Gweyn is with child—a cause of celebration in many ways—but we both know the delicacy of these situations. Children die in infancy, in their youth, every day, even with the best medics the realm has to offer. And the son of a king is no exception. I love my nephews dearly and want the best for them. And you, of course."

"Yes, of course."

"And while I once worried about alliances, I feel as if there is less concern where you are involved this time around. I know you sacrificed prime in your marriage to King Lot, and it can't have been easy for you. In return, you have given me gifts I cannot repay, both in your relinquishing of the Orkneys, and with your son Gawain." He almost winced when he said Gawain, the Tournament still clearly heavy on his heart.

I nodded, deciding my part of the conversation consisted of listening to what Arthur had to say.

"I have spoken with Merlin at length, and with Bedevere and Cai of course, and we both believe the best course of action is to seek a match for you here at court, with someone celebrated, yet comfortable."

At Merlin's name the hair on my arms stood up at end; I knew the conversation would not end well, and my hope began to drain away like water through a sieve.

Arthur continued, "A good match—a *worthy* match for you, Anna. So you might find happiness, here, with your family. The knight I have in mind has a family estate, of sizable means, to which you could retreat now and again."

"Yes, my lord." I said the words, but my lips felt numb.

"Would that please you?" he asked, genuinely curious. "To be here at Carelon most of the year? I sense you are anxious sometimes to be amid the hustle and bustle of court life. We have little to look forward to until the Midsummer festivities, so it should be quiet, save if we are threatened at the borders again. My scouts tell me some of the tribes to the North are gathering... but that is neither here nor there. Anna, you would have everything you need at Carelon, and it would make my heart glad to know you were close."

"To answer your question, my lord—yes, being at Carelon would do me well. I treasure my son dearly, and I do wish to be nearer to him. When the twins are of age, I hope this will be their home. They are good and strong boys, like their father."

I meant Bedevere, of course. I feared I would cry.

He smiled, genuinely. "Anna, we have many years to make up between us," he said, reaching out to touch my hands. "I hope in the time to come, we can do just that. I will make an announcement soon as to your betrothal."

"Yes, my lord," I said, and he dismissed me.

When I returned to my chamber, I burst into tears. Bedevere held his own land, a bountiful territory called Dinas Powys in the South. But I could not escape the creeping sense of dread Merlin's name heralded.

All hope felt frail, delicate as an icicle. I had hoped that this time I would have a hand in my wedding. My first marriage was a puppet show: I was paraded about like a stunned deer, dressed and instructed. I did as I was told, and on a cold night in Orkney Lot bedded me with a few guttural groans and a handful of thrusts, before he rolled off of me, out-of-breath and reeking of stale wine. When I did not rush to him again with enthusiasm, he made it clear I did not have a say in the matter.

I could not bear such a match again.

I wrote to Bedevere, a hasty letter filled with fear. He wrote back a single line: *Trust in your own fate and do not fear the conjuror.*


IT WAS TWO days later, at a splendid breakfast, attended by everyone—including Gawain, whose nose would never be straight again, although he had recovered from most of his injuries—when my engagement announcement came.

I was seated next to Gweyn, as usual, and she was busily devouring her breakfast. Her nausea had vanished, and now she could not get enough food. It showed, too, as her hips widened, and the flesh around her cheeks and gullet began to soften and swell over the last month or so. I thought the weight did her figure well, though, truth be told. As a thin woman she was less remarkable, but the earthiness suited her remarkably.

I caught Bedevere's eye across the room, and he smiled comfortingly at me.

"How is Gawain doing, by the way?" Gweyn asked, snapping me out of my pensive state.

I sighed, looking over at my son. Words between us were few since his failure at tournament. Gawain heard King Pellas was attempting to marry off Elaine to Lanceloch, and the issue was eating at him. He blamed me for losing the little wisp. I suppose all men must find blame somewhere, even if it is not truth.

"He will mend," I said, moving a honeyed carrot around with my knife. "But he is not of good spirits. It is more than his ribs that were bruised at the Tournament, you know. And he is ever so hard on himself."

"He should be glad of his accomplishments. Though he lost to Lanceloch, he still broke all previous records on the way. Is it not enough?" She tore off another piece of crusty bread, then slathered it with butter, before delicately stuffing it into her mouth, grinning as she did so. "No, I suppose it is not. I forget how young he is!"

"The men of Orkney and their pride are legend. It is a perilous thing. I am afraid it will take time for him to recover."

"Such a shame! But time is a healer. He can make up for it. Lanceloch is an upstart, at the moment, the darling. Every one of us has faults, however. In time Gawain will discover Lanceloch's weakness." She paused, looking down the row to where Lanceloch and Arthur were talking nearly nose to nose. "He seems so young, doesn't he? But he is older than I am!"

"Who, Lanceloch?"

"Yes, indeed. It is just... he is quite innocent. I do not think he has been at any court long. It is said he spent some of his years in fosterage with Elaine of Benwick's aunt— oh, she would be yours as well!" Gweyn was delighted to make the connection.

"Which aunt?" I asked. "I am plagued with them."

"Why, Vyvian, of course."

"Vyvian?" I hadn't heard her name uttered in at least a decade. "But Vyvian is—"

Arthur stood, and I could not finish my sentence. I felt my nerves crackle; my appetite evaporated in anticipation of his announcement, and my stomach turned with every new course. Time never slowed when I needed, yet always accelerated dread.

It would come down to this moment, then. My fate, yet again in Arthur's hands. I could not say how much control came from Merlin. I should have asked Morgen, but as usual, she was nowhere to be found. Come to think on it, I had not seen much of my Morgen since my arrival. She was not in attendance at the Tournament of Lugh, nor did she dine with us regularly as Merlin did.

"My dear friends," Arthur said, holding up his goblet. "I have brought you here to make a very grand announcement."

The murmuring died down, replaced with affirmative cries and some applause.

Arthur hushed them with his hands. "You all know my sister, Anna Pendragon, once Queen of Orkney, has returned to us here at Carelon after the death of her husband, King Lot. We mourn his loss greatly, but celebrate the contribution of Anna and her son, Sir Gawain, here at court."

There were general cries of agreement, and I saw Gawain half-heartedly raise his goblet in recognition.

"But mourning, as we all know, comes and goes. Now, I am happy to say Anna is prepared to once again enter into a sacred bond of marriage, as she has told me, for the strength of our realm. Rather than see her leave us, Merlin and I have decided she is to be betrothed to a member of our own brotherhood, to a Knight of the Realm. A man of exceptional prowess and land, a knight worthy of the sister of the King..."

I caught Bedevere's eye, hoping for a smile and a look of comfort in his brown eyes. When he did not return my look, I knew something was amiss. He went pale, just as Merlin leaned over and whispered in his ear; Bedevere's hands curled around his goblet as if gripping his longsword.

My ears rang. My breath stilled. It was as if the floor itself dropped beneath my feet and I was falling.

"Anna?"

Gweyn's voice came to me as a whisper, far away.

Then Arthur finished his announcement, showering me with a beatific grin and declared: "So if you will, please, ladies and gentlemen of Carelon—let us celebrate the union of Anna Pendragon and Lanceloch du Lac."

I felt Gweyn's hands on me, pushing me to stand, and though my legs felt heavy as lead, I stood nonetheless, grasping the table to steady myself. Tears filled my eyes, and I gave a ghastly smile, wishing I had the strength to scream.

Then Lanceloch was standing next to me, holding my hand, and I saw the fury in Gawain's face, the betrayal in Bedevere's, and I wanted to faint. I wished I could. But I just stood, clenching my teeth through a haggard grin and laughing a high, strange noise. It was my curse to swoon only when inconvenient.

Knights rushed to congratulate me, and I blindly clasped their hands and kissed their faces, ever feeling the presence of Lanceloch behind me like a pillar of fire.

First, I thought: Bedevere. Then: Lanceloch is ten years younger than me. Then: My sister will be my stepmother. The shrill whine rose in my ears and I wanted to run from the hall entirely, but my legs had turned to stone.

"I have a lovely castle in Gaul," said Lanceloch, softly. His voice was gentle, soothing, in spite of my wish that it be coarse and easy to despise. He was squeezing my hand as one might to calm a child. "It is called the Joyous Guard. I can take you there, if you like—once in a while—to retreat from the business of Carelon."

I said naught in reply; I was rendered mute. I recall shaking Cai's hand as he came to kiss my cheek. I felt as if I were no longer seeing through my own eyes, and when Merlin approached me, I thought I would stop breathing for my hatred of him. I wanted to scratch his eyes out. I was so close to living with Bedevere as his wife, to a life of love and not simply duty.

The conjuror leaned over. "A second chance, Lady Anna," he said. "A remarkable gift. An unusual match, perhaps, but thank you for your agreement of re-marriage. It will keep Lanceloch precisely where we need him."

Arthur gazed only upon Lanceloch. And I understood, grappled with the fleeting hope dying in my chest like a downed bird: my brother did not want my happiness. He only wanted Lanceloch in bonds, bonds that could not be broken by another. Safe in his grasp, close to him, and I the instrument of his captivity.

IT IS A dreadful thing to marry an older man, but there is a power in knowing he will meet Death first and set you free. Marrying a younger man is like staring at your own pyre.

MY FIRST WEDDING took place upon the craggy shores of Orkney, in Wyre, not far from the fortress Lot so loved. He was King of all Lothian but preferred the desolation of the Orkneys, and our bonding ceremony reflected this: there was but a single Avillionian priest to marry us, and a handful of witnesses I did not know. Then, I had Marsa, my maid with me, but she was already ailing and could not attend the nuptials.

I do not remember what words we spoke. I only remember the cold and the dread; the chill made my teeth chatter and the salty air made my skin prickle. When he took me to bed, my feet were still numb from standing in the cold sand.

In the months between the consummation and Gawain's birth, I became a shadow of a person. Marsa died of the grippe, and my new handmaidens were as afraid of Lot as I was, and they did little more than provide for me lest they be punished.

I went away. I ate for Gawain, the child inside of me. But I did not sew, I did not read. When I wasn't sick from the child, a sign of a healthy pregnancy I was told time and again, I slept. The world felt bled of all color, leeched of joy and warmth and friendship.

Then Gawain came. Late, and in the middle of the night, squalling and raging, red as a beet, and my furious child gave me a new life. Not as a mother, no, but as a human being. His cries awoke within me a fierce protectiveness, not just of him, but of myself. Free as I was from the weight of childbearing, I began to see again. The brilliance and the stark beauty of the Orkneys, my son's inheritance, slowly came into view. The world came alive again, and me in it.

When Gawain was a year old, Bedevere and a small retinue came to Hrolf's Isle, the larger island near Wyre where we received our guests and the majority of the men lived and worked. He and his brother Lucan grew up with us in Carelon, but I had not seen him in years, since he, like so many other knights, was fostered at another court. We were so young; I, fifteen, Bedevere barely seventeen. But already, we carried the weight of kingdoms on our shoulders.

I saw Bedevere across the room, laughing his melodious laugh, his dark eyes merry and his fine form awash in candlelight and knew I wanted him. I had never desired another man before. My husband turned lovemaking into a perfunctory act of violence. I knew it as nothing else.

I left the hall in tears. Bedevere found me, crouched and

weeping, in the old Ascomanni graveyard, my pet cat on my lap.

"Anna Pendragon, daughter of Uther," Bedevere said, falling to his knees before me. "It is cold enough for your tears to freeze."

"I am frozen through," I said, gasping for air.

We were utterly alone, the wind drowning our voices.

"Impossible. You are forged from the same ore as Arthur, King of all Braetan," Bedevere said, his voice as warm as morning sunshine. "And your grandfather, it was said, was part Ascomanni himself, a great leader of hordes of warriors named Aska. Arthur told me more than once that Aska's wife, Drunna, conquered her own islands."

I had never heard that story before. "Arthur loves such tales. But he also lives the life of an exalted king and beloved ruler."

"Anna, you have the heart of a fighter. You are not alone." He paused, his hands recoiling as he brought the small lantern toward me, and I gazed up at him, surprised to see him so close. His eyes fell to my neck, where my scarf had fallen away: there were bruises there. And many more he could not see.

"I am so tired, Bedevere," I whispered.

He clenched his jaw, then reached out to stroke my cheek. I felt a reluctant fire rise within me again. "What can I do? I will do anything for you, Anna. Anything you ask."

And thus, we began. Every spring, just as the celandine and coltsfoot broke through the cold, hard earth, Bedevere would come with supplies and news from Carelon. Those bright yellow flowers, carpeting the green expanse of the Orkneys, kindled a fire inside of me and brought me hope.

And, in time, the bravery and the means by which to make my escape.

THIS TIME, HOWEVER, my wedding was the talk of Carelon. I had no time to speak with Bedevere with the dizzying preparations. I tried to write to Bedevere, but nothing I wrote made sense. I began to worry he thought I was tied up with the decree to marry Lanceloch, as if I got some cruel pleasure out of doing him ill again.

I had done it before; I suppose he was right in thinking I had again.

The longer I spent without word from Bedevere, the more my fear twisted into hatred. Men are often cruel, and though I considered Bedevere an exception, I was willing to admit an oversight. What kind of a man professes his love, but in the face of adversity vanishes from sight? He had not advocated for our union, not in a meaningful manner. He unwittingly sold me off once more.

My mind drifted away, as it had in those years on Orkney, but there was no herald of spring to bring me joy. When I was not attending dinners or sitting through planning for the ceremonies, most of which I let Gweyn control, I slept alone in my room. I longed for Bedevere, I longed for word from the twins; I longed for Gawain's forgiveness. I even wrote to Morgen, asking after her strange absence. I wished I could find comfort, connection, I wished I knew what was wrong with me, why I only drowned deeper every day.

I received no answers and no replies.

Gweyn blossomed, ever growing, her long, garish gowns always enhancing her newly rotund figure. She looked like the goddess incarnate, all breasts and stomach and hips. I had never seen her happier, and though she was cloying at times, her enthusiasm for the wedding knew no bounds.

Gawain continued to keep his distance, only greeting me while in public and ignoring my pleas to connect. I had always wanted to speak to him of womanly things, to explain to him our too-brief childhoods and innocence, our endurance during our marriages. But he went to Arthur so young. I wanted him to understand a woman's plight in the world, but I perhaps I kept too much from him too long.

Gweyn and I visited the sempstresses together each morning, checking the status of my gown. It was magnificent, done in crimson, gold, and ivory, detailed with intricate embroidery down the back, a complicated interlace of ivy and roses. A most beautiful composition, and I could not but help myself to reach out and touch the work, thanking the head sempstress. If I had to marry a man nearly young enough to be my child, I would at least look the part of a grand bride.

"Why, Anna," Gweyn said, as we walked away from my gown in progress to the tunic and sash Lanceloch would be wearing, "if I did not know you better, I would have thought you were smiling just then."

I smiled more with the recognition. "I suppose there is some surprise joy to be found, strange as this all is."

"I know it is not what you expected," said Gweyn, touching my hand gently with hers, letting the fingertips linger a moment. "You will look like a goddess of old. You're so tall, and so elegant—no man will be able to keep his eyes from you."

"I am not a woman who likes to draw attention to herself," I said.

"But you do, my dear. You are positively marvelous. And so is your husband-to-be. He is a very striking man, you know—more handsome than any I have seen, if you don't mind me saying, and Arthur is so fond of him. Do you know Lanceloch plays the lute *and* the lyre? And he speaks at least six languages? And he's been spending hours in the kennels with the hounds."

"If Vyvian reared him, then it makes sense," I said, remembering my eccentric, and thoroughly exiled, aunt. "But he is so young... and as you said, so innocent."

"Perhaps he will work hard to be a good husband, then. I know naught of your previous marriage, Anna, as you are never one to speak of such things, and no, I don't expect it. I know we are very different, and you have no use for more sisters in your life. But I do, truly, wish you every happiness this time around. I know what it feels like to be... pushed in directions you hadn't considered."

It broke my heart to look at Gweyn, the way she regarded me with complete trust and adoration. I could not bear to tell her what I suspected, that Arthur was in love with Lanceloch— and he would not suffer to have him married to some mad king's insipid daughter, or anyone else, and had therefore promised him to an old, fading, likely barren woman. In hopes, of course, to drive him into his arms. I would have done the same thing in his place and with his power.

"Well, I cannot fathom what he would want with an old woman like me," I said, shivering a little as we moved from the warmth of the sempstress' workshop into the long hallway leading to the stairs to the higher levels of the castle.

"Old woman! Nonsense," said Gweyn, waving a chubby hand in my direction. "You've retained your looks better than half the court a fraction of your age. You really ought to take a good look in the mirror sometimes. I hear your mother was the same way—she looked remarkably young for years."

"She was beautiful in ways I have never claimed to be," I said.

We mounted the stairs, and were surprised to see Lanceloch himself standing, speaking to a group of knights. He turned to us and smiled, then hurried over.

"Your Majesty, Queen Gweynevere," he said, bowing lowly to Gweyn, taking her hand and kissing it softly. Then he looked to me: "Your ladyship, Princess Anna Pendragon."

Princess. Indeed.

"Good evening, Sir Lanceloch du Lac," said Gweyn, her voice full of merriment. I do not think anyone had used my full title in a long time, and though he omitted my minor holdings, it was humorous. I was no more a princess than I was a virgin. "What brings you to this side of the castle, may I ask?"

He smiled, his amber eyes merry. Gweyn was right, he was stunning. But I would have been happier admiring him from a distance, like a fine portrait or a colorful tapestry. The thought of forcing myself to the act of love with him horrified me—how could one so comely ever concede to be with a woman like me, someone who'd borne three children and still had the scars to show? Such thoughts kept me sleepless at night.

"I was hoping to have a moment with my future wife," he said, looking on so kindly it was like to break my heart.

"Of course," Gweyn said, without my consent. "Sir

Lanceloch is a most honorable knight—none of us would deny him the joy of speaking with his wife-to-be." She could not have sounded more delighted. And slightly devious.

He walked with me to the orchid garden, an enclosed glass structure on the southeastern side of the castle, typically tended by one deaf elderly man named Hoel. We walked side by side a while, neither speaking, as we passed the blooming tumbles of flowers, all gifted to Arthur from Avillion, lovely and erotic, so vibrant and unusual, their heads unfurling and trembling as we passed.

The sun was setting over the rolling hills, painting the grass gold and blazing orange, and on the horizon where the hedgerows stretched in stark lines, fireflies danced in dizzy circles. Deep, splendid summer, full of the song of insects and the promise of fruit.

"I thought Carelon to be a cold place, from your aunt's descriptions," Lanceloch said, staring out at the sunset. His eyes were cast in its light, reflecting like flames. "She bears no love for this place, least of all Merlin. But she loves Arthur, for all his curiousness."

"You find my brother curious?" I asked. I wondered how much he knew.

"He is a man of contradiction," said my knight, shaking his head slowly. "A man half in love with life yet resigned to the gruesome truth of death and decay. He worries a great deal that his grasp will fail, and he will cease to be all he has been prophesied."

"Does he?" I asked, nearly stunned to silence by Lanceloch's poetic conversation. "I am afraid my brother does not confide in me as he does you. And my sister, your stepmother, even less."

110

Lanceloch shrugged carelessly for one speaking of the ruler of all Braetan. It was his easy way; I would later learn. "I suppose it is part of the bond of brothers in arms, I do not know."

I almost laughed at the expression but remained my calm composure.

"He believes you and I are destined to be together. And in time, we could find love, if we so seek it."

"So speaks great Arthur," I said, finding it very difficult to infuse any sense of warmth into my voice. "Tell me, Lanceloch, have you heard the prophecy Merlin gave me on the day of my birth?"

He turned away from the sun, regarding me. The light caught the stubble on his chin, turning it metallic gold. Perhaps he was a bronze statue, and not a man, I thought dizzily.

"Yes. I know of it. Merlin interpreted a prophecy, and it said you would be forgotten by all men," he said, the words like honey on his tongue.

"And you do not mind a wife forgotten?"

"You do not occur to me as a woman so easily forgotten, prophecy or no, Anna." He sobered slightly when I was quiet. "Has it been such a burden?"

"It is difficult to say," I said evenly. "I was married just shy of my thirteenth birthday and forgotten to the wastes of Orkney. I was more than a memory in Carelon before I even knew myself."

Lanceloch's eyes narrowed, wincing. "That is perilously young."

"Such is the fate of the Pendragon princess."

"Lot's reputation was known even to me, but I was too young to have known why such decisions were made.

Someday, if you should find it in your heart, we can speak of these days. As your husband, I am here should you wish."

"It does lay heavy on me at times. I have scarcely shared it with a soul." I could not say why I admitted so much to him. No one at court, save Bedevere, had ever asked about my time with Lot. "But then, even my friends here seem to forget me."

"So your curse is not always to your detriment. I hear tell you sometimes don the clothes of your maids to visit the infirm, and to speak with the cooks in the kitchens," he said, smiling wryly.

That information could have only come from one person: Bedevere. The knowledge of this cut through me.

"I used to," I replied, my voice catching in my throat. The betrayal was bitter. "I enjoy the company of common folk. And I do not like being chained to court politics."

"Here, we can make whatever life we like. You and I."

"As long as you do not mind my evening traipse through the scullery, perhaps we can come to an agreement."

He laughed, the edges of his eyes crinkling. What gods wrought him engendered him with a most wondrous countenance, striking in joy and in solemnity. It was the latter which descended upon him suddenly and drew my attention.

"Though, there is one matter I wished to discuss, Anna," he said, his voice losing its smoothness. He drew a long breath, averting my eyes momentarily. "And it concerns our marriage bed."

"I know the ways of knights, Sir Lanceloch. I am no innocent bride," I said, almost touching his shoulder, but refraining. He had a comfortable way about him put me at ease. But ease meant trust, and trust meant weakness; I could afford neither.

"That is just the thing, my darling," he said softly. "I have... I have only been chaste."

I froze in our procession, and he continued speaking as I struggled to assemble my thoughts.

"I wanted to speak to you of this before our wedding. It is something I have cherished, as a vow to Ayr, the twenty-six years of my life. I hope you will... be patient with me, in these ways..." His chest rose and fell, and he looked nervously down at his hands.

"You promised yourself to Ayr?" I said. "I thought vows of celibacy were reserved for only the most devout priests of Avillion, not the lusty knights of Arthur."

"I am an unusual knight," he admitted, rubbing the back of his head. The gesture made him look a bit like an embarrassed child found sleeping with his favorite blanket, as I had once discovered with Gawain when he was thirteen. "But once I am married—I pledge to give myself to you, should you have me. It is what Arthur wants—it is what you deserve, should you... should you desire me."

Should *I* desire *him*?

Gods damn him. He was so innocent, so pure. Listening to Lanceloch's musical voice, so fraught with emotion and vulnerability, I was mesmerized. He was unearthly. This dedication, this straightforwardness, this humility. I remembered him at Lugh's Tournament, wracked with grief over the injured opponent, taking time to see after his well-being rather than gloat over his own prowess. This man was compassionate beyond reason, his heart the strangest contradiction to the body he inhabited.

"You are unusual," I said, taking his hand in mine. It felt strange; his hands were rough, yet without the wear of Bedevere's or the papery skin of Lot. He squeezed my fingers, smiling. "Just remarkable."

# CHAPTER FIVE

## WOVEN ENDS

As THE WEDDING approached, I tried and failed to reconcile with Gawain and Bedevere. I understood Gawain's anger, and knew there was little I could do to sway his opinion. I would marry the man who shamed my son in front of the entire court. I could do nothing. Every effort I made to contact Gawain ended with his temper, the final attempt punctuated by a door slammed in my face. Were I one step closer, the impact would have broken my nose.

I suppose Gawain had much to learn about obeying the will of one's king. He was lucky of his kinship with the King, for I do not think Arthur would have been patient with any other. It would take time, and he would be tested—I held out the hope that eventually Gawain would understand the decision to wed Lanceloch was no choice of mine. He was a man grown in some ways, but childlike in others, still.

THE MORNING OF my wedding to Lanceloch du Lac, I was awoken out of a dream by a thunderclap and wind so vast it shook the windowpanes. My hands were so cold while my maids dressed me, I could scarcely arrange my crown or fix the edges of my cuffs. When a herald came in, announcing the ceremony had to be moved inside, upon Merlin's absolute insistence, the storm began pelting hail with such ferocity some of the windows in West Tower shattered.

From my own window, I could survey the ruin of Gweyn's marvelous flowered garden, the immense bower twined with white roses, deep blue valerian, and blush-colored lilies, all braided with intricate ribbon, now flopping lifeless, half-blown into a large oak tree. The delicate paper lanterns she'd commissioned from Merlin sat on the ground like bloated lumps of clay.

By the time we were ushered into Lugh's chapel, another consequence of the weather was revealed: many of the invited knights were dispatched to one of the nearby villages where a bridge collapsed, and a damn burst, flooding the town and killing a dozen peasants.

No fairy tale, that was certain. Even the chapel was awash in muddy footprints

No storm, no collection of mud, and certainly no dark sky could dim my betrothed's uncanny beauty. For regardless of the day's challenges, Lanceloch was resplendent, serious, and solemn through the ceremony, a stalwart pinnacle of knightly strength and grace. Merlin officiated, as was his duty, and the old conjuror's voice made me feel cold and alone, no matter my family and friends surrounding me. I would not meet his eye, I decided. I would not let him see my anger, my frustration. The man wielded too much power, but he could never know how it wounded me.

*Who judges the great conjuror?*

I closed my eyes as I listened to Merlin repeat the traditional marriage poem of Avillion.

*Like threads of yarn, your souls now cling—one*
*    strong strand.*
*Man and woman, woman and man, with the power*
*    of gods between—*
*Hold fast to the fiber of life, braid it about yourself.*
*In rain, in sun; feast and famine; dark and light.*
*Let no one sunder what the gods have wrought.*

I repeated the words, but their meaning was ash in my mouth. Looking at Lanceloch, I could not help but admire him—and yet, I could not put aside the gnawing feeling our union was wrong and destined for sorrow. For all these good intentions, for all my obeisance, and even for the sliver of hope kindling that Lanceloch and I might build a friendship, I knew I was naught but a pawn in Arthur's game.

Long had I heard of Merlin's famed voice, but never heard it for myself. The entire congregation went still and silent as he hoisted his ancient harp and began to sing.

The song was an old tale, and Merlin's voice was high and trilling, strained and strange. He sang a tale of Gwydion and his sister Arianrhod, the warrior's wildness and her broken virginity. She was tasked with proving her purity, and when she failed, she gave birth to two children, one of whom was a malformed monster.

It was not appropriate. But it was sung in language only my mother's people would know. And even so, the congregation was under such a spell of music they simply gawked at the old bard, eyes wide and mouths ajar. Even Lanceloch was transfixed.

I could only guess that it was a warning. That Merlin threatened to curse my womb should I stray from Lanceloch. Or that he would harm my children. And certainly, I had no doubt, the old conjuror knew Lanceloch's secret.

Every reverberating note, echoing around the cavernous chapel, made my headache, my eyes water, and my teeth throb. I was sweating, head to toe, when he finished, and nearly missed Arthur's proclamation of our union:

"Blessed be the union of my new brother, Lanceloch du Lac, and his wife, the Lady du Lac."

Another name, another life, another move, in the Great Game.

Gweyn found me at the banquet table and embraced me until it hurt. "I cannot believe this weather, sister," she said, pulling away to dab at her eyes. "I would have bathed you in sunshine and lilies. I would have piled you with flowers and arrayed your dress in carpets of ribbon."

"I know," I said, truly touched by her desire to bring light into my life. No one I'd ever met tried so hard to make me happy. "You should not weep for the weather; it cannot be helped."

"And that *song*." Gweyn shuddered, her curls dancing at her cheeks. "I will have to have words with Arthur. Letting that old menace sing about—"

"It was just a song," I said, squeezing her hand. She squeezed mine back, her fingers even colder than mine. "Gweyn, you should rest. You have the child to think of."

"Oh, if I stop decorating and indulging in delight, I will weep so much the whole castle would flood," she said, smiling through her tears. "Now, go! Dance, eat. You have a beautiful husband and a long night ahead."

I watched her go, wishing I could comfort her, before being drawn back into the merriment.

AFTER DRINKING MORE than I should to drown out the memory of Merlin's wretched song, the crowd ushered my new husband and I back to my apartment, the quarters we were now expected to inhabit together. The entire path to the apartment was littered with rose petals and lily blossoms, though many were still damp from the rain. In spite of the cheer, and the furs around my shoulders, the procession was a chilly one, and as the crowd dissipated behind us, I shivered.

At last we were alone, the last revelers' voices drifting down the dark halls and away.

"Take my hand," Lanceloch said, his cheeks flushed and his eyes alight with joy. We stood at the great wooden threshold, side by side. We were of a height, and when I turned to look at him, we were almost nose-to-nose. "My bride."

The hearth roared inside, and the room boasted tables laden with honeyed fruits, intricate breads, and flagons of ruby red wine. Lanceloch closed the door behind us and stood a moment, just looking at me.

Slowly, I removed my cloak. My stomach sank and flipped by turns, as inconstant as the sea. I felt terribly inadequate for him, yet I could not tamp the desire rising in me. His body longed to be touched and was so wonderfully carved it begged assurance of its solidity.

He was so young; too young. I felt repulsive, a practical crone in comparison. I made no motion to go toward him, no indication that I was ready for the inevitable. In truth, I was as cold and as frightened as I had been on my first wedding day, though I was far from virgin now.

"Your hair cannot be comfortable like so, twisted and tied and twirled," he said, coming close. He reached up to touch the pins in my hair and I caught his hand.

"It doesn't have to be tonight," I said, softly. He was so beautiful, but I did not want to break him. I only wanted to marvel at him, like a bronze statue in the sun. "We have time."

He gazed upon me with a look of astonishment. "I want to touch your hair," he said at last. "That is all. For right now. It is very beautiful. I watched the firelight dance down each long strand tonight at dinner, like fairy floss."

Knowing better than to deny my new husband, and feeling not a little flattered, I helped him uncoil each long twist until I stood before him like a maiden, hair falling to my waist in golden rivulets.

"A marvel," he said, taking one lock in his hand and softly pulling it over his palm. "Like spun gold."

"Thank you, my lord," I said, unsure what to do with such compliments.

"No, 'my lord,' please, Anna. Not here. Not in our home."

I blushed. Gods help me, but I blushed at his invitation of intimacy. "If you do not wish to bed me, there is no harm in waiting. However long you want."

"It's not that—I have just spent so long preparing my body for battle and no time preparing it for love." It was not the response I was expecting, but nor did I anticipate the rising passion in his gaze. He gazed at my collar bones, where a thick chain of gold fell, a blue topaz set in the middle like a strange, ancient eye.

"You do not have to love me with your heart for it to be pleasurable," I said softly. He ran a finger over the skin at my neck and I gasped of breath at the sudden touch. His eyes were possessed of the same childlike fascination as when he'd stroked my hair. "Although, in all truth, Lanceloch, I am not as experienced as some women my age."

"Your husband—was he a great lover?" Again, in that half-distracted tone.

I grabbed his fingers in mine. "Dear gods, Lanceloch, no."

"I'm sorry," he said, frowning. "You said you were young, but your marriage was long. I suppose I hoped eventually he understood the treasure of you."

I swallowed hard. "For Lot, the act of love was done only to claim me or to frighten me or to get me with child. His first wife failed him in that matter; he kept a mistress for other affections, and she doted upon him."

"A mistress? You mean—he—" Lanceloch was wide-eyed, the idea of adultery so far from his mind. That pure heart.

"Yes, a mistress. Her name was Maira, and she shared his quarters. I stayed in my own apartment, where I reared our boys, and managed the household."

"Shameful," he said. He moved even nearer to me, observing my face a moment before brushing a finger across my bottom lip, slow and searching. I would not be capable of conversation much longer. Passion unspooled within me. "Surely he knew such behavior broke your heart."

"It did not," I said. "I did not love my husband. I did not mind someone else warming his bed while I still feared he would darken my threshold."

Anger flashed across his features and he sighed deeply. "I'm sorry you did not know love. But perhaps it is a naïve thought. I find many of my thoughts are."

"I despised him in the end," I said, my voice unexpectedly husky with emotion. "I did not weep when he died, Lanceloch. He was a cruel man, in more ways than I can yet explain."

"I will not be a cruel husband," he said, taking my hand in his, and bringing my fingers to his lips, kissing them. His lips were warm, slightly chapped. His moist skin lingered a moment before pulling back, and he looked into my face, his amber eyes dark and strange in the firelight.

"You can be whomever you are with me, Lanceloch. I do not want you to pretend you love me or need me; this union was not done outside our own intentions. I know a political alliance when I see one, and Arthur and Merlin have their reasons," I said, fighting the desire and the wine within me. Heavens, the way he looked at me. "We are an alliance—and we can be friends, but we need not be lovers."

He considered it for a moment, the silence drawing out between us. I suppose it was foolish of me to hope he might feel attracted to me, but the sting of the realization was less painful than I had anticipated. What flicker of lust he kindled before began to diminish.

"You wouldn't be angry with me if I wanted to wait?" he asked, looking down at the place where my gown fastened to the kirtle. He ran his hands over the beadwork, the dragon dancing with the lion. "It is not I do not *want* to. It is only, with my vow I worry—"

"That your prowess will diminish if you lose yourself to passion and sensuality?"

He flushed in the firelight, the skin at his neck patchy and red. I wondered vaguely if he favored men, but then it occurred to me that he simply may not have understood the act of love at all. For all his passionate speech, and wonder at my body, he was very detached from desire, as if such thoughts were rare. This was strange in anyone, let alone a man of such physical ability as Lanceloch. Knights at Carelon were known often more for their dabbling with women than their work with swords of steel.

"So—we could wait?" he asked.

"Of course," I said, surprised though at the hollow feeling the words left in me. I did the best to continue smiling, trying to comfort myself in the fact he was so young and out of touch, but tears still pricked my eyes. I used the moment to reach again for my cloak, to turn away, and to feign a chill. "There is more than one bedchamber here, Lanceloch. I would be the last to intrude on your vow."

The act of love would be best kept for a later date, when we were both of a better mindset.

If ever at all.

SUMMER DEEPENED, AND outside my window the green grass withered and turned brown in the unrelenting sunlight. I heard some of Gweyn's beloved lilies died in spite of the best efforts of a handful of herbalists brought in to aid in the maintenance. I adjusted, slowly, to life as Lady du Lac. After the festivities of our nuptials, however, so little changed.

I rarely saw Lanceloch save in the evenings, and even then, often he came to our apartment well after I was asleep.

Arthur kept him very busy. My young husband was at times worried, distressed, and agitated, but I did not ask after him other than in passing. Perhaps it sounds cruel, but I knew what Arthur was after, and Lanceloch would never share with me what went on behind those closed doors. After our first night together, when he stroked my hair and gave me hope, our relations had thinned to perfunctory communication and sitting beside one another at the endless banquets of Carelon.

It was a black summer for me. I received a handful of letters from Gareth, pleading with me to take him home. I replied that, though I would if it were in my power, I was as helpless as he in the matter. Only Arthur could change the situation. Gaheris, according to Gareth, was flourishing, having fallen in love with one of Luw's daughters. I prayed her name was not Elaine. But poor, sensitive Gareth was suffering there alone without his brother to comfort him. It would get better, I assured him.

To compound matters, Gawain still did not speak to me. I wrote him—writing letters to my own son in the same castle!—but he either threw them away, burned them, or refused them outright. When King Pellas returned to his own lands with his daughter Elaine, Gawain's mood was even more morose; he was accused of inciting violence among the knights, and Arthur made him spend a humiliating evening in the dungeon.

Bedevere, too, refused company, and Gweyn was often too sick or tired. I worried after her but was not often permitted nearby. Rumors were that Gweyn often fell into oracular dazes, and the priestess of Avillion attended her every move.

I was curious, and a bit excited, when I heard Gweyn's sister Hwyfar was arriving shortly to court, from Avillion. I thought I might find the woman who was jilted by my brother to be worthy of pursuing an alliance.

But before I could think much on Hwyfar, I received a rather remarkable shock at the hands of my sister Morgen who I hadn't seen in months. I knew one thing: she was not at Carelon, for I asked after her through Anette and Jain and Culver, who by now were my most helpful spies.

I had returned to my quarters late one night, then sent Anette to sleep. She was within a few weeks of her due date and, like Gweyn, beyond the capabilities of normal movement. I worried for her, frail as she was.

Sitting in my favorite chair in the parlor, I was just about to take up my embroidery, when I noticed someone standing across from me.

"Morgen," I said, my voice scarcely a whisper. "But you are not—"

"I frightened you," she said.

I brought one of my trembling fingers to my lips. "It is not unusual for someone to appear unbidden into my midst— but they are most typically present in the castle."

She looked wild in my domestic environment, her dark hair trying to escape its braided confines, homespun gown in grey and dun such a contrast to my elegant blue and gold silks. To look at her face, none would expect we shared the same mother.

Then, her image shifted, like ink on water, and re-established itself again, the lines clearer this time.

I was so rarely in the presence of magic I came quite slowly to the realization she was, in fact, projecting herself.

"Oh, dear... you are... this is a spell," I said, sitting down across from her, peering at her.

Morgen looked weary to her bones, lines carved deep around her eyes, the trenches around her mouth more pronounced than I had seen in years. "I need to speak with you; I do not have long."

"Where are you?" I asked. Her projection gave no indication of place. How did this magic work?

"Tintagel," she said, softly. Her father's castle in Cornwall, then. Where Arthur was conceived, and our mother betrayed.

"You look unwell, my dear," I said.

"Gweynevere is going to have her child soon," she said, her voice gaining strength. She stood and turned around, then began pacing. The wightly version of herself moved along the rushed floor, but the feet were not quite substantial. It looked as though she were walking on mist. "A boy."

"Amhar," I said, hating the name still. The woman had no sense in naming, clearly. "Yes."

"She *cannot* raise the boy," Morgen said, shaking her hair so her braids waved side to side. I never once heard her speak so detachedly. I wondered if she was taking herbs to facilitate the projection. "But I cannot be in Carelon, so I need your help."

I almost burst into raucous laughter but hid it instead behind a curt smile. "My help? Dear sister... is not Margawse available?"

The image of my sister Morgen rippled, as if I had disturbed her reflection in a pool. It was strange to think she would reach for help in such an unusual way. Magic was not typically wasted on one such as me.

"She cannot help me," Morgen said, and I caught a hint of frustration, as if she were suddenly aware of how far she had to lower herself to address me in this way. "Anna, I ask you to do this because you are the only one among us who can. It is for the preservation of us all."

"You sound so riddled with doom," I observed. As strange as it may sound, I was quite flattered Morgen sought me out, especially in such an unusual way. Magic always existed on the periphery of my life, distanced to the point I often discredited it. There were times I did not believe in the powers of Morgen and Merlin, and the priests and priestess of Avillion. I believed their wiles to be just that: tricks to entice the rest of us into thinking they held more power than the average person, even if my prophecy haunted my thoughts.

Yet, I could not deny it now. It had been rumored my mother, Igraine, was descended of the same line of conjurors as Merlin, and though I did not take much stock in gossip, it was possible. Merlin, for all his meddling, only involved himself with my mother once.

"Will you help me, or will you make this more difficult than it already is?" Morgen said. I had struck a nerve.

"It depends. Am I being told, or do I have a say?"

"It would depend upon you. But I ask you first and try and explain myself. The power here drains me."

"Of course."

I folded the unattended embroidery at my lap, twisting one of the red threads up and over my fingers. The tension helped focus me on the wavering image of my half-sister as she stopped pacing and faced me.

"Gweynevere cannot be allowed to—no, let me try

again," Morgen said, wincing as she retraced her line of thought. "The child cannot be raised at Carelon."

"What are you suggesting?" I asked, somehow not surprised at her proclamation. Their marriage had been a bad omen from the beginning, with Merlin opposing it. Arthur's covetousness was the only reason it even happened; and now with the arrival of Hwyfar, matters were sure to get out of hand. "I do not see why you need me."

"I am being kept at a distance by other powers."

"I owe you nothing."

"Oh, do you not?"

"No," I snapped. "Nothing."

"You tell me, sister," Morgen said gently. "You asked for herbs, for books, and I sent them to you. You asked for knowledge, and I provided. And you returned to Carelon a widow."

Her words hung, cold. I'd not told her, exactly, what transpired the night of Lot's death. I took a long time to believe it myself, to fully grasp what I was capable of in the end.

"Continue," I said, my throat dry.

"Your maid, Anette, will give birth to her child on the same day as Gweynevere. You will take that child to the Queen in exchange for Amhar. You will bring Amhar to one of the priests of Avillion, who will meet you in the Queen's chamber."

"Morgen—" I said, trying to keep my composure, but lacking the presence of mind to do so. Gooseflesh ran up and down my arms, unrelenting. I was short of breath. Words danced in my mind, but I could not form them.

"There are eyes here. Always watching me. You know of whom I speak."

Morgen nodded. "I will keep Merlin from you." The way she said his name sent a chill down my spine; my stomach ran cold.

"Morgen, I must ask—are you in danger?"

She did not reply. "Gweyn trusts you. She loves you. The midwife assisting her is in my service. In the meantime, you'll need to prepare yourself; you will need to gain entrance to the Queen's chambers, in the event you are not allowed in."

"How will I do such a thing? I cannot just walk about commanding the midwives give me the son's heir—she will be surrounded by guards. Surely Lanceloch would see me, or someone else, and ask after—"

"You'll pull shadows, as you always do."

"Pull shadows?" I asked.

Now it was time for Morgen to smile; she even laughed a little, teeth flashing behind red, red lips. "Oh, Anna dearest sister," she said. "Have you been so blind all these years? I suppose you've always been such a simple girl, doing as you're told."

When I said nothing, for lack of knowing what to say, she continued. "You pull shadows every day. When you walk down the hall, you do it without even knowing. Our mother did it; Elaine does it. It is a family gift, allowing you to walk as if in the shadows, so people do not recognize you. Aunt Vyvian is the best of all of us. It was one of the reasons for her exile. They discovered what she could do. For she could slip inside the skin of others. This is the power of the women in our line, and the price we pay when we shape the world. She lives alone, she lives chained, because she dared to challenge Merlin."

"Morgen, this is preposterous. My prophecy—I thought—"

"You thought people simply forgot you?" she said, lightly and almost sweetly. "No, no. I am afraid, my dear, you are one of us. Your prophecy is part of it, but your powers run deep. You must only delve for them."

"Can there not be someone else?" I asked. I was frightened to use magic, and even more frightened to know I tested it the night I had gone to Lot's room. I stood there, dripping the concoction into his sleeping mouth: celandine, larkspur, nightshade, and sweet honey. He opened his eyes, but he did not see me. Yes. There was truth to her words. "I am unskilled and unreliable, then."

"Go to my quarters in Merlin's tower. Say you are sent on an errand from me. There is a small scroll with green floss on my rosewood bookshelf beside the raven's egg that never hatches. You will find better instructions there."

"I feel so unprepared. Is there naught you can teach me now?"

She shook her head. "You know I cannot."

"I have no desire to work as an accomplice to the murder of an innocent child—a wanted child—and a bold-faced lie, to my Queen, nonetheless."

Morgen frowned. "I did not speak of murder... Anna, we face a grave future if we allow Amhar to live at court. I have seen what he grows up to be. No child of Arthur's will stand the throne—and if he does, he will be the ruin of us all."

"I do not believe a word of it."

"Can you not feel it?" Morgen asked, pressing closer. Her projection glimmered slightly, edges going soft, and then returning with more definition. "Can you not feel it all around you? Every day brings us closer. His name is murmured on the winds... Carelon will fall, and all with it, if you do not do this. We do not build a future only for Arthur."

Her words gave me pause.

I had been frowning so deeply my head began to hurt, and I reached to touch the pinched space between my eyes, then startled at the chill in my fingers. When I exhaled, my breath misted. It was still summer.

I moaned. "I do not want to do this, Morgen. I only want peace."

"I will grant you a boon, Anna." She was starting to sound desperate, but she did not offer me words of comfort, and I was glad. It would have been false.

"What if I refuse?" I hissed, shivering again. My teeth were starting to rattle, and I wondered if Morgen's projection was pulling all the warmth out of the room. It was strong magic. "What if I tell Arthur?"

"You will not, because I know about your children."

"You—"

"Gaheris and Gareth are not Lot's," Morgen said. "Suppose how furious Luwddoc would be to find out he has been supporting two bastards begotten on a love-struck knight... and after all these months of feeding them and training them. It would be such a shame if he discovered Gaheris was spreading wide the legs of his most beloved daughter. The gods know, he would be positively *murderous*."

131

"You wouldn't, you…"

Gaheris couldn't have been acting in such a way—gods, he was only thirteen… But I was been the same age when I was married, and I was capable then.

My vision swam. I dug my fingernails into my palms, willing the pain would bring clarity to my thoughts. Morgen had thought this through and would have me do this at any price. I loathed her foresight, and closeness to Merlin… Merlin… If anyone knew how to get to Merlin, if anyone knew his secrets, it would be her. I could not risk her as an enemy, then.

Yes, I needed to think. I willed my mind to obey and shirk off the gnawing fear.

"Let me visit Vyvian," I said, my breath so fast I felt as if I had scaled a hundred stairs. "Grant me passage to see the Lady of the Lake, and I will do as you ask."

The request did not rest well with Morgen. I could tell how reluctant she was. But she said: "Very well."

"And my poor Anette?" I asked. "She must go childless, so a Queen can raise the child a stranger's child?"

"I will send instruction," Morgen said. "You'll have choices."

"You bring me such comfort," I said weakly.

"I will not forget this," she said.

Morgen stood a moment, then held her hands together; then the vision dissipated into a pillar of mist. The fire burned brighter, and when I walked to where Morgen had stood, I touched the ground to find it quite moist. It smelled of loamy earth warmed by the sun.

I sat for a long while in the same chair, shivering, twisting the embroidery threads between my fingers so hard I broke the skin. How dare Morgen resort to such duplicitous tactics to have me do her dirty deeds? I had agreed to something truly vile. How could I ever live with Anette again? She, who her mother named after me—little Anna— who I promised to employ and protect?

I agreed to Morgen's terms. I cast my lot. Slowly, I began to understand the power of my own choice. There was a purpose for me, after all, beyond the embroidery and drudgery of my days. A greater fate, tied not to Arthur and Merlin and their endless alliances, but to the other women of Carelon.

As I toiled over my decision, I recalled Morgan's observation: I carried the same gifts my mother and Elaine possessed.

*Pulling shadows.* I looked down at my chapped, dry hands, the fingers long and white in the firelight, and found it very hard to believe. I wanted to, of course—I wanted to assure myself I had some connection to my mother, to my aunt, to the women in my family who displayed so many more talents than I ever possessed. But I worried Morgen was simply lying to me, playing to my desires to win me to her side.

I would have to find out for myself.

# CHAPTER SIX

## FRAYED ENDS

WITH EACH PASSING day, I grew more ill at heart. I did not know if it was a result of the words Morgen left me, or simply the dread over what I must do. Gweyn was confined to her quarters until the end of the pregnancy—walking any stairs was out of the question—and I arranged to have Anette moved to the servants' rooms in closer proximity to the nursery. It would be easier that way.

In my spare time—of which I had plenty, as Lanceloch was forever occupied, and Gweyn secluded—I practiced pulling shadows with Morgen's scroll. I wandered around the castle, doing my best to go unnoticed. I found the more I became aware of my own body, the more I could change. Astonished, I looked down at my own hands to see, somehow, my rings were missing. They were but plain hands, unadorned, like some serving woman; it was no surprise I was so often overlooked.

And it was with more astonishment one afternoon, as I was contemplating Bedevere, I was addressed thusly by Sir Bors:

"Good afternoon, Sir Bedevere."

Bors continued on, but I ducked behind a doorway, breathless—I was both terrified and exhilarated. Looking down at my clothes I saw a fading glamor, the last outfit I had seen Bedevere wear. Through magic, I wore his face, his body, for just a moment. Long enough to convince Bors I was Bedevere himself.

Dangerous, I thought, not to be kept in check. I could be the death of him, or anyone.

But I tried again, this time thinking of Sir Lamorak and could not bring about the shadow, or the semblance. Perhaps my grasp on magic was more tenuous than I thought. Regardless, I had little opportunity to delve into the questions surrounding me—those would have to wait until I spoke with Vyvian—because the time for dark deeds approached.

The baby came too fast, like a torrent, and Anette could not withstand the strain. Though I did my best to give her the best treatment available to one of her station, even arranging her own room, it was not enough.

I stood by Anette's paltry bed, watching the afternoon light moving across her pale, young face, her white, parted lips. The bed, the sheets, her shift, all awash in blood, as one of her hands fell limply off the bed. I cursed the sun; I cursed the gods: sometimes Fate turns and there is naught we can do.

Why did the day have to be so beautiful? Birds crisscrossed the window, finding their nests; I could hear bees buzzing, and laughter from three stories down. It smelled of late summer and the promise of autumn, of harvest, of joy.

The world moved on, yet mine stood still. I recalled Anette as a child, lovely and quiet; remembered when she first came to me as a maid, how gentle she was with my hair, fretting to hurt me; recalled how she would listen to me read cold nights in Orkney, eyes wide and eager to know every detail.

And now she was dead. Dead as Mother, dead as Lot, dead for the carrion to take. Would he share my secret in the dark of the Otherworld? Would Anette's death darken my soul?

Jain stood still and turned to me, sickly pale. In her arms, the tiny form of Anette's child squirmed, squalling, punctuated the growing emptiness of the room.

"A boy," I said.

"Yes."

"Give him to me," I said.

Jain hesitated only a scarce second, but her defiance ate at my guilt and my sorrow. Before I could control myself, and at the mercy of considerable grief, I shrieked:

"I said give me the *child*."

She complied, and I turned away. I could feel her, staring at me from the door. "This no longer concerns you," I said, as acidly as I could—it helped control my tears.

I did not turn to see the look on her face, but knew what it would be: vacant, stunned. I hoped she cried.

*You will have choices.*

Morgen's words rang in my mind. Taking Anette's child was easier than I expected.

She neglected to tell me about Anette's fate, if she knew. She must not have known, I convinced myself as I moved through the castle, the baby in my arms, moving uncomfortably against my breasts. For the moment I could only give him warmth, although his squalling pulled at my mothering desires.

Protecting this child was paramount, and barely considering my actions, I began to pull shadows so completely around us, we became darkness itself. Closing my eyes, I put my finger into the baby's mouth, and he suckled happily, though I knew he would only be content for so long. As beautiful as newborns are, I recalled how horrid, too. I had borne twins; I knew it well. Nursing should draw women closer to their children, but the reality was raw and bleeding breasts, constant feedings, and a sense of being bled dry.

The guard at Gweyn's door stared at the place where I stood; he looked confused. I moved hesitantly, but he made no further movement. *Castle, stone… rock hewn…* I thought to myself, *flagstone, sandstone, brick and mortar. Darkness. Whispers. Nothing.*

The door opened, a maid rushed out with a basin of hot water and I slipped into Gweyn's chamber, pulling shadows around me thick as a cocoon, just as the door slammed.

My heart was still in my throat, hands trembling. The child was ready to suck the blood out of my finger, but he had not yet begun to cry.

The drapes drawn tight, Gweyn was asleep, snoring softly, her long blonde hair combed down over her breasts, her hand still reaching out to touch the crib with the babe.

"It has only been a few minutes," said a voice to my left. It was one of the nurses, whom I could not recognize. There was a wild look to her, reminding me of Morgen. A cousin of hers, I wondered. "She will sleep a while longer." Another of Morgen's tonics, then.

"You can see me?" I half whispered.

"I know you are here," she clarified.

When I did not move, she whispered, "I will take the babe."

I looked down at Amhar—the likeness to the babe in my arms was enough. The same dark hair, the same pursed lips. All but for the swaddling. I shed my shadows.

The nurse made quick work of Anette's child, cleaning him, giving him goat's milk she dribbled on her finger, grinning widely. No, I had seen her face—in Avillion, once. How, and why, was Morgen working so closely with the Holy Island these days?

Such questions were of little use. I was sweating so profusely my shift clung in a dozen places.

When the nurse finished, Anette's son lay in place of a prince, swathed in silks and gold embroidery. "I will take the other child," she said. Her very presence was calming, and the whole room smelled heady, like steeped mint and incense.

"But, I can…" I said, feeling sleep wind around me like a blanket. "I can help more."

"This will do. Morgen said to give this to you," said the priestess, handing me a crude iron key on a chain. "She said you would know what to do with it."

The key to Vyvian's gate.

I took Anette's son from the cradle and smoothed back his hair. He looked like a prince. Amhar, Gweyn's babe, lay so listless in the nurse's arm's I wondered if he was already dead. The nurse covered his face with ragged homespun and smiled.

"Gods be with you," said the priestess, and bowed her head. She sunk into the shadows and left me standing with the child in my arms, tears streaming down my face like a fool at a funeral.

I stood there until the child began to cry again and startled at Gweyn's voice.

"Anna—sister, is that you?"

"Gweyn," I said, my voice wavering.

"You—you're holding him," she said, turning to me. She smiled serenely. "I have not... seen him yet... They... I do not think I stayed awake. It all happened so quickly. My nurse gave me something to drink and..."

I could see, even in the dim light of her chamber, the heaviness in her eyelids, the darkness in her eyes. They had drugged her and taken her child.

"He is right here," I said. The fear gripped me like a vice around my heart: she would know the child was not hers.

"Can I hold him?"

I wanted to deny her but could not. I looked at Gweyn, so sweet and exhausted, so round and beautiful, so perfectly serene and in pain.

I placed Anette's child into the arms of my Queen.

She began to cry and shook so violently as she beheld her child I had to sit down. But she did not scorn me, and she did not reject the child. "He is so beautiful, Anna. Oh, gods, I never saw such a beautiful child... he looks so like his father. Do not you think?"

"Very like," I managed, kneeling on the side of the bed to admire him. All that was left of Anette in the world.

Gweynevere tilted her head, her brows furrowed, and again my stomach lurched. "But he doesn't look like an Amhar," she said, tracing the lines of his face with a chubby, long-nailed finger. He opened his lips, searching for suckle.

"No?" I asked.

139

"I think I think I shall name him… Mordred." And she pulled down her shirt, offering the babe her round breast, already slick with milk. He took to it greedily, and she laughed. "Yes, Mordred. Little Mordred. My son."

I returned to my chambers that night, and Lanceloch was already asleep. He'd left a small coronet of roses on the hearth for me. I wept, alone and in my shadows, until I fell asleep by the fire. When I awoke the next morning, he had draped me in a long coverlet and put out some breakfast. I did not hear from Morgen for quite some time.

THE FAMED HWYFAR of Avillion missed the birth of her nephew, but eventually arrived after Harvest Festivities with a troupe of actors and the most rag-tag group of priests and priestesses Avillion had ever encountered. Some shirked their white robes for more comfortable traveling attire, and more than half were fond of drink. They lingered in the strangest of places and, more often than not, stirred trouble by stealing food, antagonizing the knights, and occasionally molesting ladies at court. They turned the castle upside down, but Arthur was too busy to bother. I found it likely he gave Hwyfar a wide berth in order to make up for slighting her and marrying her younger sister. With the new prince, the whole castle was already upended.

Until I saw Hwyfar in the flesh I did not understand just how very powerful and very troubling she was. Perhaps my supposition of an alliance was ill-conceived.

Hwyfar was naught like her sister, who was all soft lines and gentleness. She was a giantess, a woman more likely to wrap her hands about the pommel of a sword than fold them in prayer. Her remarkable stature was made all the more impressive by her mane of straight red hair, nearly as red as Gawain's, and her seductive, yet muscular, frame. It was not common for women at court to tower over me, but even across a room I felt diminished in her presence.

She did not seem to deem it necessary to wear dresses, as every proper woman did. No, she preferred leather riding pants and a loose man's shirt, over which she wore a cropped tunic. Around her neck, the only indication she had any connection to Avillion at all, hung three large amber drops the size of my thumbs. Amber was precious to the priestesses of Avillion. They believed the preserved sap of the ancient trees was wisdom awaiting escape.

When Hwyfar spoke, heads turned. There was nothing demure about her, nothing sweet and innocent. In every movement there spoke the act of languid love, and passion, sensuality, painful power.

The day Hwyfar arrived, my timing was ill-fated. I informed Arthur of my intention to seek out Vyvian. He did not seem to mind, or question, but he asked I do one favor before departing, providing I travel with Lanceloch, of course.

It was Merlin who had suggested it. The gnarled old man was leaning behind Arthur, at his throne, looking at me with his shrewd, unreadable eyes.

"The Lady Anna ought to visit Lady Hwyfar before she departs," he said, his voice smooth with practiced musicality. "It would be only fitting, after all, since she is so close to Her Majesty the Queen. She may accept our gifts more readily when delivered at the hand of the King's sister."

"That is an excellent idea, Merlin," Arthur said, as bright as a sparrow. I do not think Arthur ever understood women very well, and he marveled at Merlin's insights, whether or not they were correct. "I wanted to send her some welcoming gifts. Gowns, furs, decorations... did she say how long she was staying, Merlin?"

"No indication," replied the conjuror. He was staring directly at me, as if challenging me in the silence. I did not doubt he knew about the child, of course, about Mordred— he was part of the grand scheme. But he had never spoken about it, never thanked me, and as time passed, I still heard nothing from Morgen. The last few days left me fretful; perhaps, I was misled. It felt like a strange dream.

But no. I slipped my hand further down into the sleeve of my dress and felt the biting cold of the iron key to Vyvian's gate. I had not fabricated it, nor was I losing my mind.

"I will be happy to make her as comfortable as possible," I said. Jain was attending me that day, and she shuffled behind me. Since Anette's death I forbade her to return to the infirmary, until the arrival of two of Luwddoc's nieces on his wife's side—Enid and Aileen—who would be replacing her.

Arthur sent me to the clothier, the sempstress, and a half-dozen other artisans in and around the castle, with Jain and Haen in tow. By the end of our journey, half the day passed, and we were laden almost beyond our capacity. It took four knights to help heft the various items, including an inlaid chest Gweyn commissioned for Hwyfar which looked, indeed, as if it belonged in the circus. The Avillion ideal of beauty was far beyond me.

I ordered the knights to convene at the third bell, so I could return to my quarters and refresh. Truth be told, I was intimidated beyond belief by this Hwyfar who already challenged my concepts of courtly propriety. How strange to think she nearly married Arthur. Had he known what sort of woman he had jilted in favor of poor Gweyn? I thought not. By the look on his face, he never beheld Hwyfar until the moment she burst into the Great Hall... it made for an interesting situation.

Fastening my green kirtle, and letting Jain braid my hair a little more haphazardly than I would have liked, I finally emerged and met the encumbered knights on the landing before Hwyfar's quarters. I could already hear voices, laughter, and the clink of glasses from behind the heavy oak and iron door and wondered what kind of ribaldry was going on. Gods alive, but there were both men and women in there.

When at last someone answered the armored knock of Sir Haloran, it was a short man with black hair and cool gray eyes, dressed as a cleric of some sort, with a wooden sword at his hip and a moon painted on his forehead. He was more than a little drunk, and upon seeing me, burst into laughter.

"She is wearing green!" he cackled, twirling in a drunken circle and falling straight on his rear.

The crowd burst into raucous laughter, and I stood, staring at the scene before me, doing my best to remain composed and project stately serenity. Hwyfar's room was so colorful, so garish, I found it difficult to separate the individual components making the whole. Most of the people in the room were actors and carnival folk with whom Hwyfar arrived, their motley garb a giveaway. A juggler arced flaming torches in the air before him, a pair of women dressed in little else but paint pawed at one another passionately, and an elaborate game of catch-and-kiss ran through everything else.

"Hush, Jass," Hwyfar said, batting at the short man who greeted me and was now on the ground, clutching his stomach, desperately trying to breathe through his laughter.

It took me a few more heartbeats to find my voice. The heady musk of perfume wafted out the door, mingling with the aromas of food and fruit. Hwyfar herself balanced a drink in her hand, the liquid a deep emerald green, but the smile on her full lips showed no indication its strength had affected her.

"Hwyfar of Avillion, I am Anna du Lac, sister to Arthur, King of Braetan. I come bearing gifts on his behalf, welcoming you to Carelon," I said, gesturing to the knights behind me, still straining under the weight of their treasures.

"Oh?" said Hwyfar, looking over my shoulder. She smirked. "Arthur sends me gifts?"

"Yes," I replied. "And Gweynevere, as well. Of course." She was close to me, near enough I could smell the sour reek of the drink on her breath.

Hwyfar's gaze roamed over my face, then down the front of my gown. "How sad—I had thought the welcoming gift was you," Hwyfar continued, reaching out and tracing a hand down my cheek.

I slapped it away, and Sir Haloran said, "Lady Hwyfar, you are addressing the sister of the King."

"Yes, I am," Hwyfar said. Behind her, a flatulating noise rose and the raucous crowd began cackling and gamboling again in earnest.

This only seemed to amuse Hwyfar more, and she chuckled throatily, beckoning me inside with a shake of her glass. I had no intention of entering the fray, but as there were knights behind me, both curious to see the rest of the goings on in the room and burdened with gifts, I was swept through.

My face burned with embarrassment. Who was this woman? It seemed impossible she was related in any manner to Gweyn—and thank the gods she had not married Arthur!

"Ah, such lovely silks," Hwyfar said, casually running her fingers through some of the finer examples. As she leaned over, her haphazard clothing did naught to prevent anyone and everyone from seeing her ample breasts and creamy skin. One of the knights nearly stumbled over two of the catch-and-kissers—who, from what I could gather, were only a few breaths away from the act of love—and looked terrified as a mouse.

Hwyfar surveyed the bounty and nodded approvingly. "Thank your brother for me, will you?" she said, as I made for the door, clutching onto Sir Haloran's elbow. "It will be put to good use."

I could not escape fast enough, but when I finally did, I felt faint. I understood immediately why Merlin requested I do the job; it was the sort of business no one wanted, and as I needed something from him, he found it a fair bargain. Now that I had done Morgen's ill tidings, did Merlin find it necessary to debase me so? I entertained visions of poking his eyes out with my thumbs but found myself calm by the time I reached the main hall once again, no worse for wear.

THE LONG WINTER stretched before me, and we had yet to embark to Vyvian's island.

I earned a moment of freedom with Lanceloch, but before we set out, I found myself irrevocably drawn again to Bedevere.

We met in our Enclave, by moonlight. We did not speak at first. We only made love, soft and slow, in darkness. Complete in each other's embrace, free from the momentary bonds of Fate.

"I suppose that answers my question," he said, drawing his fingers down my face. "You've never kissed me in such a way before."

"I am… unattended, in many ways," I said, burrowing my face in the soft divot of his shoulder and collarbones, trying to hide my smile.

He laughed, squeezing me. "'Tis hard to fathom you'd allow such neglect."

"I am simply honoring his vow," I said. "I cannot ask of him what he cannot give. Not after Lot. Purity runs in his veins as surely as fire in yours."

"Then he is a fool. No man of substance would turn his back on one as treasured and lovely as you."

"It isn't about that."

"But you suffer alone."

"I have suffered worse. Please, let us not speak on it."

"I understand, Anna. Though the other knights whisper if this is but a play marriage. You are often without him at events, and though Arthur insists you enjoy every happiness, I cannot speak for the rest of the court."

"What does that mean?" I pressed myself up on my elbow and looked down at his dear face. I wished he would just stop talking and take me again, not poison our moment with talk of court games.

"I'm sorry. I should keep quiet. All this talk of purity and chastity and vows makes me think of the Christ men. And they exhaust me."

I heard rumors among my own servants of Christian priests abiding among some of Pellas's envoys, the diplomats and nobles who lived at Carelon most of the year. The King did not approve of our pagan ways, finding belief in the gods to be idol worship. And yet they said he carried around beads and a picture of his Christ's Virgin Mother, fingering it with almost lusting abandon. How such behavior was not considered idolatry, I could not fathom.

"Too much purity and the knights raise their tempers, I suppose," I replied. "Is that what this is about? Are you feeling their frustration?" I began to draw my hand down his belly, but he stopped my hand.

"Anna."

He only spoke my name in the dark.

"Bedevere," I replied in the same tone.

"They say the Queen is entertaining this priest. Can you even fathom? A priestess of Avillion, raised on the nectar of the gods and the apples of the sacred grove. They say it is because Arthur defied Merlin, and he married her even when the portents were against them. Now they say their son will be raised a Christian, leading to his own life as a Christian priest. A celibate priest."

"All the better for my family, I suppose," I said, offhandedly. I was trying to make light of his conversation, but he was not in a mood.

"Our faith connects us," Bedevere said. "Our stories bond us. To Braetan. To Avillion. To the Otherworld and what comes after."

"I had no idea you were so pious."

"I am pious when I need to be. Because it keeps the peace. War is on the wind, Anna. You know that. The Christians preach peace but are quick to draw the swords. Have you not heard these whispers?"

"No. I am a shadow. I would speak to Morgen, but she is so often away." I sighed dramatically. "Besides, it is difficult to know the changing world when one is expected to embroider and gossip all the hours of the day."

He grabbed my chin and kissed me hard. But I could tell he was still angry. Still, I did not let that come between us as we entwined again, that old familiar rhythm bringing us crashing together.

When we finished for a second time, I said, "I do not think this can happen again for a while. The risk is too great."

Bedevere said nothing for a moment. I dragged my fingertips through his beard, reveling in the soft hush it made against my skin. He smelled of me and my sweat. My heart ached.

"You always come back to me," he half sang.

"Bedevere, I am not some love-sick bitch in the kennels. I am a married woman."

"Now who is the pious one? You ought to find the Christian priest. You might find him appealing."

"I have a husband, Bedevere."

"That hasn't stopped you before."

"I have a responsibility."

"No, my darling. You have a eunuch."

The Pendragon fury rose in me. I can owe it to naught else. If I had not been concerned about exposing our tryst, I would have yelled at him, grabbed his hair, scratched his skin. I could not explain why I felt so protective of Lanceloch. I could manage the teasing, but I could not manage the insult. He was still my husband.

I did not strike him. But I left and did not spare a backward glance as he begged and called my name.


WHEN AT LAST Lanceloch and I departed to see Vyvian it was late in a heady, sweet spring. The swift decision left me a bit unsettled. For weeks, I had been left to my own: Mordred was crawling about the nursery, Gweyn was so often with her priest I rarely saw her, and Morgen only wrote to me now and again. Lanceloch was so occupied with Arthur's wars, and Bedevere so often dispatched to tend to one scuffle or another, it meant I spent most of the winter alone.

It was strange to find myself wrapped up again in movement, preparation, and excitement.

Since so few attended the Lady of the Lake, Lanceloch and I were given tasks in addition to our own visit. The first was to retrieve a weapon promised to Arthur, made by Vyvian's own hand. She promised the gift over a decade ago and Arthur was anxious over it. My brother, who always fancied his weaponry, was eager to see what he presumed was a sword, but not so eager as to make the trek to see Vyvian himself. The second request was from Merlin; he found one of Vyvian's books in his own collection, and he no longer had use for it. Strange as it seemed, until their falling out they were quite close; Vyvian's powers were famed, and it was only by Merlin's magic she was kept at the lake.

While the trip to see Vyvian made me nervous—I had not seen my aunt in two decades, at least, and wondered what she would make of such a strange trip—for the first time in many years I was riding without a caravan. Only Lanceloch accompanied me.

Carelon itself was a place largely devoid of magic, save that which Merlin and Morgen permitted or conducted. But it was far wilder further south and east. Together, with my knight, I supposed it would be an adventure.

It rained a fine mist when we left, and our cloaks gradually changed from light gray to dew-dappled to black in the first hour. Even so, I had to ask Lanceloch to stop after a time for my discomfort. I was no longer accustomed to riding horseback for such distances.

"I am sorry—" I said, splashing my face with cold water from my flask. It was so cold on my cheeks I shivered.

"No need, Anna. Do not worry," Lance said, vaulting off his horse with more flair than I had ever seen in casual company. He helped brush the hair out of my face, smiling at me with an even, charming look. "We are not pressed for time. We can take it at a slower pace. Only Mars was chomping at the bit to get a trot in; it is my fault."

"Give me a few days and my muscles might remember themselves," I said, kneading my thighs with the heel of my hand and wincing. "I am afraid I have been kept indoors too long without light. I have withered like an orchid past bloom."

I finally stood up straight, arching my back, and found Lanceloch was smiling up at the sky through the trees, hands on his hips. The way the shadows fell from the black branches up above us and streaked across his skin was remarkable, tracing the gentle lines of his face and brow. He looked like a thing of the wood, then, as happy as a sapling grown in the same loamy soil, a living dryad.

When he helped me back on my mare, he kissed my cheek softly. "Your cheeks are flushed," he said, placing his thumb on my chin.

I put a hand to my face, and my fingers felt hot against my lips. He was toying with me. Something about the fresh air clearly addled his brains.

"We should move on," I said, turning away to not to marvel so long on the color of his eyes, shot through with green from the reflection of the leaves. "Before we lose light."

"You are correct," he said, patting my knee. "It is only… I do enjoy this time alone with you. More than I thought I would, if I may say. That doesn't sound cruel, does it?"

"Perhaps I am not as much a bore as you worried," I said, smiling in spite of myself.

"There is more of you in Arthur than anyone understands. A forwardness, a clarity—like you're drawn in bolder strokes than the rest of us. Except when you are not; except when you are air and darkness," he said, his gaze wandering over my face. "I like that it is my secret to keep."

My traitorous heart thrummed at his words. And just like that, we were on the move once more.

The meandering forest between Carelon and Vyvian's island was maintained by an order of knights more akin to rangers, ensuring—should the King ever wish it—he could go hunting in a wilder expanse without the worry of unseemly characters. Vyvian's lake, Aurus Lake, was bordered by the forest on all sides, and should we get to her, we had to go through the wood. But it was still a good half-day's journey; she was kept close, but not too close.

Trees have ever left me unsettled. Perhaps it is their age, as they live so much longer than man… I have never been able to put my finger on it. Still, whenever I have had the occasion to walk through dense woods, I am overcome with unsettling feelings of being watched, as if the very knots of the trees were eyes.

Not so with my husband. Lanceloch took to the forest as if he were born there, and I did not have the heart to ask him to slow down for me and my tired legs. He was completely in his element, exclaiming over every new flower, vine and branch. For every bend in the road, for every overhanging verge, he had a story. For every leaf, he had a name. His herbalism rivaled even Morgen's, his imagination brighter than a bard's.

"Oh, and this was where I came face-to-face with a grifflet," he exclaimed, marking a patch of rather uninspired mud and a fallen, termite-riddled log. We decided to walk a particularly meddlesome mile, leading the horses, and so I watched him as he walked before me, narrating the scene. "It came out of nowhere, descending on me with this unnatural beauty I still cannot put words to. At first, I was not sure if I should speak to it or strike at it—the plumes on its head, I will tell you, would rival even some of Queen Gweynevere's head-dresses, it was so lovely. Copper shot with green—and the grifflet's eyes! By gods, just astonishing. Frightening, but astonishing. It had me rattling in my boots."

"How does one kill a grifflet?" I asked. I had only heard of grifflets in legend, but Lanceloch's enthusiasm made me doubt my assumptions.

His eyes were filled with childlike excitement when he turned to me, thrilled at my question. "Well, their teeth are not particularly deadly, although they can shred through your skin rather impressively," he said, kicking at the foot of one of the trees. He turned on me, poised for action, showing me the motion he made when he had been attacked. "I knew I needed to attack at its throat—for you see, it is the sound the grifflet makes that kills you. Vyvian used to tell me a grifflet could boil your brains if you let it shriek. I could see its throat bobbing up and down in its scaly, slick neck—and I only carried a pair of daggers with me, having gone to fetch mushrooms for Vyv—"

Lanceloch turned on his heel, then hopped from one foot to the other, spry as a jester. He unsheathed his sword, turning the pommel at an angle like a huge dagger. "I screamed—so loud, gods I must have frightened the whole wood. I reasoned if I screamed, the noise in my own head might be enough to buffet the noise it would give off. But for some reason, it stayed silent. Just cocked its head at me and sneered. I think it was waiting for me to do something, to attack. My threat was not enough."

Lanceloch ducked right, then left. He laughed, then pulled a dagger from his boot, flinging it into the nearest tree. It stuck into a huge knot, wobbled, and then was still.

"I took my second dagger, and got the beast, right in the throat. It was not enough to kill it, but enough to stun it long enough to eventually finish the job. I forgot to be frightened, at that point. The thing was dead, and I abandoned fear somewhere in the middle of my attack. So, I sliced its head off, its black blue blood slipping…" He paused, likely seeing the look on my face. I was white with the description.

"Apologies, my lady," he said, coming up to me and taking my hands in his. His palms were warm and dry, comforting. "I got a little bewitched by my own memory."

His amber eyes looked deep green in the shadow of the canopy above, and I could see every dark lash standing out against his complexion. Gods, but he was beautiful. And so close. I felt my stomach flutter. I wanted so to touch him, to bring him to me, to have him touch me back. I longed for the feeling of a man, and here in the wood buzzing with bees and trilling with the sound of birds, there was no better a place in my mind. Just a kiss. Certainly he could grant me so small a favor...

Gods, I missed Bedevere. Significantly more than I lusted for Lanceloch, my own husband. I could ensnare Bedevere again when we arrived back home. Or I could redouble efforts with Lanceloch. One meant mending a disastrous last argument with my lover. The other meant taking an irrevocable piece of my husband. Neither option appealed, and so I remained, a stunned creature full of wanting and no release.

"Naught to fret," I managed, weakly. I took a step back, but he grabbed my hand before I could wrest it away.

"Your pulse is racing," he said, feeling my wrist with his able fingers.

"I am not made of stone," I said, taking my hand back, gently. He let go, and I turned to check on my horse. "Or do you expect me to feel nothing?"

I couldn't look at him again, and he seemed to have gathered that conversation was not part of the bargain, either. It struck me how foolish I was letting him continue on and on with his vow of chastity and wondered how hard it would be to make him break it. What would he lose, indeed; but what would I gain?

Lanceloch's voice was more subdued when he spoke again at last. I had taken the fight out of him as with so many other knights. Were men so easy to best in games of emotion?

"You're upset with me," he said.

"My lord Arthur demands a great deal of your time," I said, as lightly as I could, ducking under a branch some strides behind Lanceloch. He was surprised at the address, and when he turned over his shoulder his brows were already knit low. He likely believed I was angry at him for his show of restrained passion earlier.

"I do as His Majesty requires," he replied.

"*Anything* he requires?" I asked.

Lanceloch stopped his horse and blinked at me, taken by the audacity of my tone. I never would have dared to speak to Lot in such a manner—but then again, we never spoke unless absolutely necessary. This foray into the woods with my new, young—but despairingly chaste—husband was quite different. I was beginning to think of breaking his vow as a personal challenge.

"Lady Anna…" he said stiffly.

"I assume he is aware of your vow?" I asked, rifling through my satchel to find an apple I had picked a few miles back. I polished it with the sleeve of my dress, and took a bite; crispy and sweet, just as I liked them.

"What are you getting at, my lady?"

"It is only you spend so much time in his company—and I know our match is not to your greatest liking. I am not a spring pear, I know the truth of it, and yet…"

"Anna, you said my vow did not bother you—"

"I said no such thing. I said I would not take it from you without your explicit consent. I am no monster. But I am a woman, still, though not in my own spring," I looked up at him under my lashes, something that Bedevere had told me once sent him into paroxysms of desire. "And no person, not even you, can fight their desires forever. If not with me, it will be with another. I do not command you."

"I did as Arthur bade, and I married you, Anna. You hold the key to my vow," he said, his voice as hushed as the leaves moving above our heads. "Not him—not anyone else. If the vow is broken, it will be with you. And only you."

He was very close, and I was so stunned by the strange turn of the conversation I merely stood gaping at him, the half-eaten apple still touching my lips.

"If a king commands his servant—"

"Only you," he repeated.

"Lanceloch, you do not need to flatter me. I am not looking for such false hope. We are married, I am your wife. I can live with not seeing you, but we must understand one another. The court speaks. Whatever our course of action, we must be united."

"Do you not see the way I look at you?" he asked. He reached up and twirled a lock of my hair around his finger, examining it as if it held the key to all his questions.

"I—" he looked me in the eyes again and silenced me.

"I desire you, Anna. Very much… more than I can explain. I did not know who I was marrying until the day we spoke in the orchid garden. You looked right into me, so plainly and truly, you spoke to me so kindly, even in the shadow of the shame I had brought to your family," he said.

"You mean Gawain…" I said, his name heavy on my lips as I spoke it.

"Of course," Lanceloch said, drawing nearer again. He dropped the bridle to his horse, and brushed his hands through my hair, tracing the line of my cheek. "But you, as well, you did your duty to Arthur—in spite of his reasoning, in spite of the sacrifice—again, after enduring a kind of darkness I will never know. I understand some of the pain you endure, because we are in both his service—we simply fight with different weapons."

I shivered, feeling as if Lanceloch were staring through me, laying me bare. His striking eyes pierced me with an innocent conviction, and my eyes filled with tears before I could stop myself.

"You long for the touch of another, I know," he said, holding my arm with his hand, firmly, as if grounding himself. "Who would not? I give you full permission to take a lover, if you cannot withstand the need—I cannot ask you to do what I have done—"

"Lanceloch!" I cried, "I am not—"

"It doesn't matter to me—I would defend you to the last," he said. "But you need only ask me, and I will break my vow for you."

"Lanceloch, I would never do such a thing."

I watched him, his lips slightly parted, eyes searching mine. He regarded me with a look of patience, of virtue, so pure it made me feel worthless, tarnished, shamed. I had only been with Bedevere since our strange marriage began, but the deed felt so improper in the light of one as Lanceloch.

How was it possible for such a man to exist in this broken,

hollow world? I hoped that Vyvian would help enlighten me in the short time we were together. For if this was going to be the shape of the rest of my life, I was certain I could not bear it.

Surely, Lanceloch had a flaw, at least one, I could use to my advantage. I only saw a man too honorable, too good, too dedicated. Perhaps there lay the answer; perhaps he was a man unable to find the center of the pendulum—all was in extremes.

When he rose, he soared; but I feared what would happen if he should fall.

"It is a challenge to me, that is all," I said at last. "A strangeness. I am unsure how to serve, Lanceloch. I lived a long life as a woman in bonds, imprisoned by fear, and this is not how I envisioned the shape of my life upon escape."

"Anna, I—" he said, looking down at the ground.

"The light is waning, husband. Let us make short these miles before darkness falls."

"Yes, of course." He breathed deeply, his hand flat on his chest, then said, "Thank you. For being my wife. And letting me accompany you here. We may not yet have answers, but we have today."

THEY CALLED VYVIAN the Lady of the Lake because she was imprisoned at the very center of a great body of water called Aurus Lake. She was, however, no simple conjuror, but a blacksmith, and the precise location of her home was far from her own decision. When Arthur ascended the throne, both Vyvian and Merlin interpreted prophecies— prophecies that, it is said, contradicted each other entirely, but neither would back down from. The argument escalated with such intensity Vyvian, in a rage, threatened Merlin's life. Merlin was never one to take a threat lightly and so convinced the Avillion priestesses to remove Vyvian from court. Permanently. Some say he ought to have drowned her. I say he would not have dared try.

Though they could not kill her—or at least, none would volunteer to do the deed—they decided, with the help of Merlin, to imprison her. She could never leave, for the water was enchanted to her, bonded with the blood of her own sisters. Should she try to escape, she would only arrive back on shore. Access to the lake was strictly regulated and permitted by one boat.

Vyvian had been let out on the occasion of Arthur's marriage, and I recalled her there, wearing glass bracelets filled with water from Aurus Lake, encircling her wrists and ankles. For whatever reasoning, however, they did not allow her to attend my mother's funeral.

Perhaps they could chain her, but I do not think they could tame her.

Aurus Lake was surrounded by cypress and alders, sinking their roots deep into the water and earth, forming a dense barrier. There was only one pathway in, and it was quiet. Bird songs still trilled, but from far away, as if they, too, kept their distance from the magic at the lake. I could feel nothing, myself, and I looked across the smooth surface of the lake and breathed deep of the wet, green scents around me.

"I should like to take a swim," Lanceloch murmured as he approached. He had hardly spoken since our last conversation. The trees dipped their hoary heads, leaves of every shade of green surrounding us. "The water here is ever cold, perfect for hot days. I used to swim to the shore and back every morning."

"How old were you when you first came here?" I asked.

"Very young. Six, seven, perhaps? I do not know precisely. It is as if my memories all begin here with the lakeshore. My feet in the mud and my head in the branches. Before my life here... well, I remember *that* Elaine—ah, your sister, my stepmother—wept to see me go, but I was never sure if they were tears of joy or of sorrow. She kissed me and told me she loved me and insisted I would make my family proud by learning the ways of Vyvian of the Lake, her aunt. I never asked what sort of bargain was struck for the match, but I suppose it was likely foreseen."

From the dark sand bank, I could just make out the island, a wisp of smoke rising into the sky from the chimney, or the forge, perhaps. The water was still like glass and the trees reflected like a continuation of this world into another. The sun was at its pinnacle, bathing the lake in golden light. A falcon cried from so high above it looked but a pinprick in the wide, blue sky.

Straight ahead I spied the gate, a rudimentary iron structure planted deep into the ground. Around one leg of the gate, and drifting into the water, a silver linked chain as thick as my wrist, tethered a slender, white boat. In spite of standing in water so long, the chain showed no indication of rust, and even in the sunlight, emitted a cold, white glow.

I handed Vyvian's key to Lanceloch, and he found the lock—square and solid as the iron gate itself—and it clicked open with one swift turn. Then he helped me into the vessel, and after a few terrifying moments catching my balance, I righted myself.

"Not a boats-woman?" he asked, suppressing a smile.

"Not in the least," I replied, already feeling the pull of nausea.

"Do not close your eyes," he instructed, as I did. "It will only make things worse. Just concentrate on the island as we approach it, and your stomach should settle a bit."

He smiled, and placed a hand gently on my knee, then picked up the oars.

In silence, we slipped across the water. Lanceloch rowed with ease and elegance, hardly making a ripple across the smooth surface. For all the purported magic charms, Aurus Lake still smelled of a lake, of fish and decay. Beneath the surface of the clear water, silver fish flit about, their scales like tiny suits of mail.

Closer we rowed, my eyes ever on the little island. It was green and sandy, set with a small cottage and smithy, and far more quaint than whimsical. Vyvian set stones around the cottage, in the same style I had seen farmers construct in the countryside, and brilliant violets and petunias cascaded out the window boxes while asters tossed their colorful heads in the breeze along the grass. I also saw a garden, set with a scarecrow, his limp arms dangling in the breeze, head lolling to one side. It bore a more than passing resemblance to Merlin, I thought.

And in between each of Lanceloch's strokes, I could hear Vyvian working, the persistent drumming of hammer on anvil, reverberating across the lake.

# CHAPTER SEVEN

## FORGED ENDS

HALFWAY TO THE shore the sounds of smiting ceased, and Vyvian emerged to greet us. A passer-by would have mistaken her for a man, considering how strong and compact she was. She had cut her hair above her ears and wore men's britches with a tunic beneath her charred leather apron. Her face was pinched and wrinkled, but kind. She looked nothing like my mother, and I felt disappointed; I hadn't realized how much I hoped for a semblance between them.

As we came up on the shore, Vyvian trotted down the pathway, and Lanceloch bounded toward her, leaving me the impossible task of steadying the boat while keeping my skirts dry. Having no experience with such things and trying to exit the boat without help from my rather preoccupied husband, I slipped, and the boat caught me in the leg, throwing me over the edge.

Thankfully the water was not deep, but I sat there gasping and sputtering for longer than was proper before Lanceloch and Vyvian noticed me.

"Oh, saints alive," said my aunt, taking one arm while

Lanceloch took the other. "Lance! You neglected your lovely wife."

I was too cold and shocked to tell if she was being facetious or not. Our horses, tethered at the other side of the lake, held any hopes of a warm change of clothes, and I shivered miserably.

"Let's get you inside," she said, squeezing a little. She smelled of fire and flux, sweat and dirt. Vyvian was the single most unladylike woman I had ever encountered. And her voice, gods, was a work of irony. She sounded as delicate as Gweyn.

The cottage was well-appointed, but as common as could be. It appeared she lived off of her herbs and fish, as dried versions of both hung from bunches in the rafters of her one-room abode. The fire was crackling and hot, though, and she brought me a warm throw she knitted herself.

Vyvian served me tea and seedcakes and wrapped my feet in furs.

"Well, now!" she said at last, when my teeth stopped clattering so much. "To what do I owe this pleasure? Lance, I cannot fathom what would have dragged you away from court!" She turned to me with a conspiratorial eye. "You know, since he was six, he has only spoken of going to court to be Arthur's champion. When I finally let him free, I think he may have jumped across the lake in pure joy."

I tried to smile. My lips were still numb. "Aunt Vyvian," I said. "It has been a long time; thank you for receiving us."

"I ought not refuse a pair of guests. Least of all a niece and a foster-son. Quite a match, though." She glanced at Lanceloch a moment, as if measuring him for some kind of change. I wondered if she knew of his vow. "But I cannot say I foresaw your match, considering how old Lot was when you married him, I suppose a second marriage was not out of the question…"

Neither Lanceloch nor I had words in reply; we caught each other's eyes, then both looked away.

Vyvian ran a hand through her gray-streaked hair and shrugged, clearing her voice amidst the silence. "I suppose this is not just a visit to tell me how much you missed me."

Lanceloch looked hurt, the edges of his eyes crinkling as if in a wince. "Vyv, you know it is not so easy to leave. It's a delicate matter."

"'Course not," she said, with a shrug. I was unsure as to how serious she was. There was no mirth in her eyes, at least, but I hardly knew the woman. I was none to judge.

"We brought a book back to you," Lanceloch said, reaching inside his satchel and producing the volume.

"Bah, I do not need old relics," said Vyvian, batting it away with her hand. "Do you see any books here, Lance? Have you ever seen books?"

"No, of course not but—"

She stood, grabbed the book, then threw it into the hearth, where it waited a moment before catching fire. I watched, mesmerized, as the expensive pages seared and singed, then turned to ash. She spat after it.

We were all silent as it burned. There was no doubt in my mind she knew precisely who sent it.

"Apologies," Vyvian said, nodding to us both. "You see, it has been oh…" She counted on her fingers, ending on her thumb, "Well, dear, suffice it to say, I have been away from Carelon since Arthur was born. And since arriving here, I have sought a stripped-down approach to life, living off the land like a common farmer, without the use of magic. It has been good to be here, regardless of the circumstance; I have been happy."

"You have?" I asked.

She raised her eyebrows as if the question was slightly exasperating. "Tell me, Anna Pendragon, why in the name of Iaia did you ever come here?"

"I… I have some questions to ask you," I said. Now that I was sitting in her parlor, listening to her disparage magic altogether, I considered my trip was already a rather spectacular failure. All I had done to get here, to get answers about Merlin and Arthur and the machinations at court. "But—"

"May I go fishing?" asked Lanceloch, apropos of nothing. He sounded as innocent as a six-year old awaiting dismissal to go chase butterflies.

We both stared at him, and he scratched the side of his face, a little embarrassed. "I have not been able to in months, and we won't have much time today—and if I am not mistaken, Anna, you wished to speak to Vyv of women's things. So—you can converse together, and I will fish."

"I do not see why not—if the Lady Vyvian has no objections?" I said, painfully aware of his youth. Under Vyvian's watchful eye it was near humiliating.

My aunt grinned widely, patting her foster-son on the head. "Of course not. You know where the poles are, Lance; and there should be a good bed of worms to the left of the lettuce."

When Lanceloch was gone, Vyvian seemed a little less comfortable. But she was kind enough, offering me broth and tea, should I need it. I was feeling much better by then;

the fire and furs having done their job. It was unlikely I would be swimming again any time soon and wondered at the senselessness of my husband.

"So, tell me," Vyvian said, sitting down across from me, and slapping her hands on her thighs. "Things are not well in Carelon. I can tell that much if Arthur is marrying his sister off to my Lance—"

I made a motion to speak, but she hushed me with a finger. The movement was so like my mother's it compelled me to silence like an obeisant child.

Vyvian continued. "But you are clearly far from miserable. Though, apparently, you've found him honorable enough not to break his vow."

"How did you—?"

"I raised the boy. I would know. Just because I no longer use magic doesn't mean I cannot see it."

"Of... of course."

"But yet you are here, which surprises me. Which is a rare occasion! You realize, my dear, if my plan won out, you and Arthur never would have been born, so it is quite curious to find you at my doorstep," she said, and there was no warmth in the words. No kindness. It was a hollow fact, and so shocking that it rendered me mute.

She sighed, leaning back in her chair, regarding the flames with half-open eyes. "And yet, you are still of my blood. So, it is possible you are experiencing a shift in your very being: this is not surprising to me, the same happened to your mother, when she began to age, when her children left, when she was widowed. You may be seeing things you can't explain, feeling intense emotions rise at strange moments." Vyvian paused a moment before continuing. "Or perhaps are even pulling shadows, now. It is the family gift. I do not suppose I ever thought it would transfer to you, what with all the Pendragon blood mingling with ours, but still…"

I nodded, wordless. She knew. It was both a relief and a wonder.

"And yet such elements are not enough to bring you here, you who have rarely seen outside the walls of stone. No, you may not love your half-sisters overly much, but I suspect speaking to them would be significantly easier than getting passage from Arthur—or Merlin—to get here. Because no one comes here without something to bargain."

"I was given clearance," I explained, a little weakly. "Certain events at court have left me… unsure as to the motivation of some."

"Merlin. You mean Merlin. Speak plainly, child."

"How much at court does he control?" I asked, my voice low.

Vyvian leveled me with an even stare. "You know."

"He has too much sway over Arthur. To the misery of all around him. I have seen things, participated in schemes… From the moment I was born, Merlin has haunted my steps, presided over the decisions which sent me into darkness. And I am not alone. Merlin judges all—but who judges Merlin?"

The memory of what happened to Gweyn, the dark deception I participated in, brought tears to my eyes, and I attempted to hide them with my hand. Morgen had asked me to help her, yes, but I knew she was moved by another force. Merlin and his damned prophecies, a latent power rising through the kingdom, perhaps.

"So the Christ's men have come," Vyvian said.

"Yes, but I do not see—"

"Remember. Prophet." Vyvian thrust a thumb at her chest. "No one judges Merlin. Though the Christians will try."

"I would have to agree. Except Arthur does not see their threat. I am tired, Vyvian, of being played as a pawn. I feel powerless to help my sisters, my children, my servants." I choked back the memory of Anette, dead and pale. "While Arthur and Merlin scheme, we must do their bidding, even after, they are impervious to the fallout."

"You will always have more power in your left nipple than that idiot Arthur does in his whole member!" she said, laughing with a high-pitched cackle. "My sister and I, we are from a strong line, an ancient pedigree. It is why Merlin was always so afraid of me, why he locked me away here. Because, frankly, I am the only one who could have stopped him."

"And why does he do this? He worked miracles to bring my father to the throne, to raise Arthur to king, but you would not bow," I said. "What prophecies moved him but not you?"

Vyvian sank a little in her chair, as if the conversation were slowly weakening her. "It is difficult to explain, of course. There are thousands of prophecies, from all corners of Braetan, old and new, spoken and written, every day. Some choose to read what they want, to hear as they see fit. Merlin is one of those. Oh, he is powerful, and capable. He has to be admired in many ways; he has ushered in an era of peace and prosperity unlike any we've ever seen. And he is loved for it."

"Not by me."

"Clearly. Tell me, Anna, why do you hate Merlin? I have reason enough for both of us, let alone the pain your mother suffered as a result. A lack of his own consequences and his meddling at court is one thing, but there is rage within you beyond such reasoning. Speak, my dear. I am here to listen."

I did not hesitate. I told her about the burden of my prophecy. About Elaine, and about Lot. About the years of pain, the decades of being ignored. Then I told her of sending my son away, and isolation in the following years. I told her of Bedevere, how he was the father of the twins, and how I never allowed myself to love him, for fear of never truly having him. I shared the story of abuse at the hand of Lot, of working with Morgen to poison him. Then I spoke of what had befallen me when I returned to Carelon, of the tournament and Lanceloch's arrival—how Arthur, clearly, was in love with him, and only married me off to keep him close. How my new marriage cost me the love of Bedevere and my son Gawain.

Then I told her about Amhar and Mordred.

By the time I finished telling my story, I sobbed into the blanket like a child. I never shared my struggles with anyone in such detail, and though she spoke little, her demeanor changed significantly throughout the telling. I think Vyvian saw me differently once I'd finished my tale.

She leaned over and took my cheek in her hand. "Such madness wrought; such pain endured."

The acknowledgement set my heart at ease. "I feel as if I am powerless, aunt. And I am so tired."

"You have choices, my dear. Lanceloch was right about that, at least. Most times he is as dull-headed as an ox, but he has moments of brightness. Too virtuous for his own good,

I say; it blots out his sense. But you have let your prophecy define you and have failed to see the benefit. You desire to rid Carelon of Merlin's clutches, to free yourself and your fellow subjects from his whims. This is a noble calling, and one you inherited from your mother, and from me."

"My mother?"

"You hardly knew her, of course. But Igraine loved her husband Gorlois. She came to me when she saw visions of her dead husband, and Merlin lurking in the shadows. I petitioned Merlin, reading him the runes I saw. Like your mother, like the Queen, I could portend the ways of Fate. Merlin has never been able to do such things, though he can interpret them. Our power could not stand against Merlin's vision and Uther's violence. Your mother fell ill shortly after you were born."

"She faded away, over years."

"Her mind faded away, along with her body. It was Merlin's curse to her, and to me. Along with your prophecy, an attempt to punish the line of Igraine."

"I, too, fade." I did not want to ask the question, but I pressed onward. If Merlin did not give the prophecies, then it well could have been hers. "My prophecy. Was it one you gave?"

Vyvian shrugged, then looked a little helpless. "I gave many prophecies, child. Merlin interprets them. So many things I see never come to be. But Merlin's power lies in shaping prophecies, often to his own bidding. I am the sunlight; he is the stained glass."

"So he chose to grant me this prophecy, to strengthen it and direct it."

"Precisely."

Tears rose again in me and I cursed the welling of emotion. The longer I spoke with Vyvian, the more I was reminded of my mother. "You didn't have to tell him."

"Oh, but I did. When I was young, as a priestess of Avillion, I was tasked with writing down all my prophecies and sharing them with Merlin. Yours came years before you were born, before he was certain about you and Arthur."

"I cannot escape it."

"No, but you must remember the words: you will only be forgotten as *yourself*. Anna Pendragon will be forgotten. But it does not mean you cannot fashion yourself a new mantle to wear."

"What do you—"

"You already pull shadows, do you not?"

"Yes. Morgen helped me."

"Good, she's a talented witch, that one. But there are secrets I have kept from her, too. For I know the threads of her fate, and this kind of magic would undo her."

The hair on my arms rose.

"I have a…" she paused, looking out the window. "I have a few books. Just a handful. I know, I know, I said I do not work magic and I do not keep books, and it is mostly true. Always exceptions; there are always exceptions. Some books, and some powers, are too dear, or too potent, to suffer destruction. I only keep books bonded to my own blood, and not even Merlin could take them from me. He sends me books because he knows I have more, volumes he has tried, and failed, to seek out. The one you brought has a powerful spell emblazoned in its pages. No matter. We are safe." Her voice took on a haunted tone when she spoke, and I shuddered. Vyvian raised a finger. "One book still in my possession speaks of an ancient magic, akin to your ability to pull shadows. It is similar to what Merlin used to transform the face of Gorlois in the way a pyre is similar to a candle; it is women's magic."

"Transform... you mean, I could wear the face of another?"

"Oh, it is not so simple. Even Merlin could only make the vision passable for a brief time. But that is because he was a man dabbling in our magic, so it is not surprising he was marginal at the incantation."

I knew the story of my mother, and how she bedded my father not because of love, but because she mistook him for her own husband.

"But I couldn't fool everyone. I'm barely good enough at hiding in shadows." I was growing more and more confused, my recent emotions leaving me with a feeling of helplessness and fear. Vyvian's solution felt too easy.

She sighed, taking in my face again. "You are *forgotten*. The moment you walk from one room to the next. Oh, people know who you are, but the details, they fade. It is how the world sees you. Do you ever wonder why your children rarely seek you out? Why even Lance looks at you as if he sees you for the first time each day?"

"It is a curse," I whispered.

"If you let it. But what if you were to look different—to carry about you the visage of another? You could have your own history, your own experiences... a new body, a new history, a new name."

"A new name?"

"A name that would *not* be forgotten. A name that would give you the tools you need to get close to Merlin, to answer your questions."

"Is he a corrupting force, Vyvian? Is my family in danger?"

"He does not need to be a corruption for danger to arise. And he can be a good man, yet in need of a hasty death." Her words cut sharper than any blade.

Vyvian made another pot of tea and continued to steal glances at Lanceloch as he set up his fishing rod. I considered her words. If I could get close enough to Merlin, if I could test my suppositions. I could free the kingdom. My sisters, my children, my brother... we no longer would be at the mercy of his whims.

"Of course, there are rituals to follow, and important limitations to keep in mind," she said. "Magic done foolishly and sloppily is a danger to everyone."

"I have time."

"You'll need it. But you come by your gifts honestly. Your sister Elaine showed such promise. I hear she is a Christian now. Such a waste! How could she forget?"

I had not heard such rumors, but I pushed away the ugly feeling of abandonment I felt rising in my chest. "I am ready to try."

Vyvian nodded. "It will take great conviction, and above all *certainty* that you have no other choice. And of course, once you snare the rabbit, you'll need a cage should you decide the world is better off without Merlin Taleisin. I will leave that up to you. The book itself has many intriguing examples."

An overwhelming tide of emotion rushed over me: no one in my family had helped me in such a way before, nor hinted at my potential.

"You look stricken," Vyvian said.

I was afraid. "Can you not see the threads of Fate? Will I succeed?"

Her expression was sad. "The choice no longer lies with me. I once tried to pull at the strings of my own fate, and this is where I fell."

She went to the mantle and felt around at some of the masonry, then stopped and pulled out one of the stones, removing a very ordinary looking brown leather-bound volume no larger than the palm of my hand. I was curious, but not altogether convinced.

Vyvian looked down at the book, turning it over in her hands before giving it to me, spine up. There were no words written there, but rather a series of elaborate silver swirls pressed directly into the leather. She glanced out the window.

"I do not wish Lanceloch to know about this," she said. "It is not that I do not trust him, only that I know his heart. He believes I have given up magic entirely—which I have, in practice—and would be quite disappointed to know I was helping you in this matter."

"We are not as yet so close," I assured her. "Ours will always be a fraught alliance."

I opened the book, turning to the first page. There were few words, some faint symbols, and half a sketch; but as I tried to interpret them, the ink swam before my eyes. It was as if the pages had been soaked in water, markings smearing this way and that.

"Not an easy matter just to pick it up and read it," continued Vyvian, a smile forming on her thin lips. "It will not come easy, Anna. Harder than it ever came to me. I had training, years of it. But your mother refused to let you to the wolves at Avillion, and in some ways I do not blame her."

"Mother wanted to send me to Avillion?" I asked, snapping my head up from the reading, and finding Vyvian leaning quite close to me. She straightened.

"Of course she did. She did not want you raised at court, not as Uther's daughter. You would have been given the freedom of choice if she sent you to Avillion—though of course, if you're one of Leodegraunce's daughters, that decision is apparently taken from you in the name of growing a greater Braetan—instead of having to endure what you did."

I found it challenging to envision my mother's concern for me. "I did not know she... considered such things," I said, tactfully as I could.

This seemed to amuse Vyvian, and she chuckled a bit.

"Ah, Igraine was a complicated woman, my dear," said Vyvian, pouring herself another clay mug full of tea, and then picking out some of the leaves before flicking them into the fire. "As sisters, we could not have been more different. Her beauty launched a war."

"But you would have had her stay with Gorlois."

"I would. And she would have sent you to Avillion, and never allowed you to marry Lot. All shifted because of Merlin's power at court."

"She did not love my father, I know."

"Igraine and Gorlois were more in love than people even deserve to be. And yet... Uther defiled their union. He died young for it, for deceiving your mother, and I will never understand how she came to believe the lie. Because she did. She forgave Uther, and loved him, in her way. And loved you. But I see you have her strength too, for you love your sons fiercely."

"Merlin always told me the deception was the only way to bring about Arthur's birth," I said. I closed the book, and ran my fingers over the smooth leather, feeling the grain of it beneath my skin. It was surprisingly warm. "When I had the courage to ask. He said, sometimes, 'Fate is a demanding mistress, blind to love and desire.'"

Vyvian puffed up her lips. "Merlin wanted *Arthur*, that is all. He worked to woo Igraine from Gorlois for years. We both knew Arthur had to be born of Uther and a woman from our line. So, when it seemed Igraine would not relent in her affections for her husband, I offered... well, myself."

"Yourself?"

"The same. And Merlin would not accept this."

"Why in the world not?" It scarcely made any sense.

"Because..." she shook her head, and for a moment, I saw the beauty she once must have possessed, before time and hard work had changed her body. It was in the softness of her jaw, and the delicate arc her hand made in the air. "Because I was his lover. For a time. I was seduced by his power, and he by mine..."

"This family," I muttered, and Vyvian laughed.

"Suffice it to say, in spite of rumors of his infallible nature, the man is quite mortal. Powerful, yes. But painfully mortal. Though I suspect he might realize he has grown immortal after all these years. Such is the burden of being a legend in one's own time." She rested her cup between her hands, warming her palms. "Then, I dared to challenge him in front of Uther, at court. And Merlin did not like it. He accused me of practicing as a skin witch—which is not untrue, but still not flattering of my many talents—and charged me as an apostate. Yes, he judged me and punished me, and no one stopped him. Not even Igraine, my own sister."

"All to keep you quiet," I said, feeling the price of it. The book burned in my hands, and I began to doubt my capabilities. Would I be willing to go against this man who had defeated such a brilliant woman as Vyvian? If I failed, surely it was exile or death. "What did you see, Vyvian?"

Vyvian did not reply. "It matters not. There are some shadows I cannot shake, nor burden you with. I accepted my diminishment, and as you are here, I can see Arthur and Merlin have begun to forget to fear me. Which is a relief and a welcome thought. It means they do not see you for your power, either. Here, I have nursed thoughts of revenge as you have in Carelon. But even after a while misery makes poor company. I am not entirely without influence. He could not write me out of the story entirely, after all. I told Merlin his interpretations were too rigid, the outcomes too flimsy. He refused my advice. And now, still, he fights for control of his prophecies and makes himself a monster. To some extent I see my own prophecies unfolding before me. Arthur was Hwyfar's. Gweyn was a priestess. He broke Avillion the moment he refused change. And now behold! More Christ men every day." She sounded a bit like Bedevere.

"But now, you see there's a chance. In me. For retribution. For you, for my mother, for my sisters..."

"Yes, Anna. A chance. A slim, delicate chance. It is likely that the transformation will take longer for you than most, and you must be prepared to sacrifice everything for it. Not just yourself, but your marriage, your relationship to your sons, your mind and body. And for that, you must contemplate a great deal. You have the implement in your hands, in your very soul, dearest child, but it will be by sweat, blood, and tears that this comes to be."

My anger and trepidation subsided, replaced by an eerie calm. I could hear the lake lapping on the shore outside, accompanied by the trilling of birds and Vyvian's melodic wind-chimes. I noticed Lanceloch, bare-chested in the sun, pull a shimmering salmon from the waters, laughing with as much joy as a child with his first catch.

I did not know what else to say. I knew this path would not be an easy one, but I already heard more than I bargained for.

"What do I do with the book?" I asked.

"Learn how to read it. Then, you can begin."

"How do I read it?"

"That puzzle, I cannot tell you. It is different for everyone."

"I see."

I was nearly dry by now and the shivering abated. The fire had done a rather impressive job of drying my clothing, but I would be glad for the spare cloak in my pack on the opposite shore. We could not stay much longer.

"There was one more thing," I said, rising and walking to the window to look across her garden. It may have been a prison, but it was a lovely one. Then again, so was my own.

"Oh?" she asked.

"Arthur mentioned something of a weapon, an implement you were fashioning for him. He asked me to inquire about it," I said, knowing so little in the ways of arms. I couldn't even recall if he had said what it was. A sword? A shield? It was all brutality to me.

Vyvian began to laugh. Within a few heartbeats she was

doubled over, laughing so hard tears sprung to her eyes.

"Oh, oh dear me," she said at last, her breath raspy. She fanned her face with her hand, tears coursing down her cheeks. "He really—he really thinks—oh, men! *Men!*"

I was quite confused. "Vyvian—"

"Anna, Anna dear. Your brother! He is purported to be greatest King of an age, but gods..." she said.

I had no mind to what she was getting at and waited for a further explanation. What was unclear to Arthur was even foggier to my mind.

"Lanceloch, dear," Vyvian whispered. "What did Arthur think he was when I sent him to court? A plaything? Well, no, don't answer that. I think I know."

Startling, I looked again out the window.

"You mean...?"

"I trained Lanceloch. I *fashioned* him with my own hands. A weapon! Oh, gods, the King has no sense of metaphor."

"I think... perhaps he was expecting a sword?"

Vyvian frowned, but her eyes were still merry. "Of course he did. So literal. As if the King has need for another sword! While Merlin is still lurking at Carelon, Arthur will be kept under lock and key. Merlin will never allow his golden child to wield his own sword, which is precisely why I had Lanceloch trained as I did, to be his arms, his protector."

"But why should Arthur need such a thing?" I asked.

She paused and turned to me, her eyes unfocused. "Because war is coming, Anna. War is on the wind. And we will both have to wait and watch."

I shivered, not wanting to hear a word of war, for it would mean ruin. Bedevere's warning returned to mind. The thought of sending my sons to battle, or Lanceloch, made me ill. I had heard of the skirmishes with the Ascomanni but blocked them from my mind. Ignorance, while it is still an option, brings about a certain cloak of calmness to one's disposition.

"Come. Let me find him a sword you can take, and we can pretend it is suffused with magic," she said, taking me by the hand, smiling again. "You can even give it a silly name. Call it what you will. And I can give you and Lanceloch some parting gifts. I suppose you will not be able to stay for supper."

The smithy was dark and dank, but having never been in one before, I had no idea whether it was common or not. Everything seemed hard and strange to me, odd implements lining the walls, the dirt floor, the weapons in progress. Most of what she made, however, were smaller things— gates, doors, trellises, the scrollwork a beautiful mingling of darkest iron and space. It was artful if not a bit crude.

Vyvian rummaged in a series of velvet lined drawers, poking about the weapons, testing their edges. Lanceloch had seen us depart, and after a dip in the water, he joined us, drying his hair with a scrap of cloth from the smithy. He still stood bare to his riding breeches, and I tried my best to avert my eyes; I'd not observed the glory of him since our wedding night. But capturing his form again, bronzed in the golden sunlight and supple from swimming, made my pulse quicken.

"This one should do well for you, Lance. What are you carrying these days? Still the bastard sword I sent you back with?" When he nodded, she continued, and pulled a long, broad-bladed weapon from the drawer. The hilt was wrapped with copper wire and the pommel impressed with a large cabochon of amber. It caught the light, and as it did, I saw the scrollwork, etched along the weapon's blade. It looked like a somewhat stylized version of stags' horns.

Lanceloch took the blade reverently, drawing his hands alongside it. "I never saw you work on this," he said.

"That is because I did not start it 'til after you left. I have got to keep myself busy these days with no one to drill," she added with a sad little smile. "And... hmm... there was something I made a few months ago as a commission from King Marqus, but he refused the last payment. It is not easy, of course, taking on such work from a distance, but it is the only connection I have with the world beyond... but perhaps Marqus was not worthy of such a weapon."

She pulled a wrapped weapon from the drawer and slowly removed the covering. "Perfectly balanced," she said, grasping the hilt. It was by no means as ornate as Lanceloch's new sword, yet the metal's color was so white and pure it dazzled like moonlit water. She ran her hand down the center indentation on the blade, then showed us both the design on the bottom of the pommel: a dragon in a circle, eating its own tail.

"Hopefully he will not read any irony into it," she added, bringing it to one of the many tables in the smithy, and matching it—after two failed attempts—with a leather scabbard and buckle.

"And one more thing," she said. "Something for my niece. I am thinking a small dagger—" She glanced at Lanceloch, who nodded, as if he knew.

Vyvian retrieved a delicate scabbard, woven with silk flowers, from a drawer hidden beneath the desk. Drawing out the blade, I saw how tiny—and gods, how sharp it was.

"This was mine," she said. "In another lifetime. It saved

my life more than once, too. Keep it as your own; keep it near yourself. You never know what dangers might find you on the road to Carelon."

We departed and leaving was far more difficult on Lanceloch than me. I sensed he wanted to stay, not so much for Vyvian, but for the peacefulness of the place. I could not say I blamed him; though I knew little of his daily dealings at Carelon, I knew the strain it put on him, saw the fatigue in his eyes when he returned from long days of politics and sparring.

And now, with the rumor of war on the horizon, it was likely even more difficult for him to contemplate leaving this perfect peace. I think it was the worst of it: Lanceloch loved living on the lake, loved it as purely as one can love anything. More than he loved me, more than he loved Arthur... and it was a greater shame that Vyvian kept him for with the sole intention of giving him away, a gift to a greater man.

Perhaps Lanceloch and I had more in common than I thought; we were both gotten and sold in our lives. Not even Vyvian was guiltless in the game.

When we arrived back at Carelon, the streets were quiet. There was no indication of a storm in the sky, but we both noted the curious silence. It hung around us as we progressed up toward the castle.

"News of war?" I asked.

Lanceloch leaned forward on his horse, running his hand down the side of his neck, then tangling his fingers in his mane. "I am not certain, milady."

"The castle is only this quiet if someone has died, or if death is coming," I said, feeling the book pressing against my breast; before we left, I placed it in the lining of my cloak to ensure Lanceloch did not see it, and I did not lose track of it. It was not a settling feeling; the book was still warmer than I was.

By the time we were brought before Arthur, it was full dark, and the stars twinkled outside the arched windows. The King stood with Bedevere, Merlin and, to my relief, Gawain, before a large map, moving pieces across it with a long wooden implement I had once seen my father use.

When he saw us, his eyes softened, and he embraced us both.

"It is the Ascomanni," he said, a growl to his voice, gesturing to the map with a sweeping motion. "We had a regiment at the borders in the North, and Ascomanni ships came out from nowhere. Only a handful survived; it was over a week ago, but their messenger was fleet-footed."

"Ascomanni have landed?" Lanceloch said, holding Arthur by the shoulder. The two men locked eyes, as if they understood the significance of the act more than the rest of us.

"It is good we have delivered your sword safely to you, then, my lord," I said, kneeling before Arthur. "I present the sword Caliburn."

Understanding the symbolic nature of the gesture, I suppose, Lanceloch removed the sword from his back, and unwrapped it before handing it to me.

I took the sword, remarkably heavy in my hands, and presented it to Arthur, trying to make more of a show. I remembered my mother presenting my father with a similar sword, once, when I was a child, and thought it might bring the same memory of pageantry to my brother.

Lanceloch stood by me, straight and strong, and I looked up into Arthur's eyes as my arms shook with the weight of the sword.

As soon as Arthur saw the weapon, his face lit up with joy. He caressed the blade as if it were as fragile as ice and smiled—at me. He smiled directly at me. Over his shoulder I caught sight of Merlin, and he looked slightly concerned, but said nothing. For one strange moment, I wondered if he could sense the presence of the book in my cloak, or if he had somehow seen it.

I could still hear Vyvian's voice in my head, and it was a mighty comfort. *Suffice it to say, in spite of rumors of his infallible nature, the man is quite mortal. Powerful, yes. But painfully mortal.* I smiled at Merlin, graciously as I could.

"Thank you, dear sister," Arthur said. "For delivering this—and Lanceloch—to me. I trust your visit to our aunt was worth the trek?"

"Indeed, my lord," I said, standing. "It did her much good to see Lanceloch again, and my heart is peaceful. I thank you for the boon."

When I left, I felt light on my feet, somehow, though I tried not let it show. Gods knew, it was not the time for joy. But wars came and went; treachery within the walls of the castle, if not cut out, would fester and tear down the foundation bit by bit.

# CHAPTER EIGHT

## A FINE END

IT WAS TO my surprise, as the days and weeks unfolded before the mass deployment North, to hear Arthur was, in fact, planning on commanding the troops from the field rather than from the throne. I thought, initially, his behavior was flying in the face of Merlin's wishes, but I was informed later, while lunching with Gweyn, it was not so.

"Oh, Merlin was quite adamant about it," said Gweyn. Mordred was off with the wet-nurse, and we both sat eating figs and honey while the knights drilled down on the green. From the distance, I couldn't recognize one from another but had my guesses as which three knights were at the front: Gawain, Lanceloch, and Bedevere. In spite of Arthur's favor for Lanceloch, he still included Gawain in nearly all of his decisions, and I heard, my son would command the front regiment during the campaign.

Perhaps war would do him well, if he survived the aftermath. Perhaps he would learn to treasure family more. My anger regarding Gawain quelled to general disappointment and in many ways, I felt he was already dead to me, ignoring me as he did. War taught Lot the importance of home fires and good food, he once said. Gawain would do well to learn the same.

"Adamant?" I asked, flicking out the stem of one of the figs. It was not the best crop this year, unfortunately, and I went to grab some of the bread and honey as I spoke, hoping it would improve the flavor. "Merlin rarely seems *adamant* to me. More like... vaguely officious."

She grinned and turned to her side. She already consumed most of the figs, and I had no complaint. Though Gweyn shed the obvious curve of pregnancy around her middle, she showed no sign of slowing her voracious appetite, owing to the demands of a nursing mother.

Hwyfar lounged nearby, to my chagrin, carousing with her courtiers before a yellow and green silk tent, playing the harp and singing every now and again. As much as I detested the woman, I could not deny her voice was lovely. And on this day, it did add a rather enchanting feel to the season.

"The old man is not so terrible," Gweyn said. "He has been ever attentive to me since Mordred was born. And I could scarcely believe it, but the other day no matter what I did I could not get him to stop crying. I tried everything! Then, Merlin and Arthur came in—I was such a mess, crying into my pillow as the nurse tried to quiet him. But not one moment in Merlin's arms, and the child was silent—cooing! Quite a little miracle."

"Astounding," I said, nibbling the edge of the bread. It was not so bad. "But I am still surprised he is letting Arthur go afield. It seems a large risk to put one's king in such a precarious situation."

Gweyn shrugged, as if the idea of losing Arthur in a grim battle was no concern of hers. "Merlin believes the King is only as strong as the people who are loyal to him, and that Arthur ought to show himself to be a true warrior, rather than his father before him—"

"Uther Pendragon fought bravely at the Battle of—"

"Which was *before* he was king," she pointed out. "*Before* Arthur was born. Since Arthur's birth, all eyes have been upon him, and we must not forget. At least, that is what he tells me. He says he has waited his whole life to prove his mettle, and it is the first time in his life Merlin has given him a blessing to go. He is a good fighter—I have seen him practice."

*Loving a fight and being a good fighter are not the same,* I thought, but smiled at Gweyn regardless.

It was then I noticed one of the knights breaking from the group. He moved at an impressive pace, and halfway to our knoll, he removed his helmet with a frustrated wrench.

It was Lanceloch. I should have guessed by his stride.

By the time he arrived where we were, he was crimson faced.

"Lance," I said, now calling him by the name Vyvian had. Somehow, after seeing him that day on the island, I felt it was a more proper name for him. "Whatever is the matter?"

"I have been dismissed for the campaign," he said, the words clipped, his eyes blazing.

"Why?"

"What for?" Gweyn and I asked simultaneously.

"Your Highness," he said, dipping into a stiff bow by Gweyn. She held out her chubby hand to his, and he kissed it without looking up. "Begging your pardon for my rash behavior. I am only surprised."

He wiped the back of his gauntlet across his forehead; I doubted it would be much good, and so I rose, and put my hand on his cheek, calming him. I was reminded of Culver calming the horses when they got caught in a storm. Taking my handkerchief, I wiped the sweat from his brow, then, because we were in the presence of others, kissed him softly on the cheek.

Lance smiled, grateful, his eyes showing the kindness he so often bestowed upon me. "Thank you, good wife," he said. I couldn't comprehend the difficulty of walking about in the equivalent of an iron cage in the searing sun, let alone under emotional duress. Even in my silk and linen dress, I was sweltering.

"It is not... it is not that I have dishonored the King in any way," he said, taking a deep breath. He smelled of sweat and blood, and there was a streak of dirt below his chin where his helmet rubbed against his skin. It only served to make him look more roguish. "He wishes I stay behind to ensure the safety of the Queen, her sister, and the King's sister."

"Which is a responsibility most frequently bestowed upon Sir Cai, his steward," I said, perhaps too quickly. Gweyn looked at me oddly. I fumbled for the right explanation. But the attention did not linger long on me.

Hwyfar was now approaching us, her long green gown clinging to her body, leaving no doubt of the exact flawlessness of her form. She wore a sweet smile on her lips, and had I not known how deviant she was, I might have mistaken it for genuine congeniality.

"What's this I hear?" she asked, voice husky as usual. Her eyes were half-lidded, as if just roused from a nap for more drink. That was her way; she always looked as if she had just been bedded.

"My lord Lanceloch will be attending the castle while King Arthur takes the knights to war," I said, coolly as I could. I was still standing next to Lance, and grasped his armored hand, almost possessively. He was one treasure she could not have. "The King believes his skills are far and away the most superior of all his knights, and therefore, he will be able to command in his absence, keeping us safe."

Hwyfar raised one red eyebrow, her smile unfaltering. "Delightful. At very least we will have a semblance of normalcy here at court. With all the knights away, it will be an undoubtedly boring experience day to day."

"Oh come now, sister," said Gweyn. "If it will be so dull, I am sure you could always return to Avillion. Surely they would welcome you home with open arms."

Hwyfar chuckled. "Ah! I believe, dear sister, you are stuck with me for quite some while. So long as Father is still upset with me, there's no hope of my departure. But I do hear he may yet be sending Mawra to us."

"Mawra?" I asked, exchanging side-glances with my husband, who was still gritting his teeth. He widened his eyes slightly, clearly as thrilled as I at the prospect of yet another of Leodegraunce's progeny.

"Our middle sister," said Gweyn, sighing lightly. She was ruffled, I could tell, as her cheeks flushed deeper pink than usual; she called over one of her maids, who adjusted the awning over us, and began fanning herself fretfully.

"She is the difficult one," said Hwyfar, with an insidious grin.

\* \* \*

I SCARCELY SAW Lance the next few days as he was briefed on all the important matters of state while Arthur prepared to leave for the North. He returned at night, or at least I presumed he did, for I found remnants of his visit in our apartment—clothing disposed, half-eaten husks of bread, the like—but I never saw him. He returned long after I fell asleep and departed before I rose again in the morning.

Feigning illness, and having Jain corroborate my claims, I took it upon myself to study the book Vyvian had given me. Though I had yet to make up my mind on the subject of murder, I was curious to learn Merlin's secrets. Arranging myself in a chair, I poured myself a glass of wine and leafed through the first few pages. Before I committed myself to the task entirely, complete understanding was paramount. I needed to get close to the old conjuror to judge him and my disguise would have to be foolproof.

I understood, then, my calling: to measure Merlin's sins against his triumphs and hold him accountable. For myself, my mother, and all the women bruised and broken in his wake.

I felt giddy at the prospect, but my elation quickly turned to frustration.

Once again, the words inside the tiny book swam, making me woozy. I looked away to the fire and then back. Still the same result. Vyvian said I had to figure out how to read it; that was my first test, my first trial.

If it was a puzzle than surely there were circumstances that changed the print. I turned it upside down, I held the pages up to the candle. I saw naught.

I dripped a few sprinkles of water on the page, but the letters went unchanged. Then I tried wine, even a bit of ale I had sent up, thinking alcohol might reveal the message. Feeling frustrated, and perhaps a little giddy, I then rubbed bread upon the vellum pages, only to get some unhappy crumbs into the spine and binding.

If not food, then perhaps more elements? I brought it closer to the fire, but when the book became too hot to touch, I reasoned any more exposure would render it impossible to read. And though the puzzle was likely difficult, it was bound to be manageable.

By the time I heard a knock on the door—I tried everything from ink to soil to rubbing one of my diamond necklaces over it—I was half asleep. Culver was there, as well as my personal guard, and he opened the door. I was surprised to hear Lance's voice, and dismissal.

I heard the door down the hall shut, and I rose, stowing the book under the pedestal of a bronze unicorn I brought with me from Orkney.

"Lance? Is that you?"

He stood in the hall, leaning against the side of the wood-paneled wall, his head down. The light from behind cast him in silhouette, and even in casual dress his beauty was startling.

Lance's habit was to go straight to his room, which was on the opposite side of the apartment, but here he was, just a few steps from my room.

Glancing up at me, I saw tears in his eyes.

"Lance—"

He rushed me, enveloping me, burying his face in my breast, his arms about my waist. There was no time to present myself and felt embarrassed immediately; I was still in my day-robe, and my hair was down.

But this did not seem to matter to him. Carefully, gently, I ran my hand over the strong shoulders, the indentation down his spine, the curve of his lower back. He simply held me, breathing deeply, as if he were steeling himself for something.

It was then he began to kiss me, to move slowly up the length of my neck. I felt the breath go out of me; it had been so long since I felt the touch of a man, and certainly ages with an unfamiliar form. I knew the contours of Bedevere's body as well as my own, but Lance was still a mystery. He continued to breathe hard, his breath tickling the delicate hairs at my neck and ears, causing gooseflesh to rise on my arms.

I could feel his passion harden between us, and I gulped, trying to steady myself on legs gone weak. "Lance... you do not... you said..."

"Damn what I said," he whispered, letting go of me with one arm, and shutting the oak door behind him with a kick of his leg. The iron latches shook. "I do not care. Anna, I need you."

Something had changed in him.

"Lance, I promised I would not take this from you," I said softly. "You seem upset."

His arms trembled as they held me firm. He searched my face, his expression softening.

"Breathe for me, Lance."

Dropping his head slightly, Lance's great shoulders rose and fell, the grip on my arms relenting. "Anna..." he said hoarsely.

"I am your wife, and I will do as you ask. But I will not do you the discourtesy of what was done to me," I said. "It is not the same, and I was but a child. I can be more than a vessel for you, I can be your guide."

"Please, Anna," he was almost begging. "Guide me to you. I can bear it no longer."

I needed no more permission.

Through tears, I brought him to me, and with touch alone I told him a story of pleasure. I opened myself to him, gave him time to understand, and when at last we came together he spent himself after three thrusts.

"My brain feels as if it's made of spiderwebs and down," he said at last, still breathing ragged. "You are like silk and honey, and warm as a hearth. Gods, Anna."

"It is part of the joy of it, the gods' gift to us," I said, gently stroking the line of his cheekbones. "Iaia, too, rejoices."

"You moved so differently. And the sounds you made... I have heard such things before, of course, but it is different, knowing you," he said. "At first, I thought you might be in pain."

"'Twas not pain, my dear. I promise I will bite you at the first sign of pain."

"Then perhaps I ought to test the boundaries of pain and pleasure," he said with a roguish wink. But his merriment faded swiftly as we fell into silence.

"There will be other joys," I said. "For now, sleep."

I began to sing a song without words, a tune my mother hummed. It reminded me of green glades and rolling hills, bright cliffs, and the sapphire line of the sea.

When I was done, he was asleep, his breath deep and even as a child's.

I remained awake beside him a few hours, my mind racing with thoughts of love and betrayal, until I, too, fell into the dreamless dark.

LANCE STILL SLEPT when I awoke the next morning. Accustomed to rising early, I began to stir, but he grabbed my hand as I tried to move away. I startled, reaching for my robe.

"Not so quickly," he said, pulling my face down to his and kissing me sweetly. I never had occasion to wake up in such a way as this and was unsure what to do. Bedevere and I always bedded in secret, leaving our separate ways when the deed was done, and I was altogether baffled when he approached me so gently. I was disheveled and unwashed, but it did not matter.

I could not help but kiss him back. He looked up into my face, and sat up with me, running his hands through my hair, down my shoulders, then over the curve of my breasts. He drew a finger languidly over my nipples, then brought his lips to them each in turn, eliciting a low moan from me. My body betrayed what sense I had left, and desire rose in me, coiling between my legs, my skin flushing.

"It was so dark last night," he said, pushing me back to the bed, trailing kisses down between my breasts to my stomach. "I could scarcely enjoy the view of you."

"There is not much to see," I said, gasping as he slid his hand up between my legs. The night before, I told him what wonders lie within, how a skilled lover could bring his beloved to passion with no more than words and his fingers.

"The windows cast shadows all over your lovely freckled skin. And you have stripes, silver, like a tiger," he said, chuckling. The lines left by two pregnancies. I never considered them silver, but somehow shameful. Like the spent skin of dried fruit. Lance only marveled, slipping down further, the warmth of his breath tickling the hair between my legs. "The light turns all your hair to fire."

"Lance..."

"I know you think me unskilled in love, and in some ways I am. But I have read books, and heard stories," he said, pulling me across the thick furs so my legs were on either side of his dark, curly head. "Of how a woman tastes, and how a patient lover can tend to her..."

Bedevere had never dared.

I flushed at Lance's words, clutching the thick coverlets in my fists, unable to keep from smiling, from moaning.

"My lady does not argue for once," he said.

One smooth stroke of his tongue and I was undone, words vanished, and my body writhed and responded, twisted and moved, until I broke in a wave of pleasure. Wily Lanceloch was not as innocent as I thought, and it drove me mad with my own wanting.

Still catching my breath, I brought him to me and gently turned so he was now upon the bed. "Let me show you another way," I said.

He looked at me, amber eyes dazzling with desire, watching me. I felt strange, as if he were trying to look into me, to challenge me somehow. I could not explain the feeling; I cannot, even now.

I let my hands rouse him even more, watched as his body responded to my every touch, and then I fell down upon him, thrusting his passion into my own. He roared, I gasped, and we let the push and pull of our bodies guide us to completion.

When we finished, I lay awhile on his chest. The sounds of drilling knights drifted up through the windows and I thought of Bedevere: thoughts of my knight were accompanied by a pain coursing through my chest and arms, as if I were bruised and broken beneath my skin. I did love Bedevere. Of course I did. I always would. But I could not have him now.

My eyes filled with tears, but I could not weep; not for my husband. I knew, as sure as I knew my own fate, he would not be mine for long. This joy was hard won.

Still, I would not let the joy pass unseen. I watched Lanceloch as he lay, eyes closed, a smile on his fair lips, as if all that was good in the world was truly ours.

I turned my face from Lance and feigned sleep until he left, kissing me softly on the forehead before departing.

WE RECEIVED WORD later the same day from Arthur: we were summoned to another imminent feast, in honor of Ayr, our warrior-god. I knew it was in hopes of suffusing his knights with hope and strength, but I felt a foreboding. Bedevere would be there, and Gawain as well; though neither of them had spoken to me since my wedding, I still held out hope I might raise their notice at least once more and feared at the same time I would not.

For their sakes I did not want to appear so happy or too beautiful at the feast, yet I did not wish them to think me miserable; a woman, they say, tells her whole life in the clothes she wears. I wore a dark blue gown, a gift from Gweyn, and wound a long string of freshwater pearls around my neck. I needed to make a good impression. Gweyn's sister Mawra arrived the evening before, and I had not the occasion to meet her since. They said she was the troublesome sister, and indeed she arrived on the wings of war.

I was instructing one of my new handmaidens, a young girl named Fauna, on how to set my curls right, and what temperature to get the irons—hot enough to steam a bead of water, but not to make it sizzle—when Haen entered stammering a few words I could not decipher.

"Speak up," I said, staring at him in the mirror. "Or I will have to call Culver up from the stables to translate for you."

"Your, er, your son is here," he said, blinking nervously. He rotated his hat in his hands, over and over.

"My—son?" I asked.

"My Lord Orkney." He was as astonished as I was. "Gawain, Your Highness."

"Well, show him in," I said, swatting Fauna away, and telling her to leave me.

I tried a few breaths in and out, hoping for calm. But I already felt tears threatening my composure; I thought long about the departure of my eldest son but knowing he stopped to see me—even if he came to scorn me—filled me with apprehension.

I held onto the hope that so long as he considered me at all, there was a chance he might love me again.

When he stepped into the room, I first glimpsed him in my copper mirror. He was losing the fullness of youth already, the lines of his face delving deeper and eliminating all sign of his once boyish face. His lips were turned down, almost pouting into a frown, but he was clean, well-dressed; his hair was cropped so short the curls were all but gone, and it made him look fierce.

I finished clasping the pearl earring I was fidgeting with and turned slowly, putting the mirror down.

"Gawain," I said.

"Mother."

I stared at him, and he at me. Would that I had a knife, I might have been able to cut the air with our gazes. For once, I was at a complete loss for words, practically paralyzed by his presence. What was I to do? I, who nursed him and cared for him, who dressed his wounds, and taught him to be brave, and right, and true? It seemed impossible I should be made to feel guilty over circumstances beyond my control.

"I spoke to Arthur," he said, pulling a chair over and sitting across from me. He put his hands on my knee, and I marveled at how large they were, how thick the fingers, how broad the palms.

"You did," I said.

"He told me Merlin insisted on the whole marriage— your marriage," he said, clarifying. "The one with Du Lac."

"Yes. Of course he did. As my marriage to your father. Are you in the habit of knowing women who have a choice in these matters? Merlin sees all, orchestrates all, in Carelon."

"But…" he paused, letting his head drop slightly, averting his eyes. I wanted to reach out and smooth them from his brow, kiss his temple as I once did. I used to kiss him in his sleep, and he would smile, then begin to suckle, as if he knew I were near. My heart ached for a moment as I mourned the babe now lost to the man.

I leaned forward. "But what, dear?"

"Arthur indicated that yes, Merlin advised him in the matter, but it was far more complicated than it appeared. He had me understand King Pellas was attempting to marry Lanceloch off to Elaine, of all people, and to prevent... well, to prevent Lanceloch becoming an ally of another king, he arranged the marriage with you," he said, choosing his words carefully.

"That is... the most of it," I said.

He cracked something of a shy smile, a look I knew was reserved for me alone. For whom among Arthur's court would believe Gawain to be shy other than me? "I was foolish. I thought when you went on your errand with Du Lac to visit Vyvian you were engaging in a tryst like some lovesick maiden," he said, wincing as he said it. "It ate me up inside. But then Gweyn intervened after hearing me let loose some rather unkind accusations on Du Lac's part, and I'm sorry."

Indeed.

Gweyn. Mercurial, curious Gweyn. I had her to thank for this. As usual, it was the women of the castle who moved the knights, our pawns, in the grand game, when they were not paying attention.

Gawain cleared his throat. "She took me aside and explained you were both on an errand for Merlin, and you had little say in the matter, and I ought not interfere. She said only the most wonderful things about you, and I began to feel, well, like a boor for doing as I have for so many months."

He almost grinned again, gooseberry green eyes glinting under his dark eyebrows. There, my mischievous little boy.

"I do not hold any love for the man, mind you, Mother; I doubt I ever will. But I realize now this was not your fault. You must be miserable with him! And I have left you to suffer so long. I am a poor knight to behave in such a manner. And a pitiful son."

I watched Gawain, wondering if he would ever make a woman happy, wondering if any man could make any woman complete. Were they all so blind to blame us for the weaknesses of our sex? To blame us for forming alliances we could not prevent? I wanted to bat him about the head, to curse him for his blindness, to call him the names I never had strength to call his father. I wanted to transform myself.

Instead, I let the silence grow around us like an invisible fog.

"I am, as always, at the mercy of the decisions of my lord, Gawain. You must try to understand."

"So you do not love him?" he asked, too fast. Then added, "Du Lac, I mean. This is a marriage of convenience, not of love."

Though I wanted to, I did not defend Lance. Gawain would not understand. He was stubborn in such a way that even the most logical arguments made little sense in the wake of his temper. My son grew to wisdom, I think, but in his younger years there was little between his ears not impaired by the constant battering of his armor.

I should have told him Lance was a good man, a true man, and would be a worthy friend if he only let him in. But like his father, Gawain would listen to no reason if it did not come from his own thinking. If he and Lanceloch would ever be friends, it would take a long while. Perhaps even then I knew such attempts would be in vain.

I chose my words kindly. "I have come to know Lanceloch in the last few months," I said. "I do not love him—not in the way I think you mean. But as the sister of Arthur, my dear Gawain, love is not a luxury I have oft been afforded."

"You loved Bedevere once," he said.

"I—what?"

"He…" he paused and shook his head. "He told me, about before you were married to Father; how you thought you would be married to Bedevere, that the papers were even drawn up at one point. But then, something happened, and you were sent off to Orkney instead. He said it was difficult on you. On you both."

I had never told Gawain and never thought Bedevere would have spoken about it either, yet there it was. To my surprise, on the heels of Gawain's apology, I felt a glimmer of hope Bedevere would come around, too.

"It was," I said, whispering the words, as if the walls could hear me. "Bedevere and I were once quite enamored of one another; I fear we have gone our ways in the years since, and I do not think of him as I once did."

"He is a good man."

"I know," I said, and wished it was not so true. Had Bedevere truly left me, or had I left him? Had I ignored him when I married Lanceloch, for fear of his judgement, for the hurt in his eyes? It was likely.

No, it was more than likely. It was true.

"My darling, what has passed has passed," I said, rising from my chair. Gawain helped me, and he twirled me about, smiling.

"You look beautiful, Mother," he said.

"Thank you, Gawain."

And he embraced me and kissed me upon my cheek.

So, it was well that day, in spite of the sorrow of his leaving. Were we to linger on the possibilities of death and injury, we would likely both have wept until we were dry. As it was, we left healed, forgiven. For a while, at least.

Things were never easy with my eldest son and me. But it was a beginning

AND SO THEY left, a great retinue of armored knights below a hundred billowing banners, to fight the Ascomanni. The castle felt empty; Bedevere never said goodbye, and my thoughts often turned to him. Lance was moody and often absent, and only came to me when he wished for affection, rarely for conversation. But as the weeks passed, even that stopped. He became obsessed with the tactical positioning of the regiments and studied the stream of messages in and out of the castle into the late hours of the night from the study in our apartment. I ordered Haen to attend to him, but he was most typically ignored.

I thought of my sons, of Gareth and Gaheris, and wondered if Luwddoc was sending troops to bolster the lines in the north; I sent word to Orkney, hoping we could spare a few hundred spears. They were but a day's march from where the breach was, and I hoped no one had been lost to the Ascomanni barbarians. While small raids were seen now and again during Lot's reign, there was never such a breach before.

Immersed in dark thoughts and feeling the pull of loneliness, one night I decided to go to Lanceloch, to check on his progress and see if there was aught I could do for him. I had all but abandoned Vyvian's book, and due to the attention of the court being centered mostly on Leodegraunce's girls, I found myself more comfortably in the shadows again. I did not wish to draw attention to myself in the least and only managed a passing introduction to Mawra. Truly, I did not feel, after Hwyfar, I could manage another sibling, by blood or no. I already felt as if I were Gweyn's mother, and I certainly needed no more children.

I presented myself to my husband, hoping my presence would be appreciated. It was all I could do to cheer him up, and I longed for human contact.

"The night is late, Lance," I said, standing at the arch to his room. He had ordered a table brought in, and his bed was shoved up against the wall. The surface of the bed was strewn with maps and papers.

He was uncommonly disheveled, his cape forgotten and thrown in a pile by the door, tunic open and untied at the collar. In the last months he had let his hair grow and it gave him a strangely wild appearance, like a man lost in the wood or belonging to it.

"Not now, Anna, please," he said, not looking up.

I had yet to enter his room but rehearsed the words to myself before drawing up the courage to interrupt him. "I know you want to help by poring over the correspondences and immersing yourself in the maps," I said, taking a cautious step in. "I know how it fee—"

"How it feels?" he yelled, his words so full of bitterness I staggered away into the shadow of the arch as if they had been poison-tipped arrows. "You think you know how it feels, Anna?"

"Forgive me, Lance—"

"You dare to tell me you know what it is to carry the

burden of a kingdom on your back—left to the squabbling nobles at court, and that madman Merlin—while all those dearest to you fight at the hand of marauding barbarians?"

"I did not mean—" I was losing, quickly. I tried to back away, to run. I did not want a confrontation. I realized I should have stayed in my room; only loneliness inspired the departure from the comfort of my room, and it was a deception. Jain was occupied, Anette was gone, and I had no one.

And I knew the look in his eyes. I had seen it in Lot.

But now Lance was standing, stalking toward me. We were of an even height, but he seemed to tower over me. He grabbed me by the wrists, and his hands were cruel.

"You, who spend more time arranging your clothing than pondering anyone else! You live a life of ease, Anna; you have nothing important to give other than your title, and so you have done your duty," he said, pulling me close. He looked frenzied, exhausted; even in my terror, I pitied him. Part of me, some dark part, thrilled at the attention even if it was tinged with violence.

"Lance—I—"

"Get out of my room!" he shouted, shoving me. I tried to move, but my legs were frozen. I was too shocked, shaking, numb with it all, to do anything. "Or have you something else to tell me? To inform me of how I am somehow failing as your husband. I have given your family everything!"

My eyes burned, but tears did not fall. I still could not move; my legs trembling so. For the first time I understood he had not broken his vow with me; I was merely a reaction to that sundering of power.

A reaction to Arthur.

That was why he had been so insistent, so passionate.

Words escaped in anger before I could rein them in; the only weapon I knew, released as surely as a hidden dagger. "Next time you need to release yourself of guilt, bury yourself in another Pendragon."

Gods, I deserved it. He slapped me so hard I fell to the ground. I heard him cry, saw the fear in his face, the tears fall from his eyes

"Anna, please. Anna, I'm sorry!"

His voice was choked by sobs.

"You don't deserve this. You don't deserve me. I'm broken… I'm sorry…"

I scrambled away, soundless and gasping for air, until I got into my room. I barred the door from him, though he knocked, begging for a response, until the eleventh bell when he went back to his work.

When he left, I let the tears come. I screamed, I threw the blankets from my bed, I smashed a vase. I sobbed, choking on fury, until I knocked over my favorite unicorn statue. When I went to pick it up, I cut my hand, and it sung in concert with the pain coursing through my whole body.

As I staunched the blood with the hem of my dress, gritting my teeth against the pain, I noticed Vyvian's book had fallen to the floor.

The pages opened and rustled at me with whispers of their own.

Through blurry eyes, I picked it up, and brushed my trembling hand over the page. In an instant, the pain was gone.

And the words were clear as if they'd just been written with fresh ink.

# CHAPTER NINE

## A BLOODY END

AFTER ABOUT AN hour of reading madly, the words of Vyvian's book began to fade again, swimming away like fickle fish. I could not absorb much, and what I read had been quite disturbing: a long list of warnings. It appeared there were hundreds of things not to do, and when not to do them. I could barely contemplate it all before the book was once again rendered unreadable, and I gave up, returning the book under the unicorn's pedestal.

If pain is what the book needed, it would have to wait. Exhausted, my hand throbbing, I contemplated my own fate, my own prophecy, and my own plan. Lance knew Merlin's wretchedness, he said as much. He was not a monster, but he could be monstrous. He had struck me, and that wound would never heal.

But to play the game, I could not afford a long, drawn out feud with him. I was not the first bruised wife, nor would I be the last. I knew in my heart we would never be the same though no one would ever know the difference.

\* \* \*

THE NEXT MORNING, Fate had its own ideas. I spent the first few hours after dawn preparing for a discussion with Lanceloch, establishing new limitations on our arrangement, clarifications on our roles. His violence gave me room to bargain.

I was walking from my room through the apartment when I was struck with a wave of nausea so powerful I doubled over and vomited directly on the carpet; there had been no notice, and I sat there, sputtering, while Fauna dashed to get something to clean it up with.

Lance, departing for court himself, caught up to me, pure concern flitting across his amber eyes. My heart soared to see it in spite of myself. He cared, even when his heart was ruined.

"Anna—Anna, are you quite alright?" he asked, his words full of apologies I did not allow him to make.

Damn the gods. Of all the inconvenient times for this to happen. How was it I bedded Bedevere close to twenty times since arriving at court and never once conceived, and yet after a handful of occasions with Lance I suddenly became fertile as a new goddess?

He helped move my hair out of my face, and in spite of my attempted refusal, led me to the soft mattress in my room, ordering one of the manservants to get Jain.

I did not need Jain to tell me I was pregnant.

"Do you think it was something you ate?" he asked, taking my hands, and trying to look me in the eye. I stared at the furs atop the bed, watching the way the light changed them to an almost metallic red, remembering with regret how we had shared our bodies together not long ago.

"Unless I ate a baby," I said.

He did not catch on until I looked at him, brow raised. He could not be so dense.

"You—you mean?" he stammered, then dropped to one knee, pulling my hands even closer to him. I smelled like vomit, and I cringed at the thought. "You mean you're with child?"

"Yes." Speaking it made it no easier, but my courses were late, though I had simply thought it was due to the stress of recent events and my age.

A child. Sometimes Lance struck me as more childlike than even my youngest sons. He was gawking, hands held just so, hovering over my stomach as if he expected me to swell to size right before his eyes.

"You cannot see anything yet. You will not. For a few months at least." I paused, not wanting to touch his hands, but feeling compelled to do so. He was the father, after all. If I was blessed enough—though I was not sure "blessed" was the right word to use on the subject—to carry another child to full term, and not have them suffer the ends of so many, I would be delivering a child sometime in the late summer.

The medic came in, a red-faced man I did not know; Jain was occupied. I turned away. I did not wish to be relegated to the prodding and poking of his sort, that was for certain.

"Your Ladyship, Lordship," the medic said, clearing his throat. I wondered if he was part of the dregs Arthur left us, after taking more of the qualified medical staff with him on the campaign.

"My wife is with child," Lance said, and I could hear the emotion in his voice. Men were always like this with news of their progeny. I once felt joy at the realization of pregnancy, relief from Lot's attentions—but now I felt hollow, destitute. I did not want another child. Women my age did not often survive the childbed, their hearts unable to hold up against the strain, their bodies already weakened from years of carrying children before.

I was still fit but had no mind for child-rearing.

"Oh," said the medic, blushing even more red. He mopped his forehead with the back of his hand. "If that is the case, there's little I can do but make you comfortable. I can send a midwife, if you desire, and see if she has any herbs to allay your pains." The medic's gaze rested on my cheek, now swollen from Lance's attack.

Lance saw it, too.

"Thank you," Lance said, when I did not respond. "Yes, please. Send the midwife."

My thoughts spiraled down and my vision blurred, and I could not look at Lance again. So I turned to the window. Frost clung to the pane like crooked fingers reaching toward the warmth inside.

LATER THAT AFTERNOON the midwife arrived. At first, I took no notice of the woman as she moved about me. The news of my pregnancy was not a welcome one, and I still felt as if I would never keep food down again. It had not been so bad with the twins, but I was happier then, in some ways. Perhaps the reason for my comfort lay in their paternity, in knowing Bedevere's children would represent our love together into another generation.

"You'll need to stay off your feet," said a familiar voice. "No trips to see long-lost aunts, no traipsing through the woods…"

Morgen.

When she turned to the side, I saw she was pregnant as well—and at nearly seven years my senior I was beside myself with surprise. I must have goggled at her, for she smiled a little, the lines around her eyes creasing. Aside from the swell of her condition, she looked much aged since the last time I encountered her. Her jet-black hair was shot with gray about the temples, and she was not wearing her usual robes. For all intents and purposes, she looked exactly as a midwife ought to, down to the knotted belt and flat-footed shoes.

"Yes, it seems you and I will bring children into the world before the next autumn," she said, rubbing her stomach thoughtfully. She looked serene, content. So unlike her.

The last time we spoke, Morgen orchestrated the greatest betrayal against the crown imaginable: switching innocent babies at birth. I felt dread cling to my chest but did not want to let it show. I had not seen her in Carelon in ages and could not understand her sudden appearance.

"Naught helped me in the first weeks," she continued, natural in conversation as if we had last discussed the weather. "Not as far as the nausea was concerned. There are some teas which may help for a time, but you likely saw the limits of their power before."

I shuffled a little uneasily on the bed. "You're not wearing your usual robes."

"I am a midwife," she said, producing a few packets of tea from the satchel at her hip. Morgen glanced up at me, and I thought I caught something like pain in her eyes. But it faded away, and she smiled instead. "Merlin has released me from his service, and so, I have taken up the position of first midwife."

Quite truly, I did not know what to say. Merlin apprenticed Morgen when she was barely of age, and I scarcely saw them apart after. I never anticipated her release; she was meant to replace Merlin when he was too old or had passed on. And, I knew her so little—less even than Margawse.

"Are you quite well, then?" I asked her.

She smiled, and I was now certain it covered her tears. "Midwifery suits me, and the castle is in need of good direction," Morgen explained. "And now that I am no longer apprenticed to Merlin, I have a significantly larger amount of freedom. Which is welcome."

"Surely Arthur's sister deserves—"

"I requested the reassignment and he consented. There is no shame in it; I oversee all births at the castle, and as such, it is a great honor."

"Is there anything—"

Morgen shook her head, and took my hand, feeling for my pulse. She brushed her fingers over the delicate skin at my wrist and patted me. "You'll deliver well; you're strong. Young enough. I only advise you take it very easy."

"Easy? Like you?" I joked.

"It is different with me," she said. Her voice was tender, and she took my hands in hers, squeezing my fingers. "I have no husband, no title. But you—you have Lanceloch, raised by our own aunt. He is a good man, most times, Anna. Treasure him as you can, even if it is not in love, and he will do well by you."

I knew Morgen had the Eye—she often saw things, as Gweyn did—but I squirmed inside, hoping she did not know what transpired between Lance and me. It was not unusual for a man to strike his wife; Lot struck me often, but he was one such man, brought up to see women as chattel, possessions, minds to shape and not to respect. Lance knew better. With him, it felt as if I'd awakened a facet of his personality, an insidiousness within. I knew Lanceloch could summon violence on the battlefield but bringing it into our marriage bed would not do.

"Thank you, Morgen."

She let go of my hands and took a deep breath. I thought for a moment she might cry. She shook her head instead. "It will be another boy. Send him to his father's people. Promise me that." Her voice was grave, knowing.

I had no desire to raise another child. And Elaine was childless.

"Of course," I said.

OVER THE COMING months, I suffered. I can say it no other way. News from the North was varied; it seemed that victory was ours, but hard-won. Lance was by turns attentive and distant, and our relationship bruised over but did not heal. We lived separate lives unless we engaged in passion, lightning and thunder on separate courses.

Carelon was quiet. I spent my time weaving and embroidering, often reading poetry and saint's lives of early Avillion. I avoided Vyvian's book for the time. Though I had new reason to doubt Merlin's motives—that being the mystery of Morgen's ostracization—I began to think, as the pregnancy progressed, that my furor was hasty. Merlin traveled between the front and Carelon, and I had only seen him in passing, now he scarcely seemed the monster I made him out to be. I thought often of Anette's child, as he grew under the care of Gweyn, and wondered about Amhar on Avillion. Though I tried to ask Morgen on one her visits to me, she would not say.

My mind went soft with pregnancy, and I lost myself for a while.

In the early Spring, Morgen gave birth to a daughter, Llachlyn. She was dark and small as her mother but born a bit too soon. We worried for weeks that she would not live, but eventually, she began to thrive, mostly at the hand of Margawse, of all people. Morgen explained that with so many children being born—a result of the mass deployment of knights—there was little time for her to raise a child, and Margawse was more than willing to lend her hand. She never had children of her own, and I think it did her well to see the line of Cornwall pass to another girl, though I highly doubted Margawse's motives.

As with my other pregnancies, I felt during the course of growth that I was someone else. I did not think as usual, did not aspire to do much else than sit quietly and read, to meditate, to walk about the castle premises. Even Lance's moodiness did not bother me. I spent much time with Gweyn, and her sister Mawra—who in spite of Hwyfar's warning, seemed as docile and bland as the Queen—and we watched Mordred play about his great playroom.

It was two weeks before the child was to come, and all about me was stifling discomfort. Summer was on its way out, and the leaves were beginning to change, turning the green to gold and crimson. We awaited the return of Arthur and his knights with caution. There were many casualties, horrific stories, but no real news. We did not know who numbered among the living.

I prayed to Iaia, mother goddess, every day for Bedevere. I did not think I could endure his death, not with so many unspoken words between us.

When the knights finally arrived home, they came in erratic numbers. Arthur had sent many wounded men first, and so the medics—and even the midwives—were kept busy. I worried that when the time came for my child to be born, there would not be enough staff to attend me. I was already feeling a weight below the womb, warning me that the time was growing nearer.

In the matter of a few hours, I learned that a handful of knights I knew well had been gravely injured, including young Lamorak and Palomydes. Though I could have easily slipped in among their ranks in the infirmary, I continued my daily walks throughout the castle, attended by Fauna, and when she could spare the time, by Jain. We made the same circuit every day, and it was beginning to bore me.

I was thinking that I ought to sit down a while on one of the garden benches, when a familiar voice called my name.

I turned to see my Bedevere, leaning up against a tree. His arm was wrapped to his side, the fingers protruding black and bruised. A scabbed line ran down the side of his face as well, healed and puckering, yet his face was as dear as ever his eyes deep wells of sadness.

"Bedevere," I managed, as Fauna helped me to my seat. I heaved a sigh, but Bedevere was approaching me, his gaze resting on the swell of my belly. Over the last few months I ventured just once a day from my apartment, and those who encountered me never looked with such astonishment.

"Anna… Lady Du Lac," he said, correcting himself. He used my first name, and Fauna gave him a very confused look.

"You'll excuse us, Fauna," I said. She attempted to say something, but I held out my hand. "I will meet you within the hour back in the apartment. Sir Bedevere is more than capable of arranging an escort for me if needs be."

When she departed, we were nearly alone. I could hear the clipping of a gardener in the distance, but as most of the knights were in the infirmary or visiting their families, the lower garden was quite deserted.

As his brother died a few years before, Bedevere had no family left; only me, and Arthur.

He stood beneath a willow and had to move the long tendrils of leaves aside to come up beside me, which he did with a low grunt.

"It hurts," I said.

"Quite," he replied, moving his bandaged arm gently. "Broken. Along with my shield. The bones were set at the field, though, by a very capable medic we since lost. A right shame, that."

"It will mend?"

"It will. In time. I tried to stay with the rest, but the King would not have it. He worried it might fester and wanted me in the care and cleanliness of the castle." I knew it must have been a horror by the sound of his voice.

"How many did you lose, in all?"

Bedevere stared out across the high-headed sunflowers and squinted. "For certain, at least two hundred. We buried them, when we could. But by and large they were peasants, foot-soldiers. A few knights, but none you held dear."

"Gawain?" I asked, and my voice caught in my throat, tears coming unbidden.

"Fit as an ox. He fought well. Commanded an entire

retinue. Lot would have been proud to see him. He will be arriving with Arthur." Bedevere rolled one of the narrow willow leaves between his thumb and forefinger. "I rode forward with Palomydes—who shouldn't have taken the saddle at all, in my opinion—to see the injured on their way first. Arthur was detained dealing with Hrapnar, the King of the Ascomanni. We ended surprisingly peaceful, after the bloodshed. Hrapnar is even sending a handful of knights to Arthur as a pledge of faithfulness. His best."

"And how do they compare to our best?" I asked, glad for the change of subject. My relief at Gawain's well-being was like a cloak of warmth about me.

"Middling. But fierce. Strong men, hard men. But desperate and hungry, too. I helped convince Arthur that if, perhaps, we deal with them more as a nearby kingdom rather than a threat, it would end better. They live in desolate conditions and love their land. Arthur doesn't want their damn islands, but he wants their respect. It is a good compromise."

I nodded. "Fascinating. I learned less than that from Lanceloch, so the information is appreciated."

He cleared his throat and looked down at my belly again. "I take it has been a good pregnancy?"

"I am bigger than a henhouse and fit to bursting. I have sweltered through one of the most stifling summers in recent memories, and I had no desire to have a child again, if that is what you're getting at," I said, rubbing my hand over where my navel was protruding. I could feel the child inside move, the surface of my stomach rising and falling strangely.

"Lanceloch is pleased?"

"Overjoyed." I wanted to tell Bedevere how distant Lance

was, how unlike himself. But I could not. In another world, perhaps; but it was not his burden to bear, nor mine to give. It was difficult enough for Lanceloch among the knights, and Bedevere's influence was great. I took a breath and continued: "He has been very occupied with the war, as it has nearly consumed every waking moment of his life—between that and keeping the castle safe. Lance would have been happier afield."

"He loves him," Bedevere said

I startled, turning to him so suddenly that he had to catch me. "What did you say?"

Bedevere looked weary, but continued. "Arthur loves Lanceloch, always has. What has transpired between them, only the gods know. It is quite torturous to see. I believe Arthur simply felt more comfortable having Lanceloch here; it meant he would be safe." He spoke quietly. "I know this as his closest friend, and I know you must suspect. He is your brother after all; and Lance is your husband." The last word was not without its barbs.

I nodded, looking down at the rings on my fingers. Gifts of guilt from Lance.

He turned to me, eyes soft, warm. "I hope… I hope you can stand to be my friend once again, Anna. I fear I have made a mess of the only love I am bound to ever have."

Why did everyone always want something from me? Lance wanted a child. Arthur wanted obeisance, Bedevere wanted friendship. Morgen wanted my compliance, and Gweyn wanted me as a sister, a mother, a friend.

"Bedevere, we are ever the hazel and the hawthorn, bisected by a great wall," I said. "I have missed you."

"And I have missed you, my darling."

The wind moved his hair, willow frond falling into his beard. He looked so dear.

"I am glad you are back safely," I said, rising slowly, using the back of the bench for support. Bedevere couldn't have helped me if he wanted to, as his good arm faced away from him. As I moved, I felt a pressure at the base of my spine. I would not be able to tarry long. "And though I wish to speak more, my body betrays me; would you see about sending Morgen to me? I am not well."

WHEN IT CAME time for the birth, I was surrounded by familiar faces: Morgen and Margawse, foremost, as well as Jain. In spite of the difficulties with my half-sisters, I could not fathom anyone else with me.

And as before, the pain was so complete, so surrounding, that I scarcely knew where or when I was. Both times before, I birthed children among strangers, or those who might as well have been. With Gawain, the process was a horror. The groping, the blood, the leather lace between my teeth, my own screams dulling my ears. He had been large and turned. I fully expected to die that night. I was still a child, myself, my body not yet full grown.

This time I felt less fear, but still vanished into a world of excruciating pain that surrounded me like a red light, a searing force that began in my womb and radiated in every direction, all the way down to my fingernails, which I raked across the bedsheets. Morgen brought me a stick to bite upon, but it did not help. I wanted to die, and part of me hoped I would.

And all at once, in the middle of the birth, I thought of

Gweyn, and what she had gone through. How they had drugged her, and taken her child, and how I complied. Though the memory of the pain from prior childbirth was distant, I somehow attributed my current suffering to that sin. I wished I could change the past, shame building within me that I allowed such cruelty to befall Gweyn.

"Oh, gods," someone said, and my attention lifted from the cloud of pain. I saw the look in Morgen's eyes, saw the way she exchanged glances with Margawse.

"What?" I demanded, my voice so raspy that it sounded like the croak of a crone.

Then, I lost consciousness.

I dreamed, or so I thought, that Morgen was weeping, and Margawse grabbed a handful of flesh and blood from bed, then left the room; it was the last thing I saw before I plunged into darkness, cold and complete.

I decided that I had died, and it was a relief.

"ANNA."

*Mother.*

"Anna... wake up."

No, not Mother.

My sister. Elaine.

My eyelids were heavy as lead. Sunlight streamed in my window, falling upon the bed, and I remembered what Lance said to me the first morning I awoke next to him. That he thought I was beautiful. I wanted to burst into tears, except that my once-favorite sister was sitting at the edge of my bed, watching me, and I had enough years to atone for without weeping before her.

She was edging toward fifty, and though I had not seen her in over twenty-five years, little about her changed save that her skin seemed thinner, somehow. Elaine was still delicate, her small nose and pursed lips giving her an air of aristocracy none of her sisters possessed. She was short, slightly round, her dark hair tied neatly behind her head, caught with a net of pearl and floss. As always, her clothes were quite modest, muted grey and black with a white collar of beaded fabric.

"I am here, Anna."

I squinted. Everything seemed too bright.

"The child…" I said.

"The boy is fine," said Elaine, and something about her syntax sent a shiver through me. So when she said, "The girl was born still," my heart had not so far to fall as it might have.

"Twins," I said.

"It is common, especially in women who have borne twins before," she said, as if she were the foremost subject on the situation. "You carried them to term, or at least… the boy thrived. The girl likely died some weeks ago. It is difficult for us to know when, of course. But the boy thrives."

"Lance?"

"He has named him Galahad."

Gods, I had been carrying around a dead child in me for weeks. If I still possessed any energy, I would have wept to the heavens. I felt scoured out, empty as a hollow gourd. What did the gods expect of me that I would be made to endure so much?

"It is a good name," I said, turning from her. I asked, "Where is he?"

"With my handmaiden, Elsa."

"Children have a way of going missing," she said lightly, smoothing the furs with her small, deft hand. She gave me a look that said she knew the details of Amhar and Mordred's births, and I turned my weary eyes from hers. "I wanted to be here, to make sure you hadn't changed your mind. Time is pressing, and I have a wet-nurse prepared for the ride. He will lack for naught."

"I thought there might be more time. A year, a month…" I had written to Elaine, months before, asking her to foster our child, as agreed with Morgen.

"Anna, you know this is best. You know it. Don't pretend this is about the child. Because it isn't. It's about you."

"So you come to tell me," I said, my lips trembling so much the words tumbled out like hailstones, "that one of my children is dead, and the other is to be taken."

She tilted her head, birdlike, as if perplexed at my stunned reaction, as if she could not fathom for the life of her why I would be upset. "Anna, dear. It is cause for rejoicing. Galahad will be well taken care of."

"He is *my son*," I said. "I should take care of him. And you are a *Christian*." Confusion surrounded me, my body weak, my mind reeling with such grave tidings.

I lost a daughter.

"Still, I have agreed to send him to Avillion when he is ready." She did not sound happy about it.

"No," I said, trying to rise on the bed, but feeling the pressure of my stitches. I fell back on the pillows, gasping for breath. The world began to darken around me. "Please, Elaine… Just let me see him."

I did not want another child. My pregnancy was long and

painful, and the prospect of a child weaning and teething... I wished, more than once, for an end to it. It could be done. I knew the herbs. I knew the spells.

Except, I had not. Perhaps because I loved Lance, in a way I saved only for him. And that changed all. Knowing our daughter was born dead, waking to this too-bright world, thrust into another season at Carelon, my brain was on fire with grief and fear.

"I had a daughter..." I whispered the words.

"Elsa. Bring the child."

A figure, blurry against the sunlight, darkened my vision a moment. Then I felt the welcome pressure of a baby in my arms, and was surrounded by the newness of him, that undeniable scent. He was not large, as his brothers had been, but dainty in a way that spoke of his father's blood. A head of black curly hair, pursed lips, and a contented expression. My other boys screamed their way into the world for days, but little Galahad was mild and content and darling.

I understood, as well, that I could not rear a child and grow my own magic. Elaine was right. Fosterage, it would be.

"Love him, sister," I said to her, handing Galahad back after one kiss to his forehead. "Love him and bring him back to us a shining man of substance, burnished brighter than even his father."

# CHAPTER TEN

## BEGINNING

AND SO IT was, bereft of both my youngest children, that my life at last became my own.

It is strange to think, I know, that one's life can begin after having borne five children, after two marriages, and countless losses. But upon the death of Blancheflor—for I named my only daughter as such—after relinquishing Galahad, it became quite clear that my life had been spared for a purpose.

I dallied too long. Vyvian had given me the keys to Merlin's judgement, and I nearly tossed them away, for what? For the hope of love with Lanceloch? For hope that I could win him from Arthur? For a life as an old mother?

No, the only love left in me was for my sons, and they would need it very little in the coming years. The twins did not write, though I did, and Gawain... Gawain and I would try and fail the rest of our lives to mend the rift between us. Brokenness was all we could ever hope for.

\* \* \*

As ICICLES HUNG from the moss-covered gargoyles outside my window, I stood, stark naked and breathed as if for the first time. My feet were numb from the cold, such that my fingers had gone white; moisture gathered beneath my nose. My hair, having grown long, tickled the back of my knees. Gooseflesh rose all along my skin, but I did not shiver. I grasped the iron grate at the bottom of the windowpane, and felt the bite of metal, reveled in that pain.

It was my pain, my chosen pain.

And I would need the pain. I was reading the book.

When I sat down with the book once again, fingers barely complying with my commands to turn the pages, I found, rather quickly, that page turning was not necessary, as the very same sheaves I had read nearly a year before were filled with new words, new concepts. It had progressed beyond the warnings from before and was now centered around one idea: a name.

For, to be someone else, as Vyvian said, I would need a new name. If, by some streak of brilliance I was able to manage the complicated spell, I would appear as someone else entirely. None would know.

Every spell of this sort, this shadow pulling, required a name.

And as surely as I knew my own name, I knew this one. *Nimue*.

The name came like a trickle of melting snow, clear and complete. I sat, saying the name to myself, over and over, feeling the tickle of the consonants and the fullness of the vowels. Nimue. Nimue. Nimue. I began to see her—she was younger than I, with a fuller figure, and short, compact frame. Her hair was tousled and dark, and her eyes slanted, wild.

Pictish, perhaps. Beautiful, but distant, as if beauty were not something that she considered important, yet written in every curve of her, from her sensitive lips, to the swell of her hips.

When the pain faded, so did the vision. Realizing that more physical cold would do me harm—the book reiterated the importance of a sound mind and body, and I did not dare disregard its advice so soon after birth—I put a robe on and went in search Vyvian's dagger. It had been some time since I had seen it and wondered if Fauna or one of the other maids accidentally placed it among Lance's things.

I did find it, however, folded in one of my drawers, underneath a scarf I'd forgotten about, a gift from Lance on some occasion that escaped me. I slid the dagger from its sheath, and turned it in the light, watching the vivid cold glint of the winter sun.

I would have to find a way to manage pain, and prolonged pain—but also pain that could be overlooked. It had to be something easily hidden that would not make it difficult for me to walk or go about my daily activities with lingering issues.

Sticking the dagger between my thigh and the cushioned side of my chair, I lowered my arm down, so that the skin above my elbow came in contact with the blade. A little gauze, and an old scarf meant that I could absorb any spilled blood.

And so, with a deep breath, I lowered my arm onto the blade, harder, until I felt the abrupt piercing, the dagger parting my skin and entering my body. I gasped, grit my teeth, as tears sprung to my eyes.

It was good; it was very good.

Looking at the page, the letters were brilliant once again.

\* \* \*

I HAD GIVEN explicit instructions to Fauna to leave me alone, and to only come if called. And I must have frightened her, for that is precisely what she did. As to the others in the castle, it was unlikely that anyone—save perhaps Bedevere if the mood struck him—would interfere.

As I read, I learned much. But it was not easy; this was no matter of a month, or even a year's worth of work. These rituals and spells would require endless hours of refining. And even then, after I learned to cast an impermeable shadow—the sort that would not fade away in bright light or to the touch, as the only way I knew how to work the magic—there was still one problem.

Though I trusted in my prophecy to be forgotten, I still did not want to appear suspicious. If I was to become someone else, this Nimue, it would have to be convincing. So I not only had to learn how to weave her shadow, but also to cast my own if needs be. We needed to appear together, or at very least, in two places at once, on occasion. I could not just escape to the Joyous Guard, as I hoped.

But before any details on that matter were to be attended to, I had to learn the rituals and gather the components.

I had to dig up a grave.

The ritual required the bones of a woman to use as, as crude as it sounds, a palette for Nimue. This magic was very specific in that it could not be done simply by wanting, or by talent; it was component magic, dark magic of a sort, according to the book. Trickster's magic, women's magic, whispered from the line of the goddess Cayell herself, the shifting, dark-haired goddess of war.

So one night, I made it appear as if I were going to bed early, and when it sounded as if Fauna departed, I left the apartment, pulling shadows so completely about me that the guard at the door had only enough time to wonder how the door opened up of its own accord. It was nothing I could maintain for long, but the book suggested the illusion in situations such as this. I enhanced the glamor with a combination of marrie root and dragonsnap, two ingredients frequently in a standard midwife's kit. I had asked Morgen for them, and she had been happy to help, glad that I was still using my "latent abilities" as she called them.

She was a puzzle. Since dismissed—rather forcefully, and on account of her pregnancy—from Merlin, she was a changed woman. Morgen was sweet to me, even considerate of my being. She often visited me when she could, making sure that I was feeling well after the birth, asking after her nephews, and offering her opinion of court intrigue.

I thought of Morgen as I slipped through the castle, cloaked, my head down, making as little noise as I could, and pulling shadows around me. As I descended into the depths, I began to think of my twins, and how they fared, wondering if they would ever believe the stories their mother would tell them when it was all over, or whether that would be forgotten, too.

And I wondered, strangely, if I would, in time, forget my own self.

The graveyard was quiet, but I was not worried about running in to anyone. For one, the only part of the graveyard frequented by visitors was the section reserved for royalty, and then only during the day.

Anette was buried among the rabble of the castle, far below my ancestors, in a crypt. I had the plaque commissioned for her myself and knew the precise location—which was a blessing. Many servants got neither plaque nor a discernible resting place. But she served a greater purpose than she or I ever expected, and I believed she deserved greater than a pauper's barrow.

At least, until now.

The common crypt was below ground and required passage through three gates. I had been down in the daylight, but never in the dark. Thankfully, there were torches which could be lighted by passing over the constant flame at the head of the crypt. Judging by the pale wicks, they were unused. I was not sure if it was because the servants and maids of the castle were too busy to visit, or if they simply did not know how to honor their dead; either way, the passage reeked. Though most of the foot-soldiers were buried in the north where they had fallen, a few lingered, and some died later.

I pulled my hood over my face a little more and continued to descend into the dark, one step at a time, shivering.

What did I expect? Ghasts? Phantoms? Certainly more than this. Once the smell dissipated, as I progressed past the main antechamber, it was dry and warm. Though my torchlight illuminated an intriguing collection of bones and bodies, there was nothing remarkable other than the fact that this was, as it had always been, a crypt. A dry, well-swept crypt.

My fear gone, I went to the corner where I knew Anette's remains had been placed. There was little left but sinew clung to the bones, and I shuddered as my fingers grazed the uneven surface. The book indicated that I needed only a few bones, and not an entire skeleton, so I took some finger bones along with a long, elegant femur, and a shoulder blade. They fit comfortably in the bag.

I was just leaving the cemetery, when I heard a voice beckon me.

"It is late for a walk."

"Gods, Lance. You scared me out of my skin."

He was carrying a single white orchid from the garden, and he was shivering, having much underestimated the chill. I hadn't noticed how cold it was, but I also dressed accordingly. He looked as out of place in the climate as the flower.

"I am sorry—" I began. I looked at the orchid, then at him again. He was here for Blancheflor. Of course he was. Good, pure, brilliant Lanceloch, far more pious than I and always striving to atone for sins he had no control over.

"Lance, it's cold," I said, pulling my satchel to the side and under my cloak. He would likely think I was on a similar errand, visiting the child's little unmarked grave.

He mistook my hesitation for emotion, and though it was hard to see much in the dim light, I could swear there were tears in his eyes.

"I speak to her, sometimes, when I feel I can speak to no other. I know it is nonsense, but she... she is still a part of us," he said. I heard the weariness in his voice, the sound of a man's soul being wrung out by the careless hands of the gods.

I nodded, looking demure. I had no escort.

"I have asked Elaine if I can see Galahad, for one month in the summer. Arthur has given me—" He cleared his throat. The silence was telling. "Permission. He has given me permission to go see Galahad, in the summer. It will be good to be in Benwick again. You can come if you would like, you know. You'd be welcome there, and the climate might suit you, warmer as it is."

Poor Lance. I have never known who to blame for his suffering. Perhaps he was destined to suffer far before I ever encountered him, before our time in the orchid garden, when I came to know him. I am always quick to blame myself. I could not pretend to love him, nor could I accept that he loved me. Did he love Arthur as the King loved him? Perhaps. Did he love others? Yes. But even in those days, before the great rift that came between he and Arthur, Lance seemed to me a man desperate for love, but either unwilling or unable to accept the pain of it.

Love broke his soul, I think.

Of course, I was none to speak. I knew I ruined Bedevere's affections for me long ago. And in the dark nights, when I could not find sleep, I envisioned the life Bedevere and I could have had, free from politics and turmoil and loyalty. A world without Arthur. A world without Merlin.

Worse even, when that dream died in a flurry of bitter memories, I thought perhaps someday I could find happiness with Lance; that I could bring him fullness.

"Lance, I am beyond traveling. I am not as strong as I was."

"Anna."

I sighed. He was being difficult, and I was freezing. "Can this wait?"

"You always delay the inevitable," he said, kicking at the pebbled ground with his boot. "You escape me, when I try to comfort you. Our child, our children—we should share in the suffering together."

"I cannot live in that darkness forever, Lance. Elaine will give him a good life."

"You deserve a good life."

"I deserve only what I can take," I said.

The wind picked up, and Lance flexed his fingers. "I am being sent away, you know; I will be gone, likely half a year. Sent to see King Pellas, to try and mend the rift between his kingdom and ours. It seems he still holds me in high esteem, in spite of... the changing world."

"Being out of the castle might do you good, Lance," I said, still conscious of Anette's bones pressing against my back. My own bones ached with the cold.

"Gods damn you, Anna," he said, though there was little fight in it. I would have taken more offense if I actually worried about the gods' wrath. "You couldn't keep the course of conversation if it was written on a scroll."

I shuffled a little, trying to keep the satchel from view as best I could. The dark was my ally, but I did not want to be sloppy. Lance would not know what to do if he caught me stealing bones from a crypt, and I had no good excuse to give.

"Lance. What *do* you want from me?"

He spoke to the ground. "You and I... almost, we were almost..."

"We cannot make each other happy, Lance. Almost is worse than had been," I said.

"You're my wife."

"I am your prize," I replied. "I am your inheritance. Your chains at court. I am everything you hate about your life, and I am well aware. I will not pretend to be any other, Lance. I cannot."

"What's to become of this?"

I almost laughed. "It is not so difficult. Simply find someone who makes you happy. Love them, cherish them. I will remain married to you as long as I am alive because it is what Arthur wanted. I will let you to your whims and wiles. But, by gods, enjoy yourself for a moment before you die of self-loathing, will not you?" I patted his arm. "I have offered myself of you, and you have not taken it. Not truly. I cannot help you out of the labyrinth."

"You will not want an annulment?"

"Do you?"

"No, but… I thought you might. After what happened."

I shrugged. "What good would it do me, Lance? It would free me up for another marriage, and gods know, it is the last thing that I want. I cannot bear it again. So long as you leave me to my things, I will leave you to yours."

"And what of Galahad?" he asked.

"What of him?"

He frowned deeper. "You'll want to see him, sometime—I could at least arrange for a short trip for you, in a few months, when it is warmer and the seas are calmer and—"

"They need a season of peace," I said. "So long as Elaine has Galahad, I know he is safe. I am used to living apart from my children."

Lance put his hand on my forearm, scarce inches from where the blade had been pressed, the skin aching in response. "It should have made us stronger, what happened," he said, smoothing his thumb gently back and forth.

"You have your duty; I have done mine," I said, and began the long walk back to my chamber. "Perhaps it is the best we can manage between us now."

I ARRANGED TO meet Morgen two days later, feigning an issue that required her attention. I had the apartment to myself, and Fauna brought us mulled wine and cider cakes, as well as some cheese from Eire by a young emissary of King Marqus.

She looked haggard when she entered the room and narrowed her eyes at me.

"This doesn't appear to be urgent," she said, eyeing the little repast.

"I want to talk," I said, gesturing to the seat beside me.

"Anna Pendragon," she said, raising her dark eyebrows. "I have never seen you so forward."

"Life changes us, blood and bone."

"So it does." Morgen sat with a rush of air, a sigh of relief. I doubt she slept much.

I poured her some wine and handed her a few cider cakes on one of the garish plates Gweyn had given me. She looked down at it and set it on her lap. I was famished and began eating in spite of her refusal.

"Anna," she said, leaning forward. "I cannot stay long—I am sorry, but Gweyn is very ill, and I have to attend her. I thought this was an urgent matter."

"Gweyn is ill?" I asked. I had been quite caught up with my own matters and not attended the Queen in some time.

She nodded, looking over her shoulder to ensure no one was guarding the door, then spoke very lowly. "She began hemorrhaging last night, and at first I thought it was a miscarriage; but it was unlikely that she was with child, and now I think it is something worse. The bleeding has stopped for now, although she has not left her bed in the last half day. The fight seems to have gone out of her, and..." Morgen broke a corner off one of the cider cakes and nibbled on it. "I do not think she wants to live."

"Doesn't want to live?" I asked, shocked still by the announcement of Gweyn's illness. "What in the gods' names is the matter?"

"When was the last time you saw her?"

I tried to think. During the beginning of my pregnancy, not long after Hwyfar's arrival. "I tried to see her, but I did not want to interrupt her family. Her sisters. Come now, she can't be that ill." I told it more to myself, guilt gnawing at me. Gweyn had been my friend, and maybe she had forgotten me.

Morgen's eyes filled with tears. I had never seen her cry, but she began to sob, head down, dark hair like a streaked black curtain.

I went down to my knees before her, putting my hands on her legs, trying to look up into her eyes. I recalled a sudden memory of doing something similar when we were so much younger. Seven years may have been between us, but we retained a certain connection, she and I.

"It is my fault that she is ill, and I ought to be set afire for it; Merlin warned me, and I did not listen. I thought it impossible—some prophecies surely weren't meant to be true," she said, as I reached up and gave her a kerchief to wipe her eyes.

"What do you mean—-Morgen, as your sister, tell me. I can help you."

"Anna, do you know why he took me as his apprentice?" she asked.

"No, I… simply assumed it was your talent."

She laughed coldly. "On my day of prophecy, he took Mother and I up to Cornwall, to Father's castle. He placed me on a rock there and called the priestesses to read their decree. When it was given to him, he refused to share it. Instead, he insisted that I be brought to him." Morgen dabbed her nose on the kerchief and continued.

"Merlin told me that my prophecy was dire. Potentially disastrous to all that he had done to orchestrate Arthur's reign and rule—he said he knew how to avert it, though, that if I would love him, all would be well. He lay with me immediately; gods, I was so young. I said I loved him, of course I did."

"Oh, Morgen," I said, remembering well the horrors of my marital conjugation with Lot. I had said things to him then, in the dark, that were just the opposite of what I felt, hoping that with a profession of love I would feel less pain.

"But he never told me what it was, what my prophecy was; at least you, Anna, know yours. I know it is a burden to you," she said, grasping my hands tight. "But at least it is no mystery. Mine came so late, and it hung about my neck."

Morgen drew a long breath. "Merlin began to tire of me when I passed my prime. He said that the danger of the prophecy was passed and did not seem to worry after me so much. He began inviting other women to his chambers at night, and at first, I was angry—furious. Jealous, of course, because even then, I thought I loved Merlin. My love blinded me to his machinations, and by the time I realized my plight he cast me out. I could not know for certain that all his decisions, his interpretations, had brought us suffering."

Love, such a strange conviction. I had no idea Morgen was so affected by it. While in Merlin's clutches she always seemed distant, so unfeeling. I was beginning to see why.

"Oh, Anna. You are the sister I can trust with this; Margawse suspects but does not know the entire truth. Will you promise to say nothing if I speak this to you? I feel it growing inside of me, choking me every day, and now with Gweyn—"

"Any secret you entrust to me I will keep safe," I said, gentle as I could. Part of me wanted to smile. It appeared that my plan was going quite well; another piece of the game against Merlin. A bargaining chip, if necessary.

I could not fathom the magnitude of that chip until Morgen spoke it.

"It happened so quickly," she said, taking her hands from mine, and drawing them down the side of her face. In that moment she looked older than I had ever seen her, but slowly, slowly, a kind of light began to kindle in her eyes.

"I do not know why my steps led me there; it was as if they were guided by an invisible hand. I slipped into his chamber, and he was alone, poring over his books, weeping about something, someone. I was so angry at Merlin, so desperate for the love of another. He kept saying, 'Lance...' Over and over, his shoulders shaking, crying until he could speak no more."

She had not said his name, but I knew she was talking about Arthur. I could see the scene unfurl in my mind;

Arthur's chambers, the low burning fire; the bed, draped in crimson and gold silks; the lines of armor on the wall. And my brother, bent over, crying like a child.

"At first, I only held him. We both wept, though with sorrow neither of us could share why. But then… oh Anna, I cannot explain it to even myself—"

"Go on," I said, my lips trembling with the words. My heart thudded in my ears as she spoke, my breath shallow.

Morgen swallowed, holding out her hands, finger splayed, as if she were holding someone between her hands. "I took him by the cheeks, stroked his face, wiped his tears. Then he looked at me, and the way his eyes caught the light, the way he saw me then. I want to say I had no choice, to blame the Fates, but I cannot. Not entirely. In that moment, we wanted each other—wanted what was never allowed, forbidden…

"And we took it. That night we took it."

She stopped crying, and put her hands down, looking straight at me. "Anna. Llachlyn is Arthur's daughter."

At first, I had no words. I rose from my chair and paced the room, then stood by the fire, looking into it. How long I stood in that dark silence, I know not.

That Morgen was our half-sister made the deed no less grievous.

"And Gweyn; how is it that her health is brought into this?" I asked, without turning around. I heard the rustle of fabric as Morgen relaxed a bit.

"Arthur was wounded during the war," she said, her voice deeper than it had been moments ago. "That pain of knowing brought Gweyn a clarity of prophecy. She claims it is from her Christ, but I know what she was. It was the

Eye. She saw her child. On Avillion. Her true child… and she saw the words of my prophecy written. *The first born of Arthur will bring his end.*"

I hadn't seen Gweyn; hadn't asked after her. I was adrift in my sorrow so long, all else was obliterated. I realized, then, my pain was a whisper compared to hers.

"I don't understand," I said. "The first born still lives. Amhar. He will come to court at some point and—"

"No. No, don't you see? Amhar wasn't Arthur's. Neither child was. She hoped it would go unnoticed, but she… she planned deeper than all of us. And Merlin did not suspect. Now, knowing she has given her life to raising a foundling, it broke something in her. She speaks only of meeting Christ, now. Refusing food. Refusing water," said Morgen. "And Arthur is already drawing up a contract to marry Mawra in the case that she does; oh, Anna, it is a horror to see how he looks upon her now. I saw the way he looked at her when she first came to court—he worshiped her."

"So Gweyn will die," I said.

"Yes. Within the passing of the next few days. The illness may have been exacerbated by her sorrow. She is too ashamed to speak of it, and it has destroyed her."

I turned to Morgen, my back to the fire, and watched her a moment.

"What has happened to us at the hands of that cruel man," I said.

"Anna, do not you see? It is far worse."

I dare near swooned at the words. "Worse?"

"The prophecy that Merlin gave regarding Arthur's child, regarding Amhar and Mordred. *The first born of Arthur.*"

"Llachlyn."

"Anna, Merlin has ever directed my steps and now, I am alone and powerless. What am I do to?" I had never seen her so distraught.

"I must speak with you of my plans, dear sister." I smiled, leaning forward to touch her arm. She flinched, then relaxed.

"Plans?"

"It seems we are all victims of our prophecies; but I am learning to find the blessing in that. Come. Let me show you something. Our aunt is a blacksmith, it is true. But she does not forge magic swords; she forges magic weapons."

# CHAPTER ELEVEN

## NIMUE

I EXPLAINED WHAT I knew, starting with my heartbreak at having been married to Lot instead of Bedevere. I progressed past every marker, indicating how Merlin seemed to loom along the way, guiding the pieces where he wanted them.

"So Gawain still sits at Arthur's side, Lot's promise fulfilled," I said, with a sigh, passing my hands over the book a little self-consciously. Morgen had not said much, and I had never been so frank. With anyone. "But, yes, Bedevere is the twins' father."

Morgen looked at me, her eyebrows up. "I do not think I have had chance to see them. Do they favor you or he?"

"I do not know. They certainly looked enough like Gawain to prevent any inquiries; either that, or Lot just did not notice. What difference would it have made? I gave Arthur that crown long ago, which was likely all he wanted."

I sighed. "I thought my sorrows would be over, coming here. But all I have found is more of Merlin's disruption and dissent. After the incident with Amhar and Mordred…"

"That is why you wanted to see Vyvian," said Morgen, smiling, as if she were a little proud of my orchestration. The grin looked so much like Mother's.

"I reasoned, if anyone in the world hated Merlin as much as me, it was Vyvian. But she seemed happy, and warned me that revenge would be difficult, and would take a long time. I waited. I have been waiting, for the right time. But after Galahad, and what happened with you… I can keep still no longer. Merlin's meddling has carved a hole in my chest, and I cannot abide by it any longer. How is it that he goes so unquestioned? He deserves judgement."

"And after that?"

"I will choose," I said simply.

Morgen exhaled, pulling her shawl around her shoulders. Her eyes became unfocused, as if she were shifting through unseen memories. "Merlin is just a man, but… not entirely just a man. It is difficult for me to explain, Anna, since you have not grown up around such things. You are treading on a dangerous path, little sister. I will help you in what ways I can—but there are some things I cannot do."

We agreed to meet again in three days' time, and she wanted to hear more of the book, and what I planned to do; I had not yet told her about Nimue. She had pressing matters to attend to, and until Gweyn was healed, she would not be free. Chances were, even after that she would not be free. Morgen struck me, for the first time, as a woman with great conscience. Something she likely inherited from her father, since I remembered none of it in my mother.

That night, however, Morgen woke me in my chambers. Her voice was soft: "If you have words you'd like to say, she is conscious for now."

We made our way through Carelon toward the Queen's chambers. The moon was full outside, casting silvery shadows through the narrow windows and doorways as we walked, side by side. Both of us pulled our own shadows, without a word, and moved like ghosts together, silent and full of dread.

I tried to recall the last time I had seen Gweyn. From a distance, perhaps. With her sisters. Laughing. I felt what, betrayed? A silly feeling. I now recognized it as jealousy. She displayed such an easy comfort with her sisters, those famed daughters of Leodegraunce, and my relationship with my own was so fraught. I avoided them for they made me sad, sad to miss a piece of joy only known through such sisterhood. Foolishness. Gweyn would have loved me as a sister; I only kept her at a distance.

When we entered her rooms, the smell of sick pervaded all. I knew that scent and understood what it meant. A black-robed Christian priest snored near Gweyn's bed and I did not need to ask if Morgen had prepared him a draught.

Gone was the splendor of Gweynevere. Gone was the luster of her hair. Gone was the fullness of her cheek, the sweetness of her lips.

Yet when she opened her eyes, they saw me.

"Anna," she breathed.

"Gweyn…" I could not manage more than that.

Gweyn licked her dry, thin lips, and Morgen gave her a sip of water. We watched as the Queen painfully swallowed. Finally she said, "I thought we would have more time, you and me. I thought we would become old maids together. Raise our sons together. I am so sorry I could not stop him."

"Do not strain yourself, my Queen," I said, taking her

frail hand. "I regret nothing, save that I did not spend more time with you."

"I dream he is in here with me," the Queen continued, as if I had not spoken. "Standing like a vulture, waiting for me to die. He told me when we married—he told me I would die. He told me I would never carry a child of Arthur's." She winced. "My Eye showed me the truth before it went dark, before Christ delivered me from that dark burden."

Morgen and I exchanged glances. She said softly, "She has been speaking like this all evening. It is why I wanted you here."

Gweyn squeezed my hand gently. "But I have seen you, sister. And I have heard your name in the halls when they think I am not listening. They still pull at the strings of Fate, straining and stretching the fibers… but they do not know what we have done."

The Queen gasped, and for a moment I was certain the end was nigh. A pair of moths flitted in the moonlight by the window, ghostly white wings like little apparitions in a dance of death.

"Shh, sister," I said, tasting my own tears. "You have burned so bright."

"The vulture and the eagle, they do not see. While they pull at the threads of Fate, together we have woven a great loom, dyed in our blood and the blood of our children." Gweyn's gaze slid to mine. "But no more. You will judge, Anna Pendragon. You will know the time and the hour."

Gweyn shuddered, her head turning to the side. Morgen reached down to smooth back her hair and dry the sweat clinging to the Queen's once fair brow.

"Gweyn, I am sorry," I said.

A faint smile crossed her lips, and Gweyn's gaze met mine. She saw me, saw through me, saw into me. "I forgave you the moment I met you. I knew what would come to be. You were my sister then, my sister now. I pray you reach heaven, for you will exact judgement on earth as our Lord has anointed you."

And she fell into a deep sleep, the moths at the window now a cloud of gamboling spirits awaiting her end.

I HEARD THE bells ring at the temple the next morning, and knew the Queen was dead. They had rung the same melody with my mother's passing. I stood, staunching the blood from the wound at my arm, and went to the window. Winter still weighed heavily on the world, the landscape frosted and brown. The sky was slate gray, with low hanging clouds in the east. I tried to recognize a hint of spring—a sprig of green grass, a crocus, the blush of buds on the tress—but I saw naught but death and desolation.

ONCE GWEYN WAS dead, her part of the tale was over. The other daughters of Leodegraunce soon rose to the top of court, and though I had expected Hwyfar to object regarding Arthur's decision to marry Mawra, she did not.

With Gweyn's departure, Carelon lost its joy. It became a harder place. Slowly, many of her garish additions were removed, first one at a time, and then entire wings were changed for Mawra's more subdued style.

At the time I couldn't fathom why Hwyfar had ever warned us against Mawra; from the very beginning, the day after her marriage to Arthur, she seemed a shining example of Queenhood. Mawra shone, having the delicacy of Gweyn and the fierce red hair and complexion of Hwyfar. She was shrewd and insisted on being involved in nearly every part of the castle goings on. She wanted to change the way the servants were dispatched, and suggested renovating part of the north wing to accommodate the growing number of children of royal descent. Mawra wanted to excavate part of the cemetery to make room for more of the recently fallen and expand the crypts; she wanted to open trade with Avillion and expand our agreement with Eire. And she wanted Arthur to officially recognize the Christians at court, in honor of Gweyn.

Mawra was a much better match for Arthur. She grounded him, she drilled him, she pushed him, much in the way that Bedevere did, except with more force. Unlike Gweyn, Mawra did not coddle my brother. He suffered Gweyn for her beauty, but he feared Mawra for her wrath and her cleverness. Bedevere always had good ideas, but never outright said them; the effectiveness of his influence on Arthur had to do with the phrasing of his ideas. He always orchestrated it in such a way as to make Arthur believe he had come up with the idea himself. Mawra, from what I heard on occasion from Cai, was absolutely forthright. She pressed Arthur to make better decisions, to ponder from a philosophical point of view.

The more I heard about Mawra, the more I wanted to get to know her.

Most days, Lance and I lived in our separate worlds. I do not blame the man; there was little left between us that hadn't been either ruined by ourselves, or by Merlin's foretelling. We made an uncomfortable truce, but a truce it was. Divorce did not behoove either of us, and I hoped he had moved on past his gallant misgivings of infidelity and found someone to make him happy. Though Bedevere had sought audience with me a half dozen times since Galahad's birth, I only encountered him at funerals and the few festivals I attended, and always then at a distance. I became a faded member of the extended household and did not miss a life of pageantry, banquets, and tournaments.

One strange night, after walking the orchid garden, I found Lance in our quarters, waiting for me.

"Anna," he said, coming up behind me, taking my arm gently. I was with Fauna, and I dismissed her while I had an excuse to extricate myself from his touch.

"I did not expect to see you, Lance," I said, going to the chair by the fire in our common room. He was so frequently absent I felt a little off put by his presence.

But that was nonsense. I was moody and melancholy, having felt that way much since Gweyn's death.

"I am just seeing after you," he said, going to stand by the fireplace. In silhouette I could see how defined his muscles still were; he was clearly taking care of himself, in spite of the lack of tournaments or actual war. It struck me as strange to think that he had once been undefeated, and now was relegated mostly to the causes of state and the whims of Arthur.

I gave him what smile I could, which was marginal. "I am well as I can be," I replied.

"You seemed quite distraught at Gweyn's funeral. I have been worried."

In any other man such a statement would have sounded disingenuous, but not with Lance. No matter the wounds between us, all the barbs and bruises that weighed us down, he cared. It would have been so much easier if he were able to be as distant as I.

"She was a good woman. And a friend," I said. "I had little time to tell her how I admired her; but such is the way of death. It is rarely convenient to those of us who live." I brushed my hair back from my face, undoing some of the braids Fauna placed so meticulously. "But Arthur seems to be happy enough with Mawra."

"He grieves for Gweyn, still," Lance said, turning toward the fire. For one strange moment I recalled the first night after our wedding, in this very room, and him bathed in the light of the flickering flames—I actually pined for it. Part of me would always desire and pity him. The feelings of both so strangely intertwined that I could never tell where one began and the other ended. "But I think he struggles, too. Mawra brought him unexpected happiness. I do not think that he and Gweyn had the smoothest of years, especially since Mordred was born."

"And how is the boy?" I asked.

"He is quite attached to Mawra and Margawse. He has taken to playing with Llachlyn quite a bit—Arthur finds great joy watching them play together."

"That is wonderful," I said, with every attempt at sincerity. "I have not had occasion to speak to Arthur much; I think he forgets I haunt this wing."

"Anna, that is morbid. He loves you. He only wants to ensure you are given space as needed. You've been through trials of late that would break a weaker soul," Lance said, as kind as ever. I could see his face pinch with pain for me.

"And you?" I asked. "How fares your happiness?"

He linked his hands behind his back and leaned forward a bit on the balls of his feet. Then said with a smile, "I think I have found a bit of love, at least. Something to last a little while."

"Good," I said.

I had ordered him to find love, but I suppose I harbored a strange delusion that he might never find it, that I would be the love of his life. His admission still stung.

"You deserve happiness, Lance," I said, kissing his forehead. "Good night. May you find peace in your dreams."

Before he could reply, I left for my room.

I sat on my bed and felt a surprising weight gone from my shoulders. Time was moving, and Nimue awaited. I let the last lingering hope tethering me to Lanceloch du Lac flit away, like a salmon freed from the line.


GATHERING ANETTE'S BONES was just the beginning; the rituals were long and complicated, and keeping up appearances at court was still important for me, though I felt no desire to outside of necessity. Morgen was an essential reason for any success I had, and though she was hesitant to give me any direct advice in the way of the rituals, she always knew where to find components. We spoke little, but when we did, she was eager to know about progress.

Morgen also helped me with the problem of being in two places at once. Not only could she pull shadows, but, as she had once done, she could project them as well. She learned, with practice, to project a vision of me. The specter would not be able to interact with anyone but could be easily seen and controlled; all she needed were a few locks of hair, some blood, and a personal possession of mine; I gave her the unicorn statue.

As for *who* Nimue would be, that was a bit more complicated. She had to be credentialed, but not royal. I decided to announce her arrival as a distant cousin on Lot's maternal side; his mother came from an extremely large family, but of whom most were dead, or illiterate. She would be my new lady in waiting, and everything—eventually—would go through her to get to me. With Morgen's assistance, my melancholy and illness would appear to worsen over the course of the year.

It was three years to the day of Gweyn's death when my plan finally came to fruition. Oh, there were goings on at court, of course; births and deaths, marriages and annulments. But I spent the majority of those years studying, painfully working through the incantations, applying salves to my wounds, and doing rituals to combine the proper implements and components for the final draught. There was no space for mistakes. Morgen was my guide, my helper. She spent her time cataloguing Merlin's movements, drawing intricate maps of his tower and spell books, and making excuses for me whenever possible among family and the court.

There were a handful of limitations when it came to the use of the potion. The first batch would last only a year, so my time was finite. The book also mentioned that it was occasionally erratic and may exhibit a cumulative effect; it would not wear off as quickly even if I took the same dose over a long period of time. I had enough components to make another draught if necessary, but it would likely take another few years to accomplish again, and there was no guarantee the final product would be the same.

Still, it was better than nothing. Considerably better. I found a deep well of patience inside myself I had not known existed. Vyvian lived alone on an island for decades; I could spend a few years to gain the knowledge we all deserved.

I had gone over the words a thousand times, but I was still nervous. It was a new moon, and the castle was abuzz with the arrival of King Uriens and his entourage, as well as news of a new and rather astonishing knight who refused to reveal his parentage, name, or face. Ah, those were such days.

But I wanted none of it.

The last step of the ritual was the combination of dry ingredients with a mixture of wine, blood, and saltwater. I traveled with Bedevere all the way to the marshes for that, and once I combined it with the other two liquids, the stench was nearly intolerable.

As I sifted the sand and bone and ash, the result of countless rituals themselves, into the goblet and stirred, I reminded myself to breathe. The book warned about the taste, the smell, and the resulting pain. But if I did not take heed, the final product—Nimue—would not be as persuading as she ought to be.

So, I mixed, and I spoke words of a language I had no right to know. Then, I poured, into a small, green-glass cup, and brought it to my lips, hesitating only half a heartbeat before swallowing. It tasted simply sour at first, a bit like bile, but the flavor changed as it made its way down my throat, giving way to bitter, to sweet, to cloyingly sweet; it was one moment like fire, another like refreshing cold water.

Then the burning began. I doubled over as it seared down my throat into my stomach, sending tendrils of cramping down into my womb, and further down my legs. My arms went slack, and I tried to fight against it, but it was quite overwhelming for the first few minutes; I did not cry out, I only gritted my teeth.

I had to master this rising tide of power; according to the book, it was up to me to shape my body, and I needed a clear view of Nimue to do that. If I concentrated on the pain, I would never make her convincing. The potion could only do so much.

Swallowing back the bile that threatened to rise, I stood in the middle of my room, and stared at the single candle burning by the bed. My skin felt as if someone had placed coals on every inch of it, and I could no longer bear the pressure of clothing. So, carefully, I stripped myself of my gown and my undergarments. It was winter, but I felt no chill. I began to run my hands over my body, cringing at the pain. It was torture. Every hair, every imperfection on my skin was like a searing, open wound; the palms of my hands carved rough routes across my thighs, my stomach, my cheeks.

I couldn't let the pain overwhelm me. I wanted to. Part of me was frightened, terrified that I had made the wrong choice. The more I ran my hands across my body, the more the pain intensified. I began to cry.

And then, when I thought the pain would consume me outright, it broke. My body was infused with a sudden flush of excitement, and my mind awash with clarity. "Nimue," I whispered, and saw her again as I had before, only in my mind.

Now, I traced the lines I saw with my hands, pressing and pulling at my flesh. I started with my face, remembering the details—the eyes, the nose, everything reacted like clay beneath my fingers. I moved to my arms, my stomach and spine, shortening my body, feeling my bones settle and sink. I needed more flesh, so I drew my hands over my breasts and nipples, willing them to fill out, as well as my belly, my buttocks, my thighs. Nimue was earth, and I was afire.

## ~ *Nimue* ~

NIMUE OPENED HER eyes and felt the pressure of rushes at her cheek. She turned her head, squinting through a curtain of tangled hair, palms pressed to the ground. Her shoulders ached, as if she had carried a burden many miles, and she was possessed of a pressing hunger.

But to get food, she would have to stand.

Still shivering, she rose to her knees, then sat back on her heels, surveying the room. It was a strange, familiar place: mistress's room. It was cold. Confused, Nimue looked down at her body and began to laugh.

She was naked.

Stretching out her arms, she reveled in the softness of her skin, the suppleness of her flesh. She ran her hands over her breasts, sweeping the nipples, then pressed her fingers down over her stomach, her pubis, her thighs.

Soon, she needed the comfort of another. This new body ached with wanting.

*Soon, soon*, said her mistress, her voice as soothing as mother's milk. *First, dress. I have left a perfect piece for you.*

A dress hung over the side of the bed, silvered silk with interlace about the neck, and Nimue went to it, slipping the delicate material between her hands. Her mistress had been kind to provide such a remarkable dress.

Nimue pulled the dress overhead, shimmying as it fell down over her body. With a few, swift motions, she tied the laces impressively tight to better accentuate the curve of her hips, the swell of her breasts. The feel of the fabric against her skin reminded her again she so desired a sweet mouth to devour in the act of love.

*You're lovely. Not too lovely, just lovely enough. Different enough. You've an earthiness that will do you well; your face will be remembered at court.*

*But first. Something red, I think, to complement the hue and tone of your skin, my dear. I never liked the necklace much, as it did nothing for my complexion. But it was a gift by my departed husband. It is in the third tier in my jewelry cabinet, just to the left of my dresser. You can take it.*

Nimue found the necklace quickly and tied it about her neck, noting just how well it complimented her features for a moment in the copper mirror.

Ah, but she was hungry.

*Go to the parlor; I had Fauna bring you some food.*

Yes, there: a delightful spread with honeyed toast, buttery cheese, and enough wine for two. She ate it all, indelicately, brushing the crumbs from her chest and sucking the honey from her fingers.

*Feels so much better, doesn't it?*

Such exertion required a moment's rest, and Nimue tiptoed to one of the larger chairs, the one likely reserved for the mistress's husband, and slipped comfortably into it, wriggling her bare toes into the carpet, giggling as the coarse wool fibers tickled the soles of her feet.

Then she began to laugh, and her mistress laughed with her.

It was so good to be alive.

*It will not be difficult to find Hwyfar, and she is the first on our list. She will adore you; let her in, but not too much. She is a work in progress.*

*There, do you hear it?*

There was music and laughter coming from her left, and Nimue felt drawn to it; she liked finding it rather than relying on the directions the mistress had given her.

A constant stream of circus folk and curious priests made their way in and out as Nimue navigated toward Hwyfar's room. She had to step over three cats to get to the main door, and another bolted across her feet when she was greeted by one of Hwyfar's servants.

*It is hard to believe, I know, but the first time I visited Hwyfar, it was even more chaotic than this.*

Peering into the room as the servant ushered Nimue in; she had to draw a breath in to see the place, such a marvelous sight it was. The colors, the silks; it was very like a dream almost remembered.

*Ah, there she is.*

Sitting across the room on a long, plush chair, a perched white peacock eating from her hand, was Hwyfar.

"The lady Nimue," said the priest, in announcement. "Lady Du Lac's servant."

When Hwyfar looked up, it was under her long lashes, as languorous as a lioness. Her clothing did precious little to cover her strong, lithe body, which moved just beneath the flowing material. It was the middle of winter and yet Hwyfar wore no shoes, and as she brought her feet to the floor, an anklet around one tinkled gently.

"Goodness, come in dear," she said, gesturing to the vacant spot beside her.

*You feel that? She has got a power in her, Hwyfar. But do not let her pull you in too close. Not yet.*

Nimue felt her knees go weak. Incense wafted about the room, both holy and profane, mingling in an enticing aroma that clouded her thoughts, pushing her mistress's voice to a whisper in the back of her mind. As she sat down on the springy sofa, Nimue's heart beat faster; Hwyfar smelled of jasmine and musk and a tumble of red hair corkscrewed down between the woman's white shoulders, bouncing as she tossed her head.

The mistress had been adamant: to get to Merlin, Nimue must get to Hwyfar. She must know everything that went on in Carelon, and Hwyfar kept secrets not even Morgen knew. Nimue was happy to oblige, glad of the challenge.

"So this is the lady Nimue who we have heard so much about," Hwyfar said, reaching out to brush her hand across Nimue's cheek.

*Yes, I did my best to herald your arrival…*

Nimue smiled; her body responded with heat, heat everywhere, but she stayed composed. It was restraint amidst the passion that would make succumbing so sweet. "Good evening, Lady Hwyfar," she said, liking the sound of her voice. Hushed, almost, but with a strength to it. "I am here on behalf of my mistress, to deliver a message, if you will have it."

*Hwyfar only desires those things which are out her grasp. Do not let yourself fall too quickly into her snare, or else she will tire of you and throw you to the wolves.*

Hwyfar's smile wavered as Nimue handed her the rolled-up piece of parchment. It was a list of silks and laces, attainable only from Avillion, that her mistress had drawn up weeks before, to be used for Mawra's Midsummer dress.

Hwyfar continued to read and nodded. "All simple enough. It might take a few days for me to gather everything, but it will be done, of course. And you can let your mistress know that I will be happy to aid her in any other way she requires; the dress is for my sister, after all," she said running her hands through her curls, white fingers emerging suddenly from the red waves. "Can I get you something to drink, little one?" she asked, tilting her head toward Nimue.

"I have just dined," she replied.

*Very good… yes, quite.*

"You are comely for an Orkney raised lass," said Hwyfar, tilting her head to get a better look at Nimue's face. Nimue felt the woman's eyes tracing the lines of her face, and it kindled her desire ever further.

"As are you, Lady Hwyfar," Nimue replied. To her surprise, Hwyfar grinned brilliantly in response, red lips spreading over her teeth.

*Compliment her, Nimue. She is ripe for it.*

Nimue continued, leaning forward ever so slightly, first batting her lashes and then directing her dark eyes skyward to the resplendent Hwyfar. "I am but an Orkney girl, raised among the rock and salt; but you—your eyes are like to still the hearts of all who see them. It is a wonder you have yet to marry, I say, but my mistress says you simply live for the pleasure of life."

Hwyfar grinned, settled a little in her chair, then reached out, tracing her fingers along Nimue's shoulder, "Such a wonder. I have only just seen the Orkney boys for the first time today, and I say you bear little resemblance to them."

*Yes. The boys. Ask her about my sons.*

"You've seen all of Lady Anna's sons?" Nimue asked, placing her hand demurely on her thigh, but in such a way as to brush Hwyfar's as well.

"Yes, of course. Just arrived this afternoon with a rather remarkable caravan. They certainly do not favor the Pendragon side," she said, smiling wolfishly. "Curious. I had never met Lot, but I heard he was a diminutive man. These boys are quite large, Gareth even taller than Gawain, with dark hair and eyes. Quite marvelous. At a scarce sixteen years they're the talk of the castle. You ought to have a look for yourself."

"I ought to," Nimue replied. "I have been so busy attending to my lady that I have failed to find where they're staying."

"With Gawain, of course," Hwyfar replied casually, flicking a feather from her shoulder. It swooped up and fell softly to the pillows. "He will be quite possessive of them, now that they're here, I am sure."

*Trying to sway them from me, I suppose. He has been so remote, so dark.*

Hwyfar's hand now found its way to the crook of Nimue's neck, fingers twirling around the strand of hair there. Nimue felt the response in her body, and it was powerful, like an unexpected tide.

*Perhaps you shouldn't have had so much wine.*

"I am sure you have things to do," Hwyfar said, leaning even closer. "But when you find yourself with time, you may always come see me. I have a feeling," she said, so close, Nimue felt the brush of her lips on hers, "we will become quite good friends, little Nimue."

*It is time to leave... Nimue.*

*... Nimue. Now.*

Grasping the cushion, and pulling herself back, Nimue rose and smiled. "Indeed," she replied, standing on shaky legs. "I will return again—to arrange further for the Queen's dress. And for more conversation."

"Wonderful," said Hwyfar, reclining back on the sofa, and picking up her reading. She grinned over the pages at Nimue, and then went back to her task.

GAWAIN HAS BEEN *given a rather impressive accommodation in the castle, mostly due to his heroics during the border wars three years ago. I have seen him on occasion over the last few years, but he has been, in most ways, entirely distant. When we are not yelling at one another, we are silent. I suppose I should learn to accept that which I have rather than pining for that which is lost.*

Nimue ran her fingers over the letters intended for Gawain. Her mistress had described her boys, unfathomably large in comparison to Nimue. Yet she did not fear them.

Still, Nimue could not help but startle at the figure that greeted her at the door, the young Gaheris, she surmised, or else some gigantic hero of old. Not only was he large, he was remarkably handsome to Nimue's eyes. He looked like a bolder version of Arthur, stronger and broader across the arms and chest, with dark hair instead of auburn. And when he smiled...

*Yes, he is remarkable, is he not? A far cry from the scrawny lad I left to Luw. But no. Do not even think on it, Nimue. You may have all others, if you desire, but not this one.*

"I bring word from the Lady Anna du Lac," Nimue said, half tripping on a curtsey.

His face was remarkable, the strong Pendragon brow combined with Bedevere's soft lips and large eyes, her mistress said; his father's presence was not overwhelming, but Nimue thought it improved significantly on the matter. His body was corded with muscle, yet he stood lightly, with the with the grace of a dancer—like Lanceloch once did.

"That must be the new maid," Nimue heard a deeper, slightly slurred voice say from inside. "Bring her in, Gaheris. Might as well."

*That is Gawain. And he sounds drunk. Steel yourself, Nimue.*

Gaheris gave an embarrassed smiled, ushering her in. Though Gawain's quarters were sparse as a soldier's, and a complete contrast to Hwyfar's bedecked palace, there were pieces of furniture here and there that spoke of taste. A shield here, a helmet there; on the wall a drooping, faded tapestry.

*I think he has lost his pride. Or else it is been slowly eroded away... I am not blameless, but there is a point where a man walks his own path and can no longer hold others accountable for his mistakes.*

Gawain stood by the window, a clay goblet in one hand and a corked bottle in the other. Gods, but he was a sight.

His hair was red as blood, his green eyes in stark contrast. Just like holly berries and leaves. He was handsome to look upon, though not as delicately wrought as his brother Gaheris, in a powerful, passionate way.

When he saw Nimue, his eyes darkened.

"I hear tell you're from Orkney," he said, as if it were the least interesting bit of information he had ever heard in his life. "Gaheris and I will have little in the way of the place to share with you; I suppose you were too young for me to notice, and too old for him."

*I hope he doesn't mean for that to sound as lewd as it does.*

"Begging your pardons, Sirs," Nimue said, producing the roll of paper and handing it to Gawain. He rolled his eyes, and then indicated with a flick of his neck that Gaheris was to take it.

"So you're a cousin?" asked Gaheris, sweet and gentle again, clearly trying to make up for his brother's transgressions of hospitality. He smiled at her with something like relief.

*Careful, Nimue. I have not had many occasions to be around Gawain when he is drunk; but I knew his father enough to suspect it is not something you want to suffer alone.*

"Distant," Nimue said, folding her hands together, and leaning forward on the balls of her feet. She knew the words well and recited them by rote. "On your father's mother's side. A second cousin—but still. I am very thankful to have been brought here."

"Strange. I did not see you come in," growled Gawain, placing the bottle down on one of his square, unattractive tables and taking a somewhat misguided step toward Nimue. He needed no help but righted himself rather inelegantly. "Strange, that."

"I came in the fall," Nimue said, continuing to grin. She would not be intimidated by an Orkney drunk. "I stayed with a cousin of my mother's, not far from here. When the Lady Anna was ready for me, I simply took a carriage in from town. It is easy to go unnoticed; Carelon is quite a grand place, in every sense of the word."

Gaheris's features spread in a delighted grin. "You are quite right on that account! It is a magnificent place," agreed Gaheris. "I am still getting quite lost—why, just yesterday, I found myself completely turned around. Thankfully, Sir Bedevere helped me—"

*Bedevere.*

"Bedevere?" Nimue said, interrupting him awkwardly. Both sons stared at Nimue for the impertinence. "I, I mean *Sir* Bedevere. I am still learning... but I have heard so much of Sir Bedevere, of his heroics on the field and his exploits."

"Not nearly so many as Lanceloch—" started Gaheris, who then turned rather white, and stopped. He cleared his throat.

Nimue helped finish the sentence, stepping between he and Gawain. "Oh, Sir Lanceloch is no war hero like your brother Gawain," she said, falling into another curtsey. "He is now a warrior of the state, so says the Lady Anna."

*Good! Smart girl. Stray always from the subject of Lanceloch, if at all possible.*

"And we always listen to the Lady Anna," said Gawain, diffused for the moment. He snarled, snatching the letter from Gaheris with his scarred hand.

*You see that scar? I was told he received it on his last campaign, and that it was Palomydes who had prevented the deathblow intended afterward. And do you know what he did in repayment? He challenged Palomydes to a duel for interfering with the will of the gods. What a foolish boor he has become. Gods, Nimue, but he is only twenty-four...*

"So, Mother wants everything to go through you," Gawain said, taking a deep draught of the liquor he held in hand. He wiped at his mouth, managing to refrain from spilling. "How charming of her. She commands, we obey."

"The Lady Anna is not well," Nimue said gently. It was important they believed it.

Gaheris looked concerned, hurt, but Gawain's eyes were hard and lifeless as green marbles. "No surprise there," he said. "Such is what happens when you breed with buggerers."

"Gawain, perhaps you've had enough—"

"No—not nearly enough," Gawain said, pressing closer to Nimue. He towered over her, smelling of vomit and sweat, as if he had been sick in his clothes yet not changed. She wanted to weep for him, for she could see the pain written in the lines of his face.

The mistress was quiet; waiting, watching.

Nimue flinched when he grabbed her cheek with his rough hands, squeezing her chin and face. He could snap her neck, there was no doubt.

"Sir Gawain—" she tried to say, and saw Gaheris at the corner of her eye, saw him stiffen and shake his head.

"Tell Mother," Gawain said, his words cool and clipped, "that if she sends you back in here, she will be nursing a grandchild within the year." He widened his eyes, leering, the whites a mad swirl of red veins.

Nimue stumbled back, right into Gaheris. She gave him a frightened look, pleading internally for the mistress to help her, but the response was still silence.

She stopped, breathless, in the hallway, only to hear the door creak open and Gaheris emerge.

"Nimue—I am so sorry," he said, his eyebrows pinched.

*How like Bedevere he looks.*

"No, no," said Nimue, forcing a smile, smoothing the front of her dress. "I grew up in Orkney—I know what liquor can do to a man. I will come back when Sir Gawain is more agreeable."

"It is not—it is not just that," said Gaheris, leaning on the stone wall, watching Nimue in the flickering torchlight. Ah, there was longing in his eyes, and Nimue felt the pull of it as surely as insects meandering toward the flame. "I am afraid he and Gareth had a falling out—you might want to tell Mother if you see her. And Gareth's gone! No one knows where to, and we are to be presented at court tomorrow for all to see. Arthur's furious, and Gawain blames himself, and he is certain that Mother will have his head to it."

*Brothers by blood and bone.*

"What happened?" asked Nimue, reaching out to touch Gaheris's shoulder.

"It was such a nightmare. They resorted to blows and…"

"Blows? But you've scarcely seen each other in the last four years. What—" Nimue was beginning to feel a little sick to her stomach. She could feel herself fading, and there was an ache in her lower back that had not been there before.

"Gareth wanted to see Mother," said Gaheris, shaking his head. "And Gawain said some unkind things. Gareth was worried; we'd heard she was not well, and that… Well, you know more than the rest, do you not? Gawain did not even ask, the boor. But how is she?"

*Gods, what a miracle I have in Gaheris. He loves me still.*

Nimue wanted to take him into her arms, to embrace him, to assure him that all was well, flourishing. Instead she said, "She is quite changed since the birth of your brother, Galahad. But she is stronger now than she used to be. Though she prefers the quiet darkness of her room to the constant motion of court."

"I hope to see her soon," said Gaheris. "And when I find Gareth, we will seek her out. In the meantime." He indicated the door and laughed a little bitterly. "I have got an angry bear to tame."

"Take care that you do not bate him," she said, softly. "And I will bring the message to your mother. She will be glad to hear of it."

"Bless you, Nimue," said Gaheris, taking her hands in his, and kissing them.

# CHAPTER TWELVE

## GARETH

*~ Anna ~*

BY THE TIME I returned to my room, I was so winded and in pain that I could scarcely think straight. The book often spoke of pain, and it seemed to me that my life was now made of it. Gareth was missing, Gawain was drunk and despondent, Gaheris was caught between. I thought my transformation into Nimue was done at the right time, but I began to doubt myself. My sons needed me, did they not?

But what good could I do, as their mother? How could I help them, when I could scarcely help myself? No, perhaps Nimue could be their advocate; perhaps there was a way I could exact my revenge and be present for my sons at the same time.

Looking into my mirror, I saw the last glimpses of Nimue's face fade into my own, felt the excruciating lengthening and changing of my body back to its frail self. My skin sagged, my muscles ached. I collapsed on the bed, every vein in my body wrapped in fire, and wept until I fell asleep.

"Anna."

I opened one eye, then the other. It was Morgen, standing over me, her expression stern, concerned.

"Morgen," I said, turning, woozy. I wanted to throw up but refrained from doing so only by virtue of my constitution. "I am sorry. I am a little disoriented."

She placed three pouches of herbs at the table beside my bed, then lit a small candle which sent out a citrus scent immediately; it helped my nausea considerably.

"It will not get easier," she said, frowning so that the line between her eyes deepened. It was dark out, and she had lit a handful of candles, keeping the room bright enough, but just barely. "These herbs will help. As you asked, a few knights and a handful of ladies saw your form walk the hall while you and Nimue visited with Gawain and Hwyfar."

"Thank you," I said. She brought me something to drink and held it to my lips.

"Otherwise... how do you feel?"

"Better than when it wore off; it was quite a horror," I said honestly. "But I slept remarkably well. No dreams at all." I sipped: it was mint tea, tinged with honey, and drinking it did me a world of good.

"Well, that is good at least," she said, then smiled a little. "And your transformation?"

I could not help but smile. "It was marvelous."

"And you are still in control of her?"

"Entirely."

Morgen looked appeased, and she sat down at the edge of the bed, running her hand over my arm, lovingly. Like a proud mother. "I know where Gareth is, by the way."

"You do?" I said. I had not told her what happened, but it was likely the whole castle was abuzz with it by now.

Morgen nodded, laughed a bit. "He is in the kitchens, scrubbing dishes, if you would believe it. A clever disguise, but I saw through him. No pot-scrubbers would ever have shoulders like that!"

I laughed. It felt good, but my lungs were sore, still.

"Well, I have plenty of the draught—"

"Anna."

"You—what?"

Morgen looked very much like Mother, then, her eyes up, her chin pointed down. "You cannot escape into Nimue every time there is confrontation. Especially with your own sons just arrived."

"But—"

"I am sure being possessed of a younger, fresher body is exhilarating—but this is dangerous magic. And you are far from experienced. Take today's success and wait until you require it again. Remember your task." She gestured to the maps and notes we had collected on Merlin's habits, the mounting evidence, and the small portrait of Gweyn.

I thought about Gawain's warning, and knew she was right. Though I could feel Nimue beckoning me back, I would have to wait. She was not my errand-girl.

"Thank you," I said, taking her hand.

"I will not always be here to be your conscience," Morgen warned, holding my hand for but a heartbeat before letting go. "And this will only become more difficult as time progresses; and the closer you are to Merlin, the more challenging to maintain the ruse. So, rest yourself. Keep yourself—remember yourself, above all, Anna Pendragon."

When she said my name, I shivered.

\* \* \*

So, I ACCOUTERED myself for arrival to the kitchens for the first time I recalled, without pulling shadows, with no glamor other than those I was born with. I had ventured there on occasion during my childhood, when Millie worked as head cook and would sneak me bits of bread and cake when no one was looking. There was something devilish about being able to eat dinner before my father, King of All Braetan, did.

I smiled at that thought as I did my hair in the mirror, having told Fauna not to report back to me until much later. I found Haen, however, and ordered him to send word to Sir Bedevere that his presence was required; if he was not available, then I would require Sir Cai as an escort. If neither were free, then I told Haen to use his wits to find me a decent companion to the kitchens. It was so rare that I left my room these days I wanted it to appear that I had taken every precaution in terms of my safety.

To my utter surprise, it was Lance who showed up, tailed by Haen who looked both confused and a little chagrined. It was absolutely the worst choice I could think, owing to Gawain's present perception of his stepfather, and I shot Haen a look that I hoped might wither his testicles. Alas, I was not Morgen, and such abilities were quite beyond me.

"Haen tells me you require escort to the kitchens?" Lance asked. He looked remarkably handsome that evening, dressed in scarlet and white, his heavy velvet cape clasped at his shoulder with a marvelous brooch I recalled giving him some years back. A birthday present, I thought—one that was my father's.

I glared again at Haen.

Lance gave me one of his smiles, these days so rare, and continued: "I overheard him attempting to convince Sir Palomydes, but the poor fellow looked straight out of his head about it. No one has heard from you in weeks, and you're all of the sudden out for a stroll to the kitchens?" It would have sounded condescending from anyone else, but he said it with a glint in his eyes. He knew me better than that.

"It is Gareth," I said, saying my youngest's name with a sinking stomach. He would not be happy to see me. Or perhaps he would. Either way, it was a problem I had not taken into consideration, and as time passed, I was becoming more and more irritated thinking of him scouring pots.

"Gareth—the one just arrived? Already causing trouble?" Lance, who had grown up with brothers, clearly found the situation amusing.

"Yes. Gaheris is with Gawain." I once thought it clever to name all my sons so similarly, but was regretting it as, in my anger, the name differentiation came out almost comically. I also thought, quite suddenly, that Lance had named Galahad—he adhered to my naming convention without consulting me at all. I felt strangely guilty for not noticing it before. "Gareth, as you heard, ran away after he and Gawain, apparently, resorted to pommeling one another like squabbling peasants."

"It was in the middle of the courtyard," added Lance, as if I required the extra elucidation. "It was quite impressive. I do think, with a little more practice, Gareth might have had a fighting chance. His form is remarkable—both the twins, by the look of them, will be taller and stronger than Gawain."

"I am glad they provided you with a moment's amusement, Lance—but truly, I need to find Gareth. He is hiding out in the kitchens, of all places, scrubbing pots. I daresay he thinks he is mighty clever but forgets that his Aunt Morgen has a habit of collecting her herbs there, and she spotted him."

He held out his arm, and I noticed how our clothing clashed. Why had I chosen not to wear my blue gown? It would have made a much more impressive statement, even if it was only a trip to the kitchens.

Gold would have looked particularly nice with his crimson.

It was quite close to the dining hour, and we descended into the kitchens with Haen following behind. The scents of dinner even made my mouth water; I couldn't remember the last time I ventured to the dining hall for a proper meal. Likely one feast or another, of a mandatory sort.

"You look lovely," Lance said, leaning to my ear. I felt my face flush, and turned away, apologizing under my breath.

He grinned, squeezing my arm a little. "You know, it will do you good to get out a bit. You once said so yourself, and you were right about me, then."

I glanced at him, seeing him so close for the first time in a long while. He had been given special quarters upon his return from Benwick, after a rather unsavory and unsuccessful attempt to woo Pellas to the crown, to allow him to work in quiet. As a result, he stayed within our apartment only a few nights out of the week, if at all.

Millie had long since died, but part of me couldn't help looking for her face amidst the crowd of servants as we entered the main pantry and workspace of the kitchens. From the central room there were three others, including the bakery, the butchery, and a room dedicated to the finalized products, the fanciful cakes and dainties that Arthur and Mawra were so fond of.

Upon seeing us, quite a few stopped short, and one man dropped his platter entirely, likely recognizing Sir Lanceloch du Lac on my arm. The clatter garnered attention of those whose had not already been won.

"Where is the head cook?" asked Lance, addressing a sallow-faced woman carrying a breadbasket. She blanched another shade of parchment, and gestured to a tall, lame woman, leaning on a single crutch.

Her name, it turned out, was Laira, and she was unimpressed by our arrival. At first, she acted as if we were mad, then called aside one of the scullery maids, who informed her that, yes, a new pot scrubber was assigned to them earlier that day, but she had no idea where he went.

Once we were led to the right place, it was apparent Gareth was not cleaning pots at the correct station; he would have towered head and shoulders above the rest of the servants had he been, and I would not have required anyone to point him out.

"We called him 'Beaumains'," said the scullery maid, as we began to widen our search.

I could not help but laugh. "Why is that, pray tell?"

Her eyes glinted. She was a pretty thing, and I wondered if Gareth had noticed. "For such a big young man, his hands were so delicate and white." I think she almost blushed as she said it.

We eventually found Gareth assisting one of the cake decorators, standing guard over a toppling cake that rose higher than his head. When he saw me, a flicker of confusion rested there for a moment, then a flush of red, and the resolve of recognition.

When Gareth and Gaheris were younger, when I left them, they were alike as peas, but the years between had changed them. Gareth was not as dark as Gaheris, and not quite as handsome, I did not think. Yet he possessed a gentleness, a softness in his face that was quite endearing to me. His eyes were dark, like Gareth's, although his hair was more auburn. He chose to keep his shorter than Gaheris, yet it was still long enough to be pulled back. Nor was he quite as muscular as Gaheris, but longer of limb—just a bit. I would have to examine the two side-by-side to make a final analysis. Still, I did know, looking at him then, that I produced a remarkable set.

"Mother," he said, his eyes settling on me only a moment before recognizing my husband. "Sir—Sir Lanceloch, sir." He fell to one knee, his hand on his breast, until Lance held him up. For the way the young knights adored my husband it would have stood to reason that he was a saint, or king.

Lance reached down and helped Gareth to his feet, then gestured to me.

Gareth smiled, and came to me.

I embraced him, and he held me, if not a little awkwardly. I had last held him four years before, and he was barely of a height then. "Gareth. Come, let us go somewhere more private. This is scarcely the place to have such a conversation."

"Where are we going?" he asked, looking around as if I were to produce a magic room to retreat into.

"Your brother's room. Lance, while you're here, please join us? You are part of the family, after all. And if this goes well, we can all have dinner with the rest of the court. It will be a lovely reunion."

THE TREK TO the other side of the castle, to Gawain's quarters, was long, and by the end I was weary enough to have to lean on Lance. Gareth continually stole concerned glances my way, but I smiled and pressed on. From the look of him it appeared rumors of my existence had implied I was near death! Ah, well, I was to prove them wrong. If I was to be successful in my business with Nimue, I needed to ensure my family could hold strong—likely without me for a time.

Initially, Gawain refused our entrance. But, seeing as the liquor had subsided significantly from his blood, he relented when I pressed him. As much as he avoided me—a habit he inherited from me, and something I could not fault him for entirely—when under my fire, he reverted to my darling eldest son, who truly only wanted to please me.

When I saw Gaheris, I was able to embrace him as I wanted before. There were tears in his eyes, and to see the look of relief in his expression upon seeing Gareth assured me that their bond was still strong. That was important. Luwddoc had not been a man of means or status, not after I handily dissolved his brother's kingdom with one sweeping gesture, but he was a man of great heart. That was why I consented to their fosterage. I knew in that single look that my decision was well founded.

And, of course, Lanceloch needed no introduction; it was apparent that the twins were as equally awed by his presence as I had thought.

"Mother—about earlier, with Nimue," said Gawain,

coming closer to me, taking my hands. He cupped his enormous pair around mine, his brows pressing together with worry.

"We all have bad days," I said. "She said you were indisposed—and perhaps you had celebrated a little too handily at your brothers' return. I suspect you will apologize to her immediately upon seeing her next?"

He faltered a bit, eyes moving side to side as he processed what I said. "Of course," Gawain said, squeezing my hand in thanks. "She is not with you now?"

I shook my head. "She is a lady in waiting, dear; I have her running errands as she ought. Now... tell me, Gawain, where is the decent furniture?" I asked, gesturing around.

"I, uh," said Gawain, staring at the two chairs in the center of the room and the rickety table between. "I have not gotten to that part yet."

"Three years," I said to him, folding my hands at my chest and shaking my head. "Three years have passed, and the best you can do is assemble, what, old crates?" I clapped and turned to Haen, who had come in with another servant of Lanceloch's. "Haen, bring some chairs. Nice chairs. Red will do—but keep them sturdy, mind you. No flimsy Avillionian affairs."

Gawain frowned, then looked out the murky window.

"As we wait for seats," I said, walking a semi-circle in front of my sons, admiring them though they likely did not know it, "I need to settle some matters with you all. Gareth and Gaheris—I am overjoyed at your return, as is your step-father." Lance nodded, smiling as comfortably as he could

I was not as tired as I had been the night before, but it would not do without a little pity. I gestured Lance over to me. He complied, a little concerned, but I continued speaking anyway, trying to ignore the look of pity in his eyes. Good, they were paying attention.

"I am not well," I said simply. "It is why Nimue is here, why I do not leave my room often. Lanceloch knows this, and he has kept me to my own, allowing me to live my days in peace, as I desire, rather than be bothered with the gossip and stress of the court. You are not women; you cannot understand what it is like…" I wanted to say, *to be forgotten*, but the words caught in my throat. Even my sons forgot me.

"I thought she was a *servant*," said Gawain. Gods, but he was sulking.

"She is a *kinswoman*," I corrected, holding up a finger. "She is my lady in waiting, and my proxy. I trust her to make decisions on my behalf, and to leave me in peace. But that is not to say that I will not be here for my sons, should they need me."

Gareth look relieved, Gaheris a little confused. Gawain just stared.

"Which leads me to the reason I walked all the way down to the kitchens and up to your… quarters," I said, trying to stress to Gawain how important the appearance of his apartment was in the grand scheme of things. I stared at him. "The King would be ashamed—ashamed, I tell you— that you ever lay a hand on your brother, and in public of all places! I am mortified. Gods know I have reached out my hand to you all again and again, only to be brushed aside, but if this is how you conduct yourself at court, I will not hesitate to use what power I have to influence Arthur. Knights do not behave like common peasants, resorting to fisticuffs before half the realm."

I took a deep breath and turned to the twins, who were almost shoulder to shoulder; Gaheris's mouth had gone agape, and I wanted to laugh. Apparently, my little speech actually frightened him.

"You two are on the brink of manhood. Your uncle Luwddoc gave you his food, his drink, his shelter, his attention and expertise so that you would honor him." As I said this, some strange expression flitted across Gareth's face, but was replaced by a steely set of his jaw. I would enquire later. Perhaps as Nimue. "I want to express how important first impressions are at court, and stress that every eye will be on you, judging you all the more because you are Arthur's nephews. It is not fair, I know, but it is the reality of the matter."

"Yes, Mother," said Gaheris, averting his eyes altogether. "I am sorry—I am terribly sorry."

"You have nothing to be sorry about, Gaheris," I said, turning to him and cupping his cheek in my hand. "You were a peacemaker through this. It is most admirable."

"Thank you, Mother," he said, meeker than I would have liked. But he almost smiled.

"From now on, I do not want to hear word of this. If anything happens, I promise you, either Morgen or Nimue will know, and then *I will know*. Can I have your word? All of you?"

They consented, even Gawain. He looked me straight in the eye; he meant it.

"Lance?" I said, beckoning him forward. He did not hesitate as most men would have; I was throwing him to my brood, but as always, he was up for the task.

"It is not my place to lecture you," he said, his voice low, tolerant. He fit his hand over the pommel of his sword, swaying from side to side a bit. He looked to Gawain: "Least of all to you, Gawain. I know there has been little love between us since your mother and I married—but you have to understand, I admire Anna Pendragon a great deal. I have seen what she has given up for the love of her realm, for her King. We would all do well by learning from her example. And if she needs peace and quiet, by gods, we'll give it to her."

"Thank you, Lance," I said, softly. It was a most impressive piece of improvisation.

"Which is why," continued Lance, "I will be taking Gareth as my squire tomorrow, at your knighting. I know, it is a bit of spoiling the surprise, but I want you to know how important it is for me to prove to you—to you all." He addressed Gawain this time. "To prove how much I value the contribution of this family, how much it means to me, as the father of your half-brother, that we remain steadfast as a whole."

I wondered if Lance had any idea what Gawain called him earlier in Nimue's presence. Of course, he couldn't have known. But still, words said in drunkenness cut no less deep, not for me. Gawain was drunk, and testing Nimue.

"I will be taking Gaheris," Gawain said, with something that resembled a grunt.

"You weren't going to tell us?" Gareth asked, still recovering from the shock. Lance had yet to take a squire; it was a remarkable honor. I was just as surprised as he.

"Arthur said we should only reveal it if necessary, that... well, you know, he loves a good surprise," Gawain said, smiling a little. The expression changed him utterly, sloughed a decade of worries off his brow. I wondered if he would ever settle down with a good woman to bed, the same one every night; but even then, I knew him to be a man of inconstancy. It was better that he please a woman every now and again than subject one to his temper and infidelity every day of their married life. I had made the right choice in my counsel to him.

When we finished talking, Lance embraced all the boys. He was scarcely five years older than Gawain, and yet the age between them seemed so much more considerable. Perhaps it was marrying me, or the suffering we'd both gone through, but he had become more of a man than I ever expected him to be. There was softness within him once, in his manner, in his hesitation; but not now. No, he was strength and hardness, tempered now and again with kindness, pity, mercy. I wondered how similar he was to an actual sword, thinking about what Vyvian had said so long ago, how he was Arthur's greatest weapon.

THE NEXT DAY I attended the boys at their knighting, dragged from my depths by a very insistent Lance, who— as unusual as it was those days—actually slept in our apartment. He promised he would let me alone once the excitement died down, but after the speech to the lads, he said, I had to back it up with my support. Chances were, they'd forget in a matter of days, though Lance promised to be there a constant reminder to their oaths.

I had not expected Lance to come to my side so readily, not to mention take Gareth under his wing. It was a brilliant stroke. The boys needed reining in, and Gareth practically worshipped Lance. He and Gaheris possessed the frames, but not the form. Not yet. And Gawain and Lanceloch were the best in the knighting business. With no sign of war, at least for now, I knew I would be able to go about my business in relative peace. Knights, as I knew so well, were kept busy, constantly training and perfecting themselves. It was part of Arthur's hold on the minds and imaginations of the whole realm. To see a knight was to see a shining representative of the great King. Or so he thought.

He had many ideas, my brother, many of which of course are well known.

After my first foray as Nimue, I felt untethered to my own life. Morgen was right: I wanted to be back in that young, fresh body again. But the incident with my boys made the transition more difficult. I was exhausted in a thousand ways, even though I had worked very hard to maintain my strength.

The second time I transformed was not, as I thought it would be, out of simple desire, but rather necessity. For my plan to work, Nimue needed a life, and she needed to be seen.

Because, you see: Merlin was about again.

Merlin often traveled in those days, finding that now his greatest prophecy—the one about Arthur being the rightful ruler of all Braetan—had come true, he had a great deal of time on his warty hands. Not to mention he disposed entirely of Morgen and her ill-gotten child. No doubt he was trying to unspool that catastrophe and feeling lonely.

I heard that Merlin returned and was staying not far from Hwyfar's quarters, with a group of purported Ascomanni soothsayers, remnants from the last war. According to Morgen, he had acquired a new interest in various methods of prognostication, stemming from his failure to prevent Llachlyn from being born and what those ramifications might engender.

According to Morgen, Merlin was certain that the girl would be no threat, since she was no man. How wrong he was to be.

In truth, I worried that Nimue would not appeal to him, or that he would intimidate me, and I would lose control of my guise. Gods, he frightened Morgen, and she was more accomplished than I could ever dream of being.

The transformation the second time, however, was quicker and less painful, which gave me hope. Perhaps my body was getting used to being stretched and molded. Almost immediately, I was suffused with a feeling of exhilaration, euphoria. I had not lost consciousness, either, which made the transition easier. I simply changed into Nimue and let her work as I watched.

~ *Nimue* ~

IT WAS MORNING, bright and beautiful, two days after the twins had been named full knights, and as Nimue walked about the castle, taking in the sights and sounds, she caught a whiff of fresh earth from outside; spring was coming. Gods, had she ever felt spring before? When had she last splashed in a stream, or run in a field? It was difficult to say. Before life with her mistress, her memory was a long, cold winter, full of darkness, waiting for spring.

"Pardon me, milady," a low voice said as Nimue, not paying attention, nearly lost her balance and careened directly into him.

A little dazed, she turned and hit the stone wall, knocking her head considerably in order to compensate. It was far from an elegant move.

"Are you quite well?" he asked

She blinked through double vision to see a dark-haired knight staring down at her, a cruel scar down the side of his face; but he was no ugly man. He was thinner, less brawny than some of the other nights, and old as Arthur at least. His lips were quick to smile, and his eyes were kind.

*Bedevere. Gods, it is Bedevere.*

"Be… Best Sir—I am sorry," Nimue said, catching herself.

"I do not believe I have the pleasure of your acquaintance," he said, taking Nimue's arm carefully, appropriately.

*He is a remarkable fellow, Nimue. Courteous in every sense. That I have corrupted our love is no trivial fact, but you can trust him. Be at ease.*

"Nimue, Sir—"

"Bedevere," he said.

"Sir Bedevere?" she said, falling into a low curtsey, far as she could manage—which was far, what with the limber legs. "It is an honor. I have heard so much of you from my mistress, the Lady Anna du Lac."

"Ah, so you're the Nimue she mentioned," he said. His eyes kindled when she said, "Lady Anna."

*Damn the man, but he does not relent.*

"The same," Nimue said.

"I would offer you escort, but I have been summoned to the King himself. Are you lost? Perhaps I could find a stray knight to conduct you safely."

"No, thank you," Nimue said, dipping into another superfluous curtsey. "I am summoned elsewhere, myself.

To meet with Lady Hwyfar, on a matter of the Queen's dresses." It was half true; she did intend on seeing Hwyfar, as soon as she had managed a glimpse or two at Merlin.

He looked a little surprised but nodded. "Well, far be it from me to judge an Orkney lass. I have no doubt you've tricks up your sleeve. But if you desire any escort, please, do not hesitate to let me know. And you—if you would, let the Lady Anna know I hope she is recovering well. It was good to see her sons' knighting ceremony. They will make us all proud."

*Gods, he knows. How could he not? Gaheris favors him so very much.*

"Yes," Nimuë said, forcing the smile. "Of course, I shall let her know this evening when we are to have our tea."

"Excellent. And if there is anything she—or you—require, do not hesitate to seek me out," he added, a little desperately, perhaps.

*Oh, Nimuë. I wish I had the strength to have done with him, completely. I have tried, gods; I have tried. But Bedevere has a habit of lingering, of returning again and again... and my heart is bruised from it.*

It was not far to Merlin's chambers, but Nimuë did not want to appear suspicious, so she wandered a little. Since Bedevere's appearance, the mistress had gone quiet.

Hwyfar's room was around the corner, and the door to the quarters Merlin had taken—far from the tower that was his own, which was strange in and of itself—was barred shut. She thought she could smell sage burning. It would be quite remarkable to see what was going on inside.

Nimuë found her way to one of the large stained-glass windows overlooking the southern rise. She could see a vague hint of green on the grass now, here and there, as if the blades of vegetation were beginning to remember what they truly were. The sun helped. Today was warm enough to shirk furs and blankets, and she had worn a simple pair of wool-lined slippers, comfortable and practical, but a little daring, too. They went only to her ankles, and beneath her dress at least a foot of skin showed. Today's dress was green, a brilliant emerald, tight about the waist and breasts. It was the height of fashion, a gift from Hwyfar.

"It is quite a view; rather easy to get caught up in it."

Nimue did not have to turn to see it was Merlin; she could feel him behind her, sure as a pillar of ice. She had been made for this, and hatred burned already in her breast. Instead of turning in awe, or admiration, as with Bedevere, she decided on a different approach.

"Even now it is so much greener than Orkney," she said.

"I have only been to Orkney once," Merlin continued, the low resonant voice surprisingly warm. "And even then, in the summertime, it was far colder than my liking. I think, one of these days, I shall retire to the Continent. I hear Gaul is significantly less severe."

She turned, then, summoning all the warmth and charm she had never allowed herself, and looked to Merlin. He was but a breath away from her; she might have been able to kiss him if she leaned closer.

"I am Nimue," she said, smiling.

"Nimue," he said, as if the name tasted sweet. "A rather unusual name for an Orkney lass."

"Unusual?"

"It is beautiful," Merlin said. His eyes were brown like an oak tree, his skin chapped and dry from recent travel. His hair had grayed considerably, but he still possessed an eerie quality of youth in spite of it. Then again, perhaps he was the sort of man who was never young to begin with.

"My mother," she said. "She wanted a name... a name that would be remembered."

He added, with a smile, before departing: "I will not forget it."

*And so, it begins.*

# CHAPTER THIRTEEN

## HWYFAR

### ~ *Anna* ~

MY SONS HAD many adventures outside the castle walls, and undoubtedly those will be the ones you hear of most often. Much killing was done, but always in Arthur's name, and always seen as an act of bravery and honor. In truth, I always had a difficult time imagining war. I was forever on the inside of Orkney Castle or Carelon, never with eyes for such brutality. We women know the long-suffering of it, the festering wounds and injuries that never heal, the scars left on the skin and the soul.

Peace, though, reigned most supreme, and unfortunately peace makes men uncomfortable. Once Arthur's knights secured the borders, most kings—save for Pellas, Pellinore, and Marqus—surrendered their thrones and crowns, Carelon grew quiet.

For my part, I was much too busy for my liking but knew it must be so. Two months passed and I had not made much progress with Merlin, save a few glances of recognition. He was certainly not as smitten with Nimue as I hoped and knew I would have to work harder. But so lay the problem: I struggled with my transitions.

I could not deny the strangeness. Though transitions were easier, I grew restless. During transformation, I hardly felt any pain. But Nimue lingered longer, and when I was back to myself again, I felt so weak and desperate, so terribly depressed, that I wanted to slink right back into her skin again. I took stern talk from Morgen, but it made little difference.

Whenever I became Nimue, I found her urges to be quite meddlesome. Her first thoughts were of food and of coupling, and the pull was such that it was nearly impossible to ignore. As Anna, I was tepid—I hardly ate, and I certainly had no relations with men. What good would something like that have done anyway? Little, I am sure. But Nimue—with Nimue it was as if I were tasting and feeling everything for the first time; every scent, sight, and sound was more intense, more fulfilling and arousing.

I craved that feeling, even if it was through her.

I know in these days of stalwart denial, we so rarely talk about carnal occurrences. Perhaps it is because there is shame, knowing that it was part of what made Arthur's court so decadent and contributed toward its untimely decay. I suppose we blame everything on what was lost. But I tell you, then, there was no shame in it.

I have spoken of Arthur's love for Lance, and perhaps I have been crueler than I ought. Arthur, I believed, really and truly loved Lance—and Lance him—though it was never an issue I bothered myself with. I know they were intimate, but Lance never explained it to me, likely thinking

I would be scandalized; they were far from the only knights at court with such dalliances, and I do think that Lance's intimacy in return was more of a loyal reaction than one of passion, especially considering what later happened with Mawra. If he went to Arthur's arms in those days, perhaps I drove him to it. I have thought many a time in my life how strange it must have been to bed a sister and a brother, so very alike in feature.

Regardless, Hwyfar became quite dear to me, as Nimue—and in a way as Anna, too. Though I was having more and more difficulty in containing Nimue, and in remembering exactly what I had done while transformed, the moments with Hwyfar were always the clearest.

Hwyfar was simply intoxicating. She was all softness and luxury, from the smell of her skin to the dimples in her cheeks, she was a miraculous angel of sensuality. And Nimue lost herself to her, completely. She had never known comfort as such, never known the touch of another to be so delicate, so considerate, so knowing. Perhaps that was why Nimue found it hard to be on task with Merlin.

### ~ Nimue ~

HWYFAR'S ROOM WAS a den of wonders, always hosting a far-off dignitary with magical prowess, or enchanting storytellers and acrobats. But when she wanted Nimue alone, it was so. In the quiet, in the stillness, and the burning of incense, they delighted in one another. Whatever food Nimue wanted, whatever music she desired, whatever softness to her lips, Hwyfar was always there.

Nimue began to love her.

They were still intertwined, their breath ragged and tinged with laughter, when she spoke words that changed Nimue, that reminded me of her mistress's cause, what she was made for.

She had dallied enough in the last three months, and it was a fortunate, if not shocking, revelation.

"I wonder about Lance and Mawra," Hwyfar said, stroking Nimue's back lightly with the tips of her fingers. Nimue felt something like a dart of fire shoot up her spine, warning me. "I mean, they manage in secret, of course. But everyone knows. The way they look at each other—why, it is as if the air between then would ignite with but a flicker of flame."

Nimue tried not to tense, but she felt the tightness in her chest nonetheless. The mistress did not know, and the knowledge hit her like a fist to the stomach.

"Oh yes," she said, trying to answer as she should.

"Mawra tells me the most sordid details," Hwyfar said, reaching up to brush some of her dark red hair from her brow, deepened to brown with sweat. "The things they do. She says he is insatiable, like a man possessed. Not that she minds; she has always been a bit of a vixen herself, before she was married off to him. Of course it complicates matters, considering how much Arthur favors Lance. Such intriguing bedfellows."

"It seems unlikely that Lance could have... such a duplicitous nature," Nimue said carefully, turning onto her stomach. She looked into Hwyfar's remarkable eyes, feeling the pull of desire still there, wanting to kiss her full lips again. But she restrained. "I have only heard most kind things on my mistress's behalf."

Hwyfar's eyes widened, as if she realized to whom Nimue belonged just then. "Oh, gods, Nimue—I am sorry. I did not mean to imply—"

"It is nothing of consequence," she said, finding what truth she could in the words. She cooed, running her small hands down Hwyfar's neck and shoulder, to the rise of her breasts. "I know that since Galahad's birth, my mistress has... given Lance something of a blessing to take a lover, should he need it. But I do not think that she had expected it to be the Queen, is all."

The effect of Nimue's hands seemed to tame Hwyfar a bit. Hwyfar's white freckled shoulders dropped down, tension released. "Yes, I know. I have the greatest respect for your mistress and miss her dearly—but I understand she wishes little to do with the court, and I do not blame her. I would do the same, were I in her place, considering all she has endured."

"You used to live in Avillion," Nimue said, resting her chin on her hands, and lowering her eyes a little. Staring into Hwyfar's eyes was unsettling sometimes. "Why did you come back here, why not stay? Surely you would have been spared the strangeness of court, the sorrow... People always say Avillion is so full of wonders."

"If by wonders, they mean apples, then yes," said Hwyfar with a straight-toothed grin. She pressed Nimue away gently and rose from the bed, wrapping one of the long silk blankets around her middle and going to sit at her vanity. She possessed the most miraculous mirror Nimue had ever seen, polished so clear that the image was nearly the same as the subject. Even her mistress's costly copper mirror sported a significant warp to it; this was nearly as clear as a reflection in water.

Hwyfar twisted her red hair up behind her head, a few curls falling down to the nape of her neck, and then secured it with a long pin set with a turquoise bauble. "Avillion has orchards, thousands of them, covering nearly every bit of the island. Where there are not apple orchards, there are temples. We have some livestock, but as most priests and priestesses shun meat, the majority of our food is vegetable, and often quite boring. It is said that meat clouds the mind of a seer, making them sluggish and often incorrect."

Nimue slipped to the side of the bed, her feet dangling over the edge. "Apples and temples," she said with a smirk.

"On Avillion we make the prophecies, but rarely do we live them. It was not the case with my sisters and I. Leodegraunce, our father... it is complicated. We all had prophecies read, as your mistress did, as princesses. It was important, our father believed, in spite of his plans for us to be priestesses as our mother was. Of course, celibacy was never necessary, and he wanted to marry us off, if we desired it."

She sighed, leaning over the back of her chair, pretty lips pursed in thought. "And we all did. We told him so—we wanted to be married. But our prophecies made it complicated."

"What were your prophecies?" Nimue asked, innocently.

"I cannot tell you that—or at least, none other than mine. Mine was simply this: 'King's companion'. Which made it quite apparent, to my father, at any rate, that I would make the perfect wife for Arthur; I was younger than him enough to be appealing, and certainly more beautiful than my other two sisters."

Nimue did not argue.

Hwyfar shrugged. "When I came to court, Gweyn was my lady in waiting. And with one look, Arthur was smitten with her. He wanted her as any powerful man wants dainty, lovely things. I think, seeing me, he was afraid. I am nearly as tall as he, and I met his eye. I was not the sort of woman he wanted."

"Were you angry?"

"I was angry enough to return to Avillion. But…" Hwyfar drifted off, turning back to the mirror, and seeming to address herself there. "Eventually I came back. I was having bad dreams, nightmares, really, that something terrible was to happen to Gweyn." A muscle tightened in her jaw when she said her sister's name then, and Nimue thought she caught a glimmer of tears in her eye. "So I came back to Carelon, and it was welcome. My father had been a boor the entire time I was in Avillion and realized that though I was a priestess in name, I would never be one again in heart."

"Why not?"

"They do not like my prophecies," she said as if it were a silly, useless little detail. "They told me my prophecies were too mundane—in the case of what weather might befall us. And all for the better. I was more interested in earthly delights rather than apples and temples, as it were. Once in Carelon, I found a home I could actually enjoy, where I was left on my own. I think Arthur only tolerates me because he is frightened of me."

Hwyfar stood and went to her window, drawing the thick curtains aside a moment, bathing the room in sunlight. It turned her hair to burnished copper. It was deep spring, but a chilly afternoon and drawing the shade brought was like a breath of cold air.

"Then Gweyn slipped away from me. She said, after Mordred, Arthur would not touch her. He acted as if she... as if something were wrong with her. I tried to instruct her as best I could, informing her of some of the more unique aspects of lovemaking, hoping that her knowledge would help. But it did not. When she fell ill, it was as if her body were destroying itself from the inside. It started with a miscarriage, but it would not end. I do not know if that child was Arthur's; I dared not ask. I only know that my poor sister died in a kind of pain I could never know. I tried, I tried to reach out to her—it is why Mawra was brought to court. I had written our father, begging that she come, to try and help Gweyn. But..." Hwyfar pressed her hand on the window, the pane fogging up around her, from the warmth of her fingers.

Nimue stood and went to her, quietly. She was weeping, and Nimue tucked her head into the space between her shoulder blades, brushing her lips against the smooth, freckled skin.

"I stood outside her room when she died," Hwyfar said. She was shivering now. "And I saw Merlin, and he asked after us. I told him what happened, and he said nothing for a moment; I would have done anything to have heard a kind word as I stood there, my shift covered in my sister's blood. But he shook his head and said, 'We are all at the will of prophecies, Hwyfar. So take your sorrow for the moment and return with your head high. Even ends are beginnings.'"

She laughed, bitter and short. "Would that I could have clawed his beady eyes out!"

Her cheeks were streaked with tears, the skin red as if burned. But Nimue brought her to her lips, instead, drawing her in completely, and comforted her in the only way she knew.

AFTER DEPARTING HWYFAR'S apartment, Nimue meandered through the grand courtyard and sat beneath the largest apple tree—one brought from Avillion. She closed her eyes and let it rain blossoms upon her shoulders, the sweet musk surrounding her, reminding her of Hwyfar again. Nimue breathed in and out, lulled to near sleep by the creak of the tree's branches and the hushing of leaves above her head.

"Ah, it is little Nimue," said a voice she knew: Lanceloch.

Nimue opened her eyes, brushing petals from her face, and beheld Lanceloch standing before her, his brilliant red cloak pinned with a clasp unfamiliar to her. It looked suspiciously Avillionian.

He was smiling though, as purely as sunlight. "Be careful! They say women have strange dreams under apple trees."

"Do they?"

"You seem sad," he said, tilting his head to the side. "May I sit with you a moment?"

"Of course, Sir Lanceloch," she said, remembering her manners. She bowed her head, courteously, then looked up into the branches. "I already have strange dreams, I suppose... Did you come here to enjoy the blossoms, as well?"

He smiled a little. There were lines around his eyes Nimue had not noticed the last time she saw him, but in spite of that he looked rested, refreshed. "No, I came to find you, my dear. I ran into Hwyfar, who told me you were doing errands for Anna this morning."

"You were looking for me?" Nimue asked. To her knowledge, no one had gone looking for her before. Especially not the most famed knight of the realm.

"Yes, indeed. The King is asking after you."

"The—King?" she asked, stuttering from genuine surprise.

"He has heard such remarkable things about you, and he wanted to meet you. I think he has some concerns about your mistress, and desires to hear your perspective."

"He sent *you* all the way to find me?" she asked. If only her mistress were here; she would be so surprised.

"Well, considering I am responsible for your safety, I suppose it is a good approach," he said, his amber eyes measuring her. She wanted to weep, seeing him. He looked at her as one might a daughter, or a niece, a look both paternal and compassionate.

Then, faint. A whisper:

*Gods, it would have been good to see him with Galahad.*

Sir Lamorak was at the door to Arthur's chambers, and let Nimue in quickly with Lanceloch on her arm.

When Nimue first beheld her mistress's brother that day, she was in awe of him. He was beautiful, in face and form, broadening with age across the chest. His close-cropped beard gave him an air of stateliness, a bit like the portraits she had seen of Uther Pendragon in the great hall. But still, his eyes were so like her mistress's, especially when they first looked upon her, that Nimue fell completely silent and forgot to curtsey at all.

"My Lady Nimue," he said.

The words alone were enough to remind Nimue of courtesy, and she fell into as deep a bow as she could. The

King had been sitting in a fur-trimmed chair, but he rose and went to her, taking her hand and helping her stand.

"Your Highness," she said, feeling her heart flutter in her chest. His hands were warm, dry, surprisingly powerful.

"Please, take a seat. Are you hungry, thirsty?" he inquired, sitting again himself. Nimue noticed that he limped slightly but said naught.

"I am fine," she said, taking the proffered seat and folding her hands one over the other.

She was suddenly glad to have taken extra time dressing after her earlier dalliance with Hwyfar; she had been quite disheveled before. The gown was now spectacular, sewn of ivory and red silks, given by Hwyfar herself.

Arthur laughed, leaning over, and picked an apple blossom out of Nimue's hair. "You were down by the tree?"

"Yes, Your Majesty," she said, smiling instead of blushing. "Enjoying spring."

Lance was still in the room, and he strode to the fire, warming his hands; he looked exceedingly comfortable. He looked over his shoulder, grinning a little.

"I used to do that," continued Arthur, leaning back on his chair. "Of course, the tree was smaller, then—though it is pruned every year, of course. But there's something rather magical about being under the limbs of a tree shedding blossoms; it soothes the soul."

"That it does, Your Majesty," Nimue agreed.

He folded his hands together, making a little steeple with them, his smile fading away. "Thank you for coming to see me," he said, his voice gentle and lulling as the branches of the tree itself.

"It is my honor, Your Majesty."

"As Lanceloch has likely told you, I was hoping you might speak with me a bit about my sister, Anna. I know she depends on you a great deal these days."

She nodded, keeping her features impassible. It was easier to do than she had thought. "I am honored at that, as well. She has been a most gracious mistress."

"I am certain she is," Arthur said, and his eyes pinched, as if he were in pain. He took a deep breath. "It is only that I worry about her—I simply do not know what to say to her. I thought perhaps you could be a bridge between us; I feel she has slipped away from me, and I cannot find my way back. She is... the closest family I have."

"Most days, she is simply quiet," Nimue said, the truth as she made it to be. "She likes to read, to embroider. She just has no taste for the... intricacies of court, I do not think."

"She spoke with her sons a few months ago," Lance said. "She seemed well but frail. She is distant with me..." He trailed off, exchanging a look with Arthur Nimue did not know how to read. "I suspect that is only a fault of mine."

"She bears you no ill will, Sir Lanceloch," Nimue said, sweetly and convincingly as she could. It was mostly true. "She is only..."

"Brokenhearted," Arthur replied. He leaned his head on his hand, his chair creaking a bit. It was a strange chair, looked to be made of the skins of a few different animals patched together.

Arthur sighed and looked around the room, as if expecting to see someone. "Merlin is not here today," he said, and Nimue caught relief in his tone. "I have no idea when he will be back, but he seems altogether unconcerned about Lady Anna. I have consulted him, and he continually changes the subject. I know she is not the most renowned of the ladies at court, but I cannot help but feel guilty for her pain. Feel guilty for what might have been. Lance shared with me some of the difficulties Anna endured as a young bride, and I am shamed. As a man, as her king." He took a deep, shuddering breath. "As her brother."

Nimue continued to watch Arthur, nodding her head as he spoke. She reached inside herself for the voice of her mistress but found it still absent. Or mute.

"I have four sisters," he said, his tone indicating that he was trying again. "I never knew Elaine. Margawse is quite her own woman, and though I have certainly tried to give her the space she needs, Morgen and I..." He licked his lips, his tongue very red against his skin. "We do not speak much. But Anna is my full sister. She has both the resilience of our mother and the forwardness of our father; she is the closest living creature to me in all the earth, and I feel as if I have pushed her further away than them all."

Lance was now standing off to Arthur's right, head down, his hands clasped before him, listening. Nimue supposed he had heard this speech before.

"I have ever listened to Merlin, as my father did before me. And I have not questioned his decisions. Save once. With Gweyn. But now, as I lay out his judgements before me, I see how time and again, Anna has fallen by the way, brushed aside like chaff. He did not consider her as a person, but rather a means to an end. My heart told me, ages ago, differently. But Merlin was so adamant.

"I remember," he said, a soft smile brightening his countenance. For a moment he looked as brilliant as the sun; it was remarkable. "I remember when she fell in love.

With Bedevere, of course. Gods, we were so young then. I wanted nothing more to give my best friend my sister—to join them together. I had the power to do it—one stroke of a pen. But Merlin swept in, speaking of doom, and frightening me to the core. But doom came, anyway. I have denied her happiness at every turn by listening to Merlin. And now, in my hour of need, Merlin deserts me for his tower and I am left with clear eyes."

Nimue waited a breath before speaking as her head was spinning. Would that she had asked for wine earlier; she could have done with something to calm her nerves.

"The Lady Anna," she said, "bears no ill will to you, Your Highness. She is simply weary of the world, I think. She is comfortable, though."

"Is she happy?" Lance asked. He seemed ill at ease, wringing his hands.

"I do not think she has ever aspired to happiness. Contentment, perhaps. Justice, at times," Nimue replied. "I bring her news of her sons, and what goes on at court, but I do not think hers is a heart to know of quests and adventures these days. She has spent most of her life here, or else at Orkney Castle."

Arthur drew his hands down his cheeks. "I do not wish her sorrow to turn inward. Not like with our mother, or with Gweyn. I have overlooked too many dear women, and I fear I will pay the price for it."

"She will be well enough in time, Your Majesty," Nimue replied. "I promise you. She will regain her strength. I will see to it."

"Your saying so is like a sunbeam to my heart," said the King as he held out his hand, rings glittering in the light.

"But there is yet another thing, as well; I have a favor to ask of you, and only hope that you consider it, though you are free to refuse."

"Of course, Your Majesty. Anything you require."

"Merlin has asked after you," he said, dropping his voice lower, then clearing his throat as if the request had left him parched. "He seems to think you are rather unique. These days, the man is a mystery to me, and I know there's a certain level of strangeness with him and his visits abroad. He will not speak to me on the subject of his transience in and out of court, but I supposed if you could get close enough."

Lance finished, as the King faltered for the right words to say. "You could perhaps report to us. Let us know his mind. We have begun to suspect he is not of a sound mind; you understand. See if he will speak with you. Listen. And then tell us, without embellishment or detail."

Nimue flushed with pleasure.

It was perfect.

"Yes, Your Majesty," she replied. "Anything you ask of me, of course."

"Then I will make the arrangements to allow you passage into Merlin's quarters should it be required, and he will be informed of my consent—providing the Lady Anna can spare you."

"I am sure she will," she said.

Later, Nimue found Morgen among the midwives, sorting herbs and commanding the women there with her mere presence. They seemed shadows in the wake of her radiance; she was smiling, at home.

When she saw Nimue, Morgen gave instructions to the

slight girl beside her, and approached, reading the young woman's face as best she could.

"Lady Nimue," she said.

"We need to talk," Nimue replied.

Morgen took her hand and squeezed it.

"This is the part I need to learn from you," she whispered. "I have got the prey. I need the snare."

# CHAPTER FOURTEEN

## MERLIN

Nimue was given a special key and a bottle, within which was slipped an elegant piece of parchment. The parchment was marked in extremely small script, and she could tell nothing other than the color of the ink: deepest red, almost brown. When she arrived at Merlin's tower—for he had once again taken up residence there—she was to use the key on the main door, and then slip the bottle through a small opening beneath the latch. Then she was told to wait.

She hadn't much time to contemplate the oddity, when she heard a grinding noise followed by a light cough. Then, a plank in the oaken door moved aside, and Merlin's black-brown eyes narrowed down at her.

"Good morn—" was all she managed before the slot closed again, and the door opened with an impressive groan of the hinges.

He was standing there, smiling, the little bottle in one hand, and his staff in the other. Some have speculated the staff itself was made of a holy, or gods-touched material, of such a miraculous quality it granted command of the weather and channeled strange power. However, Nimue doubted it from the beginning. He was simply old, and likely injured at some point; she came to know for a certainty he had significant problems with gout, and severe arthritis. The staff was a necessity.

"Nimue," he said, the smile deepening further than she had ever seen. "Come, come in! I am overjoyed you have come to pay me a visit. Please—just through the hall there, and to the right. You'll see the parlor."

Her mistress warned her Merlin was made of lies, and his home was a den of deception, as well. But it did not appear forbidding. The walls were dark stained wood, and unadorned; the floor was cedar. It smelled fresh and clean, as if someone had just been through to catch all the dust. The parlor itself was unremarkable; dark knotted carpet over the rushes, three angular red chairs and a narrow table, a low burning fire. She could smell citrus, and out the rather large windows, Nimue noticed the blooming apple tree in the courtyard. Even in the past few days, its beauty somewhat diminished; the blossoms were nowhere near as dense as once were.

She had expected more. Certainly more books, trinkets, oddities. It is what people assume of wizards. But from what she observed, Merlin's taste in decoration was rather straight-forward. Clean lines, simple fabrics, a hint of comfort and sunlight. But nothing extravagant. No Avillonian extravagance, no sensual pageantry like Hwyfar.

"There we go," Merlin said, gesturing to one of the red chairs. "Please, do take a seat. If you've made the trek all the way here, you're likely exhausted. Your cheeks are even flushed."

Nimue grinned, finding courage in the smile.

"It is a lovely view," she said.

He went to the hearth and removed a kettle of warmed water, then looked around, as if confused. He spotted what he was looking for—a tea set, resting on a small table with some lemon cakes and lavender sprigs.

"Not a bad view, no," he agreed. "Though I have seen it for the better part of my stay here, and I am afraid in contrast to the many wonders around the Islands of Braetan, it rather pales in comparison. It is an Avillionian blood apple tree, did you know that?"

"I've never heard of blood apples," she replied.

Merlin went about making the tea in such a way she surmised he did it often. She had not seen any sign of servants, either. Though she couldn't fathom he did his own cleaning. The place was more immaculate than her mistress's apartment was.

"Tea?"

"Certainly."

"Not too long of a steep, and it will be just right. I made these lemon cakes just this morning, but I am afraid they turned out much less fluffy than I had hoped. I fear I picked up the hobby of cookery far too late in life."

Nimue hardly knew the right response. The image of Merlin in an apron with a mixing bowl was too absurd to even comprehend. So instead, she nodded politely and accepted the plate of lemon cakes he put before me.

"The tree itself was brought here, oh…" he said, standing again by the tea cart, figuring on his fingers. "Hmm, decades ago. Before Arthur was born, when Uther was just building Carelon. I think he had a tryst with someone. I forget her name now, there were so many!"

"But he was young. Insatiable, and resilient. An impressive man in many ways, Uther Pendragon, but sadly soft in the brain a bit. I think it likely had to do with all the jostling about in armor fighting the Ascomanni." He knocked on his head as if it were a helmet and grinned toothily; he was missing some teeth, black holes among yellowed pegs. "Regardless. The tree came to us on Midsummer Festival from that woman... what was her name? Gods, I cannot remember anything these days. He planted it amidst the scaffolding and masonry and proclaimed it would be an enduring symbol of their love."

"Their love?" she echoed, politely eating some of the cake. It was harder than it looked and sweetened with so much honey as to make Nimue's lips purse, and she quite liked sweet things.

Merlin laughed as if Nimue had just made a marvelous joke, and she chuckled a bit with him. He said, "Oh dear me, no. It lasted a scant few months, perhaps. Uther was never a man for the long-term, at least not until he saw Igraine the first time and—oh, here I go again being rude. And I think I have let the tea leaves steep too long."

He examined the clay teapot, a most rudimentary version that would have looked at home in a cattle-herd's house. Pouring the tea for her, Nimue watched the steam rise from the cup and mingle with the white hair on his beard, and she wondered what in the name of the gods he wanted her for. For a moment, she had the uncomfortable image of a small gadfly caught in a spider web, shaking and trembling, then at last going limp, too tired to give up.

But no. She could not let such thoughts invade her purpose. Arthur commanded her. Anna made her. It was not time to back down now.

Merlin was lies. He had wrought deception on everyone; on her mistress, on Hwyfar. It was time to be done with it. To know at last.

"Here you go," he said, handing Nimue the tea in a cobalt glazed mug. The inside was unglazed and a brilliant red. It smelled of lavender.

"Thank you," she replied.

Merlin then took his tea, and his cake, to his seat, and arranged his robes a bit before relaxing his shoulders and taking a sip. He looked a harmless old man, there, the steam rising around his nose.

"Do you like it? The tea?"

"It is good," she lied. It tasted a bit too much like a perfume she had been given by one of her adoring knights and ruined what there was left to redeem in the lemon cakes. "Quite floral."

He smacked his lips together. "Yes, it is floral. But I think I shall relent a little next time with the rosehips. It is a little stifling for me, quite truly. Though perhaps I just let it steep too long."

His eyes were hungry for her, and he watched her, unrelenting. She knew this game. He could be both an old, ailing man, and a predator. He could be a good man, and a calculating man. Judgement was not in extremes but in the balance, each grain of sand against the measure of his intent.

DISTRAUGHT AND UNSETTLED from her meeting with Merlin, Nimue decided to use what time she had left in her day, before her mistress returned, to visit Hwyfar; she was in possession of a bracelet which allowed her full access into her lover's room, whenever she needed it.

And she was in need. Hwyfar was the only comfort she knew amidst the well of darkness she felt deepening around her. With her mistress so often absent, Nimue felt alone, adrift. The pressure from Arthur and Lanceloch, the continual advances of knights at court; Nimue sought Hwyfar's den of pleasure and attention for balance, for indulgence, for grounding.

But when Nimue stepped onto Hwyfar's floor, she knew immediately something was amiss. There was no laughter, no music, no sweet scents of exotic perfume.

The hall was empty.

Nimue rushed to the door with trembling hands and found it open, the room scoured clean of all else familiar, down to the gray stone.

Hwyfar had gone. Without word.

### ~ *Anna* ~

THAT EVENING, MORGEN found me in my room. I was feeling poorly, having had another treacherous time coming out of Nimue. I ordered Fauna to draw me a bath, and though she inquired after Nimue, I pretended not to hear her. The stupid girl asked too many questions; I was going to have to have her replaced sooner or later if she kept it up.

"What do you mean 'nothing of consequence'?" Morgen demanded, lips pressed tight so the wrinkles around her mouth deepened. "You were in there for three hours with him, and you what, talked about the weather?"

I was weary, and Morgen was in no good mood. Why was everyone so demanding? Summoning what strength I could, I rose from the bed and took my robe, shivering as the cool material slid across my skin.

"*Nimue* was in there, yes, and I mean just that," I replied, coolly. I looked down at my wrist as I pulled it through the sleeve of the robe and noted how bony it had become. Gods, whatever volume of food Nimue consumed seemed to do naught for me; I was on the verge of wasting away. I was feeling a little feverish, too; but no appetite to speak of. "They spoke of very simple things. He was interested in the weather in Orkney, who her family was, what sort of business they did. I think he just wanted to hear Nimue speak."

"That doesn't sound like the Merlin I know," she said, even and sharp at the end. She was cross with me, of course, because she loved Merlin still. In spite of his brash behavior toward her, and the misery he had caused. Fools, all, we women of long-suffering love.

I sighed. "Morgen, can this wait? I am weary down to my bones."

"You are always tired. You're dabbling in magic much more taxing than you can handle," she countered, putting her hand on my arm. "You're frail. Your skin is flaking all over your face. And—gods, Anna, you're bleeding through your gown."

Morgen pulled her hand away from my arm, and it was red with blood. The wound on my arm I most frequently used for reading the book had apparently burst through its stitches.

She sat me down like a little girl who'd fallen and scraped her knees and did not say a word until the wound was cleaned and the stitches attended to. Out of habit now, Morgen brought her midwife's basket with her every time she visited me; she was getting used to the fact I was broken on some level or another almost every time I emerged from Nimue.

"Does the book mention anything about this?" she asked. "Anything you can do? You're thin as a rail, you can hardly see straight, and you're bleeding all over the place."

"I feel fine…" I said, as she wrapped my arm and pulled the sleeve of a new robe down to my wrist, patting my hand. "I mean, when I am Nimue—I feel fine. It is only on this end."

"*This* end is the one with your true body," she said, warning me. Her eyes searched mine, back and forth. "If you forget—you could emerge out of her into darkness or death. Anna, you cannot fade. You have sons—you have family. They still need you."

I tried to make the laughter sound lighter than it felt, but Morgen read the expression in my eyes anyway.

"You're so like Mother," she said, rising, putting her basket back together. She wound the catgut and placed it gently within.

"That is ridiculous," I said. No one had ever said such a thing to me before; it was always the Pendragons to whom parallels were made. "I am not a thing like her."

Morgen pulled the cowl up around her head, scarlet against her white streaked ebony tresses. She looked severe and wild, the Morgen I remembered when I was younger. "Do you know what it was like when she died, Anna? Do you know what kept her holed up here?"

"No, I was not here," I reminded her.

"She believed no one cared for her, that her children were

off living their own lives. In spite of the fact her daughters—some of them anyway—made every effort to bridge the chasm between us. She pushed all of us away, wanting to wallow in her own despair until it consumed her. Anna—"

"Morgen, I am not Mother."

"You might not look like her, but you're still her daughter. She cared for you, Anna."

"Mother never cared for me as I cared for my children!" I shouted, standing up too fast. I was dizzy immediately and had to brace myself with the bedpost. I wanted to vomit. "She looked at me... I was always wanting, never lovely enough or clever enough. Do not lie to me! She did not *want* me, Morgen."

Morgen looked for a moment as if she might correct me but dropped her gaze to the ground near my feet. When she looked up, there were tears in her eyes.

I had not wanted Galahad, as Mother had not wanted me. Morgen could not lie to my face about such things, not when the knowing clawed at me every day.

"You are right," she said softly, and I could tell she felt the pain of it. My sister, all these years, so distant from me and yet, she held some kind of pity for me as well. "I cannot argue with you on that count. After Arthur, she would have... well, time is passed. She is gone. I only worry after you."

"I know," I said, and wondered why I could not weep. Anger seemed to have burned away the tears.

"Nimue cannot live forever," Morgen said.

"And neither will Merlin."

\* \* \*

## ~ *Nimue* ~

MERLIN FOUND NIMUE, weeks later, as she was doing errands at the market in Carelon. She was examining a long bolt of cloth she had spied the day before, something her mistress thought would make a pretty dress for Llachlyn—a pale rose red silk with yellow interlace embroidery about the edges. Nimue was worried Morgen might not like such attention lavished on her daughter, as more than once she balked at her mistress's gifts. Nimue supposed it was because her mistress lost a daughter so young, perhaps she hoped Llachlyn might fill up the hole left by Blancheflor.

"In the market for some cloth?" asked a deep voice behind Nimue. She did not need to turn around to see it was Merlin. She had felt him approaching.

"I did picture you in such a lovely shade of red," she replied, looking over her shoulder and grinning. He looked a little more severe than the last time she had seen him, owing mostly to the black skullcap he wore. It was studded with silver stars and looked almost regal in the open market. He most certainly did not belong among colorful folk surrounding them.

"Nonsense, Nimue," he said, savoring the name once again. He almost always spoke the name whenever he could, which was an odd habit; it worried Nimue a little. As Morgen warned her, Merlin had a most unusual way with people. He was all about seeming; and he seemed, to Nimue at least, to be nothing more than a slightly befuddled old man with an eye for rounded young lasses from Orkney.

But it did not explain her hatred for him. Everything

about him discomfited Nimue, and yet she was drawn to him, again and again. There was a cruel pleasure in the pain of watching him.

*I am the judge and you are the executioner.*

Merlin continued, "You know, Avillionian monks used to wear solely such a hue, decades ago, until there was a blight on the flower they used for dye—oh, what was it called? I think it was some variant of lavender, but I cannot be sure."

Nimue drew the fabric between her fingers, judging the weight and texture. This particular merchant had a good reputation, which she knew from Hwyfar's opinion, she thought with a pang; but she was spending her mistress's money and wanted to be assured of a quality product.

Merlin reached out and selected a royal blue swath, shot with strands of gold. "Now this—this would much better compliment the tones of your hair, of your skin... fitting."

"The fabric is not for me," Nimue said, giving him a wry grin. He smiled back. "I am on an errand for my mistress. I hardly have the time to be wasting on shopping for myself."

He chuckled. "Ah, yes. I forget. You are at the disposal of the Lady Anna—or is it Lady du Lac? I scarcely see her about these days. It is as if she has vanished from Carelon altogether. Though she always struck me as a withdrawn kind of woman. Sober, in the way of Uther Pendragon's mother."

Nimue felt the skin at the nape of her neck prickle and she forced a light laugh, then let the merchant know how much cloth she needed. She handed him the money in exchange.

*Mistress? Mistress Anna?*

Nimue always sensed the mistress watching, but so rarely these days did she speak. It was as if, through

Nimue's eyes, Anna only dreamed deeply. She could have used her help, could have spoken to her about Hwyfar. But the mistress was cold and weak. And Nimue was alone.

Merlin continued speaking.

"I am sorry," he said, lowering his voice. "That was unkind of me. It is only we worry for your mistress's well-being."

"We?" Nimue asked, taking the cloth and thanking the merchant. She turned to Merlin and leveled him with a glance.

"The court," he clarified.

"My mistress is fine. She is simply weary of the court and its games," Nimue explained. "It seems everyone asks me this question. All she wants is to be let alone. Is it so unheard of?"

Merlin raised his furry eyebrows, so they touched the top of his skullcap, his forehead deepening into a dozen lines. "Unheard of? No, of course not."

"I do not think she believes she is missed," Nimue continued, walking a few paces back toward where the bakers had set up their wares. She was hungry, of course, and the smell of apples and cinnamon was almost beyond bearing. Her mouth watered and she inhaled deeply.

"Well, to be honest, she is not missed entirely," Merlin said, a little too lightly for Nimue's tastes. She turned away from him as he continued to walk along, hoping her clenched jaw would go unnoticed. The conjuror continued: "And it is not her fault, really. Some people are simply destined to be forgotten. With a court full of knights and ladies of such prowess and beauty, there are simply some who cannot measure up."

"There are many redeeming qualities about my mistress, Lord Merlin," Nimue said, making sure to smile enough to warrant a dimple. "Sometimes a certain simplicity is part of grace."

"Assuredly so," Merlin agreed. "But—well, I knew her more as a child than a woman, but even then, she was reclusive. Moody. Withdrawn. Her mother worried constantly about her because, well, I think Igraine saw much of herself in Anna, as much as she favored Uther with her looks. It is a blessing she was not born a boy."

"I see," Nimue said.

"Nimue," Merlin said, taking her shoulder. "You are a remarkable choice for the Lady Anna. I hope she treats you kindly."

"Always."

"And you are happy."

She managed a brave face. Hwyfar. "Most days. Although—"

"That is a word ripe with promise. Tell me, child."

If Nimue could have remained silent, she would have. Yet she both needed Merlin's trust and felt compelled to speak.

"I cannot help but feel as if I am meant for greater things," Nimue said. "Beyond selecting silks."

"Oh," laughed the conjuror. "I have no doubt you are correct."

~ *Anna* ~

I SAT IN the middle of my room, waiting for Nimue to leave me. She was lingering, and in her lingering, we spoke as we stared into the fire. I shivered, too cold to move.

"Merlin is difficult to unravel," I said. "But we are not making progress as I would like. My time is finite, Nimue."

"He doesn't speak to me about himself, even when I try," sighed Nimue.

"You think he doesn't trust you?"

"I think he doesn't *pity* me. Perhaps trust is the wrong word."

"He is attracted to strength, that is what Morgen said about him."

"But I'm not strong, not when it matters. I am so much younger than he is; I often feel as if he has trying to read me from the inside-out."

"Perhaps he is. You suspect he knows?"

"He sees me. Only Nimue. And when he speaks my name it is with the relish of a lover."

"Then why is it taking so long?"

"I aim to take everything from him, but I see an old man before me, palsied and worn, drawn down by the weight of his own life; he is like an oak tree, rooted to the ground, tendrils deep into the loamy earth."

"I am the judge. You are the executioner."

Nimue fell silent.

"You feel bad for him," I said.

"I do."

"Then you are of no use to me."

"I pity him, but I hate him, too."

"You hate him because I made you to hate him. But to truly succeed, you must hate him for your reasons."

"Mistress—there is another matter I—"

"You go away, sometimes. Where do you go?"

A pause. "I have lovers. Two of them."

"You do. I know this."

"But I keep their faces from you."

"You are gone for a long time, sometimes."

"I can be rid of you when I wish."

"I made you."

"I am not your flesh."

"I *made* you."

"I am not your flesh."

"I am the judge and you are the executioner."

I AM A *hollow drum, my skin drawn tight and hard against my bones, my breath like hot ash. I am bereft of life, of strength, of spirit; I am a nothing of nothings, a queen of none.*

*I see with her eyes, but I no longer move them. I am a husk of a tree, and Nimue is the ivy, twining about me, strangling, lovely and lush. Beneath, I wither and watch as the forest about me changes, the seasons shifting.*

*Morgen comes to see me, but finds only Nimue, ever Nimue. I can see her, the pinched lines of worry on her face, the concern in her eyes.*

*"Anna?" she asks, searching my face, but Nimue's answer is: "No."*

~ Anna ~

NIMUE FELT MORE love in her heart than I ever did; she was passion and light, whimsy and worry. Her heart was like a beating bird's, animal and human entwined beneath her lovely skin. Every breath she took was an ecstasy, and she cloaked herself in a mantle of joy.

I am ashamed to admit it, but I let her to it. I gave her the reins and the tether to my own life force. I was too tired to fight, knowing even then the end of the potion would be the end of her. I had bestowed my hatred of Merlin to her; I nursed it for so long, that with her passion running free I faded, always faded. But before his undoing, I had to know his faults. I needed his confession. For myself. For Gweyn. For Mother. For Morgen. For Blancheflor. And now, Hwyfar.

Though she obeyed me, she was still unpredictable. I learned the names of her lovers: Agravain and Lamorak. It was Hwyfar she had truly loved, and Lamorak, too, but it was Agravain—my sister Margawse's son—with whom she toyed, like a cat playing with a mouse. She would not relent in her flirtation with him, nor would she give him release.

She blazed like a comet, and I faded like frost in the light of the sun.

I worried, except with my fading the worry went, too. When Nimue visited the old conjuror Merlin, I would watch sometimes, hour after hour, listening as they spoke of everything and nothing. He watched her with wanting eyes, but unlike with the rest of court she was always withdrawn with him. No flirtation, no sensuality. Only knowledge.

Even so, it began to change. She knew the look in Merlin's eyes. She had to give him enough hope. She did not dissuade him, no; she lifted her skirts just so, tilted her head to the side, angling her chin so the light from the window shot through her hair. Each movement she made was measured, ripe with desire, flushed with hope.

I watched.

I waited.

I wasted.

My only hope was in patience; she could build trust and bring about Merlin's confession.

~ *Nimue* ~

NIMUE PAUSED AT the bottom of the stairs, taking a moment to tuck on her long, nut-brown tresses up into the band about her brow. She glanced from side to side, spotting the shadow of a figure coming down the hall, and dropped her hands back down to her hips. It could have been any number of people, but she hoped for one in particular: a knight named Agravain.

She was disappointed to see Gaheris, then, and she attempted to avert her eyes. He recognized her, nonetheless.

Something stirred in her, a flicker of recognition; it was her mistress, begging for something, speaking words Nimue ignored.

"Good afternoon, Lady Nimue," said Gaheris, smiling. It did him good, and she noticed the play of light from the window on his angled cheek. He was handsome. More than handsome. Dazzling. "Where might you be headed on this bright summer day?"

Nimue smiled, cheeks dimpling. "Out. To get some fresh air," she lied. "I hear you fought valiantly in the Tournament."

Gaheris's face pinched a moment, then smoothed again. "Yes—well. For a newcomer, perhaps. But I managed pretty far up the lists."

"Did Lanceloch really win the entire thing?" she asked.

"He did. Lamorak right behind him; then Palomydes. There is still some fire in the first knights of Arthur, it seems. It is a shame Gawain did not fight again, though. I had hoped he might."

"I should hope I can see it next time. The Lady Anna was not feeling well, and so I stayed with her—she is proud, though. Of you."

"I know the Tournament has never been Mother's favorite event—" He was staring at her, breathing shallow. "Gawain told me how much of a terror Lugh's Tournament was when she arrived back here years ago."

It was a look Nimue knew; he had looked at her that way upon her first outing. It was a wanting he did not know how to express, written in every line of his body. They were alone, unguarded. Only courtesy prevented anything further.

"Lady Nimue—"

"Yes?" She raised her eyebrows, having been told by the old man that it was a comely expression. She tried to do it as often as possible, now.

"Perhaps you might ride with me some afternoon? I've got three horses at court, you know, stabled and fed well. I could show you the fields beyond the castle."

Sweet Gaheris. "No, no—such a gesture is inappropriate."

"I see," he said, and she smiled to find him so beautiful when bruised. The fight went out of him, and his eyes became heavy-lidded and sad. It felt so good, so joyful, to see such an expression. To vanquish a knight. She wanted it more.

"You understand how difficult it must be for a young lady at court so far from home," she said softly, drawing her hand down the curve of his arm. It was easier because he favors his father, boring Bedevere; had he looked as much like the mistress as Gawain did, it would be more of a discomfort.

Gaheris nodded and bade her a fair day. He was angry, and Nimue was happy.

She recognized Agravain as soon as he turned the corner a few moments later, his wheat-blond hair down over his eyes, the same determined gait. He was the son of Margawse and an unknown knight, though with the progress she had made in befriending his mother, Nimue hoped to soon find out his missing identity. It would be good information to have. Powerful.

Nimue breathed power.

Agravain was not handsome like his cousins, the Orkneys, not at first glance. His face was plain, his eyes a common blue. It was only when he spoke, when he moved his hands, Nimue saw beauty; he was like a conjuror. He spoke with a liveliness and vivacity none of the other knights possessed, and Nimue admired his uniqueness.

"Darling," he said, picking her up and lacing his hands about her waist. Nimue giggled, kicking her feet in the air.

She remembered how he found her, the very first day, on her way back from visiting Gawain and Gaheris. The mistress retreated entirely, leaving Nimue alone. Though she had been crying, her tears were mostly dried, but her eyes were still red. Agravain was leaving his mother's chambers—not far from Gawain's—and they caught each other's gaze across the hall. Their first conversation was filled with such intensity that, by the end of the encounter, they had already uttered a half-dozen fevered promises. They would be together soon. Soon.

But then, Lamorak had come, so shy and sad. And Nimue had done with him what she never agreed to with Agravain. Oh, she wanted to lay with Agravain, of course she did. She always wanted it; she could find it whenever she looked for it. But Nimue preferred to keep Agravain at a distance, suffering as if on the edge of a blade. It made him more beautiful, and more devoted, knowing what he desired was but a breath from him.

With Lamorak it was different. He was older, less demanding. She melted into him; she took him with her hands, with her mouth. She marveled in the magic of their coupling. Theirs was not a relationship of words, but of actions. Nothing like Hwyfar, and their comfortable softness. But it gave her focus.

Nimue reveled in the balance of it; the wanting and the giving, the taking and the lying.

"Agravain," she said, playfully, as he brushed his whiskers against her neck, running his hand over her breast, pushing her back against the wall.

"Nimue… you must…" He was angry. So very angry.

"No, please," she said, gently at first, then again, with more strength.

He relented, a little, but did not move far; she was still pinned between him and the wall. Though not as tall as the Orkney boys, he still towered over her.

"Why do you continue this game?" he asked, voice tinged with a playfulness she found so thrilling. She purred against him.

"There is no game…" she denied, forcing her hands back. She wanted to take in the whole of him, but she did not. She breathed instead, in and out.

"I know what you've done with him," Agravain said now, his voice a growl in her ear. He pressed his armored greaves into her, and she felt her skin bruising under the pressure.

Nimue gasped as he enclosed a mighty hand around her neck. Her eyesight prickled with lights and black spots.

"With Lamorak. Or did you not know?" he clarified.

She shook her head, choking out a mangled response.

"My mother is a powerful woman," he continued, his hand roving between her legs, prodding. She would have screamed if she could, but her world went dark, those spots spreading rapidly on the periphery of her vision. "Lamorak has been a devoted friend to her for, oh, the last ten years or so. He was sent—to test you. And you failed."

He was laughing now, pressing so close she felt her spine crack against the masonry.

"The next time I see you, I am going to take you. Willing or no. I have had enough of your games, Nimue." He let her go, and she sucked in as much air as she could before falling to her knees, coughing.

"I promise you."

### ~ *Anna* ~

I WOKE UP in my bed, the covers pulled up to my chin. I was quaking with the chill, my teeth chattering.

"Nimue."

She was silent, like a child recently reprimanded.

"Yes, mistress."

"You are in trouble."

"Yes."

"And you have put me in trouble, now."

"Yes."

I sighed, turning sideways in the bed. I was ready to sleep but knew rest would not come. Not for a long time.

"Go to Merlin," I said. "And show him the bruises about your neck. Plead with him to help you. He may show you a better way to bind a man than I know; use it against him and use it against Agravain. Then we will be finished, you and I."

"I do not want to die."

"You were never born, dear. You can never die."

# CHAPTER FIFTEEN

## AGRAVAIN

### ~ Nimue ~

MERLIN WAS INCENSED when she told him the story; the slightly befuddled old man transformed into a furious creature, flapping his arms and growling, pacing about the room. He offered her tea three times, even though she accepted the first.

"And you will not tell me who did this to you?" he demanded, turning to her, his usually sallow cheeks crimson. She thought the color did him some good, made him look lively, and she almost smiled.

"You'll do terrible things to him," she insisted. "But he is one of Arthur's knights, I—"

"Yes, child?" He knelt and looked into her face, his gaze as impenetrable as cured wood. His knuckles were knobbed, twisted, and she had never noticed before—it looked as if his index finger and middle finger on his right hand were growing at different angles. The ends tapered rather delicately, and she wondered what his hands looked like in youth. He must have been spectacular to look upon, then. With those striking eyes and the sharp features since eroded with wrinkles and wear, he would have been rather handsome.

She took a deep breath, feeling the air tickle her throat. He was burning more incense, and she had not yet told him how much it bothered her.

"I want to do it myself," she said, taking his head in her hands, palm to cheek. She smoothed the skin there, above the bristles of his beard, and he closed his eyes in response—just like a cat stroked between the eyes, she thought.

"Yourself, Nimue? How do you mean?"

"I mean," she said, delicately, lightly, as if speaking of the weather, "I want revenge on him; he has mortified me and threatened me. Surely you know of ways I might be able to…"

She let the words hang in the air so the conjuror could make the connection himself.

He bowed his head, thinking.

"You were not born to a prophetic family," he said, rising slowly, as if in grave pain. "In that way, you are like me. You live not knowing, always wondering what you are, who you ought to be. I was born in a small village, the son of a cowherd and a milkmaid. Did you know that?"

Nimue shook her head. "They say you have always been," she said.

"I was born, and I will die. I am old, though, older than I ought to be. I have seen Uther as a babe, and Arthur grow to manhood. He is my greatest vision, you know. I have staked a great deal on him."

"He is a good king. Braetan is at peace."

Merlin frowned, the hair at his chin deepening into his beard. "I do not know what is wrong with me lately, except I feel as if my abilities—my visions and interpretations—have gone strange, warped. I have dreams I am lost in a wood, and when I wake, my joints are afire." He held up his gnarled hands, and she saw he could hardly move one of them when he flexed his fingers. He winced.

"Part of me," he said, going to the teapot and pouring himself another cup, "feels it is simply a part of getting older. Like this castle itself, my bones are not as strong as they once were. Every season means a weakening of the beams... All the Christians and their new temples. Their priests stalking our halls, spreading lies about purity and righteousness while slaughtering with blades behind our backs."

"You are so often away from Carelon," Nimue said. "Perhaps you ought to remain here more."

The conjuror nodded, going to the window. The steam from his mug rose and twirled around his face, dissipating entirely before it reached his eyes. The apple tree had shed its blossoms completely and looked, to the untrained eye, as plain as any other.

He spoke of this, as Nimue thought it.

"Carelon no longer feels safe, my dear. Though I have worked tirelessly to move about the pieces, to orchestrate the right prophecies, arrange the best matches, nudge Arthur toward the more just wars... I think I have lost the battle for Carelon itself. A darker power resides here, but I am blind to it."

Nimue knew that power. It had a name: Anna Pendragon. And Morgen. Hwyfar, Gweyn, Elaine, Igraine, and an endless litany of women who had run their shuttles and threads across the great loom of Fate. A color for each woman wounded: some blood red, others shimmering gold, and one jet black.

"Perhaps I am like the blood apple tree—kept about only for a short blooming period, and then destined to fall into the sleepy green of the rest of the trees and vegetation. I feel no less weary for traveling, for everywhere I go people seem to want things from me. Blessings, interpretations." He turned, the hem of his robe swishing about his feet. "Yet you do not ask me for a blessing, Nimue. You ask me for power."

Nimue felt frightened again, but she sat up straighter, leveling her chin. She would not be made to feel so common, so inferior. And so, she narrowed her eyes, taking in his form. He looked like an old man, that was all, an old man who was angry at the world. She felt less concerned and relaxed a little.

"I can ask elsewhere," she said, standing. "There are others. Morgen, for one."

"Morgen," Merlin said, between a laugh and a sneer. "You think that peddling midwife will help you for the trouble you've gotten yourself into?"

"*Myself* into?" she asked. She had not told the old man about Lamorak—she only spoke of Agravain's advances. "But you do not understand—"

"I know the way of you, Nimue. You think you cannot help it, but in every move of your body you speak the rhythm of making, the dance of mating—" He held up his hand, tracing the lines of her with his fingers, almost like a painter observing their subject. "And you do nothing to hide it—you dress just so; you speak just so. It is no surprise half the court is after you. Even the Christ priests cannot help but leer."

Nimue stilled. A thin line of fury skittered down her back.

"I am as I have been made," Nimue said at last, taking a step toward Merlin, her feet soft on the rushes. She made barely a whisper as she approached him. "I will not be ashamed."

Merlin frowned. She thought he may consider her as condescending, but she smiled to prevent it.

He did not speak. Nimue had the distant memory of finding a rabbit caught in a trap, mangled around the wickerwork, wide-eyed and trembling. It is how she saw Merlin then; ensnared. He was all eyes and still, breathing shallowly.

Nimue's breasts pressed against his arm, and he did not move to resist or to accept. The old man blinked a few times.

"You could bring me great joy," she whispered, bringing his face to hers, sliding her hand down the front of his bony chest. "And knowledge."

When Nimue fell back onto the rushes, she loved Merlin as completely as she hated him. She loved the look of loss in his eyes, the brilliance of his skin; she hated the oldness of him, the lingering scent of decay. She hated the way he rasped for air, the reek of his breath, the white hair surrounding his penis, just the same as the wiry ones sprouting on his chest.

But gods, she loved the power of it.

And hated the things he said to her. Words of love, promises. She hated the way he touched her, trails of his fingers lingering like the slime behind a slug.

He was a man, like the rest, weak to her power, only wanting to take from her.

When it was done, Nimue took account. She felt more hate than love, and hate is a bitter drug. It made her dizzy, darkening her vision.

She had power, too. A new capacity within her, spooled up and prepared. "Tell me your regrets," she whispered to him.

"I will tell you," Merlin said at last, brushing his fingers through her long hair. "At night, when I try and find peace through sleep, I see their faces. Pale and wan. The faces of those I have broken in order to raise a kingdom. I know it is the price. But I am so weary, Nimue. It is how I was made, and yet I cannot escape it. I am guilty. But I do not regret it. I have forged a dynasty in their blood."

NIMUE WAS QUIET, studying Merlin's lessons, nursing her fury toward Agravain. He was no simple task, no easy man to humiliate.

The old man called it projection, when she cast an image of herself as full and bright as can be. She did not do it much at a distance, but close by it was not so difficult. All she had to do was concentrate, holding the sachet of herbs between her hands, and direct the image of herself with her mind.

He told her she was uncommonly gifted.

She knew many things. She knew, from previous conversations with Hwyfar—before she left and broke her heart—that Margawse favored Lamorak before her and was certain she did again. But not in such a way Agravain suspected; she had long taken Lamorak, and many other knights, to bed.

A simple illusion, she decided, would be easiest. Her hope was to embarrass Agravain, discovering his mother abed with Lamorak. So she crawled to the same nook where she waited for Agravain so many days before and projected an image of herself, walking the halls. Nimue marveled in the look of her own body, so round and lovely in a remarkable green dress. The image was captivating.

Then came the sound of feet.

"Nimue?" asked a voice, trailing behind the image of her.

Nimue directed the image into Margawse's room, the door left slightly ajar by a simple spell, then released it entirely.

The source of the voice, though, was not Agravain.

It was Gaheris.

He disappeared into the doorway, just as Agravain turned the corner, following Gaheris at a furious pace.

"Gaheris—you—"

Nimue ran out from her enclave. "No, Agravain, do not go in there—do not—"

"You harlot," he growled at her, throwing open the door with his hand.

Then: "Gods, Mother!"

Nimue ran away, a flurry of swords in her wake.

### ~ *Anna* ~

IN SPITE OF my increasingly frail state, I had to go see Gaheris, who was being kept in a room in the North tower—the sort nephews of the king go to when they've killed their own kin; which meant, compared to most, the accommodations were rather impressive. I did not see much as Nimue—after returning to myself I recalled only clouded memories, vague and fleeting. I had to hear Gaheris's story; though I doubted he would be brought to the gallows for it, I worried for him.

How had it gone so wrong? Nimue did not give him any inclination of affection, and yet—by her account—he continued to seek her out. He wanted her, hungered for her, and though he had never shown much in the way of directness as Agravain had, he had resorted to such violence to protect her.

Sir Dinadin and Sir Escloval were guarding the door, and I noticed Dinadin's eyes widen when he saw me. I looked awful, I knew, but it was all the more embarrassing when someone as familiar as Dinadin noticed.

"Lady Anna—should you be about?" he asked.

Haen was with me, holding me fast. I was about ready to collapse from the effort of the walk from my quarters, winded and weary.

"I am fine, Dinadin," I said, gently as I could. "I am here to see my son."

"Of course."

He opened the door for me, revealing the steep-ceilinged room. It was well-appointed, but a little stark for my tastes. The sun was setting, but he had no view of it, though the sky was orange streaked.

Gaheris sat at a writing desk, penning something, his head down. His hair fell over most of his face. For a moment I was breathless at the beauty of him in that pose. His back arched, his shoulders strong; I never would have pictured my youngest as such a remarkably formed man.

I realized he was weeping, however, and asked Haen to

wait outside. He seemed a little concerned, but I waved my hand at him. No, this was my son, and my business alone.

"Gaheris," I said, coming up behind him. He started at my touch, as if he had not seen or heard me, and then turned, burying his head in my stomach.

I ran my hands through his hair, smoothing his brow, as he wept. He was warm, and huffing like a horse run too long, the sorrow was from so deep inside. I have found in my life men so infrequently weep, and when they do it is with a kind of relish and release; it can be quite overwhelming for them, and those about them.

"Mother, what have I done?" he asked, looking up at me. His eyes still swam with tears.

"You killed Margawse," I said, tempering my words with no feeling. What feeling could I give him? Margawse was my sister, and his aunt. It was a grave offense.

"She came at me," he said, bowing his head again, spit falling from his lips. "I entered the room—thinking, I do not know—I thought Nimue was there. I was confused— then Agravain was behind me, screaming things. They all came after me, intended to kill me, I think. Agravain said as much—he said horrible things about me, and Gawain— Mother, I couldn't let him."

"You subdued him, and Lamorak. They have both fled the castle."

"It was a horror," he said, his voice barely a whisper, ragged with weeping. "A complete horror. She was at me, all smoke and shadow. There were teeth, and gnashing— Mother, she was like a strange serpent made of nothingness. She shrieked at me, clawing my eyes and my..."

I could see the marks on his face as he looked up at me, the trails of her fingernails down his cheeks, and raked across his neck. It looked as if they'd been done with blades, not nails. One, in particular, about his temple, was deep enough to have needed stitches, though none gave them to him; he had been removed, in a frenzy, from the scene.

"I did only what I thought—she was killing me, somehow. I could feel my youth, my life, draining from me—I wanted to give up," he said, taking my hands, and pressing them to his lips. "I did not realize I had beheaded her." He swallowed. "Until I looked down at my feet."

"You protected yourself as any person ought to have. Do not torture yourself so."

He trembled, looking up at me, like a child reprimanded. "Did—did you see her body—after?"

I had. What remained of Margawse was a withered corpse, a head of long, white hair, and sunken eyes. I always suspected her beauty was unnatural, but I never fathomed she resorted to such dark pathways to power.

Then again, perhaps it simply ran in the family.

"Yes, Gaheris, I did," I said gently.

"Was she a witch?" she asked.

I shivered as he said the word. "A sort," I replied. "But she is gone now."

"Are they going to kill me?" he asked.

"I do not think so, Gaheris. That Agravain and Lamorak have disappeared is distressing. They will go to Lamorak's father if they can. But they are running from something. I suspect more died along with Margawse than her beauty," I said. "Dark shadows are afoot in Carelon in these strange days."

"Arthur must be furious."

"He is, I think. But perhaps a little relieved, as well. Margawse and he had a complicated relationship." Which could be said of Arthur and all his sisters.

He looked past me. "Where is Nimue? Is she well?"

"Nimue is very distressed over what happened," I told him. "She—and the entire court—have heard you reported seeing her that day, and yet Merlin attests to the fact she was with him, accompanying him on a walk through the orchid garden. Many people saw them both. But, unfortunately, many of her hard-worn friends are looking at her rather... doubtfully." It was not entirely a lie, but it would suffice. "Oh, Gaheris. Why did you have to pursue her so?"

He paused, lifting his head from me. Gaheris pushed himself up from the desk, and I saw what he had been writing. Just letters. Letters intertwined, of all sorts. The script was beautiful, but it made little sense to me.

When he stood, I had to look up into his face, and he smiled, even a little. "She reminded me of home," he said. "Of Orkney. I know, I know. It is a desolate place, but when we were young, it was as comforting as anything else we knew. And I thought if she got to know me, I could share that with her, and we could comfort one another. But she wanted naught from me."

"Her heart belonged to another."

"To Lamorak? To Agravain?"

"Not exactly," I said, kind as I could. "She told me Agravain threatened to force her to the act of love, you know. She was frightened by him; in a way, you have done her a service, as much as you have threatened her reputation."

"He threatened to rape her?" Gaheris asked, stiffening, his nostrils flaring.

"Gaheris—calm yourself. It is over. They are gone."

"Gods, this is a horror."

I felt the ground sway beneath my feet, and Gaheris helped me stand. He was crying again. "I am so sorry, Mother—and to have made you come to me in this hour, you must hate me."

"I can never hate you, little sparrow," I said, the name I had once given him. "But I do need my rest. There will be a trial, but I do not think you have to worry, Gaheris. There are greater things in this world for you than this."

Gaheris took my hands, leading me to the door. "Thank you for coming to see me, Mother."

"There are no thanks required, my son. It is what a mother does. Perhaps someday you will know part of it."

WHEN NIMUE CAME to me again, it was late at night. I had been dozing on and off, which I was in the habit of doing in the evening hours as the sun set. I possessed little strength for anything else—and yet, every hour I spent without her, I gained a sliver more of strength. I hoped over time the slivers would converge, and I would be resilient enough to go on without her.

It was becoming more and more apparent that life with Nimue was simply too dangerous. I had given her too much free rein, and could not control her; now she was, truly an entity other than myself. I knew, in my heart, I created her, and she would be forever part of me. But I feared if she grew too strong, I would no longer be able to resist the temptation to slink into her supple skin forever.

I saw her limned in the flames of the fire that night, two days after the debacle with Gaheris. She stood, a woman of fire and smoke, visible perhaps to me only. There was no one else in the room with me, and she spoke with whispers.

"I cannot let you out again," I said to her, closing my eyes. But the image of her was already burned in my mind, and regardless I could see her.

"You will fail if you do it without me," she reminded me, her voice like reeds on a riverbank.

"I know the spell."

"But you do not have the love. Merlin doesn't trust you, and he does not love you. You will be his, completely—he will burn through you and leave you naught but ashes."

"You think there is another way? He is already plotting the prophecies of the next generation—he hardly sleeps, hardly eats. He will undo us all." I held up my hand. "Perhaps I made you hate too much."

"And love too much."

"I am sorry…"

"Judgement will win out. It is all I had to begin, and all I will have when it ends."

"And Merlin?"

"You have judged him."

"I have."

"Then the rest is mine."

She was right. I could not be judge and executioner.

I feared letting Nimue out one more time would kill me. I was already so frail; Morgen had wept when she saw the remnants of my wasted body, cursing Arthur and Merlin, pleading with the goddess to give me strength.

But I cared naught for the empty goddesses, for Iaia and

her ever-open arms. No, the gods and goddesses had left me but shambles of a life, and I made my own goddess, in my own image: Nimue, a Queen of Fire.

MERLIN, EYES FEVER-BRIGHT, rode behind Nimue, his arm around her shoulders, running his crooked fingers through her long hair. They came to the top of a rise in the land, just within sight of Carelon; they were alone.

Nimue hummed softly under her breath, her head leaning against his breast.

She had emptied herself for him, filling her heart up with his dreams; she was his mother, his daughter, his sister, his lover. She was everything for him, every woman he ever dreamed of, wrapped and bound in flesh. In every line of her, she was made for him: the curve of her cheek, the swell of her breasts, the rise of her hips.

I made her for him. A gift. A trap. A sacrifice. A great tapestry: the threads of Fate in a binding spell, the fury of generations lashed together in retribution.

And when they lay together, he was lost as no man has ever been lost: bewitched, besotted.

Yet, the feeling within Nimue's own heart was complicated as the twining circles in the interlace of Avillion tapestries. She could not take herself from it, could not separate the love from the hatred, could not tell when one began and the other ended. In the same way, she loved and hated herself for it; she hated her own weakness but loved the power. Even the power of hatred.

"The grove is not far," said Merlin, pointing ahead. His long white hair fell down his back, lifting in the wind, streaking across Nimue's face. For a moment, she appeared as an old woman, then the image was gone. "And it is one of the only places the Christ men won't follow."

There was no one to see it but me.

The trees, below, marked the beginning of the wood, a semicircle of wondrous oak and yew, sprinkled with holly and hawthorn. It was late summer, and a hint of gold caressed the tips of the foliage, some red as rust. Birds, fat with feed, flitted from branch to branch, still hungry for more. The ground smelled of life and death, of growing things and squirming things.

And one tree, greater than the rest, rose high, gnarled with the ages.

"The oldest among us," Merlin said, when the horse came to a halt. He gingerly dismounted, and then helped Nimue down, letting his hand linger at her side a moment. He gestured to the enormous oak, shaggy with moss; a large hole on one side opened to the East, large enough for a man to sit inside.

Nimue walked to the tree on light feet, springy against the soft, loamy earth. The wind breathed life into her, strengthening her.

"Can anyone see us from here?" she asked, turning to him, tilting her head to the side so her long hair fell back from her delicate neck.

"They could before," said Merlin, holding up his hands. He closed his eyes, connecting fingertip to fingertip, then smiled, muttering words lowly. "But now they cannot."

"No?" she asked, taking a step closer to him, winding her fingers under the belt at his skinny middle. She pulled him toward her, and he laughed.

"I have made us a little bower, Nimue," he said, tracing the lines of her face, his wizened fingers cold and hard as wood.

They kissed; they became one. She brought him into her again and again, her back against the oak tree, her hands splayed at its sides, pulling the energy of it into her.

She loved him, she hated him; she could not be without him. Nimue knew the words she must say, could hear the words imploring in her mind. She had been betrayed by all but him: Hwyfar, Arthur, Agravain, Lamorak, Gaheris, even me. She did not want to die, but she did not want to live in this cruel world.

"I have come," she said between breaths. "To capture you…"

Above, the oak shuddered, though it seemed impossible to her that their act could shake it.

I felt it all, twice over; my own body, her own body…

He did not stop, he continued to press into her, to lose himself in the softness of her.

"I will," she promised.

His hands roved over her, and he was infused with a strange vigor.

"Did you—hear me?" she gasped, as he pressed her, so hard she could feel the back of the tree dig into her spine. *I have been here before*, she thought. *It will be the same with him, as it was with Agravain. I will be used and left.*

"I am your end," Nimue said, tears streaming down her cheeks. "I am your executioner."

Merlin whispered into her ear, his voice like the surging water on the ocean. He said:

"I know."

He did not relent, and she could not escape him. She felt herself slipping away, grasping the words to say but finding her mind gone eerily numb; her body was afire with a feeling more akin to anger than passion. She could no more rid herself of him than she could uproot the oak tree.

*Say the words.*

"No," Nimue whispered, her lips trembling.

*Speak the words you were born to speak.*

She cried out as one pierced with a blade.

*I will make you say it.*

"I bind you," Nimue said, tears falling on her tongue as she spoke. The words were not loud, but a thunderclap punctuated her command. "I bind you by the sky."

"Yes," Merlin said.

"I bind you by the sea."

The oak tree shuddered again, followed by another crack; the branches were moving above their heads, swaying back and forth as if part of the rhythm of their lovemaking. Their hate-making. Their fate-making.

"I bind you to the earth."

*Yes. Speak the words. Let your purpose be complete.*

"I saw... I knew," Merlin said, his face to hers, his eyes as dark as rain-stained oak bark. "I knew I would forget you... until this moment..."

*It cannot be.*

"No one will forget me," Nimue said. She raised her head, screaming as he finished into her, feeling the ache of it radiate through her body, past her womb, past all thought and being.

"I bind you to the tree!" Nimue shouted.

*Yes.*

Then: "I bind you to me!"

The oak opened like a leather purse, lips wide and wanting.

"I have made us a bower," Merlin said. "And it is finished."

And darkness took us all.

# CHAPTER SIXTEEN

## ANNA

"Anna."

No more. I could take no more. I was certain I was dead, and Nimue's final decision—to bind herself to the tree, and to Merlin—was my undoing, too.

I was angry to wake up to the world. Too real, and too cold, as it was. It seemed cruel.

"Anna... are you awake?"

A man's voice. The right voice. A better voice—a better beginning.

"Bedevere," I said.

He began to weep, taking my hand—which he had already been holding—and pressing it to his brow, then kissing it over and over.

My body felt as if I had been burned the night before, my skin tender in every place, my muscles tight. Even my bones ached, down to the very smallest. I felt like a dried husk, something left in the herbalist's drawer for use another time; I wondered vaguely if I would rattle upon being shaken.

I let him weep as I continued to breathe, taking in the cool air. It was unseasonably cold in the room, and I wondered how much time passed. I remembered so little of the last months, as I was locked in Nimue's power for most of it.

But I did not sense her presence, did not feel the need of her. Much like after childbirth, I felt a sudden momentary pang of longing: I missed the sensation of her moving within me. Some of the draught still remained, but it did not matter. It would not work. She was gone from the world. Her magic had evaporated with Merlin's last breath. Our great tapestry consumed in flame.

Bedevere stopped crying and looked to me, the dark lashes around his eyes clumped together in perfect triangles. There was gray at his temples, a streak of white on each side, and it did him a world of good; he looked beautiful, his features more pronounced than I recalled.

"I can scarcely believe my eyes," he said, smoothing my fingers with his hands.

"Nor can I," I admitted. I glanced around my room, squinting; it was very late.

"They told me you had awoken," he explained. "And I came to see you—you've been ill for quite some time. None of us thought you'd manage through the fall, but you... persisted."

With my free hand I reached up, touching my face. Skin and bone, sinew and veins. But very much alive, indeed.

"I am hardly more than a wight," I said, turning away. I felt the distant pining of hunger but said naught. "When— when is it?"

"Deep winter," Bedevere said. He frowned. "Christmas, almost. What we call Yule. What do you remember?"

Would that I could have told him everything. I had enough memories for two lifetimes, now.

I thought of Nimue's face. How I marked the look of ecstasy written in the delicate brow, the full lips. She wanted Merlin's love as much as she wanted to destroy him. And she bound them both, to each other. His spell, her power. Forever.

She had been my instrument, but gods, I had loved her, too.

"Very little," I lied. A first lie. It tasted familiar, almost comforting; what else had I ever done to Bedevere but lie to him?

"Haen and Fauna found you," he said, smoothing the coverlet with one hand, averting his gaze a moment. "You went missing—Morgen said you mentioned going for a ride, to see if you could find Nimue and Merlin, but we found you by the Grove, by your horse, completely unconscious."

"I do not think I found her... Nimue..." I said, my throat catching with emotion.

Bedevere's face fell. "No. No one has."

"Merlin is truly gone," I said.

It had not been a question, but he answered the same: "Yes. Morgen lingered a while, trying to help Arthur when she could but after... after two months, she decided to take Llachlyn to Avillion. She felt she would be safer there."

"Safer?"

"She was concerned she would be influenced by the Christ's men here at court. Anna... you are weak. I should wait to tell you these things."

"No," I commanded, grasping his hand with strength even he could appreciate. I felt the certainty of it fill me with clarity. "Bring me some water. Some bread, perhaps. Then you can tell me."

I ate, I drank, and I felt better. The wine made my cheeks flush, and my heart beat faster, and though I was weak, with Bedevere's help I was able to sit back up in bed.

"Every able-bodied person in Carelon went searching for Merlin, and until the snow came, they searched. But we found no trace. No notes, no cloak. The last person to see them together was a young knight named Tristan, who made note of the color of Nimue's dress in the distance as he was on post. They had been heading toward the Grove, then…" He trailed off, sighing. "Now, of course, the entire court believes Nimue was some witch, who tried to kill you and somehow snared Merlin. Everyone knew he was besotted with her."

"Yes," I said slowly. "That is close to the truth; she was dabbling in difficult magic, I know. I tried to convince her otherwise, but she was persistent."

"Arthur was heartbroken, but I think a little relieved, as well," Bedevere admitted. "He has ever obeyed Merlin—but now, I hear he's considering converting. Penance resounds with him. My lord is dragged down with guilt."

Something else was wrong, something he was not saying. The words were there, I could tell. He was holding back.

"I should wait," he said again, shaking his head. "You must be exhausted, Anna. I fear I will never hear the end of it if Arthur discovers I distressed you in any way—"

The apartment was so silent; of course, that was it.

"Lance," I said, feeling the loss of him before Bedevere spoke his name. My knight frowned immediately, giving away the truth to my guess.

"He has gone to the Joyous Guard; Ban of Benwick is dead, and he will be staying for a time to sort matters out.

He will return in the spring. I have sent word to him."

"You spoke with him," I said.

"We had much to say," Bedevere replied, running his hand across my knuckles. "He made me swear by my blood to watch over you."

"I would like to see my sons," I said.

"Gawain is here, as is Gaheris. But Gareth went with Lanceloch, of course… You must rest, Anna. You must gather your strength."

I laughed, but it was bitter, a laugh that longed for true joy. "I have no strength to gather, Bedevere. But with you here… I suppose I can take some from you. If you'll give it to me."

He leaned down and kissed me between my eyes, soft and sweet as a lover's first.

I was not thinking of Bedevere, though, as he kissed me gentle. I thought of Arthur. I realized I had done more than kill Merlin. I robbed Arthur of his power. I inadvertently pushed Lance away, who would someday steal Arthur's queen and bring the nation to war again, within itself. I set a new future, guided by a new Fate, in motion.

Perhaps it was Arthur I wanted revenge against the whole time; perhaps I was just too blind to see it. And perhaps I succeeded there, as well. I was afraid to accept it, though.

IN THE WEEKS that followed, Bedevere came to me every day. Eventually I was strong enough to walk about the room, then walk about the apartment. By the spring, I walked to the courtyard and back. In some ways, I was more resilient in mind and body than I had been in a long time. Nimue was gone from me, but she had taken something from me, too, something I often wonder was a blessing in its taking: I no longer felt incomplete. I no longer thirsted for answers. I heard Merlin's story, and I judged him accordingly. I endeavored to do what none before me could, and I felt at peace.

For the first time in as many years I could remember, joy. When my sons saw me healed, they embraced me as they never had before; Arthur took me in his arms, and implored I meet with him, when I could. He wanted to know more of me, to learn from me. It was the least he could do, he said, since he felt as if I was been reborn into the world. He knew so little of a woman's purview, he said. It was time he understood.

There were not many days where thoughts of Nimue did not haunt me, but that was not a surprise. She was like a lost child to me—like Blancheflor, should she have lived. Nimue was of me, and she was not of me. I was forever changed by her; she burned so brightly, for such a short time, but it seemed everyone had memories of her—memories even I had forgotten.

Though thoughts of judging Merlin consumed the better part of my mind for the last decade, my part in the story of Arthur and his Knights was but the rock thrown into the middle of a clear pool. A beginning. An end.

Most often, I think of Merlin's last words to Nimue: he knew me, then. *I knew I would forget you*, he said. And then he was gone.

In that way, I suppose, we shared the burden of my prophecy. Though I had the secret of his magics.

You know, of course, how the follies of Arthur and Mawra, of Lanceloch and others—like young Tristan, and his Isolde—then later, our sons and daughters, changed the very face of Carelon. How the castle itself began to crumble and in the end, we had little left.

Such are the ways of men. In the face of peace, we will make war among our allies; and it was no different in Carelon.

There are so many more stories to tell.

But before I lost everything again, Bedevere and I came together in the spring. We sat, hand in hand in the garden, beneath the flowering apple tree, staring out at the passersby.

"You used to think you'd be forgotten," he said, blossoms falling around us like snowflakes. He squeezed my hand.

"Some prophecies can be interpreted again," I said, looking at him. I knew what I wanted in life once more; I simply wanted Bedevere.

"They can? Is that why I cannot seem to stop thinking about you?" he asked.

"I seem to think you are impermeable in the ways of prophecy, Bedevere."

He smiled, lips smooth over his teeth. "Oh, is that so? I only thought it was on account of my loving you so much. I have always believed prophecies pale in the face of love."

"Love… yes, it is a powerful, unpredictable thing." I thought of Nimue and her own sacrifice. She had given herself to Merlin, in the end. Completely.

I sighed; it seemed an unfairly beautiful spring. "But so few of us truly know it. And most of those who have, have been broken by it. Like Arthur. I cannot see how any of this will end well, Bedevere. Is it selfish of us to love so much?"

"Selfish, yes. But it gives us all something to fight for, doesn't it? I will not give you up again, Anna."

"I do not want you to," I said. And, gods knew, I meant it. In the moment, I truly did.

# ACKNOWLEDGEMENTS

THIS EDITION WOULD not be possible without my readers. They are my champions, my inspiration, and my strength. In particular, I'd like to recognize E. J. Dawson, Dino Hicks, Kendra Montgomery-Blinn, Chelsea Banning and P. L. Stuart.

Big thanks to my agent, Stacey Graham at 3 Seas Literary, my fantastic guide forward through this unpredictable journey. I'm so glad we found another across the vastness of the internet. My weird adores your weird.

To David Thomas Moore and the team at Solaris for giving Anna Pendragon a new life and believing in the vision of Carelon across the whole series. I can't wait to continue the adventure together.

To my many professors of medieval literature and art across my years of study, but especially Dr. Kelly DeVries and Dr. Kathleen Forni at Loyola University Maryland.

To my husband Michael for being my pillar of love and support; to my son Liam, who is now almost as tall as Gawain but was running around in diapers when I began this book; to my daughter Elodie who still believes in fairies and is growing into a fierce, brilliant young woman. To my parents, John and Johanne Barron, who never doubted me a single time, and to my sister Llana, who walked with me in the distant realms of our imagination for years.

To the Yonder crew and Noir at the Bar, and especially Eryk Pruitt and Shawn A. Cosby, for welcoming me and this story of vengeance and grit at live readings in Hillsborough.

To my departed Aunt Corinne, who sent me my first illustrated copy of King Arthur's tales when I was twelve. You continue to inspire me, even now.

To Jennifer Hansen, my soul friend. For so much, always.

And lastly, to the millions of invisible women throughout history men have forgotten. We know our truth, and we know our power. Let us never doubt our influence.

*Natania Barron*

# ABOUT THE AUTHOR

**Natania Barron** is an award-winning fantasy author long preoccupied with mythology, monsters, and magic. Her often historically-inspired novels are filled with lush description and vibrant characters. Publications include her 2011 debut, *Pilgrim of the Sky*, as well as *These Marvelous Beasts*, a collection of novellas.

In 2020, Barron's *Queen of None* was hailed as "a captivating look at the intriguing figures in King Arthur's golden realm" by *Kirkus*, and won the Manly Wade Wellman award the following year.

Her shorter works have appeared in *Weird Tales*, EscapePod, and various anthologies, RPG, and game settings. In addition, she's also known for #ThreadTalk, which dives deep into the unseen, and often forgotten, world of fashion history.

Barron lives in North Carolina, USA, with her family and two dogs. When she's not writing, you can find her wandering the woods, tending her garden, and collecting rocks.

🐦 @nataniabarron
📷 @nataniabarron
♪ @nataniabooks
🌐 www.nataniabarron.com

# FIND US ONLINE!

## www.rebellionpublishing.com

/solarisbooks /solarisbks /solarisbooks

# SIGN UP TO OUR NEWSLETTER!

rebellionpublishing.com/newsletter

# YOUR REVIEWS MATTER!

Enjoy this book? Got something to say?

Leave a review on Amazon, GoodReads or with your favourite bookseller and let the world know!